BECKETT PEARCE

NINA LEVINE

authorninalevine@gmail.com

www.ninalevinebooks.com

This is a work of fiction. Names, characters, places, and incidents are a product of the author's imagination. Locales and public names are sometimes used for atmospheric purposes. Any resemblance to actual people, living or dead, or to businesses, companies, events, institutions, or locales is completely coincidental.

ISBN: 9780994585837

Cover Design by Letitia at Romantic Book Affair Designs

Proofreading provided by Read by Rose

To all the Jennas out there.
I wanna be like you one day.

1

BECKETT

I slam the door of my Rolls-Royce shut and stalk to where Johnson, my head of security, is waiting for me in the alley behind Amorosis, the Italian restaurant I frequent.

Reaching him, I take the dossier he holds out and glance down at it. "Did this turn up anything new?" I already have my suspicions, but it'd make my day if he had a different answer to give me.

A shake of his head confirms everything I thought.

I don't bother to flick through the documents. "I'm done. Make sure this gets out."

Johnson nods as he slides his sunglasses into place. "I'll handle it."

He walks to his motorcycle while I enter Amorosis through the back door.

"Yo, Becks my man," Matty, one of the dishwashers, greets me. "You see the game?"

I nod, to which he says, "The fuck, man? I'm pissed. They should have won that game." Matty loves his Yankees and is always fired up when they lose.

"I agree. Sanchez—"

He cuts me off. "Right? Sanchez had it. They got screwed over."

Frankie, the manager, joins us. "Matty, you running your mouth when you should be running your hands all over those pots?"

Matty grins. This is a common conversation between these two. "No need to get pissy, Franks. I'm on it." To me, he says, "Don't leave without seeing me, my man. We've got shit to talk about."

I nod before winding my way through the kitchen and out to the front of the restaurant where I'm meeting Annabelle. She's waiting at my usual table and waves me over when she sees me.

Standing, she makes a fuss with a hug and kisses. "It's so good to see you," she gushes. "We've got so much to discuss."

I'm not sure what exactly she wants to discuss today, or that I have time for it, but Annabelle's an old friend so I agreed to this lunch. She'll be disappointed, though, if what she wants to talk about takes longer than forty minutes as that's all I'm willing to allocate.

We sit and I order drinks before asking, "What's going on?"

Her eyes light up as she rests her elbows on the table and leans forward. "I'm organizing an art auction for charity, and I want you to be involved. We've managed to secure paintings from that artist you love, O'Keefe."

Christ, this is the last thing I have time for. Or any interest in. "I'll attend, but that's all."

Her face falls but she recovers fast—a specialty of hers. "I thought you could emcee the gala. It'll be fun." She reaches across the table and touches my arm. "Please, Beckett, for me."

Another specialty of Annabelle's is manipulation. It's only our history that helps her with me. If not for that, I'd have no qualms saying no to every request she sends my way. "When is it?"

A smile fills her face; she knows she has me. Leaning back

in her seat, she says, "Next month. I'll send the details to Louise."

The waiter delivers our drinks and takes our order, after which Annabelle sips her wine and says, "Now, tell me everything you've been up to and don't leave anything out. I heard you were seeing Natalie Gareth. I'm interested to hear more."

"You know better than to listen to the gossip, Annabelle. You also know better than to expect me to share intimate details."

She waves me off in the way only she does. "Pfft, since when do we keep anything from each other?"

I'm saved from answering that when my assistant Louise sends me a text.

Louise: *I just got a call from YR Magazine. They want to move the interview and shoot up this afternoon. I can rearrange all your meetings if you're good with this. They want you there in half an hour.*

I hold my phone up to Annabelle. "I have to make a call."

She nods and I step away to call Louise.

"Remind me why I agreed to this damn interview and photo shoot," I say when she answers. *YR* hounded me for almost a year to do an interview. I know it's going to be a farce; they sold it as a business interview, but really, they only want a shallow look into the world I inhabit, which is something I don't ever care to discuss.

"You know why you said yes, Beckett. You don't need me to remind you." Louise's cool efficiency and lack of emotions is the very reason why I hired her and the number two reason why she remains working with me after five years. The number one reason is her unmatched talent for getting the job done.

"Reschedule my meetings." I have a feeling I won't be in the right frame of mind for them after I do this interview. Normally, I wouldn't reschedule for something like a magazine interview, but I just want this over with.

"Yes, will do."

"I'll leave now. Let them know I may be late depending on traffic."

She agrees and we end the call.

I make my way back to Annabelle. "I have to leave."

"Oh no. Really?"

I nod. "My appointments this afternoon have been rearranged."

"Fine, but we need to reschedule this lunch. We're way overdue for a catchup. Even your mother agrees with me on this."

My mother and I will be having words over that. "Call Louise. Set it up."

She stands and places her hands to my chest. "Next time, no interruptions."

I agree, to keep the peace, and leave her to head out the back to where Davis, my driver, is waiting for me.

I don't see Matty on my way out, but I do locate Frankie. "Tell Matty we'll talk next time." I know Matty wants to go over his investment goals with me, something I want to encourage him in.

Frankie agrees, and I exit out into the warm New York sunshine. June is my favorite time in New York. Not too hot, and the summer crowds haven't fully invaded yet.

"Traffic's a little heavy," Davis says as I slide into the back of my car. "I'll work my magic to get you there on time, though, boss."

I meet his gaze in the rearview mirror, taking in his wide smile. "I know you will." If there's one thing Davis is good at, it's getting me places on time when there wasn't any chance in hell of that happening.

He pulls out of the alley and heads in the direction we need to go. I open my emails and work my way through the ones that have come in while I was with Annabelle. Running my gaze over my inbox, I see it's going to be a long afternoon and night between the interview and these emails.

The last email I open before I arrive at the magazine office concerns the asshole I want nothing more to do with. The asshole who stole ten million from me. The asshole I told Johnson to expose to the world. It turns out the world already knows about his dirty deeds and doesn't care. This new information is enough to ruin my entire day.

I reach for the scotch in the back of the car and pour myself one.

God knows I need it.

Declan James, the ten-million-dollar thief, has just gotten himself engaged to Katie Stein. Everyone knows that anyone tied to the Stein family is gold, which means Declan's sins are as good as wiped now.

I stare out the window at the streets of New York as Davis navigates us through them.

I throw some scotch down my throat and wonder, not for the first time, how I allowed Declan to do what he did.

He won't ever do it again.

Not to me; not to anyone.

I'll make sure of that.

No one fucks with me and gets away with it.

Not even my best friend.

2

JENNA

One should not, I repeat *not*, agree to be a wing woman on a Wednesday night. Especially not when your friend is known to party until the small hours. I may not have had anything to drink last night, but crawling into bed after 2:00 a.m. midweek never works out well for me.

Ugh.

Please kill me now.

The headache I've had since I woke up at 5:58 a.m. (and do not get me started on that wake-up time; a girl should never be awake that early), is likely to kill me. That's if Shona doesn't kill me first.

"Jenna, seriously, the next time Marisa asks you to assess the guy she wants to date midweek, say no if you've already agreed to spend the next day with me. We had goals today, girl-friend, and you're letting the team down."

I flop down onto the sofa in her boyfriend's office and groan. "I know. I'm sorry! But you know how good Marisa is at convincing people to do what she wants. I had no hope." We were supposed to find outfits today for Shona to wear on her upcoming weekend away with Graham, her boyfriend, but all we managed to do was spend three hours wandering around the mall with nothing to show for the trip except one dress. I mean, it's a stunning dress, so there is that, but it's not really what Shona was looking for.

Shona joins me on the couch. "All I know is that my fashion stylist extraordinaire friend better be back on her game by Saturday when we go shopping again."

"Wait, we're going again on Saturday?" I rub my temples. How do I not recall planning this with her?

"Yes, I've just decided. Graham's working all weekend, so it's the perfect time for us to go."

"Okay, it's a date, and I promise there won't be a hangover in sight. I'll be in bed by nine on Friday night so I'm bright and sparkly for you. We will definitely find you the perfect outfits to wow Graham." I glance around his office. "Where is he by the way? He never leaves you hanging this long." We've been waiting here for almost ten minutes; it's unlike Graham to keep her waiting.

"He said he had a meeting today that may run late." She leans over and takes my hat, settling it on her head. Angling her jaw, she says, "I need one of these. I love it so much."

"I saw a gorgeous gray one yesterday. With a beige accent. It'll look amazing on you. Especially with that white dress we found last time we went shopping."

Her eyes light up. "Yes. Perfect. The only fedora I have is that one we bought when we were in LA last year. I prefer this wide brim style more."

Graham strides into the office, his eyes going straight to Shona. The way he looks at her is everything I've ever wanted in a relationship and never found. That saying "you have to kiss a few toads to find your prince" has been my experience, except you'd have to substitute the words "a few" with "a lot" to more accurately describe it.

Shona returns my hat before leaving the sofa and moving to her boyfriend. "Hey, baby."

His hand slides around her waist and he kisses her. "Sorry I'm late."

"All good. We kept ourselves occupied."

At her teasing tone, he says, "Jesus, should I be worried?"

I laugh as I stand. Shona has been known to occupy herself in ways that mess with Graham, like that time he kept her waiting for forty minutes and she opened a million tabs on his computer (tabs drive him crazy in the way minimalism drives me crazy), rearranged his perfectly arranged desk drawers, and ordered bunches of balloons for his office that said *Damn You're Fine*, *I Love Your Ass*, and *Let's Fuck*.

Meeting Graham's gaze, I say, "You should be very worried."

"You know I blame you for her bad behavior, don't you?" he says to me.

I grin and sling my bag over my shoulder. "My work here is done." I lean in close as I walk past him. "But FYI, your woman had bad behavior nailed by the time I met her. We're equals in that department." It's true. I met Shona five years ago through the hairdresser we both use, and she was already known for her sassy and bold ways. Her personality was what drew me to her; her way of loving big that matched mine made me hold onto her tightly. I don't often meet people like myself, and while we're different in many ways, we love the same way.

"Goodbye, Jenna," he says.

I blow a kiss at Shona. "I'll see you Saturday. And I'll have had all the sleep and be more alert than you've ever seen me."

Shona points her finger at me. "You better be, girl, or we're gonna have problems."

Blowing a kiss at Graham, I say, "Goodbye, Graham."

Exiting his office, I do my best to ignore my headache. It just won't let go. I'm pretty sure I'll be spending the rest of the day in bed feeling sorry for myself.

A text comes through as I step out of the building and into the blinding sunshine. *God, why couldn't you have turned the sun down today for me? Just a little.*

Tilly: Jenna, babe, I need your help with something. Today. Urgently. I'm about to call you. IF YOU VALUE OUR FRIENDSHIP, DO NOT IGNORE ME.

Jenna: Just so you know, I have the headache from hell today.

She calls, and I answer on the first ring. "Clearly I value our friendship more than my health. What's up, Till?"

"Holy fuck, the world has lost its shit today. Did you see the news about Declan?"

"This is what's urgent?"

"Well, no, duh, but seriously, did you see?"

"No, and I don't want to know, okay? There's a reason he's my ex. I've removed him from my soul and am working hard on recharging my vibration after he wrecked it." Yes, I've started using terms like "recharging my vibration", and no, I don't really know what they mean, but they sound good. Positive. Like I really do have my life together.

"Okay, well, I'm going to ignore your request because I feel like even though this is news you don't want to know, you'll thank me later. I'm pretty sure you'd rather not walk into a room and be blindsided when someone mentions this to you." She pauses. "Declan and Katie Stein are engaged. And Declan stole ten mil from Beckett. I've just sent you the tea."

@THETEA_GASP

#BECKETTPEARCE IS ten mil poorer today. His (old?) bestie, @declanjames is ten mil richer. It seems that's how you build wealth these days. Just take it from your friends. @katiestein doesn't care though. We hope she gets a prenup before she marries the thief. That's right, friends, we're serving the tea here first. Katie & Declan #4eva

. . .

I ALMOST DROP my phone as I read @thetea_gasp's post. They're the biggest celebrity gossip account on Instagram and they always have the news before anyone else.

"Declan stole from Beckett?"

"Girl, did you hear what I said first? He's engaged to that bitch."

"I don't care about that. I told you I was done with him the minute I discovered he cheated on me."

"Well, yes, but we all know that being done with a guy and actually being 'done' with him are two different things. That was only five months ago. Are you really over him?"

I sigh and press my fingers to my temple, massaging where the headache has increased its assault on me. "Yeah, I think I am. I mean, we weren't in a great place for a while; I just wasn't ready to face that. Katie did me a favor to be honest."

"Wow, you're a better woman than me, Jenna Blaise. If Declan was my ex, I'd be planning ways to remove his balls from his body. Actually, I probably would have already done that."

"We both know you would have ripped them off and sent them to Katie in the mail with a big 'fuck you.'" My mind is still busy trying to wrap itself around the fact my asshole ex stole from his best friend. Not that I was a fan of Beckett's, but stealing from your best friend is the lowest of low. I can't help but wonder how this happened and what Beckett's response was. These are things that Tilly isn't likely to know or care about, because she's more about the society gossip, so I don't bother to ask her for more information.

Tilly laughs. "True. Right, back to business. I need you to style a shoot for me this afternoon. Our stylist came down with food poisoning at the last minute and my boss has threatened me with career death if I can't fix this. Say yes, Jenna. I need you more than I've ever needed you."

Tilly is the most dramatic girl I know, and that's saying something because I know a lot of dramatic chicks. So I know she's exaggerating solely because of this personality trait. Also, her boss adores her; there's no way he'd ruin her career or fire her or do anything to her if she couldn't replace their stylist this afternoon. These are the reasons why I feel justified in saying no to her. The main reason, though, is that with this headache, I'm not convinced I'd do a good job for her today.

"I can't. Not today."

"Why? And don't tell me it's because of your headache. I've seen you make magic happen while suffering from one of those."

Ugh. She's going to be relentless over this. I know it. "Tilly, I didn't get much sleep last night. Between that and my headache, I'm not convinced I can do a great job for you today."

"Seriously, Jenna, you could do this job while giving birth. Be here ASAP."

She ends our call before I can argue with her. Staring at my phone, I mutter, "You are the worst human alive, Tilly Fallon, and I will find a way to hurt you."

It looks like I won't be spending the day in bed, but rather I'll be styling some young rich asshole instead. I love my job, just not so much when I have to work with the kind of people the magazine Tilly works for bothers with.

I knew I shouldn't have gotten out of bed today.

3

JENNA

"You're not serious?" I say to Tilly as I stare at the man she's directing me to. I then look at her and add, "Like, for real, at what point did you think it would be a good idea *not* to tell me who I'd be styling today?"

I arrived at the *YR* offices less than ten minutes ago and am ready to walk back out. Spending time with Beckett Pearce while dealing with a pounding head is my idea of hell on earth. Something Tilly is very aware of. I'm already calculating ways of hurting her worse than I already planned to.

She grips both my arms as if she's about to give me the pep talk of all pep talks and says, "Just go in there and pretend he's someone else. Like, Chris Hemsworth. That should get you through the afternoon."

"Nothing, and I mean absolutely nothing, is going to get me through the afternoon if I have to talk to that man."

Tilly cocks her head. "What is it actually that you don't like about Beckett? Every woman I know would die to spend an afternoon with him."

"That's because they don't know him like I do. He's arrogant and superior and overbearing and controlling."

"Those words mean the same thing, babe."

"Yeah, well that's because he's those things multiplied by a thousand. You should have told me who I'd be working with, Tilly."

She manages to look regretful at that. "I'm sorry, but I was desperate. Please don't leave. Please, please, please. I promise I'll make it up to you."

"Yes, you will." I take a deep breath and steel myself while looking at Beckett again. "Okay, I'm going in. Pray for me."

"I'm on my knees."

The thing about Tilly? I can't not love her, even when she does stuff like this, which she often does. She's been the kind of friend to me that I adore and need in my life: always there at the drop of a hat when I need her. Tilly and Shona got me through my messy breakup with Declan when so many others dropped me because I no longer had anything they deemed of value, i.e. a wealthy man who could open doors. I'll never forget what they did for me.

Straightening my shoulders and gathering my inner strength, I walk to where Beckett is waiting. Not that he's waiting—this man doesn't wait for anyone. No, Beckett Pearce enters a room and takes command of it simply by existing. Declan was up there in the realm of arrogant assholes, but he was never on Beckett's level. The difference between the two of them? Declan had to put effort into everything he attempted; Beckett never had to try.

As I move closer to where he's resting his ass against the makeup vanity, I lament the fact Beckett is the best-looking man I've ever laid eyes on.

Tanned skin.

Brown hair that's the perfect blend of styled and "fuck it, I just got out of bed."

Killer stubble that's a little more than a five o'clock shadow but not a full beard.

Strong jaw.

And those eyes.

I don't even want to talk about those eyes.

They're the brightest shade of blue and they're so wasted on him.

Also, don't get me started on the dark blue suit he's wearing today. Or the fact he's wearing a vest. A man should always wear a three-piece suit in my opinion. I could ogle a good suit for hours, and this one's right up there for me. I just don't want to ogle it on him.

Beckett's eyes meet mine right as I'm admitting to myself just how fine he looks today.

He doesn't smile.

Not even a trace of a smile hits his face.

"You should fire your stylist," I open with when I reach him. Glancing at his shoes, I add, "I would have chosen the brown Alessandro Galet Scritto Oxfords for you. So much more personality in those. These are a little minimalist and bland."

"Hello to you, too, Jenna," he drawls

I dump my bag on the vanity next to his ass, doing my best not to check out said ass. I fail epically. Beckett's ass is an eleven in a ten world. I've always thought so. And that has always pissed me off.

"I have to say, I'm surprised to see you here. I wouldn't have picked *YR* as a magazine you'd ever agree to doing an interview with."

He casually crosses his feet and arms after placing his phone in his pocket. "I have my reasons."

I bet he does. Beckett doesn't do anything without a clear and calculated goal.

God, we're not even a minute into our time together and I've had enough.

"Right," I say, glancing at the clothes hanging in the corner, "let's get you suited up so we can both get out of here as soon as possible."

"That would make my fucking day," he says, and I detect

the first note of turmoil I've ever heard come from Beckett's mouth.

Although I may not particularly care for the man, I care for all my fellow humans when they're suffering, and I have to wonder if he's suffering at the moment, thanks to his friend. Wait, are they still friends? Hmm, I say no. No one steals ten million from someone and still gets to call that person a friend. Not even when ten million is a drop in the bucket to that person.

I stare at Beckett a little longer than I mean to while processing the decision whether to ask him about this or not when he arches his brows and says, "Are we getting to work or not?"

And there goes my desire to ask him how he is.

Without another word, I head over to the suits. There are six to choose from, and I search for the ugliest. I mean, he's already dressed to kill in his own suit; he hardly needs to wear one of these, so it would give me great joy to choose the worst one for him. The problem is I would never compromise my job for my dislike of a person. There's no way I'd ever dress Beckett in the shittiest suit as a fuck you, even if that's exactly what I want to do.

"How are we doing, babycakes?" Tilly asks, coming up behind me as I inspect each suit. "Any luck with these, or do I need to put a call out for another?"

"Why aren't there any red velvet suits to choose from?"

She frowns. "Are you for real right now?"

"Yep." I look at her. "No, but don't you think he'd look great in red?"

"Good God, maybe you were right about this headache interfering with your skills today."

I eye Beckett, who's back on his phone. "Okay, tell me the feel for this piece on him, and then I'll tell you which suit to go with. But just so you know that asshole could pull off red velvet, blue velvet, green velvet.... He could even pull off a suit made from cowhide."

"That annoys you, doesn't it?"

I meet her gaze again. "Yes."

"Okay, let's get back to the job at hand. The piece on him will cover his takeover of Pride Industrial and the billion that's added to his bank account this year. We're also hoping to talk with him about his love of the Mediterranean and the yacht he recently purchased, as well as the houses he owns around the world and the lifestyle that entails."

"Good luck with all of that," I say. "You do know that Beckett despises talking about his life, don't you?" It's the one thing I respect about him. He might be rich as sin, but he doesn't flash that around.

"Yes, but he hasn't met our girl before. She has a way of getting these guys to open up. I'm confident she'll get what we're after."

When Tilly has confidence in people, it's not usually unfounded, so I nod and say, "Okay, this is the suit you want then." Pulling a dark blue Brioni from the rack, I hand it to her. This Italian brand speaks the money, power, and success she's looking for. "We'll team it with a blue shirt and brown leather shoes."

She hands me back the suit. "No point giving it to me when you're the one dressing him."

With that, she turns and walks away from me. Of course she does; I'm the damn stylist, so I'm the one who needs to get this on him.

I search through the shirts and shoes, locating what I'm after to complete the outfit. I then call out to Beckett, "Let's go."

Without waiting for him, I head toward the area set up for him to try on the clothes.

He joins me and eyes the suit where I've hung it. "You're telling me this suit's better than the one I'm wearing?" God, could he be any more arrogant?

"My job is to choose a suit from what's on offer." I nod at the Brioni. "That's the best one on offer. Your job is to put the damn thing on and parade around in it for a bit. I really don't think it'll take it out of you to do that."

"I see you're still as angry with me as you always were," he says, removing his suit jacket as he walks behind the change cubicle.

"I'm not angry with you, Beckett. I just don't have time for your ways."

Beckett stands at around six foot four, which means he's taller than the screen separating us. He keeps his eyes on me as he changes. Something I find a little disconcerting.

"What ways are those, Jenna?" he asks, and it sounds like an actual question he doesn't know the answer to. Odd, because he should. We nitpicked at each other during the two years I dated Declan.

I hold his gaze, determined not to be the one who looks away. "Look, I've got a headache and have had very little sleep; I don't need to get into a discussion with you that will likely lead nowhere good. Let's just get through what we need to and go our separate ways again."

"I always liked our discussions," he says as he shrugs out of his shirt. "Even when they disintegrated into you lecturing me on why I was wrong about whatever we were discussing."

I've never seen Beckett without a shirt on, which means I've never seen the tattoo I'm now looking at. I try not to stare, but color me surprised; Beckett never struck me as a man who'd have a tattoo. I can't see the entire tattoo because most of it is on his back. What I can see is part of a wing. It curls around from the back, over his shoulder, ending at the base of his neck.

I desperately want to see the rest of the tattoo and have to refrain from asking him to turn around.

Dear God, Jenna. Get yourself together, woman.

He catches me staring. I mean, I don't even try to hide it. I can't, because I'm so taken aback. I had Beckett in a neat little box, and this messes with that categorization.

Beckett comes from old money. He followed his father into the family business straight out of college. He married old money at the age of twenty-seven after a suitable amount of time dating. Three years if my research is correct.

And yes, it kills me to have researched this man. In my defense, I wanted to know who I was spending time with while dating Declan. And I didn't want to ask Declan for the information.

Even when Beckett divorced his wife just over two years ago, he did it respectfully, making sure their family names were kept out of the gossip columns as much as possible. My research couldn't find the actual reason for the divorce, so that shows how well he managed it.

Beckett is controlled. Focused. Disciplined.

He's discreet in all things.

Cold and calculated in the way he executes his moves.

Beckett is too buttoned up for me.

I like my men to be looser, more openly passionate, more of a free spirit.

The kind of men who are tattooed.

I never imagined Beckett as that kind of man.

He doesn't say anything while I gawk; he simply continues changing. And continues watching me. And that right there has me in a fluster. Because he's not just looking at me, he's trying to unmask me. He's trying to get a feel for me. For my thoughts. I don't know how I know this, but I do. It's right there in his eyes. And holy hell, it's making me all kinds of confused and on edge and perplexed. And damn him, it's turning me on —in a completely not turned-on kind of way, of course. I mean, Beckett Pearce irritates me. He doesn't freaking get me hot and bothered.

Right, time to take charge of this situation.

I turn and search the room for Tilly. When I spot her, I

glance back at Beckett and say, "I'll leave you to finish chang-ing. You don't need me for this." Then, without waiting for his response, I turn away again and stalk in the direction of my friend.

She looks up as I approach, a frown crossing her face. "Whoa, babe, what's this all about?" she asks, her hands motioning in circles at my face. "You look like you're about to make a declaration or something."

"He's dressed. Sorted. My job here is done." I'm aware my words leave my mouth a little breathlessly, but I ignore that and charge on. "I'm going to leave now. Feel free never to hire me again. Especially if the job involves a rich asshole."

She stares at me silently for a beat, her face expressionless, before her mouth tilts into a smirk. "Oh, my darling, I think you like yourself a rich asshole but don't want to admit it."

My eyes widen. "I do not. He might be hot, but a girl needs a lot more than hot to go on. Like, maybe some personality and a lot less arrogance."

"Beckett has loads of personality. I'm not sure how you can be so blind to it."

"He might have something you like, but he has nothing I like. It's called taste, Till, and we all have different tastes."

The photographer cuts in on our conversation, saying to Tilly, "How did we go with finding a model? I'm about to start and would very much like to try the shot I mentioned to you."

Tilly pulls a face. "I'm working on it, Jacques. Just waiting to hear back from the girls I've reached out to."

Jacques frowns. A deep frown that borders on pissed off. "My dear Tilly, that is not the answer I was looking for." He throws a glance around the room, settling his gaze on me. He runs his eyes over my body before nodding and jerking his chin at me. "You." He looks at Tilly. "She's perfect for this. Get her dressed."

He strides away from us, leaving me with a bad feeling about what just transpired.

"Uh, what just happened?" I say to Tilly.

She takes hold of my bicep and leads me toward the changing cubicle where I left Beckett. "You just scored a new job."

Beckett steps out from behind the screen, filling my sight with a whole new level of hot. It turns out I'm even better at my job than I ever thought. The Brioni suit fits him in a way I don't see often. It's like it was made for him. It makes me want to peel it off him slowly.

Good God, I need help.

He looks at me expectantly, those blue eyes of his boring into mine. "Is this the look you were going for or do I need to try another one?"

Oh, buddy, you have no idea.

"It passes," I say.

His brows arch. "It only passes? Surely we can do better than that."

"It's good. You don't need to try another."

"Jenna," he says, his voice deep and smooth and way too sexy for me. Like, did he just drop it an octave or whatever those things are called? "Good isn't something I ever strive for. If this isn't the best we can do, we're trying another."

Goodness, will he just let this go already? I glare at him. Maybe there are daggers in my glare, I can't be sure, but if there are, he deserves them for being so good-looking. "This is the best we can do. Trust me on that." *Why the hell is every word I'm uttering today all breathy?* I need to seriously work on that.

Thank God for Tilly. She takes over the conversation, throwing directions at Beckett like a pro. "You're good to go, Beckett." She points to where Jacques is setting up the shoot. "You can head over there now. We'll be there in a minute."

His eyes remain on me for a beat longer than they need to before he finally leaves us. I'm not sure what his game is today, but I'm not into all this eye contact going on between us.

Before I can spend any more time thinking about that, Tilly

says, "Right, you need to put this on"—she passes me a dress —"and I swear, if you argue with me, I will post those photos of you from that party last month all over social media."

My brain tries to process her words, but there's a lot in what she said, and my brain fails. "You wouldn't. Not those photos of me—"

"Yes, *those* photos."

I take the black dress from her, my mind slowly catching up. Looking down at the dress, I say, "Why do you want me to put this on?"

"Because, my friend, the photographer wants a shot of Beckett with a beautiful woman, and you're the most beautiful woman in this room." She takes a step away from me. "Now, celebrate that beauty and get changed, and make it snappy. We're running out of time here."

The last thing I see before I do what I've been ordered to do is Beckett's face turning to mine as the photographer motions at me, and those eyes of his that see everything locking onto mine again. And holy hell, the heat in them is enough to scorch me.

What even is today and why do I have to live through it?

Beckett Pearce is not a man I want to feel anything for. And I most definitely do not want to feel what I'm feeling.

Desire.

Red-hot desire that's more confusing to me than the most confusing questions of life.

4

BECKETT

"Jenna, I need you here," the photographer says, positioning Jenna in front of me, slightly to my right, with her face to mine. "Now, look up at Beckett and place your hand here." With that directive, he takes her hand and slides it around my waist. He then looks at me and says, "And you place your hand here," while putting my arm around her waist and positioning my hand on her ass.

As Jacques leaves us to continue setting himself up to take our photo, Jenna mutters, "This is the last time I ever say yes to Tilly for anything."

"You're not enjoying yourself?"

Her beautiful blue eyes squint with annoyance. "Do I look like I'm enjoying myself?"

My lips twitch. She might not be enjoying herself, but I finally am. Jenna, on a good day, is enjoyable; Jenna, when she's like this, is even better. Declan never did know what he had. He's an idiot for fucking their relationship up. Tightening my grip on her, I say, "No, but keep it up because I'm enjoying the hell out of it."

Her eyes widen. With shock or more annoyance, I'm unsure. "I swear, if you move that hand, I will hurt you."

"People!" Jacques calls. "Let's get started."

"Yes, please," Jenna mutters. "Let's get this over with."

I agreed to this spread with *YR* solely for the PR. I knew they'd want to discuss my takeover of Pride Industrial, which will only increase my profile. Something I'm looking to do while I prep for my next move. What I couldn't have envisioned was this time with Jenna.

I've been attracted to her since she showed up on Declan's arm over two years ago. She's the kind of woman I don't often find, if at all. Classy, beautiful, kind, and intelligent—all things that are rare in one woman. The kind of women I meet, at least.

One of the things I respect about her is the way she knows her mind and stands by it. We often disagree, but not once has she backed down on me. She lets me have my say, and then she lets loose, articulating her position so well that sometimes I almost change my opinion. I could never understand why Declan didn't engage in deeper discussions with her. Jenna is a woman I would always welcome conversation with.

Jacques starts taking photos, yelling out directions to elicit the look he wants from us for this photo. Easy things like "angle your head a little to the left" and "straighten up" and "Jenna, look at Beckett." That last one seemed to irritate her, which only amused me.

Jenna has me pigeonholed as an asshole; that much is clear from everything she's ever said to me. What's become apparent today is that she's attracted to me just as much as I am to her. Something I wasn't aware of before. I don't intend for the attraction to go anywhere, and she obviously doesn't either, but I'll damn sure enjoy every minute I have her in my arms.

The scrap of material they dressed her in is hell on a man, though. Short, black, low-cut, with a slit that reveals far too much in my opinion, it's ensuring I have to do a lot more than just parade around for this shoot, as Jenna put it when she tried to boss me earlier.

Jacques stops taking photos and comes to us. "This shot is

almost perfect. Almost. I just need you to look at Jenna like she's the only woman in the world. Imagine you're going to take her home and fuck her the minute we're done here."

Jenna inhales sharply and her body stiffens.

I could kick his damn ass for being so crude with little thought for her.

Jacques looks questioningly at me. "Yes? Do we think we can manage this?"

I let Jenna go and say, "I'll be back in a minute."

Ignoring her frown, I say to Jacques, "A word," before striding out of the room.

He follows me, joining me with a glare, throwing out, "I don't appreciate my shoot being hijacked—"

"And I don't appreciate a lack of respect for the women in the room. You pull that shit again and we're done here."

His lips flatten. "I'm the one in charge here and will not be spoken to in that way. And I'll talk to whoever I want in any way I want. If that doesn't make you happy, feel free to leave."

I nod. "Got it. We're done."

I stalk back into the room, pulling the suit jacket off as I make my way to the change area. Jacques comes back in, ranting about a lack of respect for his creative process. I pay no attention to his bullshit.

I've stripped out of the jacket, shoes, and shirt, and am undoing the button of the pants when Jenna slips behind the screen. "Umm, I don't know what happened," she starts, pausing as she takes in my naked torso. "Good God, how often do you work out?" Her eyes find mine again, and before I can answer her question, she carries on, "As much as this pains me to say, please don't leave. Tilly's worked her ass off for this and we've come this far; let's finish what we started."

"You want to continue working with that asshole, yet it pains you to ask *me* to stay?"

She grimaces. "That is a good point. Sorry. He's a worse asshole than you."

"Jesus, Jenna." I shake my head. "At least I can count on you to be honest. But I have no intention of going back out there. And you shouldn't either."

Her grimace turns to a frown. "You're doing this because of what he said?"

"You act like that surprises you."

She nods slowly. "It kind of does."

I work my jaw. "I've never tried to change your opinion of me, but I'd rather you not think of me as a man who's okay with another man speaking like that in front of a woman." I jerk my chin at the screen. "Now, can I finish changing so I can get the hell out of here?"

"You're pissed off at me?" She seems confused by that.

"Yes. I'm pissed off that you think so little of me."

She takes that in and turns it over for a beat before saying, "That's fair and I apologize. I was just a little surprised is all."

"And there it is again," I say, astonishing myself at how much her reaction is affecting me. "I'd rather you not be surprised. I'd rather you expect me to feel strongly about how women should be treated."

Understanding of what she said flashes across her face. "Oh, God, I'm sorry. Shit." She stops and takes a deep breath. "Look, let me just mention again that I'm not at my best today, so my brain isn't working fast or well. And I'm just going to shut up now before I say anything else offensive."

I nod and wait silently for her to leave me to change clothes.

"Oh," she blurts when she realizes what I'm waiting for. "Yes, I'm going." She turns to leave, but then stops and looks at me again. "Are you sure there's nothing I can say to convince you to stay and finish this shoot?"

"Nothing. I'm done here."

"Okay. Disappointing, but I get it."

Jenna leaves and I finish changing. As soon as I exit the changing cubicle, Tilly zooms in on me. "Beckett, I'm sorry this has happened. Please tell me if there's anything I can do to change your mind."

I shouldn't have said yes to this in the first place. Publicity of any kind is something I always avoid. The magazine caught me during an off moment where I thought something good could come from an interview.

I eye Tilly. "This isn't your fault. It's simply differing principles at play. We're not a good fit, so it's best if we don't continue. Send me the bill for your team today and I'll take care of it."

Jenna meets my gaze, and with a lift of my chin at her, I exit the room.

The fresh air as I step out of the building is a welcome change to the bullshit of the photoshoot.

I loosen my tie.

Who the hell was I kidding when I imagined I'd make it through that?

I pull out my phone and shoot a text to Louise.

Beckett: Expect a bill from YR. Whatever it is, pay it.

Louise: It didn't go well?

Beckett: I shouldn't have agreed to it.

Louise: Or maybe this has to do with the news about Declan today.

Fuck.

Beckett: Just pay the bill.

I shove my phone back in my pocket and eye the bar down the street. It's been a long time since I've blown off work for a drink, but that's exactly what I need right now. Something to take my mind off the fact my best friend is still fucking with me even after I've erased him from my life.

5

JENNA

Today has been a shitshow of epic proportions and it's not even three o'clock yet. After Beckett left the shoot, Jacques had a meltdown of egotistical proportions, and then Tilly lost her shit. I quietly changed out of the gorgeous black dress that had been mine to wear for too short a time and tried to calm Tilly down. That was a useless endeavor. She was too far gone by the time she started ranting at Jacques for being, and I quote her directly, "a fucking sexist, racist, assholey, misogynistic, sorry excuse for a man."

"Do you want me to stay?" I ask after Jacques finally leaves. The only good thing about all this is that focusing on Tilly's problems has helped me forget my headache. The pain has almost completely eased.

"No," she says, agitation clear in her voice and body as she glances around the office anxiously. "You go. I've got a lot of work I still have to get through this afternoon." She throws her arms up. "The first of which is to fix this mess. God, I should never have hired that asshole for this job. His shoots haven't been great lately." She shakes her head. "I've really fucked this up."

"Till," I start, but she cuts me off.

"Jenna, no," she says, taking a deep breath. "I'm only just holding myself together here. I love you to death, but if you keep trying to make me feel better, I really am going to lose it, and that is not something anyone needs to see right now." She takes another long breath. "I'll get through what I need to and then I'll go home and put myself to bed where everything always feels better. And then tomorrow, I'll get up and make everything okay again." She steadies her gaze on me. "I've got this. I promise."

Right.

She's right.

Tilly is good at putting herself back together when life takes a detour. And she really does hate it when people don't listen to what she's telling them she needs.

I nod. "Gotcha. And yes, you do have this. But you should call me if you need me, okay? I'll come straight to you wherever you are, and we'll get through this together." I pause before asking her the question on the tip of my tongue. "How much trouble are you in here?"

She stares at me. "A lot."

Oh God. Tilly can get away with a lot because her boss loves her, so this is not good.

I nod again. "Right, I'm going so you can get your head together."

"Thank you."

I wrap my arms around her. "Call me later to let me know you're okay."

After she agrees, I leave her, walking as fast as possible out of the magazine offices. I know that I didn't cause this problem for her, but I feel a part of it and need to put as much space between me and that problem as possible.

I text Shona as soon as I'm outside.

Jenna: Holy shit, this afternoon has been the worst. I need a Shona debrief. What are you doing?

Shona: I'm doing Graham. On a plane. To Vegas. I'm sorry!! I can call you for a debrief if that'll help?

Jenna: No, you should keep doing what you're doing. But, since when were you going to Vegas today?

Shona: Since Graham told me he'd booked a surprise trip for us. I'll be back tomorrow.

Jenna: Don't do anything I wouldn't do.

Shona: Permission noted. Love you.

Shona: PS Day drinking fixes everything.

Jenna: Permission noted. Love you too xx

I stand on the sidewalk, trying to ignore the worry running through me. I can cope with bad things happening to me, but I don't handle it well when they happen to my friends and I feel unable to help.

Shona's right. I need a drink. A drink will help calm me.

I'm surveying my surroundings when another text comes through. Thinking it's Shona, I open it instantly, not paying much attention to the sender.

Declan: I'm going to need that necklace back that I gave you.

I stare at the screen as my brain kicks into gear.

What the hell?

I stare some more, my chest growing heavy with anger.

That anger turns to rage the longer I stare.

This asshole cheated on me for God knows how long. Possibly the entire time we were together if my gut is right.

He cheated on me with a friend. Granted, she and I weren't close, but I thought we were friends.

He very publicly announced his relationship with her two days after we broke up.

He's now engaged to her just five months after said breakup.

And now he wants the necklace he gave me back?

"I fucking hate you, Declan James!" I scream at the top of my lungs, not caring that the people walking past are gawking at me like I'm insane. Clearly, it's the day for meltdowns, and I'm embracing mine.

Stabbing at my phone, I type out a reply to his message.

Jenna: You can't have it. It's mine.

Declan: I have the receipts for it. I also insured it. As far as the law is concerned, it's mine. Or at least that's how the story will go.

My chest squeezes with more rage.

Blinding red rage that makes me want to wrap my hands around his neck and squeeze the life out of him. Until he's choking and begging me for mercy. At which point, I'll squeeze harder and make him hurt as much as he made me hurt. And I won't let go until—

Shit.

I'm losing my goddamn mind.

You need a drink.

Stat.

I eye a sports bar down the street.

Perfect.

Two minutes later, I push the door open and make my way to the bar. The bartender is either really good at his job, or the look on my face is enough to tell him not to mess with getting me a drink.

"What'll it be, beautiful?" he asks, his attention completely on me as if I'm the only person in here. I'm not. The bar is actually quite busy. It's also noisy in a way I'd normally like, but right now, with my meltdown in full force, it's far too noisy for me. Agitatingly so.

I dump my purse on the counter and pull up a stool. "Shots. I want your most lethal concoction. And I want three of them."

"Bad day, huh?"

"The worst. Like, on a scale of one to ten, I'm at a twenty."

He grins. "Gotcha."

Without another word, he gets to work. Five minutes later, he places three shots of amber liquid in front of me. I didn't bother to watch him make them, distracted by the screens filled with sports, and I don't bother to ask him what's in it before downing the first one.

"Holy hell," I say as it slides down my throat. "What was that?" I can't decide if I like it or not. I'm fairly sure it had Jäger in it as well as some cinnamony, pepperminty alcohol. I'm not generally a Jäger fan, but this hit the spot in all the right ways.

"Liquid cocaine. Jäger, cinnamon schnapps, peppermint schnapps, and I threw some Bacardi in there for you, too." He grins again. "You know, because your day is at a twenty."

"You," I declare as I pick up the next shot in line, "are my new favorite person." I throw the second shot down my throat without hesitation.

His grin turns into a devastatingly gorgeous smile that would make any woman want him. I'm in the middle of a meltdown over a man, though, so I don't want any man right now; I just want his shots.

"I'll be back," he says, pointing at the third shot. "I recommend you don't drink that one straight away. The two you've had have enough firepower to mess you up. You maybe don't even need that third one."

Oh, I need it.

He has no idea.

I watch him move to the other end of the counter and then stab at my phone to pull up my messages.

Jenna: Expect a package on your doorstep tomorrow.

Declan: Glad to see you came to your senses.

I pick up the third shot and throw it back.

Jenna: Oh, I did that five months ago when I kicked your ass out.

Declan: Don't be dramatic, Jenna. It doesn't suit you.

Jenna: Do you know what doesn't suit me? Letting a man like you order me around. I might be sending you a package, but it won't have a fucking necklace in it.

God, is it hot in here?

I remove the black blazer I'm wearing and hang it on the

back of the barstool. My execution is a little off, though, and it lands on the floor.

"Shit," I mutter, sliding off the stool. Again, my execution is off, and I stumble and almost fall flat on my ass.

"Darlin'," the bartender says, "You okay?"

My head snaps up as I lift my blazer off the floor. Meeting his gaze, I say, "Okay would not be my word of choice, but I'm getting there. You should make me more shots."

He lifts a brow. "You sure about that?"

I settle the blazer in place and climb back onto the stool, nodding. "Absolutely. Three more of those bad boys and I'll be more than okay."

He doesn't look convinced, but he honors my request, and I soon have three more shots lined up, ready to help me wipe this day from my memory.

I've almost got a shot to my mouth when Beckett's deep voice sounds from behind me. "Jenna."

I turn to him. Why is he here? As soon as that thought hits my brain, another one quickly follows. Possibly the same reason I'm here. Declan. "Beckett."

He runs his gaze over the shots in front of me and then the one in my hand. "I see you're on a mission."

"Are you judging me?" He totally is. Fuck him. This is an out-of-character afternoon of drunkenness for me.

"Not judging. Simply wondering if you need three more when you've just slammed three down in rapid succession."

I slam the fourth one down and then say, "That sounds an awful lot like a judgment of some kind."

He places his hand on the back of my stool and leans in close... and damn him for smelling so good. I do my best to ignore what his scent is doing to me while he says, "No, it sounds an awful lot like concern. I don't judge people I actually care about."

My thoughts are like a knot of twenty necklaces I can't sepa-rate, so I have trouble dissecting what he says. I must have misunderstood, because I could swear he just said he cares about me. It must be that voice of his. And that delicious scent. "What cologne are you wearing?" I demand, my brain latching on to the one thing it *can* make sense of. I'd bet my last dollar he's wearing Royal Oud. It really is sex in a bottle and one of my favorites with its rich wood smell.

He doesn't answer me. He just continues watching me intently for what feels like lots of minutes, when more likely it's only moments. Finally, he removes his hand from my stool and signals to the bartender. "Add her drinks to my bill and bring us two Macallans."

"The same as before?" the bartender asks.

Beckett nods as he pushes my shots away. "Take these away."

"Ahh, no, don't take these away," I say. Eyeing Beckett, I add, "And I can order and pay for my own drinks, thank you very much."

He looks at me. "You don't drink Macallan anymore?"

Macallan is my favorite scotch, and I really, really, *really* want to tell him I no longer drink it, but I can't bring myself to do that. "I do. But I also drink liquid cocaine, and you would do well to remember I'm not a woman you can order around."

His lips twitch. "Liquid cocaine, huh?"

I glare at him. "Yes."

He glances at the bartender again. "Bring the scotch to my table." He then picks up my shots and looks at me. "You good to walk?"

My head has started feeling all fluffy. It's exactly what I was going for, but now that Beckett's here, I wish it wasn't so fluffy. I need to be able to make sense of what he's saying and doing. Something I'm not doing too well at. It's like he's three steps ahead of me and has already moved on by the time I catch up.

"I can walk, but why do we need to walk? There's a perfectly good stool next to mine if you insist on sitting with me."

"We're not sitting here," he says in that self-assured, decisive, annoying way he has.

"Oh, really? And who made you the boss?"

He gives me a look that holds a little exasperation. Good. I'm glad I put that on his face. "By my calculations, you're going to finish these shots in the next fifteen minutes, at which time you're likely to fall off that damn stool if you remain on it. Get your ass up and move to my table so I can at least keep an eye on you and make sure you're okay."

Oh. My.

Usually I dislike his commanding ways, but this is a different kind of bossy, and I think I like it.

Good God, it must be the alcohol speaking.

I do not like Bossy Beckett.

But he has a point. Infuriatingly so. I do feel messy and not too stable on this stool. "Fine, you win, but only because you're actually right for once." I look back at him as I take my first step away from the stool. "Grab my blazer, too. I cannot lose that. And where is this table of yours?"

He takes hold of my blazer with a shake of his head. I think I see more exasperation in his eyes, but maybe I'm wrong. That's highly likely because it's official: I'm drunk.

This day was supposed to get better after entering this bar. Instead, it's going in a whole other direction thanks to Beckett showing up. I've achieved my goal of settling myself down a little, but now he's here, I wish I hadn't done such a good job of it because who knows what I'll say in this state. Especially when instead of feeling the dislike I usually feel for this man, I'm feeling a whole lot of lust.

Oh God.

Please help me.

6

BECKETT

I watch Jenna take a seat in the booth I've occupied since I entered the bar. It's the last booth, in the corner, and thankfully away from most of the noise.

Jenna's movements aren't smooth, and she lurches into the booth, landing with a thud. I like the fact she makes no apologies for the state she's in. Instead, she owns it and doesn't give me an inch when I do something she doesn't like.

After I deposit her blazer on the seat next to her, I sit opposite her and place the shots on the table between us.

She leans her elbows on the table and says, "Why are you in here? Don't you have work to do? I mean, I've never once known you to take an afternoon off to drink."

"I've never once known you to do shots like it's your job."

She removes her elbows from the table and leans back in her seat. "Good point. Ugh. What a mess of a day."

When she reaches for one of her shots, I place my hand over hers as my eyes bore into hers. "Declan?"

She stills and doesn't say anything for a long moment before nodding and pulling her hand back, minus the shot. "You too?"

The bartender arrives with the Macallans. After he leaves, I pick up my glass and drink some of the scotch. I nod. "It's been a hell of a day."

Jenna exhales loudly and pushes some strands of her long, blonde hair from her face. "That's an understatement." She picks up her phone and taps it a few times before passing it to me. "Look at what that asshole sent me."

I take the phone and read through the messages Declan sent her today. They add to the anger swirling inside me. I don't know how many necklaces Declan gave her, but I'd bet a good chunk of my cash on the one he wants back being the one I paid for. He'd given me some bullshit about being good for the fifty thousand because he had an investment about to pay off. I'd known in my gut it was a lie, but I hadn't wanted to face the fact my best friend of fifteen years was doing what so many others always tried to do to me. I hadn't wanted to acknowledge that for a long time. In the end, it turned out Declan took far more from me than money.

The only thing that cuts through the anger I'm feeling is Jenna's response to his messages. I hand her phone back. "Don't fucking give him that necklace."

Surprise fills her face. "Wow, that might be the most emotion I've ever heard from you. I'm impressed."

I throw some more scotch down my throat. "You have me neatly boxed, don't you?"

She doesn't react to that question, just says honestly, "Yes." And then, "Although, I never picked you for having tattoos. That threw me a little. How many do you have?"

One of the things that always fascinates me about Jenna is how I never quite know what I'm going to get from her. It's refreshing in a predictable fucking world.

"I think I'll keep you wondering."

A smile tugs at her lips and she points a finger at me, circling it in the air. "Oh, that's fun. Who knew Bossy Beckett had it in him?"

"Bossy Beckett?"

She shrugs. "Well, you have to admit you like bossing people around."

"It's my job to boss people around, Jenna."

"So, what, you figure you'll just do it 24/7 in case you forget how to?"

"This may come as a surprise to you, but I don't go through life ordering everyone around."

"Uh, yeah, you do."

"Trust me when I tell you that if I did do that, we wouldn't be sitting here having this conversation."

"Because you would have ordered me to shut up?"

Keeping my eyes glued to hers, I drain my glass and place it on the table. "No, because I would have sent you home by now where you'd be a hell of a lot better off than sitting here getting shit-faced."

"Oh," she says, annoyance settling over her beautiful face, "I see. You're the kind of man who likes his woman to be at home, not making any noise."

"Have you ever seen me treat a woman in that way?"

"The only thing I've seen you do, Beckett, is sleep your way through Manhattan. This is a learning opportunity for me today. Please continue to enlighten me."

"I think it'd be a waste of my time."

"Well, we're both here trying to kill time while forgetting what Declan did, so I'd say it'd be a perfect use of time."

"Do you know what I think?"

"I never know what you're thinking. It's both frustrating and interesting."

That piece of information intrigues me. I doubt she meant to share it; the alcohol she's consumed appears to have loosened her tongue. "I think you want to figure me out, and I think that annoys the hell out of you."

She stares at me for a long beat. She then picks up one of her shots and throws it back, pulling a face as it goes down. "You really are the most arrogant man I know. That's what *I* think." Moving out of her seat, she stands. "I have to go to the restroom. While I'm gone, you should make yourself useful and order me another drink."

With that, she makes her way to the restroom while I do my best, and fail, to remove my eyes from her spectacular ass.

Christ. What am I doing here? Blowing off work in favor of drinking is one thing. Drinking with Jenna Blaise is a whole other thing. One I'm not convinced is a very well-thought-out idea, because as much as she's throwing walls up at me, I know they'd be easy to break down if I wanted.

And there's the danger. Jenna's better off with those walls up, and the fact I'm even thinking about knocking them down should have me walking away. Instead, I find myself drinking the scotch I bought her and thinking about her ass and what I'd like to do to it.

7

JENNA

"What are you doing, Jenna?" I ask as I stare at myself in the restroom mirror. "This is Beckett. Arrogant, bossy Beckett, who you can't stand. Remember him? Remember all those times he condescendingly went out of his way to explain things to you that you obviously didn't understand? Oh, and what about that time he took over your dinner party and insisted on getting caterers in because he didn't think you could manage? You cannot sleep with him today. Not under any circumstance." I drop my head and suck in some deep breaths. Why does the room have to keep spinning? Like, it needs to just stand still already.

"Girlfriend," the girl standing next to me says, looking at me with concern. "Are you doing okay? You need me to get someone for you?"

I lift my face to look at her. "God, no. The only person out there who you could get is Bossy Beckett, and I do not need him coming in here and taking charge."

She laughs. "Okay. But maybe you need Bossy Beckett because you don't look so good."

I groan. "It's those cocaine shots."

"Oh girl, they are nasty. You only need a couple of them and you're good."

"Yeah, I've figured that out now." With every passing second, those shots are doing more damage to my ability to think and to make good decisions.

"Right, so," she glances at the door, "I'm gonna go. You're good? You don't need help?"

I step away from the mirror and nod while straightening my clothes that feel a little rumpled. "I'm good. Thank you."

With one last smile, she exits the restroom and I follow her out, thankful for the blast of cool air as I step back into the bar.

I walk back to Beckett's table, doing my best to ignore the way his eyes track my every step.

What is going on with us today? I've known this man for almost two and a half years, and not once has he ever looked at me this way.

I want him to stop.

You are such a liar.

No, I'm drunk, and I've had a shitty day, and so what if I think he's fuckable? That doesn't mean I want him anywhere near me.

Yep, liar.

I reach the table, noting that Beckett is halfway through the drink he bought me. Probably a good thing. I certainly don't need it.

"I'm going home," I say. "Thank you for the drinks and the conversation."

He holds my phone up. "You might want to sit down to read the message that just came in."

Declan.

I take my phone, muttering, "The next time I see him, I'm going to do serious damage to his balls."

Declan: It won't be me ordering you to return it, Jenna. Either you send it back, or the police will be paying you a visit.

My head snaps up and I stare at Beckett. "Scratch that, I'm going to actually rip them from his body. How dare he?" Before

I realize what I'm doing, I'm sliding back into the booth. "How the hell did you keep him around as a friend for so long?"

He arches a brow. "It seems we have something in common after all."

"Yeah, shitty judgment. But seriously, how many years did your friendship last?"

He takes a sip of his drink. "Fifteen."

"Wow. And you didn't know he had this in him? No, ignore that question. You're a smart man, so I can't believe you didn't know." I rest my arms on the table and lean forward. "Why did you maintain the friendship?"

He takes his time answering, and I give him the space to collect his thoughts because this is something I've wondered for months. Maybe longer if I'm honest with myself. I'd suspected the worst about Declan for months before I finally allowed my eyes to open to the real man I was dating. Finally, Beckett finishes his drink and says, "History and loyalty. And I didn't want to believe what I knew to be true." He pauses. "Something that seems to be my downfall with the people I love."

I'm stunned by his admission. I mean, I asked him the question, but I didn't expect the kind of answer that revealed a part of his soul. I can't be sure, but I think he's referring to his ex-wife, too. Because I've had enough to drink to switch my filter off, I say, "How did he manage to steal ten million from you, though? That just doesn't seem possible." From everything I know about Beckett, he's ruthless in business and never lets anything get past him.

"It seems it is possible when I care more about a person than my money. I won't make that mistake again."

"You're not going to tell me, are you?"

Again, he takes his time deciding what information to share. I've almost given up on ever knowing the answer to my question when he says, "His scheme was elaborate. The financial records were manipulated, and the accounting firm he used was complicit, something I struggled to believe due to their reputation."

"So, what, you'll never see the money again?"

"I don't expect to."

Beckett's sitting in front of me answering my questions matter-of-factly like he's relaying the facts of something that's not personal to him, but I see the effort it's taking him. For the first time ever, I see the battle behind his perfectly put-together composure. And also for the first time ever, I don't want to be as hard on him as I usually am.

"He's full of shit with this police threat, isn't he?" I ask.

"Tell me, if you're done with him, why do you want to keep the necklace?"

I don't want to answer that question. But he's been honest with me, so I'll be honest with him. "Declan never gave me anything while we were together, except for this necklace. It's probably not worth anything to anybody but me, although if he wants it back, maybe it is, but regardless, receiving that necklace was a moment in my life where I felt seen." I swallow down the emotions choking me as I share something so intimate and raw. "Life isn't about how much money a person can accumulate or how much power they have, life's about seeing the people who love you and loving them back with all your heart. And as much as he's a lying, cheating asshole, in that moment, he showed me that he actually did see me and know me, because he gave me something I would have given myself." I swallow hard again. "I haven't had many of those moments in my life, and I don't want to give this one back."

Beckett listens intently and doesn't respond straight away, which makes me feel all awkward after sharing what I did. Desperate to fill the silence, I say, "We should eat. I haven't eaten since breakfast."

"Jesus, no wonder those shots hit you straight away." He stands. "What do you want?"

I open my mouth to tell him I'm capable of ordering for

myself when I remember I'm trying to be nice to him. Not that I think I'm ever rude to him, but I know he likes to take charge, so just this once I'll let him. "Maybe just some fries. I'm not sure I trust this alcohol in me to play well with too much else."

He leaves me to order our food, and I pull out my phone and send a text to Tilly.

Jenna: Are you good?

Tilly: No. They want me to get Beckett back, and I'm pretty certain that's never going to happen, which means I'm not certain I'll keep my job. This is the worst mess I've ever made.

Jenna: I'm with Beckett. Do you want me to ask him?

She calls me. "Ah, why are you with Beckett, and how did that happen?"

"It's a long story that I'll tell you next time I see you, but seriously, I can talk to him if you want. See if maybe there might be something that would convince him to come back in." I'm not sure why my mouth is moving and saying these things because I have to agree with Tilly that I don't think there's a chance in hell of this happening. However, I'll do anything to help her, so here I am.

"I don't know, Jenna. I don't think it's a good idea. I think it might be best to give him a few days, and then I'll reach out to him."

"Okay, but if you change your mind, just text me. I can try to work my magic on him. I mean, Beckett might have a reputation for never giving an inch, but surely he can be reasoned with."

As the words leave my mouth, Beckett slides into the seat across from me, and if the look on his face is anything to go by, he heard every word I just said.

"I've gotta go, babe," Tilly says. "I'll talk to you tomorrow."

"Yeah, me too," I say slowly before ending the call. Placing the phone down, I say to Beckett, "You heard all of that, didn't you?"

He nods. "I'm interested to see what this magic is you're going to work on me."

This day has been all too much for me. From the little sleep last night and headache this morning, to letting Shona down, to having to style Beckett for a shoot I wasn't even supposed to be at, to the news about Declan, to getting drunk and spending time with Beckett, to feeling things for him that I do not want to be feeling. I just want to go home and sleep it all off. And forget any of it ever happened.

"You know what?" I say, feeling every honest thought I've had today bubble up. "I don't think my magic will ever work on you, but for what it's worth, Tilly's boss is pressuring her to convince you to still do that interview, and I told her I'd see if there's any way for her to make that happen. I know what your answer will be, though, so let's just pretend we never had this conversation. And I know you just ordered food, but I'm done here. I'm drunk and I just want to go home. Alone, because there's no way you and I are ever sleeping together even though you might just be the hottest man I know, and God knows I could do with some good sex, which I have absolutely no doubt you'd be able to provide." I point my finger at him. "And if that is ever repeated, I will deny it. You only heard those words because I'm drunk. I will forget them by tomorrow." I stand and reach for my blazer. Once I've got it on, I open my purse and pull out a wad of cash. Placing it on the table, I continue, "I'm sorry Declan deceived both of us, but after listening to you today, I think he betrayed you worse. There's a code between friends and you don't shit on that code." My voice softens. "I hate that for you, and I hope it won't stop you from letting new friends in, even though I suspect that's exactly what it will do." I run my fingers through my hair, willing myself to shut up. I've already vomited enough words all over the place. "Ugh, and now I'll leave you in peace. Don't drink too much. He's not worth it."

With that, I leave him and walk as fast as my drunk legs will carry me to the front door.

Did I really just say all that to Beckett?

God, you were supposed to help me here.

Epic failure, lady.

I'm out on the sidewalk and five steps toward the taxi I spy ahead when a strong arm comes around me and pulls me close to a hard body. Beckett's body.

"What are you doing?" I ask

"I'm making sure you get home-safely."

I shrug out of his hold, stumbling as I do so. "I'm good. I'm going to grab that taxi." And die all the deaths this day has bestowed upon me.

"You are so far from good it isn't funny," he says, and I swear I detect frustration in his voice. "For once, just let me do something for you."

"Honestly, I'm okay. I can get in a taxi and make it home all by myself." I meet his gaze and suck in a breath at the look of pure determination on his face. It's the look I've seen on him a hundred times before, and when Beckett wears it, he doesn't take no for an answer. I exhale and mutter, "Fine, help me into the taxi if you must." When he continues watching me with that same look, I add, "Thank you."

With a shake of his head, he says, "I'll do better than put you in a damn taxi. I've got my driver waiting."

Before I can resist, he takes hold of me again and guides me into his waiting Rolls-Royce. He rattles off my address for his driver, and I refrain from asking him how or why he knows it. That is a question for another day, and if I'm lucky, there won't be another day with Beckett.

We ride in silence, and I try to ignore the heat between us. I know I'm not imagining it, and while usually I'm more than good with this kind of thing, I'm not with Beckett. I'm confused by it and want to avoid even thinking about it. Impossible to do while he's sitting right next to me.

When we arrive at my building, he exits the car and helps me out before walking me to the door. When we reach it, I turn to him and say, "Thank you for the ride and for making sure I got home safely." I can't get the words out of my mouth fast enough.

He moves into me. Close. Like, close in the way I think he might kiss me. He doesn't, though. He simply nods and says, "Thank you for making that shoot half bearable."

Totally not what I expected, it throws me. With nothing to say to that, I turn to enter my building, more than ready to be alone, but Beckett places his hand on my arm and turns me back to him.

"Declan's full of shit with that police threat. He didn't pay for that necklace." He pauses. "It's yours. Don't give it back if you don't want to."

With that, he leaves me staring after him as he makes his way back to his car. If I were a whole lot less drunk and a whole lot more sober, I'd work my way through what he just said. Since I'm neither of those things, I enter my building and tell myself I'll figure out what he said tomorrow. The best I can do today is guzzle some water—a lot of water—and pray I don't wake with a hangover tomorrow.

8

BECKETT

"I'm not saying you shouldn't invest in it," Mac, my CFO, says. "I'm just saying take some more time with this decision."

"And I'm saying I don't need any more time. We're doing this."

"Christ, Beckett." He rakes his fingers through his hair. "I don't know what's gotten into you these last couple of weeks, but you're making the kind of decisions I've never seen you make. Rash decisions that may lose you a lot of money."

Mac has worked with me for three years and I trust him implicitly in this position, but I don't always agree with him. The last two weeks, I haven't agreed with anything he's advised me on, but I respect the hell out of his opinion, even when he refuses to let up about it like he is this morning. "It wouldn't be the first time I've lost money, Mac."

He moves from the sofa across from me and walks to stand in front of the expansive floor-to-ceiling window of my office that overlooks Manhattan. Gazing out at the skyline, he takes a few moments to consider his thoughts before looking back at me and saying, "Is that what this is all about? Declan?"

"Jesus," I mutter, leaning forward and loosening my tie. "I told you I don't want to discuss him. And no, for the record, this isn't about him. This is about the possibilities I see in these investments that no one else does. That's always been my strength and you know it."

"I do, but let's not forget the strength I bring to the table." He pauses. "Neither of us could have seen what was coming where Declan was concerned. Not when the financials were so manipulated. But I don't think you even care about the money. I think you're messed up over the friendship, and I don't blame you one bit for that. However, that's even more reason for you to listen to me on this."

My phone sounds with a text and I allow it to distract me. Anything is better than thinking about Declan.

Ruby: I don't suppose you have twenty you could spare me?

Beckett: Thousand or million?

Ruby: Ha. Minutes, smartass.

Beckett: When?

Ruby: Now.

Beckett: No, but yes.

Ruby: Best brother in the world.

Ruby: Don't tell Elon I said that. I'll deny every word of it.

I stand and meet Mac's gaze again. "I'll take today to think it over some more, but I don't expect to change my mind."

He nods. "I don't expect you to either because you're a stubborn son of a bitch."

Ruby enters my office as Mac leaves and dumps her purse on the sofa before flopping down onto it herself. With as much dramatics as I'm used to from her, she says, "My life is over. I need you to tell me how to fix it."

"Is this a coffee or scotch kind of 'life is over?'"

"Eww, keep your scotch to yourself. This situation calls for tequila."

"So, coffee?" She knows I don't keep tequila here.

Waving me off, she shakes her head. "I gave up caffeine a week ago."

I sit. "What's going on?"

She groans before exhaling a long breath. "Mother. That's what's going on."

"What's she done now?" These two are always at it; I've lost count of how many times this year Ruby has come to me like this.

"She told me I need to find myself a husband." Her eyes widen. "Can you believe that?"

I can.

My mother comes from some of the oldest money around and there are certain expectations held for daughters. Sons, too, but we get off easy compared to the daughters.

"I take it you told her your thoughts on the subject?"

"I wouldn't be your sister if I didn't."

I chuckle, some of the tension in my body easing. Something my sister is good at helping with.

"Was Dad around for this conversation?"

"Yes. That's why I'm in this state. If it was just her, I'd ignore her, but when Dad's involved, well, we both know what that means."

We do. And it doesn't surprise me. Ruby is nearing thirty and has spent her twenties indulging her desire to paint abstracts and sleep with any man who makes her feel good. She's lived in New York, LA, Paris, London, Amsterdam, Sydney, Berlin, and Rome. She's blown through millions, tried nearly every drug out there, drunk her way through what feels like a hundred messy breakups, and landed on my doorstep every time she's had her heart broken. I love my sister, but I spend far too much time worrying about her, and while I don't think she necessarily needs a husband, she needs to stop messing around and figure out her life.

"You want me to talk to Dad." It's not a question; it's a statement about what I assume this conversation is actually about.

"Would you?"

I shake my head. "Cut the bullshit, Rubes. I wasn't asking."

"Fine. Yes, I'm here to ask you to please talk to him. I would love you forever if you fix this for me."

"You already love me forever for all the things I've done for you. And just to be clear, I'll fix this for you on one condition."

"God, you sound more like him every day."

"I want you to sort yourself out."

"I'm trying. You get that, right?"

"No, I don't get that. What I see is a woman going from country to country, from man to man, from party to party, with no idea what she wants in life except for a good time. That's not what life's about, Ruby."

"That's where you and I disagree, big brother. If life isn't about fun and beauty and happiness, you're doing it wrong."

"They'll cut you off."

She shrugs. "Do I look like I care?"

"You should. You've never had to work a day in your life. You won't know what the hell's hit you without those millions in your bank."

She stands, anger strewn across her face. "I didn't come here for a lecture. And for your information, I *have* worked a day in my life. How do you think all my paintings came into existence?" She jabs a finger at me. "*This* is what's wrong with our family. Too much emphasis on money and appearances and not enough on finding ourselves and authenticity. Oh, and thank you very much for being just like them and not acknowledging that creativity is a worthwhile way of earning a living. You have no idea how much I've actually made from my art, because you never cared enough to ask, and I don't care enough about money to share."

Before I can stop her, she grabs her purse and stalks out of my office, slamming the door on her way out. My sister is as stubborn as everyone else in our family. Christ knows where this will all end up.

My phone rings, distracting me from thinking further about this situation.

"I've got Annabelle on the phone," Louise says when I answer. "Do you want me to put her through or take a message?"

"Christ," I mutter, taking a seat at my desk. "Put her through."

It's been two weeks since our lunch when I agreed to emcee her gala and she's called me three times since then to go over details. Details I don't need to have any hand in.

She comes on the line, bubbly as usual. "Beckett, how are you?"

"The same as when we spoke yesterday."

"Oh, darling, I'm sorry to interrupt you again, but it's important. You know I wouldn't bother you if it wasn't."

"What is it, Annabelle? I'm in the middle of something I need to get back to."

"Right, I'll get straight to the point. I'm organizing the rehearsal for the gala and want to work out what time on the Friday before works best for you."

Why the hell did I agree to this? "Louise runs my diary. You know that."

"Well, of course, yes, but I thought this was more personal than work, so I thought it best to run it by you."

"No," I say, barely containing the snappish tone on the tip of my tongue, "this needs to go by her. I'll put you back through."

"Oh." I don't miss the disappointment in her voice. "Okay, that sounds good."

Without another word, I send the call back to my assistant.

This is the last time I'll ever allow our history to dictate my response when she asks a favor.

Turning my thoughts back to Ruby, I call my father and wait for his secretary to put my call through.

He comes on the line faster than usual. "I suspect you're calling on behalf of your sister."

"Correct."

He sighs, and I imagine him sitting in the big office chair he's had for decades, placing his glasses on the desk, and leaning back with that impatient expression on his face I know so well. "Your mother is adamant this needs to happen, Beckett."

That's his way of telling me he doesn't want to back down. My father might be the power behind the name, but my mother holds just as much power in her own way.

"Ruby's not going to give her what she wants. Are you ready for the ramifications of that?"

"Your sister might be flighty, but she's not foolish. I made sure of that. She'll come to her senses."

"I think you'll find her senses are much different than yours."

"Beckett," he starts, his voice taking on the authoritarian tone he uses when he doesn't want to be challenged. I'm not in the mood for it today, though, and cut him off.

"I don't disagree with what you're trying to achieve. However, you're going about it the wrong way. Try a new approach. She won't put up with this one."

A text comes through on my cell, jerking my attention from my father.

Declan: We need to talk.

"I have to go. Think about what I've said."

I end the call and snatch my cell phone up.

Beckett: I don't have anything to say to you.

Declan: It seems you've had a lot to say to Jenna, though. Our usual café in half an hour.

There's no rational reason why I go along with his request, but I do, and half an hour later, I enter the café we've spent hundreds of hours in discussing all manner of things. He's waiting at the table in the corner, his back to me as I move toward him. Every cell in my body is on alert in a way I've only experienced with one other person in my life. The two of them make a good pair, both fucking me over in ways I never saw coming. The fact they did it together at times shouldn't have surprised me when I discovered it recently. The fact it did shows just how much work I have to do on my ability to shut down threats.

I slide into the seat across from him. "Say whatever the fuck you need to say and make sure you get it all out because there won't be another opportunity for you to say anything to me."

Smug amusement settles on his face, and I work hard not to smash a fist through that face. "What upset you more, Beckett? I'm betting it's the knowledge your wife fucked me more than she did you."

I'm out of my chair, with my hands gripping his shirt, and my face shoved close to his before I know what's happening. "You're a sorry fucking excuse for a man, Declan." I force him away from me hard enough for his ass to land on the floor.

Fuck.

I stab my fingers through my hair and suck in a breath.

This asshole isn't worth my time or my attention. I shouldn't have come here.

I make a move to leave when he says, "Jenna's refusing to return my necklace, which I assume is because you've gotten in her ear about it." He picks himself up off the floor. "The thing is, she doesn't want to mess with me over this. I won't hesitate to make public the sex video we made. And you and I both know that won't do her any favors or make her family happy."

I stare at the man I've called a friend since we were in high school and wonder how I could have been so wrong about him. "Christ, you really are a piece of work, aren't you?"

He shrugs. "At least I accept who I am. That's more than can be said about you."

"I don't know what you're talking about, Declan. The only thing I know is I should never have trusted you."

His lips pull up in a sneer. "Tell me, Beckett, did you want to fuck Jenna the entire time I was with her? Or maybe, *did* you fuck her?"

My chest fills with the kind of anger I've never experienced. Not even when I discovered my ex-wife's cheating ways and kicked her out. That anger pushes itself through my skin, crawling all over me as I snarl, "I'm not good at betraying the people in my life. I've never touched Jenna or anyone else you were with for that matter."

"And yet, here you are looking out for her when no one asked you to. Your hard-on is showing, my friend. And trust me, she's not worth it."

The rage snaking its way along my skin twists and snaps, and I finally give in to my urge to inflict pain. I punch Declan and knock him to the floor again.

"Fucking hell," he grunts. Standing, with a bloody nose, he gets in my face. "You think you're untouchable. A god. But you're no better than any of us, and you're certainly no better than me. All these years, I've lived in your shadow. I'm fucking done with that now."

"You think marrying a Stein is what'll give you the power you desperately want?" I shake my head. "You've got a lot to learn about power if you do."

That angers him and he shoves me back against the wall. I'm not oblivious to the fact we have an audience, but at this point, I don't care. "Fuck you, asshole. And tell Jenna to give me that necklace or else that video goes live."

"You want the fifty k, Declan? You got it. But she stays out of it."

His eyes go wide and his grip on me loosens. "Fuck me." He takes a step back, whistling low. "Okay, we have a deal. So long as that cash shows up today."

I grab him by the collar and pull his face back to mine. "If that video ever sees the light of day, you will regret that." My eyes search his, anger bleeding from them and every pore of my body. "Am I understood?"

He nods and jerks out of my hold. "Yeah, you're fucking understood."

"Good." I straighten my shirt. "Now get the fuck out of my sight."

I watch him walk away, my mind a wreck of thoughts I'm not sure I'll ever untangle and make sense of. A wreck I'm not sure I want anything to do with.

The only thing I know with absolute certainty is that I'm better off without the mess a best friend and wife can inflict upon a person.

9

JENNA

"Oh my God, Mom, no. You know what I think of auctioning women off for dates to raise money."

My mother presses her lips together in the way she does when she wants me to know I've disappointed her. "Jenna, darling, this is for a good cause." She checks her watch before glancing around the restaurant. "And we only have thirty minutes until the auction, so please, we need you to hurry up and work this argument out of your system and agree to help us."

My sister Kristen lifts her shoulders and pulls a defeated face. "If I have to do it, you should too."

I look between the two of them, fairly sure I already know the outcome of this conversation and wishing I was stronger against my mother's attempts to turn me into a "real" Blaise woman who offers her services willingly to a good cause that also benefits the family name. "You two planned this, didn't you? You invited me to this 'lunch,' telling me to dress up because you know I love to dress up and eat, when all along you wanted me in your auction." I point a finger at my sister. "And don't play the victim; we both know you love these events as much as she does."

My mother looks bored. "Darling, you *are* aware we're raising money for animals, aren't you? I know this is a cause close to your heart."

Damn her.

She's got me there, and she knows it. It's why she looks bored with the conversation already. She's just waiting for me to agree to something she knows is a given.

"Fine," I mutter, throwing them both a glare. "But this might be the last time I ever attend any 'lunch' you invite me to. Dinner too. In fact, don't ever invite me to eat with you again because I won't come."

Kristen grins. "The kitties thank you."

I smack her arm as Mom leaves us to share the news with her committee. "I'm serious, Kris. I detest the idea of auctioning off women. I mean, why aren't Grayson and Oliver here being auctioned off too?"

"Ha. You know Mom would auction them off in a heartbeat if she could."

"Exactly my point. Our brothers get out of it, but we don't. This is sexist bullshit."

She waves me off. "It's some harmless fun to raise money for a worthwhile charity."

There's no point trying to argue with her, so I let it go and say, "I'm not getting changed or doing anything to my hair or face. Whoever 'buys' me will have to agree to fork over the cash with me looking like this."

I manage to catch her full attention with that. And I want to high five myself for putting that horrified expression on her face. "You're not being serious?"

"I am."

She blinks slowly before dropping her gaze to my shirt and then my skirt and then my shoes. "Jenna, there's no way any man here today is going to pay for a date with you if you wear that outfit up on the stage."

I shrug. "Suits me."

I send all the thanks out into the universe that I chose to wear this outfit today. A pink tulle skirt that sits just above my knees paired with a white T-shirt that says *You Want A Perfect Girl? ...buy a Barbie*, a black biker jacket, and black and white chucks.

"Dear God, are we even related?"

"I almost wore my *Cocks Rock* tee, but I didn't think Mom would appreciate sitting across from me at lunch, staring at it. As it turns out, she and I have hardly spent any time together; I could have worn it." I fluff my hair. "My hair looks good, though, don't you think?"

With a shake of her head, she says, "You are too much."

I wish you were too.

I also feel the "are we even related" question with Kristen. We really are polar opposites. The thing is, though, that she fits into our family far more than I do. Our oldest brother, Grayson, works with Dad in the family publishing business. Oliver, our other brother, works his ass off in his tech company. They both toe the family line. And Kristen socializes her little heart out, making our mother proud. She's engaged to Johnathon Swindle, soon to be married, another thing that makes Mom proud.

Then, there's little old me who can't find a man to love her, who insists on building a styling business her parents disapprove of, and who doesn't do anything in any order that her parents would support. I'm the daughter they explain away as free-spirited and frivolous. I mean, I own those things and celebrate them, but I wish those things didn't put distance between us.

Kristen leaves me and I send a text to Shona.

Jenna: I'm being auctioned off for a date.

Shona: <insert sarcasm> Ooh, this sounds like fun. <end sarcasm>

Jenna: Exactly. I wish you were here.

Shona: I don't. How did you get yourself into this?

Jenna: My mother. You know I can't say no to her.

Shona: It's something we need to work on.

Jenna: Can we start tonight?

Shona: Yes. Unless of course you're on that date tonight.

Jenna: Nope. You know I don't play easy to get for any man. Not even one who pays for me. Oh God, that sounds disgusting.

Shona: So you're gonna make him wait?

Jenna: Of course.

Shona: Attagirl.

Jenna: Mom's approaching. Gotta go.

Shona: I'll pray you don't get some sugar daddy who slurps his drinks and has big slimy hands.

Jenna: Jesus. Make it stop.

"Jenna," Mom says, motioning for me to come with her. "We need you out the back." She stops and frowns as she eyes my clothes. "I think we might need you to change that outfit."

I cross my arms, settling in for a fight. Me saying no starts now. "No. You either auction me in this, or you don't auction me at all. And this isn't up for debate."

My tone obviously says it all because she looks at me wide-eyed like she's never seen me before. She doesn't say anything for a few moments; she simply stares at me in silence. Then with another hand motion, she says, "If we must."

I'm all cool composure as I follow her out of the hotel restaurant to the ballroom where the auction is being held, but on the inside, I'm doing cartwheels and fist pumps. It's kind of sad, though, that I'm a twenty-nine-year-old woman who can't say no to her mother easily. I hand out noes to everyone else no problem, just not my mother.

Definitely something to work on.

I admire the pink balloons and beautifully decorated room as we walk through it. I'm always a sucker for sparkle, and they've done a great job. The area behind the stage is busy with rich girls dressed to impress. They're primping and fussing like their lives depend on it. I have no doubt many of them have fully bought into the idea that they might find their future husband today, and while I don't discount that idea, because it's been known to happen, I wish I couldn't taste the desperation in the room. I wish that finding a man to marry was something that happened by chance for these women, a blessing to cherish, rather than an endgame they pursued with relentless determination.

I head over to where Kristen is fixing her makeup, paying no attention to the looks of disdain sent my way. I don't care what these women think of me. I never have.

"You look beautiful," I say, meeting her gaze in the mirror.

Her features soften. Compliments always achieve that with her, but I really do mean it. My sister is one of the most beautiful women I know. "Thank you."

Glancing around at the twenty or so girls waiting to go out on the stage, I say, "Any idea the order this is going to go in?"

She nods slowly. "Umm, I hate to break it to you, but you're going last. Because of your outfit."

I expected that but hoped I was wrong. I just want this over with. Still, I'll take it in return for not changing.

Taking a seat, I wait my turn.

It might just be the longest afternoon of my life.

I count the girls as they go out. There's twenty-two here for this, including me. Not only will I be practicing my noes with my mother after this, but I'll also be having words with her over the fact she didn't really need me in the auction. Not with the bid amounts I'm hearing come through. The highest bid so far has been one hundred thousand, with the rest not far off that. By my calculations, they've raised almost one and a half million by the time they get to me. Not bad for an afternoon of food, alcohol, and schmoozing.

"And last but certainly not least, we present Jenna Blaise." The emcee's voice filters out to where I'm waiting, and the woman manning the back of the stage motions madly for me to go out. I do as directed, and a moment later, I'm blinded by the spotlight on the stage.

"Fuck," I mutter, holding my hand up to shield my eyes, forgetting they attached a microphone to my shirt.

The emcee coughs and I realize my faux pas. Smiling out at the crowd, I say, "Sorry, but at least you guys all know what you'll get with me." I wink. "I look pretty, but there's some dirty underneath."

My mother is going to kill me.

Oh well.

I embrace this fact and make that death worthwhile, especially after the laughter I get to my first remark. Part of the auction involves the men being able to ask me questions, and I field some boring ones to begin with. They soon loosen up, though, and we begin to have some fun.

"What's your dream date?" one of the guys asks.

"A backward date," I say with a sexy smile. It's time to have a little fun with them. "First, a bath together, with rose petals and candles. Then some wild sex, followed by dessert, preferably chocolate, and then dinner."

"How do you deal with jealousy?" another man calls out.

"Honestly, I don't give a man reason to be jealous, and my ideal man wouldn't give me reason either."

"What about football? Are you good with your man putting it first when a game's on?"

I look out in the direction of where that question came from, but the lights keep me from being able to see much. "I love football so we're good. But if I'm in the mood to get a little frisky while the game's on, we're getting frisky."

Laughter fills the room and the emcee steps in. By the sound of her flustered voice, she's dying a little over my answers. "Ah, thank you, Jenna. We'll open bidding now. Let's start with ten thousand."

Hmmm. I'm not sure whether to be offended at that amount or not. They opened bidding for every other girl at twenty thousand.

This is an auction for a date, Jenna.

You hate these things, remember?

Right, yes.

The bids for me, however, come in thick and fast, and quickly move past the highest bid of the day. When I hear three hundred thousand, my eyes go wide.

Holy shit.

Now I just feel uncomfortable.

"Three hundred and ten."

"Three hundred and thirty."

"Four hundred thousand."

We're down to two guys bidding now. I can't see them, but I can make out the two voices.

"Four hundred and fifty."

"Four hundred and sixty."

Good God.

And then a third voice cuts in. "One million." And fuck me if I don't recognize that voice.

Beckett Pearce.

You have got to be kidding me.

The room turns silent after that, and the gavel comes down.

And I owe Beckett fucking Pearce a date.

10

BECKETT

Jenna glares at me. "What the hell was that?"

She's asking me a question I don't know the answer to, but I give her one anyway. "A tax deduction." That's true. Mac told me to find some more deductions.

Her glare remains in place. If she knew how much I like it, I'm certain she'd wipe it away. "Bullshit. And what are you even doing here? This does not strike me as the kind of event you would ever grace with your presence."

"I could say the same about you." Never in a million years would I have picked Jenna for being willing to get up on that stage and auction herself off.

"Don't change the subject, Beckett. I asked you a question."

I give her the only truthful answer I have. "I needed to see you. Your assistant told me where to find you."

That removes the glare from her face. In its place settles a look of confusion. "Why would you need to see me?"

I eye the people around us. Too many to be having this conversation. We require privacy for this. "How about we go on that date now and I tell you why?"

She shakes her head. "No, no date today. But that shouldn't stop you from telling me the reason for this visit."

I cock my head. "So I pay one million for a date and then have to wait to be told when I can have it?"

"Yes," she snaps. "That's exactly how this works."

"Perhaps that condition should have been explained before bidding started."

"Perhaps we can cancel your bid."

I fight the smile threatening my mouth and say, "What I have to tell you isn't something you want me to say in this room. I guarantee you that."

"Is your driver waiting outside?"

"Yes."

"We'll talk in your car."

I hold out my arm to indicate I'll follow her. A moment later, I've got my eyes on her ass and am reminded of the day two weeks ago when I last dedicated time to the same thing. Today, she's covered it with a pink ballet skirt. Two weeks ago, it was a short, black, leather-looking skirt. Christ knows what she'll kill me with on our date.

Halfway to my car, she turns and faces me, walking backward. "You just had your eyes on my ass, didn't you?"

I can't fight the smile this time. "Any man would." I drop my eyes to her T-shirt. "I'm surprised they approved this shirt for the auction."

"What? You don't like it?"

My smile remains in place. "On the contrary, I do." I also liked her black AC/DC shirt she wore when I saw her last. Not because I like that band, but because I like the way she wears clothes like she's giving the middle finger to the world she lives in.

She keeps taking steps backward while narrowing her eyes on me. "You really mean that, don't you?"

"Jenna, you should know by now that I only ever say things I mean."

"Hmmm." She doesn't say anything else before turning back around and giving me her ass again.

Davis is waiting outside the car by the time we reach it. He opens the door for Jenna, and she climbs in while I head around to the other side.

Once we're both settled, she turns to face me, bringing one leg up onto the seat, getting comfortable, and says, "Right, let's hear it."

"Where do you want Davis to drop you?"

She frowns. "We're just talking. I don't need a ride."

I don't know why Jenna fights me on every damn thing, but it's something she's always done. Even when it's clear she could do with my help. "Humor me."

It's clear it pains her to say it, but she says, "I'm going home."

I meet Davis's eyes in the mirror, and he nods before starting the car. I then say to Jenna, "I saw Declan yesterday and want to tell you what we discussed because it concerns you."

I don't miss the way her body stills at that news. "Okay."

"The necklace situation is sorted out. He won't ask you for it again. However, he mentioned a sex video you two made, and—"

She holds up a hand. "Wait. Why won't he ask me for it again?"

"I've taken care of that."

"Yes, but how?"

"I originally bought that necklace. Declan never paid me back for it. He knows he has no leg to stand on when it comes to that." I don't want to tell her this, but I'd rather this than share the fact that necklace only meant cash to Declan. If there's one thing I know about Jenna after our conversation two weeks ago, it's that she wants to feel like more than a woman who can be bought. She wants to feel like more than a moment that meant fuck all to the man she thought loved her.

Her disappointment is clear in her eyes. "I think I knew you paid for it after we talked the other week, but yay me for once again ignoring the truth that was plain to see."

"Don't do that."

"Do what?" she says bitterly. "Pretend to be anything but the woman who refused to see what was right in front of her?"

I work my jaw. "Don't take the blame for what he did."

She stares at me and slowly nods. "You're right. He's a piece of shit; I'm not. I gave my heart fully, and it's not on me that I expected the same in return. That should be a given in any relationship."

"It should." I can't agree with her more on that.

"So, the sex video?"

"You need to be aware he's threatened to make it public. I've shut that down and am hopeful he won't ever make good on that threat, but I want you prepared in case he does."

Her brows pull together. "How did you shut that down?"

"Let's just say things got ugly between us and he lost his cool. His threats were thrown out when he was pissed off. I countered with threats of my own. Threats I'll follow through on if needed."

Jenna has the look in her eyes that says she's got a thousand questions ready to fire. The only other woman I know who hounds me with so many questions is my sister. I'm usually good with this, but not so much today. I don't want to get into this necklace business with her. Not when the full truth of it may hurt her. "This makes no sense, Beckett—"

"The only thing that made sense yesterday was me punching him."

This catches her attention, drawing her away from whatever else she wanted to ask me. "Shit. You two really got into it, huh?"

"You could say that. And now we're done. And so is this necklace business."

Her features soften and she looks at me with gratitude. "Thank you."

I don't let her eyes go. "You deserve better than him. I hope you know that."

She smiles. It's something I'm not the recipient of often, and fuck if I don't like it. "I do know that, but thank you for saying it. Being cheated on is like a punch that's hard to recover from. It messed with me for a while, and to be honest, it still is, but deep down, I know there's a good man out there waiting to give me the love and happiness I deserve." She pauses briefly. "There's a good woman out there for you, too, Beckett. I hope *you* know that."

This isn't a conversation I signed up for. Dragging my gaze from her, I look out the window to see where we are. When I see we're close to her home, I say, "I need a date for when our dinner will happen, Jenna."

She arches her brows. "Who said our date should be at night?"

"You'd prefer it wasn't?"

"Not necessarily. I'm just saying assumptions should never be made."

"Tell me what you want, and I'll make it happen."

"You mean you didn't bid because of what I said my dream date would be?"

"I've learned not to make assumptions when it comes to you."

"That's a key thing to learn about me."

"Well? I'm waiting."

"I actually think I'd like to see what your idea of a date is. I'm going to leave it up to you."

"That'd be a first."

"One you'd do well not to fuck up."

My lips twitch. "Noted."

Davis pulls the car to the curb outside her building, and she grabs her purse. With one last look at me, she turns and exits the car, and I'm left wondering what I've gotten myself into. A date with a woman who's always disliked being in the same room as me. A woman who clearly wants love in her life. A woman I have no intention of pursuing a relationship with. This can only get mixed-up from here on out, yet I can't bring myself to stop whatever this is.

@thetea_gasp

#BECKETTPEARCE DROPPED a cool mil on a date with @jennablaise this week at a bachelorette auction #gasp #his-bestiesgirl. One might recall these two were spotted together a couple of weeks ago getting cozy in a bar. Beckett isn't known for going back for seconds. Could we be sipping this tea for a while? #staytuned

Tilly: Beckett's playing hard to get. I don't think he's going to change his mind on this interview. The good news is that I think my job is secure. Don seems to have moved on from the bad mood he was in over this fiasco.

Jenna: I've got my date with Beckett tonight. I could put a good word in for you.

Tilly: No. I think I'm actually good if he never does it. Like, I just wanna forget the whole thing happened.

Tilly: Have you found out where he's taking you for this date yet?

Jenna: No idea. All I'm hoping for is some good food and to make it through the evening without wanting to stab him in the eye.

Tilly: You've managed to spend time with him twice now without stabbing him in the eye. I think you'll be fine.

Jenna: There's a difference between wanting to do it and actually doing it, Till, and trust me, I wanted to do it plenty.

Tilly: This is what all good love stories are made of, my friend.

Jenna: What? Assholes and the women who spend their lives going crazy because they're in a perpetual state of 'what the actual hell am I doing with him?'

Tilly: I can't wait to hear how this date goes. I predict your clothes are off faster than you can say asshole.

Jenna: Nope. I bought a new red suit and it's not leaving my body.

Tilly: The fact you bought a new suit for Beckett tells me everything I need to know. Text me as soon as the date's over.

Jenna: I love the support you give me. You deserve a friend of the year award or something.

"Jenna," Shona says, joining me in my bedroom where she's helping me get ready for my date. "I've been thinking about which heels you should wear tonight, and I think these ones." She holds up the pair of strappy red heels I bought on her birthday weekend trip to Vegas last year.

"I'd forgotten I had these." I take them from her. "I think you might be right."

"Right? The suit is no-frills; these will dress it up. And just sayin', they'll slay Beckett. They're sexy as hell."

They're definitely that, which makes me consider whether wearing them is a smart move. I'm not convinced my goal tonight is to be sexy. I mean, there's a reason why I've chosen to wear a suit rather than a dress.

"Don't overthink this," Shona says, patting the shoes. "Wear these and stop trying to hide how hot you are. It's not like that's possible, anyway."

"I don't want to give Beckett the wrong idea," I say, being more serious about this date than I have been since he bid on it three days ago. "I'm not about leading men on; you know that."

"Beckett's a big boy. He can handle some sexy without getting the wrong idea."

She's right.

I'm not sure why I suddenly feel protective of his feelings, but I can't deny I do. Beckett might be bossy and arrogant and all those things I don't love, but he's showed me another side to himself that I actually do like.

I look at the shoes. "Okay, these are the ones."

Shona's smile fills her entire face. "Good. Now, we need to get down to business. He'll be here in forty minutes, and we still need to finish your hair."

Shona turned up on my doorstep two hours ago to help me get ready. I wasn't aware she'd planned to come over, but I love her for it because I've been nervous about this date for days. Beckett tried to plan the date for the day after the auction, and then for yesterday, but I put him off each time. I gave him bullshit reasons, but the truth is I'm nervous about it. And I find that baffling. It makes no sense that I feel nervous about spending a night with Beckett.

My phone sounds with another text.

Kristen: Are you flying single on Saturday or will you have a plus one?

"Is there anything worse," I say to Shona, holding my phone up, "than attending your sister's social gathering of the year by yourself and having to listen to everyone tell you how sorry they are your asshole ex cheated on you and then got engaged five months later? I think not."

She pulls a face. "You want me to go with you? I could wear a tux and pretend I'm your new lesbian lover. That'd give them something new to talk about."

"Maybe I should hire a fake date. A gigolo maybe."

"Ooh, that'd be fun. I would love to see him with your mother."

That thought is enough for me to rule the idea out.

My mother would fall for his charms, I'm sure of it. And I'd never hear the end of her questioning whatever happened to him. No thank you.

I ignore Kristen's text for now. I've got enough to deal with tonight. She can wait until I've gathered my strength again tomorrow.

"It's time to put the suit on," Shona says. "And then we'll finish fixing your hair."

I do as she says, and when I step out of my walk-in closet,

her eyes widen. "Wow. That suit is officially my favorite outfit you own. And I love, love, love that you're not wearing a bra. This cleavage is hot."

I look down at the blazer, taking in my bare skin where the jacket plunges between my breasts. "Too hot?"

"Never. Stop worrying. It's not like you to stress out over some cleavage on display."

That's the truth. This suit is something I'd normally wear without a second thought.

"Okay, no more thinking about this." I sit in front of my mirror. "Let's finish my hair so I can put my heels and lipstick on and get this date over and done with."

The next half hour passes by in a blur of hair, shoes, and makeup. I've just finished with my lipstick when Reggie, my doorman, calls up to confirm I'm expecting a guest. Beckett's knocking at my door a couple of minutes later.

Shona grabs her bag and air-kisses me with "Call me as soon as you get home. Unless, of course, that's after 1:00 a.m. because there's hot, dirty sex happening; in which case, you need to text me beforehand so I'm not up worrying about you all night."

I roll my eyes. "Let's be honest, you're not concerned about being up worrying over me; you just want to know if there's sex involved."

She grins. "You know me so well." Her voice softens when she adds, "Have fun. I know it's Beckett and you don't think he's capable of fun but stay open to it. Maybe he'll surprise you."

I open the door to let Beckett in, and Shona exits past him as he enters. They exchange greetings, but she doesn't hang around, and before I can catch my breath, it's just me and the man who has started doing funny things to my tummy, tonight being no exception.

If I thought I loved Beckett in a blue suit, I'd forgotten how good he looks in a black one. Devastatingly handsome are the only two words that come to mind. Besides fuckable and hot as hell, that is.

I inhale a deep breath as his eyes take me in appreciatively. When his gaze meets mine again, I throw out, "On time is a good start."

His mouth slowly spreads out in a smile. It might be the sexiest, laziest smile I've ever seen, and I hate that I want to commit it to memory. "I was given very specific instructions not to fuck this date up. Good to know I'm being scored highly so far."

"Don't get ahead of yourself, buddy. We're barely a minute in."

He continues smiling at me. "Are you ready?"

I sternly tell my tummy to settle down. Beckett is not the man to waste these butterflies on. Are they even butterflies when I have no interest in another date? I think not. I think they're some mutant insect stuck in my body that's flapping up a storm in order to escape.

I grab my purse and slip my phone in. "Yes."

He steps to the side to let me past, and as I move near him, he places his hand to the small of my back and guides me out. My heart beats faster than I ever recall it beating in the presence of a man, and my feet feel like they suddenly don't know how to move properly. Thank God for Beckett taking charge and getting us to the elevator.

As we wait for the elevator, he leans in close and says, "You look beautiful."

The next five words out of my mouth are proof I've lost my mind. Turning to look up at him, I say, "Thank you, you do too."

His mouth smiles. His eyes smile. His whole damn face smiles, and I want to tell him the date is finished and run back into my condo. Maybe now is an appropriate time to call my father and beg for an early inheritance so I can pay Beckett his million back.

"I can't say that beautiful is something I've ever been called. Coming from you it feels like a compliment," he says, that damn smile still glued to his face. How does one go about pulling a smile off someone else? I need to add that skill to my bag of tricks.

Thankfully, the elevator arrives, and Beckett ushers me in. We ride down in silence. This is agonizing for me. I'm the girl who easily fills the silence; I'm not the girl who drowns in it. Right now, though, I'm a mess of "what the hell is happening?"

Somehow, we make it out to Beckett's waiting Rolls-Royce, where he opens my door and helps me in before walking around to the other side and settling himself on the seat next to me. He and his driver exchange glances, an unspoken communication, and the car pulls out into the traffic.

"So," I say, meeting his gaze while trying to ignore the effect his cologne is having on me, "Where are you taking me?"

His phone sounds with a text. Full marks to him for ignoring it in favor of answering my question. "Somewhere quiet and relaxing."

"Intriguing. Can a girl have a clue?"

Another text comes through which he also ignores.

"Let's just say there will be lots of food for you to choose from."

Beckett has no way of knowing just how much those words are music to my ears. I'm not a calorie-counting girl. In fact, if I were to count calories, I'd be trying to accumulate a bigger number rather than a smaller one. I live for food.

Two more texts come through in quick succession.

I nod at his phone. "Maybe you should check those. Might be important."

"I suspect they're not. However, I also suspect they won't stop until I deal with them."

He sounds genuinely pained, and I have a burning desire to know who in his life is able to cause this kind of emotion in him. Beckett doesn't do emotions, yet it seems I'm learning he does.

He checks the messages and sends one back to which he immediately receives a reply. This goes back and forth for a couple of minutes, at which point he places the phone in his pocket and returns his full attention to me.

I try again for a clue as to where this date will take place. "All this food we're going to eat tonight, where will that be happening?"

"You're not good at being patient, are you?"

"No. I'm also not good with surprises."

"You don't like them?"

"Well, technically I do, but only if I don't know anything about them before they happen. This, I know about, so it's in a different category of surprise. One you should not continue keeping from me."

"Noted."

I narrow my eyes at him. "Noted as in you'll tell me or noted as in you now know but have no intention of paying attention to what I've said?"

"Do I strike you as a man who pays attention when I'm told to do something?"

Before I can answer that, his phone rings, and he apologizes before answering it.

"Ruby, can we please do this tomorrow? I'm busy tonight," he says.

His sister.

Thank you, research.

She says something, and then he says, "No, I can't change my plans. I told you this."

He listens intently to what she says next, and while I can't make out her words, I can tell she's emotional. Her voice grows louder and more passionate. Beckett remains calm, soothing almost. I wonder if this is something he's used to. Calming her down.

"I'll cancel my meeting in the morning and we'll go see them together," he says, his tone firm. "Don't drink tonight. You need a clear head for this. And you also need to figure out how you're going to get your point across tomorrow." His firm tone eases a little as he adds, "They just want the best for you. Remember that."

Wow. I've never heard Beckett like this before, and I have to admit it feels a little like the moment I saw his tattoo. The neat little hole I've slotted him into doesn't seem so neat anymore.

"Where were we?" he asks after ending his call.

I swivel in my seat to face him. "You were reminding me you're not a man who takes suggestions well."

"Right. It should be acknowledged, though, that I was willing to take your suggestions for this date into account."

"That is true and acknowledged."

"Did you get your website sorted last night?"

I told him I couldn't go out last night because my business website needed to be fixed. The way he asks the question tells me he didn't buy that reason one little bit.

"It's good as new," I say.

His eyes spark with amusement. "I bet it is."

We need a change in subject. "You know, I always wanted to ask you something."

"The only thing surprising about that statement is that there's just one item on your list."

"Smartass." I can't help smiling, though. "That time you went against your father and invested in Edge Manufacturing, how hard was that for you?" I have always wondered this, but over the last few days since he paid for this date, he's been on my mind, and this topic has been front and center.

"You've been reading up about me, Jenna," he says, the tone in his voice telling me he likes this fact.

"Oh, you have no idea," I admit, instantly wishing I could shove those words back in my mouth. Damn you filter; you need to start doing your job tonight.

He takes that in and sits with it for a moment. The look in his eyes is another giveaway as to how much he likes the fact I've done my research on him. Finally, he says, "It was both the hardest thing I've ever done and the best thing I've ever done."

And just like that, I don't regret being honest with him because it resulted in him returning the favor. And in a way I never expected from him. During the time we spent in each other's company while I dated Declan, Beckett didn't share anything raw like this. Not that I would have expected him to, but he was always so reserved. Well, except when I challenged him on something he said or did; then, he didn't hesitate to share his thoughts.

"Did it affect your relationship with him?" From what I've read, Beckett and his father had a rough time when he first joined the family company. The tension between them had simmered for a couple of years until the day Beckett ignored his father's directive and invested company money in Edge Manufacturing. There was a great deal of speculation about how that affected their relationship, but I never trust that kind of gossip.

"It did. We still maintained a united front in the business, but privately, we barely talked for a year. He pulled my power within the company during that year. Even when it was clear the investment was a good one." He pauses, weighing his words. "My father and I always had a hard relationship. Surprisingly, that investment ended up bringing us closer. It helped him see me differently. It also helped him to start trusting my ability within the company."

The car slows and comes to a stop while I'm processing everything he just said. Glancing out the window, I see we're at the Heliport at Pier 6.

Beckett exits the car and comes around my side to open my door. Holding his hand out, he helps me from the car, something I'm grateful for because my heels are sky high, and while

I'm good in heels, my nerves have the best of me tonight, and I'm a little unsteady.

Once I'm out of the car, he guides me toward the pier. It's a gorgeous summer evening with the sun throwing rays off the water as we walk to a waiting helicopter.

Looking up at Beckett, I say, "This is unexpected." I've never taken a helicopter ride and am not sure if flying in one is a good unexpected or a bad unexpected.

His eyes meet mine. "Predictability is one of my least favorite things."

"Taking risks on our first date; I like it."

My slip of the tongue doesn't go unnoticed. "First date? That implies there'll be a second." Damn him for being so attentive. Also, for having the sexiest voice known to mankind and using it against me.

"I should tell you up front that I'm not in the habit of handing out second dates easily anymore."

We reach the helicopter as Beckett says, "Smart. I'll keep that in mind."

The pilot greets us and discusses the flight with Beckett while I peer at the sleek interior. The inside of this helicopter is pure luxury with plush white carpet, white walls, six white leather seats, glossy black cabinetry and trims around the windows and seats, and a small oval table in the middle of the cabin with a dark glass top. My heart beats fast as I survey it, but I still can't decide if that's from fear or excitement. I'm leaning toward it being more to do with the thrill when Beckett places his hand to the small of my back and says, "Ready to go?"

I nod. "Yes, but I've never been in one of these, and I also have these heels, so I may need some help."

Before I know what's happening, his hands are on my waist and his mouth is to my ear. "I've got you." He lifts me, helping me into the cabin, and I settle myself into one of the super comfortable seats. A moment later, Beckett takes the seat next to me, filling the small space with his commanding presence, his intoxicating scent, and his attentiveness.

He hands me a headset. "Put these on to drown out the noise and also so we can talk."

I do as he says and then I buckle up. The pilot starts the rotor blades, and the noise is much louder than I realized it would be. Beckett and I wait while the pilot talks with whoever he needs to in order to get clearance to fly. We sit here for what feels like a long time, and I nervously anticipate takeoff. I expect the blades to whirr faster before we can take off, but they don't. Suddenly we're lifting off, and it feels like we're floating away from the ground.

Liftoff catches me by surprise, and without intending to I grip Beckett's thigh while calming myself. Once I've settled, I remove my hand and meet his gaze, my eyes wide as excitement floods my veins. "This is amazing!"

His eyes crinkle with a smile and he nods. I like that he doesn't judge me for my excitement. I'm not a woman who can hide my enthusiasm for something, and that sometimes results in people looking down their nose at me. In the circles I move in, the unwritten rule is that one should appear cool at all times. To say I fail at that is an understatement. That's not something I care about, but I have dated men who find me a little too excitable.

"Is this your helicopter?" I ask.

"Yes."

My gaze sweeps over the city as we fly over it. "If I owned it, I think you'd have trouble keeping me out of it. I can't believe I've never been in one before."

We settle into an easy silence for a little while before Beckett says, "What do you want to drink?"

I turn and find him opening a door I didn't realize existed in the center table. "What have you got?"

He rattles off a list of drinks and I choose the champagne

he mentions. I mean, my first helicopter ride deserves to be celebrated with champagne.

He pours my drink and a scotch for himself, and after I take my first sip, I say, "Are you going to tell me where you're taking me?"

"To my place in the Hamptons."

This isn't at all what I was expecting. Not that I really had any expectations. I should have known, though, that Beckett would choose subtlety over the flashy spectacle of a fancy restaurant where they know him and treat him like a king.

I sip some more champagne before giving him a smile and saying, "That's impressive."

He cocks his head and eyes me questioningly. "Why?"

"There's something to be said about a man who drops a million on a date and then chooses his own home as the venue. It's unpretentious and I like that."

The way the corners of his mouth lift tells me he appreciates what I've just said. "Careful, Jenna," he murmurs, "I might start thinking you don't hate me."

I keep my eyes firmly on his as I contemplate my response.

I want to tell him he could probably start thinking that now, but I decide those words should never leave my mouth.

We're getting on well tonight, better than we ever have, but that doesn't change anything.

This is a one-off date.

Beckett's tax deduction.

My contribution to charity.

And once the night is done, we can go back to our lives.

His phone distracts him with a text, and he glances at it. Frowning, he brings his eyes back to mine. "I'm going to have to deal with this."

I nod. "Of course."

He replies to the text while I turn my attention to the view out of the helicopter.

I'm so engrossed in the amazing scenery that I startle when

Beckett says, "I'm sorry, Jenna, but I need to go back to the city. Something's come up that I can't put off taking care of."

Turning to him, I see the worry in his eyes over whatever he has to go back for. I also see his regret over having to turn the helicopter around. "It's okay. I understand."

He speaks into the headset advising the pilot of his new plans, and after they have a brief conversation, he says to me, "I'm not sure how long this will take me. I can either have Davis drop you at home, or you can come with me, and we'll have dinner after I'm done."

This is my out if I want it. I mean, earlier I was talking about the likelihood of wanting to stab Beckett in the eye during our date. Now, I'm not so sure. On top of that, I can't deny my disappointment over the date being cut short.

I don't think I want an out.

I smile at him. "I'll come with you. You promised me lots of food tonight, and I want you to make good on that promise."

His eyes search mine, and I'm fairly certain he reads me correctly. I didn't have to say the words "I don't hate you" for him to know I don't. All I had to do was tell him I still want to have dinner with him.

Beckett drinks some more of his scotch and says, "Good," and holy hell if a delicious tension doesn't settle between us.

I thought I knew exactly how this night would go.

I thought I knew it'd be dinner and nothing else.

I thought I knew I never wanted to see Beckett again.

It's clear I know nothing.

13

JENNA

Beckett came back to the city to help a friend.

Totally not what I was expecting. I imagined it was for work.

His driver met us at the heliport and drove us to an apartment building in Brooklyn. We arrived about fifteen minutes ago, at which point Beckett brought me to a room on the ground floor that's filled with sofas, a television, a pool table, and kitchen facilities. He left me without filling me in on why he was here. It's a guy who arrives about ten minutes after Beckett left who enlightens me.

"You must be Jenna," the guy says when he joins me on the sofa where I'm scrolling my emails.

I meet his gaze and smile. "Hi."

Sitting at the other end of the sofa, he says, "I'm Josh, a friend of Beckett's and the guy that runs this place with him."

Everything Josh says intrigues me. Swiveling, I face him and put my phone away. "What is this place?"

Josh has the warmest brown eyes I think I've ever seen on anyone, and they instantly make me feel comfortable with him. Warm is a word I'd use to describe him in general too. With his casual appearance and welcoming manner, he's the opposite of

Beckett, who I would never use the word warm to describe. "Beckett hasn't told you about it?" he asks.

"Beckett and I barely know each other, Josh."

"Hmm," he says, surprise in his tone, "I didn't pick up on that from him." He pauses briefly. "So this is a center where people can come and stay when they're down and need help. Beckett and I set it up three years ago. He pays for everything, and I run the day-to-day."

This is a night full of surprises.

"When you say down, what exactly does that mean?"

"It can mean anything. They could be down financially, mentally, physically. We take referrals from many places and have a wide range of professionals who assist in helping the people who stay with us."

"Wow," I say softly, my mind exploding with what I'm learning about Beckett. "How did you two come up with the idea?"

Josh is a good-looking man with his dark hair, tanned skin, chiseled jaw, and muscles that go on for days, but it's subtle compared to Beckett's looks. However, when he smiles, like he is now, his face comes alive in a way that steals all your attention. It's clear this is a story he likes telling. "Beckett and I met in our first year of college. He was the reason I made it through, to be honest with you. He has this drive and ambition that I never had, and he helped me push harder when I needed to. I did okay for myself as a lawyer after college, but four years ago, I lost everything. My job, my mental health, and my wife. Beckett was the one who was there for me when not many others were. He got me the help I needed so I could turn my life around. I went back to work in law, but my heart wasn't in it anymore. I'd met other guys who were in similar positions as me, who needed the kind of help Beckett had given me. I wanted to do that for them, and Beckett agreed to come on board." He opens his arms wide. "And here we are."

"That might be the best thing I've heard in a long time.

What an amazing thing you two are doing." And mind blown. I'm glad I came here with Beckett rather than opting to go home. I would never have learned this side of him existed.

Josh rests his elbow on the top of the sofa, watching me like he's trying to figure me out. "Helping the people who come here is the most satisfying thing I've ever done, and I think Beckett feels the same way."

"So he's here helping someone tonight?"

"Yes." He narrows his gaze at me. "You sound confused by that."

I stare at him, processing not only his words but also the way he's said them. He's confused by my confusion, and I realize I might have been wrong about Beckett. I may have been judging him without taking the time to search under the arrogant layers I know. Sure, he's bossy and presumptuous at times, but that doesn't mean he's a bad person.

"Ugh," I mutter before leaning toward Josh and confessing, "I think I have your friend all wrong. I think maybe he's not the bad guy I've been telling myself he is for years."

He frowns. "I thought you two were friends. And on a date."

"Well, we're on a date. And we've known each other for years, but friends might be a stretch."

"Okay, you gotta help me out here. You think Beckett's a bad guy, but you said yes to a date?"

"Beckett didn't tell you about it?"

"When we spoke this morning, he told me he had a date with a friend tonight but to call him if I needed him."

"Right, so he bought this date. In a charity auction."

Understanding flashes across Josh's face, and he laughs. "Fuck me, that's totally not like Beckett and yet exactly like him at the moment."

It's my turn to frown. "At the moment? What do you mean?"

"He's going through some stuff and doing some odd things. Like buying a date." He laughs again. "How much did he pay?"

"Oh no, I'm not telling you. You'll have to ask him if you want to know that."

His eyes light up with what can only be called mischief. "It was a lot, huh?"

"You have no idea."

He whistles and shakes his head. "I like this side of Beckett. I never know what he'll do next."

"See, this isn't a side of him I know very well."

He nods like he knows what I'm talking about. "You only ever get his serious, overbearing side?"

"Yes. I know Bossy Beckett very well."

He laughs again. "I see now why you were hesitant about this date, but trust me, Jenna, there's a good guy hidden underneath Bossy Beckett. You might even like him if you give him a chance."

His phone sounds with a text, and after reading it, he says, "I have to go check something out." He stands. "Beckett shouldn't be too much longer, but I'll swing by and see if you're still here when I'm finished." He grins. "We have a lot more to talk about I think."

"It was good to meet you, Josh."

"You too."

He exits the room, and I grab my phone so I can text Shona. I'm all kinds of thrown right now and I need to get all my thoughts out.

Jenna: Beckett funds a center to help people get back on their feet. Did you know that and forget to tell me?

Shona: No. And wow. I didn't see that coming.

Jenna: Me either.

Shona: Why are you texting me mid-date? Or wait, have you already stabbed him and gone home?

Jenna: Our date got interrupted. We had to come to the center so he could help someone. I'm just waiting for him to finish up. And I don't think there's going to be any stabbing. I'm in shock and unable to pick up a knife.

Shona: So there could be sex now???!!!

Jenna: No. See: shock. No woman should ever make sexual decisions while in shock. Who knows what she'll get herself into?

Shona: Honey, forget what you're getting yourself into and just let Beckett get in you. It's been far too long since you've been fucked.

Jenna: I'm perfectly capable of taking care of myself. I don't need a dick in my life that I'm unsure of.

Shona: Oh, babe, that statement only shows me just how long it's been for you. Just let said dick into your life for one night. You'll thank me tomorrow for this advice.

Jenna: I texted you for help making sense of my thoughts, not for sex advice. Can we get back to that?

Shona: Honestly, you just need sex advice right now. We can go over the rest tomorrow. I'll swing by your office first thing with coffee.

Jenna: You are the worst best friend.

Shona: I love you too xx

I put my phone down and rest my head against the back of the sofa. Shona's right; it has been a while since I've had sex. Five months in fact. I haven't slept with anyone since Declan and I broke up. I'm not convinced she's right about me sleeping with Beckett, though. That could get messy, and I don't have it in me to get messy right now. I just want some fun. A fling with a guy not connected to me in any way. A guy whose baggage isn't labeled with the same name my baggage has on it.

Another text comes through.

Kristen: Jenna, I need to know about Saturday tonight. I'm finalizing numbers for the caterer.

There's no way I'm showing up at her party by myself. Not when everyone will be talking about Declan's engagement. I don't usually care what anyone thinks about me, but for some reason, this is different. This situation—him cheating on me and then getting engaged almost immediately—makes me feel like an idiot for not seeing what was right under my nose.

Jenna: There will be two of us.

Kristen: Oh. Okay. Thanks.

I stare at my phone. *"Oh. Okay."* I love my sister, but she takes after my mother in that she thinks I need help finding a husband. I'm tempted to never marry just to see how they handle it.

Needing a distraction from thinking about Beckett and sex and baggage and my family, I pull up my work emails again and start going through them, answering what I can. My business has picked up over the last three months, to the point where I'm going to have to hire another couple of stylists to help me meet demand. It's exciting, and not just because my goal is to expand the business, but also because I'm proving my father wrong.

When I started styling, he told me I'd be better off finding a husband. And when I started my own business a year ago, he said it would fail within the first year. He's a smart businessman who comes from a long family line of smart businessmen, so it was hard to ignore everything he said at the time and since, but somehow, I've managed to stick to my guns and do my own thing. And I've managed to do it extremely well with work coming in from everywhere, including some of the most exclusive celebrity work around.

I love my father, but he's a hard man. It's the reason why I asked Beckett about his relationship with his father. Our families are from the same world, and while I don't know his father, I find that families like ours have similar kinds of expectations for their children. I wanted that glimpse into how Beckett and his dad navigated their relationship during a time when Beckett made a choice that went against him. My father and I aren't as close as I'd prefer, and my choices in life and in business have contributed to that. I'm hopeful that will change one day and that he'll see me differently, like Beckett's father did over time.

I settle in with my emails and get through quite a lot of them over the next hour and a half. I'm so focused on them that I lose track of time. It isn't until Beckett's deep voice cuts through my thoughts that I realize so much time has passed.

"I half expected you to have gone home," he says as he takes the seat next to me.

I run my gaze over his face, noting the weariness that's crept into his eyes while he's been gone. "No, I got through a stack of emails. It was good actually. I wouldn't have wanted to do them at home, and they really needed to be done." I cock my head. "Are you okay?"

The way he looks at me tells me he didn't miss the concern laced through my voice. We share a moment over it. I don't know what the moment is, but I'm fully aware something is happening between us, and instead of feeling awkward or weird, I feel like this is exactly where I'm meant to be right now. It feels right to offer him support by either just being here with him or by giving him space to talk if that's what he needs. And, whoa, if that knowledge doesn't settle peacefully in my chest.

Beckett runs his fingers through his hair and exhales a long breath. "Have you ever had someone close who shattered and needed you in a way you didn't feel capable of providing?"

"Yes, about two years ago, one of my closest friends lost a baby. The loss sent her into a deep depression, and while she got all the professional help she needed, and she had the love and support of her husband, she needed me like she's never needed me. I felt overwhelmed and out of my depth."

He listens intently to every word I say and then asks, "How did you get through it?"

"With lots of love over lots of time. I figured out she just needed me to be there for her. She didn't need me to fix everything for her or solve all her problems. She simply needed my love and my time."

"And she's okay now?"

"Yes." I smile as I think about her. "She and her husband just had a baby a few months ago." I pause, contemplating what I'm about to say rather than just letting the words out.

"We hardly know each other, so I get it if this is weird, but if you need to talk, Beckett, I'm here and I'm a good listener."

His eyes bore into me as he says, "We need to change that."

I frown. "Change what?"

"The fact we hardly know each other."

"I'm not sure that's a great idea," I say, my words tripping over themselves in their haste to escape my mouth. It's definitely not a great idea because, hello, messy.

"Bullshit." And there's Bossy Beckett. Everything from his voice to his word choice to his body language screams determination. "Give me one good reason why it's not a good idea."

"Ah, maybe because my ex is your ex-best friend, and there's a whole lot of baggage there we're both dealing with."

His determination doesn't let up. "None of that is relevant to us getting to know each other better."

I point my finger at him. "And there's reason number two. You're way too bossy for me. I don't do well with men who try to order me around, which is something you already know. I mean, we've spent the last couple of years arguing our way through them. Why would you think it'd be a good idea to throw us together when we'd probably just continue arguing with each other?"

Heat fills his eyes. "You're feeling this just as much as I am, Jenna. You can keep fighting with me as much as you want but stop fighting your attraction to me."

Oh God.

If the way that heat in his eyes is affecting me is anything to go by, I've no hope here.

Beckett is going to boss his way into convincing me this is a good idea, and I'm not going to be able to resist him. Not when all he has to do to mess with my resolve is look at me the way he's currently looking at me. I mean, the man hasn't even touched me or kissed me or done anything to me, and I'm practically ready to beg him to lead me astray.

Right, deep breath.

If I'm going down, I'm doing it on my terms.

I stand, keeping my eyes on his. "You owe me dinner and I am more than ready for it. And let's just get one thing straight: I don't put out on first dates, not even on million-dollar first dates, so get that idea out of your mind. In fact, you'll have to work hard to even get to the first-kiss stage, so strap yourself in, buddy, and prepare for that hard work."

Beckett stands and moves into me. Dipping his face to mine, his mouth brushes my ear as he says, "You have no idea how much I like a woman who stands her ground. This won't be hard work, Jenna; this'll be a chase I'll enjoy." With that, he takes my hand and leads me out to his waiting car, his strides completely in line with the self-assured man that he is.

What the hell have I just gotten myself into?

It has to be said, though, that I like everything about what's happening.

Everything.

14

BECKETT

Jenna Blaise is the most beautiful woman I know, and only a fraction of that beauty has to do with her looks. I'm as attracted to her unpredictability, honesty, and willingness to share herself as I am to her appearance. It wouldn't matter if she'd worn the hot-as-hell red suit she's wearing tonight or something shapeless that covered her from head to toe; her beauty isn't something she can hide.

I brought her to Amorosis and asked Frankie to give us a table in the corner away from other guests. I then asked Jenna to tell me her top five choices on the menu and asked Frankie to bring us a selection of all five for her to try. Frankie always prioritizes me, so I knew he'd bring our meals quickly, but this was more important tonight. It was just after 10:00 p.m. when we arrived, and while Jenna hadn't said anything, she had to be starving. He didn't let me down.

We're halfway through eating when she puts her cutlery down and hits me with the look of hers I know means she's about to ask me a serious question. We've made it through a long round of surface questions while she's been getting a feel for me, so I've been waiting for this. And anticipating it because there's no one I enjoy this kind of conversation with more than Jenna.

"Was it a friend you went to help tonight?" she asks.

I reach for my scotch and drink some before answering. "No, my cousin. She's been spiraling for a while and came to me for help last week after her husband told her to leave their family home." I throw some more scotch down my throat as I think about Sarah's situation. "They've got two kids, both under five, and Sarah's pill addiction has gotten out of control to the point where she crashed her car with the kids in it while she was high. She was also picked up by the police for stealing clothes a couple of weeks ago. She's been medicating herself with pills and stealing for years, and her husband has told her he's done." My chest tightens as I admit, "I've tried to help her with this before, and I thought she was doing better, but it turns out she's worse than ever. I've been unable to reach her since I took her to Josh last week, and tonight was no better. I'm out of my depth here, and that's not a place I'm used to."

Compassion lines Jenna's face. "It takes a strong man to admit he feels out of his depth. I imagine you're more capable of helping Sarah than you think."

"I don't necessarily share that belief, but at the least, I'm surrounding her with the professional help she needs."

Jenna lifts her wineglass to her lips and takes a sip. "I'm surprised to hear you say you don't feel confident about something."

"Why?"

"In all the time I've known you, you've never been anything but overly confident. I've never once heard you say you were unsure of anything."

"That's because there's not much I'm unsure of."

"Surely there are things you're not certain of. Or is everything really that black and white for you?"

"If I don't know something, I make it a point to change that fact, just like if there's something I don't know how to do but want to, I change that. So yes, it's that black and white for me. But this situation with Sarah feels different. I can get her all the help she needs, but I don't know how to personally help her."

Jenna smiles and says softly, "That's because to help her personally will mean an emotional commitment, and from what I do know of you, Beckett, that's not your area of specialty. And I don't mean that in a harsh way, just a black-and-white assessment, which actually isn't my favorite type of assessment, but I think it'll probably speak to you."

She's right. In both things she mentioned. A black-and-white assessment like that does speak to me. And emotions aren't my strong suit, so what she said makes sense as to why I'm feeling out of my depth.

Before I can speak again, Jenna says, "You just need to give her lots of time and lots of love."

Coming from the family I do, time and love are the two things we were given last. Money and material possessions always came easily, but not time and love. So they aren't my forte. My ex-wife would agree with that. She spent most of our marriage screaming at me about the time I dedicated to work compared to what I gave her. Ellen may have cheated on me, but I fucked up in my own way too.

Our waitress comes to the table to check on us, drawing our attention from this conversation. When she leaves, I say, "Tell me about your family." I already know the facts that Johnson was able to compile for me, mostly to do with Blaise Corporation, the Blaise publishing empire her father runs, but I want to know something deeper and more personal than any of that.

She gives me a knowing look. "I imagine you know everything there is to know, Beckett. You're not the kind of man not to."

"Tell me something I wouldn't know."

Jenna sips some of her wine, a thoughtful expression on her face, before placing her glass down and saying, "I'm the odd one out in my family, and my father practically told me I must have done something to cause Declan to cheat on me."

I've read a bit about William Blaise being a hard ass and pushing his sons, but there hasn't been much written about his relationships with his daughters.

"I hope you told him how wrong he is about that."

Something flashes in Jenna's eyes. Doubt maybe. "Well, he and I don't have the kind of relationship where he pays too much attention to what I say. I didn't really get a word in."

This is the first time I've ever seen Jenna display anything but confidence. Even when she's expressing vulnerability, she doesn't lack confidence in herself, but everything about what she just said and how she said it shows me her father brings out her insecurities.

"He *is* wrong, Jenna," I say with conviction. "Cheating on a person has nothing to do with that person and everything to do with the asshole who cheats."

"I know." She picks at her food before continuing, "Dad and I aren't close, and I don't know if we ever will be. I asked you about your dad earlier because I'm always wondering how other people build a good relationship with their father."

I'd wondered why she chose that topic of conversation. It makes sense now. "For people like us, who come from the types of families we do with fathers like ours, I think it comes down to compromise."

Jenna's phone sounds with a text, but she ignores it and says, "As in, us compromising? I mean, there's no way I see my father compromising on anything."

I nod. "Yes."

"I'm not good at that."

"That makes two of us."

She smiles. "Yeah, I struggle to imagine you doing it. How does that work for you?"

"Not very well most of the time, but I've learned to bend for my father occasionally. It helps our relationship."

Jenna's phone sounds with another text and then two more in quick succession. "I'm sorry," she says as she reaches into her purse for it. "It may be about a job I have tomorrow morning. They often text the night before with a million questions." Her voice trails off as she reads the messages. "She has to be kidding me," she mutters before slipping the phone back into her bag. Bringing her eyes back to mine, she says, "I swear, my mother will be the death of me. That's something else for you to know about my family. If I die an early death, it'll be because of her."

I chuckle. "Are you two close?"

"That depends on your definition of close. She likes to think we are. She also likes to stick her nose in all my business. Lately, she's doing that a lot more. I think it's because I'm almost thirty and still not married."

"That's a requirement for a thirty-year-old?"

"Oh, you have no idea. According to my mother, an unmarried woman over that age is a woman destined for failure." She leans forward like she's sharing a secret. "I wasn't part of that date auction to raise money. She may have told me that was the reason, but the real reason would have been to help me find a man." Her brows arch. "I guarantee you she's at home tonight making plans for our wedding. You should be afraid, my friend. Maria Blaise is coming for you." She sips some more wine and asks, "Does your mother have similar ideas about daughters and marriage?"

"She's told my sister she needs to find a husband, but I suspect that has more to do with the fact she disapproves of Ruby's lifestyle and lack of what she deems a respectable job than necessarily wanting her married by a certain age."

"Your sister's an artist, right?"

"She paints, yes."

Jenna frowns. "Why do you say it like that? If she paints, she's an artist, isn't she?"

"Calling a person an artist implies some consistency to

their work; consistency isn't something my sister understands. She's painted some paintings and sold them, but mostly she spends her life having a good time."

Jenna leans back against her seat and looks at me like she's appraising me. "Creative people work differently than you work, Beckett. I don't know your sister, but I do know that consistency might be hard to compare between a creative type and a noncreative."

"I appreciate that, but regardless, Ruby is flighty with her art and with her life."

If the expression on Jenna's face is anything to go by, she has a lot more she wants to say on this subject. It's an expression I've seen before, and it's the expression that's preceded some of our fiercest discussions. However, this time Frankie interrupts our conversation when he joins us and says, "How is everything?"

I watch as Jenna's face lights up and she says, "Your chef is a god. This is the best Italian I've ever had. Thank you."

Frankie's a straight shooter, so it comes as no surprise to me when he says, "The best might be generous, but I appreciate your compliment. Next time you're in"—he gives me a pointed look, knowing I never bring women in a second time—"I'll have our chef make you something special that not even Beckett has had."

Jenna's a smart woman. She doesn't miss the undertone of Frankie's comment. "I look forward to trying that, and I'll be sure to let Beckett know how good it is."

Frankie's lips twitch, but he manages to keep a neutral expression. "Are you finished with your meals?"

"Yes," Jenna says. "As much as I want to eat every last bit of food on this table, I can't fit another bite in."

Frankie looks at me, and with my nod, he clears the table.

Once we're alone again, Jenna reaches for her drink and sips some. Placing the glass back on the table, she says, "I'm taking it from the look Frankie gave you that he doesn't expect to see me again here with you."

"Your directness is something I've always respected about you, Jenna."

"Hmm, you've managed to keep that to yourself all these years. I always thought it irritated the hell out of you."

My lips pull up at the ends. "That too, on occasion, but I prefer directness to the alternative."

"So, are you going to comment on what I said or just tell me you like the fact I said it?"

"You are correct. Frankie doesn't expect to see you again." I watch her closely, interested in her reaction to that admission.

Jenna smiles and displays her unpredictability when she says, "Well, in that case, I only have one question I need answered tonight before we never go on another date. How many tattoos do you have?"

"We're back to that question." She asked me this the day of the photo shoot, and I didn't answer, wanting to keep her guessing.

"Yes, and you have to answer it tonight. First date question and all."

I reach for my drink, slowly, intentionally keeping her waiting. After I drink some, I say, "We're doing a round of first-date questions?"

She grins. "Sounds like fun, right?"

"I have two tattoos."

"Oooh, where's your other one?"

"It's my turn for a question."

"Ugh, fine."

"How many do you have?" I've seen the small tattoo of circles and arrows on her wrist and always wondered if she has more.

"Three, although one of them doesn't count."

"Why not?"

"I got it at a party when I was fifteen, and it's the worst

tattoo ever. The tattoo artist shouldn't be one, and it's faded really badly now. I need to get a new tattoo to cover it up."

"How did your parents take it when they discovered you got a tattoo at fifteen?"

"I've never forgiven my sister for telling them. I was grounded for a long time. Now, my turn again. Where's that other tattoo of yours?"

"That's the kind of information reserved for second dates."

A sexy smile takes over her lips, the kind of smile I want to be on the receiving end of again. "Okay, how about this question: How many second dates do you ever make it to?"

I keep my eyes glued to hers. "I haven't dated since my divorce, Jenna."

Her forehead wrinkles with a frown. "You've been with so many women I stopped counting a long time ago."

"Not one of them was a date." I reach for my drink. "But I like that you were counting."

Her lips part as what I say silences her, and I make up my mind there's no way we won't be having a second date. The speed with which that thought settles itself in my mind baffles me, but I can't dismiss it now it's there. I may have had no desire to date for the past two years, but I'm enjoying this time with Jenna too much not to want more with her.

Jenna finishes her drink while keeping her eyes locked onto mine. I'm impatient to know what she's thinking. Finally, she says, "Beckett, I don't know if you're aware of this, but I'm not the kind of woman who does well with subtlety. I think I'm picking up on what you're saying, but just to be sure, is this a date to you?"

I don't hesitate with my answer. "Yes, this is a date."

"Right," she says, shifting her attention from me to the waiter walking past. She orders another wine, and I sit back and watch as she does something I've never seen her do. Jenna Blaise loses her cool composure, and I decide I need more of this Jenna in my life.

15

JENNA

Beckett just dropped a bomb, and he seems to have no freaking idea. He's sitting there watching me silently like he didn't just tell me I'm his first real date since his divorce.

What is this night? Like, for real, in what universe do Beckett and I go on an actual date? And don't even get me started on the fact I don't want to stab him in the eyes yet. Or the fact I desperately want to know where that other tattoo of his is.

I trip all over my words with the waiter as I attempt to order another wine. I think I manage it. The waiter seems happy enough with my order, but God knows what drink he'll come back with. And there's Becket, watching me with an expression I've never seen on his face. I have no idea what he's thinking, and that only bewilders me more.

Good God, take a breath, Jenna.

So he wants this to be a date. You can't say you're not enjoying it more than every other date you've ever been on.

My thoughts are so messed up that when Beckett doesn't fill the silence between us, I throw out, "Don't take another date for granted. We've still got the rest of the night to get through, which means there's still time for you to make me want to stab you."

The asshole grins. Seriously grins like he's having the time of his life. "Good to know. I'll be on my best behavior."

"Plus," I carry on, my thoughts nowhere near untangled, "I have a hundred more questions for you tonight. You'll probably decide this isn't the date for you before we even get through them."

He jerks his chin at me, that damn smile still in place. "Hit me."

Without stopping to put any thought into it, I say, "Do you believe mothers should stay home with their kids, or are you good with them having a career?"

"I see we're moving straight to the hard stuff," he murmurs.

"The important stuff."

Full points to him for only taking a second to answer me. "I believe women should do whatever they want to do, just as men should too. An unhappy parent can't raise a well-adjusted child." Also, full points to him for that answer, damn him.

"Agreed. And if you were a father, would you babysit your kids on a weekend your partner went away for a girls' weekend, or would you have a nanny look after them?"

"Firstly, it's not babysitting if it's your own children. And it would depend on whether I had work commitments as to who looked after the kids. If I didn't have to work, I wouldn't call the nanny in."

The waiter brings my wine, and I drink some while thinking about how well Beckett answered that question. I used the term babysitting on purpose; more points to him for picking up on that.

"Okay, next question," I say. "Imagine you're dating or married to a woman who earns more than you. How do you feel about that?"

He reaches for his drink. "It wouldn't bother me." He drinks some scotch before saying, "It's my turn for a question now." At my nod, he says, "How does tomorrow night sound for our next date?"

My eyes widen. I'm going to need a lot more than twenty-four hours to get myself together for a second date. I guzzle some more wine while trying to ignore his demanding eyes.

When I don't answer him, he says, "I'll take that as a yes."

"You shouldn't."

"I'm not hearing a no."

"No," I blurt, instantly wishing I could drag that word back into my mouth and then instantly wondering what the hell is wrong with me that I want to do that.

His brows lift. "No as in you're not free tomorrow night?"

"No as in I need to think about this."

"There's nothing to think about, Jenna."

"That's the difference between men and women, Beckett. I want to go home and think about everything we said and did tonight. I want to think about how you make me feel and whether I want to experience more of that. I want time to process every little thing before I make a decision about a second date."

"So what you're saying is, you want time to think about what you already know because you do know what you want, you're just not ready to admit it."

I stare at him for a long few moments before pointing my finger at him and saying, "See, this is the arrogant Beckett I could stab in the eyes."

He doesn't respond to that except to keep his gaze firmly on mine while saying, "And I'd let you do that if it moved you closer to accepting what's happening between us."

The way he says that, while watching me like I'm his sole focus in the world, causes me to inhale sharply. Beckett isn't saying he'd actually allow me to stab him in the eyes, but I'm hyperaware of what he *is* saying; he's going to do whatever it takes to make this second date happen.

The fact I feel that awareness deep in my core in the very

best of ways stuns me, but it shouldn't. Not with everything that's already happened between us tonight.

The simple truth is Beckett's right.

Damn him.

I already know I want a second date with him, but I'm not ready to admit it.

Taking a deep breath, I say, "I don't know what's happening between us, Beckett. What I do know is I have a lot more first-date questions for you to get through before I make a decision about a second date."

He takes that in, remaining silent for a long beat. Finally, he nods and says, "I'm an open book, but if you think you're scaring me off by asking me the kind of questions you've been asking, you need to know this about me: when I want something, nothing gets in my way or scares me off."

I've seen Beckett chase what he wants in business, and he's not lying.

I've never seen him chase a woman before, but I'm fairly certain I'm about to.

And I'm feeling a million different emotions over that, the least of which is excitement.

Damn. Him.

Because, if I'm honest with myself, I want Beckett to chase me.

Oh God, how I want that.

16

JENNA

"So you didn't sleep with him?" Shona says the morning after my date with Beckett. At the shake of my head, she says, "Tell me you at least kissed him and made out with him a little."

I continue shaking my head. "No kiss, no making out. I told him he'd have to work for it, and I meant every word."

"Wow, girlfriend, I'm both impressed and shocked." She brings her legs up onto the sofa she's sitting on in my office and gets comfy. "Right, I need a blow-by-blow of how he handled that."

Shona arrived ten minutes ago with coffee in hand, black for her, cappuccino for me, and told me she wasn't leaving until I detailed every minute of the date. First though, she wanted to know about the sex and was speechless when I informed her there was none.

Settling onto the sofa next to her, I check my watch. "I only have forty minutes before I have to leave for my first appointment."

"Well, it sounds like you can probably get through the entire date in less than ten minutes since there was no sex."

"Says the woman who kept Graham waiting before she slept with him."

She sips some coffee before conceding, "Okay, you have a point." She motions with her hand. "Start talking, and don't leave anything out."

I fill her in on the date and what I learned about Beckett. When I get to the part of the night where Beckett took me home, my phone sounds with a text. After checking it, I look at Shona and groan.

"Your mother or your sister?" she asks.

"My mother."

"She has another auction to sign you up for?"

"Worse. Probably way worse. My sister's party this weekend. I told Kristen I'm bringing someone, so Mom's been hounding me since last night wanting to know who it is."

"I told you I'm available." She grins. "We could have some real fun with that."

My phone vibrates with another text.

Mom: Jenna, stop ignoring me. I need to know who you're bringing on Saturday so I can properly prepare.

Jenna: Properly prepare for what?

Mom: I need to know who to expect so I'm prepared for the conversation. Your father is also interested to know who you're bringing.

I eye Shona, holding my phone up. "She's the most cunning woman I know."

"Why? What did she do now?"

"She just threw my father into the conversation so she can get what she wants. She told me Dad's interested to know who I'm bringing because she knows that'll mean something to me."

Shona holds out her hand. "Give me your phone. We need to finish this Beckett debrief before getting into your family drama."

I hand my phone over while muttering, "So much for a peaceful day."

"Right, so he dropped you at home and then what? Did he try to kiss you?"

I smile, remembering how Beckett handled the end of our date. "I have to give it to him. He's good at reading people. It's like he's super skilled at walking that line between pushing me for what he wants and being patient because he knows pushing will just set him right back."

"Jesus, Jenna, yes or no to the kiss? I'm dying to know here."

"No, he didn't try to kiss me, but he wanted to."

A slow smile spreads across her face. "And you were into that, weren't you?"

I exhale a long breath before admitting to my best friend the thing I don't want to admit even to myself. "I was into that, yes."

My phone goes off again, and Shona shoves it under a pillow. "Your mother is relentless."

I roll my eyes. "You're telling me."

My assistant, Cora, knocks on my office door and sticks her head in when I call out for her to come in. "You have a visitor." She glances between Shona and me. "I know you're busy, but this guy is hot with a capital H. Like, I wouldn't ever be able to use the word no with him."

"Who is it?"

"Beckett Pearce."

The faint sound of my phone buzzing with another text sounds as my brain works through the fact Beckett has dropped in unexpectedly to see me.

I'm not ready for him.

I need to finish my debrief with Shona and then spend the rest of the day processing all my thoughts.

My phone goes off again.

"Oh my God!" I motion at Shona. "Give me my phone so I can tell my mother exactly where she can shove her requests for information."

I'm not ready for her either today.

"So is that a yes or a no to seeing him, Jenna?" Cora asks.

Shona stands and hands me my phone. "That's a yes to seeing him," she says to Cora before I can answer.

"No," I say, but I'm not fast enough. Cora's already slipped back out to her desk and is no doubt telling Beckett I'm free. Meeting Shona's triumphant gaze, I say, "You will pay for this, my friend."

"Pfft, you need a helping hand with this one, and I'm more than happy to offer that help."

"What I need is a little more time to gather my thoughts."

"Honey, you're into him. You just told me that. And I think you might have finally found a man willing to push you out of your comfort zone. It's time to take a risk."

I frown. "What does that mean? I'm always stepping out of my comfort zone."

She nods. "Yes, in all areas of your life except for the men you date. When it comes to them, you always choose guys who feel safe. I want to see you with a man who pushes those boundaries." Pulling her sunglasses out, she smiles. "I expect to hear all about this later today."

"I'll be doing a reevaluation of our friendship all day, so you can expect to hear how that goes before you can expect an update on my love life."

Her grin practically fills the room. "I love you, too." With that and an air-kiss, she exits my office right as another text comes through on my phone.

Mom: Darling, you know I'm not good at being ignored.

Mom: I'll tell your sister to sit your date next to me if you don't tell me right now who it is.

Mom: And I'll put your father on his other side.

Mom: You'll be at another table.

Jenna: I was adopted, wasn't I?

My head snaps up at the sound of someone entering my office. The sight of Beckett in another dark blue suit takes my breath away. Literally. The man is far too good-looking for my health.

"You need to stop wearing suits," I throw out.

His lips curve up at the ends. "Noted."

"Which means you have no intention of doing what you noted."

Those lips of his form a full smile at that. "Now we're getting somewhere."

"Yes, I'm confirming what I already knew about you."

"Which is?"

"That you always do what you want."

"That's where you're wrong, Jenna. If I always did what I want, last night would have ended very differently." His voice deepens as he says this, and the gravel in his tone touches me in all the places I don't want it to, as do the words he utters.

Another text comes through on my phone, and in a fluster, I stab at the message to read it.

Mom: I'm about to call your sister to finalize the seating plans, my darling.

I stare at Beckett, trying to push my mother to the very back of my mind. "Why are you here?"

"To organize tonight."

"Tonight?"

"Yes, dinner."

My brain catches up with his, tripping over itself in its haste to make sense of what he's saying. "We don't have anything planned for tonight, Beckett."

"We do now." He says those three words with such confidence that it leads me to argue with him just to teach him I'm not the kind of woman he can make plans for without asking first.

"No, we don't. I'm busy tonight."

His eyes bore into mine, and the tension between us escalates to the point where I'm not convinced I can handle the heat. "Cancel whatever it is."

My phone sounds again.

Mom: This party is going to be the highlight of my social

calendar this year now that I'll have the full attention of the man you bring.

I eye Beckett, and before I can stop myself, I say, "You're coming to a party with me on Saturday, and if you say no, I will find ways to hurt you."

Amusement flashes in his eyes. "One of these days, you'll realize how much I like it when you threaten me with harm."

Of course he does.

"So that's a yes?"

"Consider my schedule cleared for you."

Ignoring the way my body likes his lack of hesitation, I type a reply to my mother.

Jenna: If you really must know, I'm bringing Beckett Pearce.

Mom: Oh my. He is absolutely sitting next to me during lunch.

Jenna: I have no doubt. Now, let me get back to work.

I place my phone on my desk and give my attention back to Beckett. "Sorry about that. My mother has been harassing me all morning about that party."

"It's her party?"

"No, my sister's. It's her annual summer party in the Hamptons. We'll take your helicopter."

More amusement settles across his face. "Will we?"

"Now is not the time to argue with me, Beckett. Not when my mother and sister are involved."

He nods. "I'll give you that, and you'll give me dinner tonight."

Giving him dinner tonight is the last thing I want to give him. But not because I don't want to see him tonight. *Why, God? Why must you force this man on me and make me like him so damn much? We need to have a big talk once this thing with him is over and done with.*

"We'll have dinner tonight. At my place. I'll cook for you."

That catches him off guard and silences him for a moment. "I'll be there at seven."

"Bring some good scotch with you. I'm all out. And try to resist the urge to wear a suit."

He doesn't respond to that, simply watches me for another moment before saying, "See you tonight, Jenna."

With that, he exits my office, leaving me to collapse onto my sofa in a mess of thoughts about everything that just happened. Between Shona, my mother, and Beckett, this morning has not gone at all like I thought it would. I'd planned to take my time deciding on a second date with Beckett, and now I have my second and third date with him organized. At the rate I'm going, Beckett will have a month's worth of dates sorted by the time he's finished with me tonight.

Most confusingly, that thought makes me happy.

I'm fairly sure I want what Beckett wants.

I'm fairly sure he could get what he wants tonight.

And I'm more than sure neither of us are thinking straight.

Bossy Beckett is not the man for me.

And yet, he's the only man I've ever dedicated this much thinking time to.

Damn him.

17

BECKETT

By the time I arrive at Jenna's condo for dinner, I'm past ready for a glass of the Balvenie scotch I brought with me. I've been dealing with Ruby and my mother on and off all day, and nothing has been resolved. I've also spent too much time negotiating a property deal that should have been a lot easier to put together. If I didn't have plans to spend the night with Jenna, I'd spend hours in the gym working the bullshit from today out of my system. However, dinner with Jenna appeals far more than a night in my gym.

"You're early," she says when she opens her door to me. "Don't you know a girl needs all the minutes up until the agreed-upon time of a date to get ready?"

I run my eyes over her, slowly, because Jenna isn't a woman to be rushed with, before saying, "Trust me when I tell you that you don't need any more time getting ready."

Her long hair hangs in loose waves, reaching down to her breasts.

Her flawless face has just enough make-up to highlight her natural beauty without altering it too much. Always my preference.

Her curves are accentuated by a tiny red dress that is all

Jenna with its teasing, casual playfulness. The amount of skin on display is something I both appreciate and will be driven to distraction by.

Heat flares in her expression, and she does what she always does when I manage to make her feel this: she fires her thoughts at me. "You're still wearing that suit."

"I know how much you like it," I murmur, enjoying the hell out of her ruffled state over my suits. I dip my face to hers as I take a step inside her condo and say, "For the record, I feel the same way about your dress." That dress comes nowhere near reaching her knees and drops low in the front giving me an eyeful of cleavage. The kind of eyeful that will torture me all night.

The door clicks shut behind me, and she leads me into her open-plan home that's filled with muted pinks, plush furniture, large flower arrangements, and music playing softly in the background, John Mayer if I'm not mistaken. Floor-to-ceiling windows give an impressive view of Manhattan, allowing the sun left over from the day in. Jenna's style isn't anything like mine, which comes as no surprise. What does, though, is how much I like it. I'm certain the only reason I do is because it's Jenna's. I'm fast discovering I like a lot of things about her.

"How many suits do you own?" she asks as I pass her the bottle of scotch when we reach her kitchen.

"I've no idea."

"So, a lot. Jesus, the torture." She eyes the scotch before bringing her gaze back to mine. "For your record, expensive scotch isn't the way to my heart."

"I do believe I was told to bring good scotch."

"I didn't mean a fifty-thousand-dollar bottle of scotch."

"This isn't a fifty-thousand-dollar bottle of scotch." Close, but not quite.

With a shake of her head, because she's no fool and knows her scotch, she points at an overhead cupboard. "Glasses are in there. You pour the drinks while I chop potatoes."

The marble island in Jenna's kitchen is filled with various ingredients for what I presume will be our dinner. "What are you making?"

"Samosas and butter chicken," she says as she starts on the potatoes.

I eye the flour on the island. "From scratch?"

She stops chopping and looks at me like I've just asked a dumb question. "It's the only way to make samosas."

I've never made them, so I have no clue. I grew up in a home where we didn't prepare our own meals. I was married to a woman who didn't cook, and I've barely cooked a meal in my life. I was impressed when Jenna told me she'd cook for us tonight.

She goes back to what she's doing while I locate the glasses and pour the drinks. Placing her glass in front of her, I say, "How can I help?"

Looking at me with an amused expression, she says, "When was the last time you prepared a meal?"

I drink some of my scotch, savoring it as it goes down. "I can't recall."

Still with the amused look, she points the tip of her knife at me and says, "How about you sit your ass on that stool and look pretty while I get these on to boil?"

"If I'm looking pretty, I'm doing something wrong."

"Trust me, you're doing everything right, Beckett. A little too well, actually."

I remove my suit jacket and place it on one of the stools while thinking about the fact something's shifted between us since I saw her this morning. Jenna's lighter, easier somehow. She's still busting my balls in the way only she does, in the way I wouldn't change, but she seems more open. At least, I hope she is. She's been fighting her attraction to me, and while I'm good to help her stop fighting it, to be as patient as is needed, I'd prefer that to not take too long.

As I'm placing my jacket down, Jenna says, "I heard the

news about Pride Industrial today. That's worth celebrating with a drink tonight." She's referring to the two-billion-dollars' worth of aircraft contracts my company won today.

I take in the smile filling her eyes as she says this. She's so fucking genuine. This is something about her that always hits me in the gut. There aren't many people in this city as real as Jenna. "You're going to help me celebrate?"

She picks up on exactly what I'm asking and lets her smile tease her lips in the kind of seductive way a man can't ignore. "That depends on your definition of celebrating."

I down some scotch, keeping my eyes firmly on her. "I think you'd like my way of celebrating."

That smile continues to play with her lips. "Oh, I have no doubt about that." Her words come out on a sexy murmur that works its way to my dick. I'm going to need every ounce of strength I have to make it through tonight because I don't intend to take this any further with her until she's ready to give me exactly what I want, and if I know anything, I know she's not ready for that yet.

Jenna places the potatoes in a pot and puts it on to boil before cleaning up after herself. She does this with such ease it's clear this is second nature to her. Once she's finished cleaning, she picks up her scotch and comes my way. Pulling out the stool next to me, she settles herself on it, crosses one leg over the other, and takes a sip of her drink while I do my best not to drop my gaze to her legs. Raising her glass, she says, "Here's to your company kicking ass." She smiles as she lets the scotch slide down her throat. I'm helpless but to take it all in. To take her all in.

I've never met a woman like her. So vibrant and honest and thoughtful. And I've certainly never had someone raise a glass to my company kicking ass.

She frowns as I watch her silently. "What? Is your company not kicking ass?"

"Yes." I smile, feeling it down to my bones in a way I don't often. "It's kicking ass. Just like yours is."

She looks at me knowingly. "I see you've been doing your homework."

"I have." I spent time today in between everything else I was dealing with checking out Jenna's company. A year old, it's doing better than most companies of that age. She has a team of ten stylists working with her, and between them, they pick up a good deal of high-end and celebrity work, which keeps them in high demand. "What's your plan to leverage the success you've had this last year?"

Her perfectly confident expression slips a little. It would be unnoticeable to most, but I've immersed myself in all things Jenna lately, and I don't miss it. "Next question."

My brows pull in. "What just happened?"

"What do you mean?"

"You're one of the most confident women I know, and when I just asked you about your business, which you should feel more than confident about, you shrunk a little. Why?"

"Why do you have to be so damn perceptive?"

"You're stalling. What's going on?"

She takes a deep breath and exhales it. "I need a cash injection if I'm going to leverage the success I've had."

"That's business 101, Jenna."

"Yes, smartass, it is, but—"

"I wasn't trying to be a smartass. I'm just trying to figure out what's going on in your mind because you said it like it's the last thing you want."

"I can either go to the bank for the cash, or I can go to my father, and honestly, neither appeals to me. I don't want to owe anyone, but I can't make the numbers work without more money behind me."

"You could look for an investor, but my advice would be to keep it in the family if possible."

"Yes, and that's why I just shrunk a little."

Of course. She told me a little about her relationship with her father last night. "You don't think he'll want to invest in you? Or you don't want to ask him?"

"Both." She bites her bottom lip, a nervous gesture I've never seen her do. "If I ask him and he turns me down, I'm not sure what that will do to me," she admits softly, giving me a piece of that vulnerability of hers that I'm drawn to.

"I can get a list of possible investors together for you," I offer even though mixing business and women is something I intentionally never do. The words are out of my mouth before I can halt them. The fact I don't care doesn't escape me.

What I've said silences her, and she takes a moment to catch her thoughts. "I didn't take you for a man who'd do that."

"I'm not."

The significance of my offer isn't lost on her, and I see the way it shifts something in her. When she speaks again, she gives me soft in a way she never has. "Thank you, Beckett, but I'm going to decline. I need to do this on my own."

"I understand that. If you change your mind, come to me."

Jenna slides off her stool and stands in front of me, smiling. "I think it's time you learned how to make samosas."

"It's not a bad idea. They are my favorite Indian food, after all."

Her smile remains in place. "I know."

Fuck me.

I didn't connect the dots when she mentioned my two favorite Indian dishes earlier. It turns out it's no coincidence that she chose them.

She jerks her chin at me and lightly smacks my thigh. "Up you get. You have work to do."

I move off the stool as Jenna rounds the island, motioning for me to follow her. When I reach her, she says, "Roll up your sleeves and wash your hands."

I try not to smile but fail to hide my amusement while I do

as I'm told. "You've waited for this moment for a long time, haven't you?"

"What? The moment I see you doing some actual work?"

"No, the moment you get to order me around."

She removes the potatoes from the stove and places them in a bowl that she puts in front of me. Her eyes find mine as she says, "I'm going to make the most of it. Now, you need to crumble these potatoes, leaving some lumps. Don't mash them completely. We want some texture in them."

We get to work, me crumbling the potatoes, Jenna gathering ingredients, both of us stealing glances at the other as we go.

I'm having trouble keeping my focus on the job she's given me. Concentrating is a skill of mine, but Jenna's slowly killing that skill. I had trouble focusing at work this afternoon too. Mac was confused when my level of interest in the contracts we won today was less than he expected it to be. His confusion matched my own, and still matches my own because here I am, unable to shift my eyes from her, my mind from her, and my desire to learn everything there is to know about her. All things I haven't wanted to do with any woman in years.

When I'm finished prepping the potatoes, Jenna heats oil in a pan and adds a bunch of different spices and other things before cooking the potatoes. She adds peas and finishes what I recognize as the filling for the samosas.

As she removes the pan from the stove, she says, "How's your cousin today?"

I rest my ass against the island and watch Jenna work the dough she made before I arrived into balls. "I spoke with her briefly. She's doing better than yesterday, and Josh is hopeful that her therapy session this morning was a productive one."

"That's good," she says before arching her brows at me. "Why is that ass of yours resting? You've got samosas to make here."

I chuckle and move next to her. Making sure to brush my

arm against hers as I do so, I place my hand on hers that's working a pizza cutter over the dough and say, "Show me what to do."

She stills for a beat, and I take in the rise and fall of her chest while I wait for her. The effect I'm having on Jenna is intoxicating. If this is what cooking together does for us, we need to spend every day in the kitchen.

"Cut the dough like this," she says, moving our hands, showing me what to do. "Then we need to get some water," she says, meeting my gaze, "and coat the edges of the dough." When I don't remove my hand from hers, she says, "I'm going to need my hand for this."

I keep my eyes glued to hers as I let go of her hand. Turning my body to hers, I bring my other hand up to her face and slide the stray hair that's fallen across it back behind her ear. No words are exchanged between us, but we don't need them; our bodies are doing all the communicating we need. And fuck me, I want to skip the samosas and move straight to dessert.

Jenna swallows hard and drops her gaze to my lips. She lingers there for a long moment before snapping back into action and issuing a string of orders for me to follow.

We finish preparing the samosas, and Jenna cooks them while I clean up the kitchen. She then heats up the butter chicken she'd already made before I arrived while I pour us both another drink. When everything's ready, we sit at the kitchen island to eat.

"I've actually never made butter chicken before," Jenna says as I take my first bite of it. "I hope it's good."

"So not only did you make my two favorites, but you went out of your way to make me something you've never cooked." My implication is clear; I don't need to say it.

She doesn't miss a beat, giving me classic Jenna. "And I can go out of my way to end this date at any point if that's your preference."

"I've made my preference very clear. I'm more interested in yours."

She keeps her eyes on me as she eats some butter chicken. When she finishes the mouthful, she says, "I think I prefer to keep you wondering."

I place my cutlery down and reach for the seat of her stool so I can pull her close. "I'm not wondering anything, Jenna, but I'd fucking love to hear the words leave your mouth."

Her eyes flare with desire as her hand meets my thigh in an effort to steady herself after I move her to me. "What do you want to hear, Beckett?"

I could play this game with her forever. "I want to hear you say you want me as much as I want you. Can you give me that?"

She drags her bottom lip between her teeth as she traces her eyes over my face. "Giving you things isn't something I ever imagined doing." The breathlessness that accompanies her words stirs feelings deep in my gut I haven't ever felt. Feelings I'd do a hell of a lot of things to experience again.

"I know, and yet here we are."

Her eyes find mine again. "I knew you were going to boss me into giving you things the minute I met Josh."

"Why then?" The way Jenna's mind works intrigues me.

Her fingers dig into my thigh. "Because it was the minute I saw a Beckett I could fall for."

She's giving me far more than I imagined she would. "*I* knew I wanted more from you the minute you stumbled out onto that auction stage."

"Why then?" She's hanging off every word of mine just as much as I'm hanging off every word of hers.

"Because it was the minute I saw you weren't just all talk about who you are. You stood in front of those women wearing anything but what would gain their approval, and you dropped an F-bomb and carried on without a care in the world. It was the minute I saw that you didn't give a shit what they thought of you, and the minute I realized I want a woman like you in my life."

"What do you want, Beckett? Sex? A few dates? A woman on your arm at events? I don't make good arm candy if that's what you're looking for."

"I don't need or want arm candy, Jenna. I want far more than that."

"I didn't think you were a relationship kind of guy."

"I didn't either." And as much as I may be puzzled over my actions with Jenna, I'm helpless but to keep pursuing her. Jenna is more than a one-night girl. She can't be just that when she's the only woman who has ever interrupted my thoughts during the day, who has ever inspired me to rework my schedule to make time for her, and who has ever had me desperate to hear her next thought.

She stares at me like she's stunned by what I've said, and I know I'm going to have to push her to give me what I want from her. I have no qualms about that because Jenna is a woman I've decided I'll always push to give me what I want. And I don't care how hard she fights me over any of it; I'll take her fight any day because everything else she gives me is worth that.

Moving closer to her, I growl, "Maybe this will convince you," before bringing my lips to hers. And finally, she falls apart in all the right ways.

18

JENNA

If I thought Beckett had messed my thoughts up before tonight, I had no idea what he was still capable of doing to them. Right now, he's taken all of them and thrown them out the window because right now, he has his lips on mine, and it's the absolute best kiss I've ever experienced.

Being kissed by Beckett is like being given a gift I never expected in a million years. The surprise and impulsiveness of it catches me in a way I didn't think possible from him. It strips any remaining hesitation I have about whatever is happening between us.

Being kissed by Beckett is something I want again and again.

Oh God, how I want this again.

The second his fingers thread through my hair, and he deepens the kiss, I surrender fully. My hands go to his chest as butterflies fill my tummy. I can't remember the last time I felt this way, like a giddy teenager dying for more.

I slide off my stool and move in between his legs, my lips never leaving his. I need his body against mine, his mouth on mine, and his scent overwhelming me in every way it is.

When we finally come up for air, I reach my hand around

to the back of his head and pull his lips back for more. We don't need air; we just need each other.

He gives me what I want but not for long. A few moments after I initiate our second kiss, he ends it and says, "I still haven't heard the words I want from you."

I keep my hand around his neck, drunk on his kisses, and needing more. "Just kiss me, Beckett. We can talk later."

He resists me and shakes his head. "I'm not kissing you again until I hear you say it."

"My God, you are the most demanding man I have ever met."

"And you are the only woman I know who doesn't want to talk."

"Which I would have thought you'd prefer."

"I think we've established you don't know me as well as you thought you did."

"No, we've established you are indeed as bossy as I always thought you were."

The bastard's lips pull up at the ends. "And here you are, demanding I kiss you. It seems bossy works well for you, Jenna."

"That mouth of yours should only be used for kissing, not bossing. *That's* what works well for me."

"I can think of other things my mouth could do that would work well for you."

At that, my brain finally loses any sense of control I had left. I mean, with all the images of Beckett's mouth flooding my mind, I have no hope of not giving in to his demands.

Gripping the back of his neck, I lean into him and finally say, "I want you as much as you want me."

The pleasure that fills his face makes me glad I gave him that, and in an instant, everything shifts for me. Where a second ago I didn't want to give in to his bossy ways, I suddenly can't remember why I felt that way or why I've been fighting this attraction so much.

He definitely took all my thoughts and threw them out the window. And the fact I don't even care anymore shows me just how drunk I am on him.

I press myself harder against him. "Now, are you going to kiss me, or are we just going to stand here arguing all night?"

"Arguing with you is one of my favorite things to do," he says as his hand glides down my back to my ass. I decide I really want his hand to be there a lot more often.

"Hmm," I murmur, brushing my lips over his lightly, "if kissing me isn't above that on your list, I'm doing something wrong."

He smiles as I give him the same words he gave me earlier. Instead of doing what I want, though, he moves his hands to my hips and lifts me to place me back on my stool. "Eat. We've got all night for everything else."

I stare at him. "You're seriously choosing eating over getting your hands and mouth on me?"

His eyes flash with his signature intensity. "If I choose my hands and mouth getting what they want, we won't be doing anything else but that tonight, and I want to spend some time getting to know you better."

And just like that, Beckett says the exact right thing that I never knew I wanted, so I stop fighting him and start eating.

～

"You know what tonight is, right?" I say as I curl up next to Beckett on my sofa with a glass of the scotch he brought tonight. I don't even care if he spent way too much money on this scotch; I'm in love with it and may just demand he always brings a bottle when he comes for dinner. Even if that will eventually bankrupt him.

He drops his gaze to my leg as it brushes his while I get comfortable. "No," he says, placing his hand on my leg. "Tell me what tonight is."

Tonight has been more relaxing than I ever imagined it could be with Beckett. After losing my cool this morning when he stopped by my office, I spent the day thinking hard about what I wanted with him. I came to the conclusion that I can't ignore my attraction to him another minute longer. I also concluded that maybe I've gotten some things wrong about him over the last couple of years.

Dinner was a two-hour affair because we lost track of time while we talked about anything and everything. We learned more about each other in those two hours than we have in the last two years. Afterward, we cleaned up together and continued talking, and while I'm desperate to kiss him again, I could spend all night discovering the things I still don't know about him.

I shoot him a sexy smile. "Tonight's our second date, and apparently, second dates are when you reveal information about your tattoos. I'm ready for a little sharing to happen."

"Is that so?"

"That is so, my friend."

Something changes in Beckett's eyes. His easy, amused mood disappears and is replaced by fierce determination at the same time that he reaches for me and brings me to straddle him. Taking hold of my hips, he growls, "I am far more than your friend, Jenna. Let's get that straight right fucking now."

Oh. My.

It has to be said that I like this side of Beckett. A lot. Like, on a scale of one to ten, my level of like is at a twenty. Growly Beckett could maybe even get away with bossing me a little.

"Noted, and when I say noted, I mean noted and I'm paying attention."

"Good." Still growly. Still doing good things to me.

I take matters into my own hands and reach for the top button on his shirt. Undoing it, I say, "I'm trying to decide if I think the tattoo of yours I haven't seen is on your ass, your leg or your back. Care to give a girl a hint?"

His hands on my hips relax, as does the expression on his face as I make my way down his buttons. "I think I'll let you find it yourself."

"I knew you were going to be like that." I finish with his buttons and pull his shirt out of his pants. A moment later, it's discarded, and I'm staring at Beckett's impressive muscles. "You know, you never did tell me how often you work out when I asked you."

"That's because you kept talking and didn't give me a chance to get a word in."

I like that he remembers our conversation. "Well, you can get a word in right now. I'm guessing with these muscles you must spend hours in the gym."

"You really want to discuss my gym habits right now?"

He's right. That is the last thing I want to talk about. I lean my face closer to his as I reach for his belt buckle. "No, there's actually something else I want to ask you." I flick his buckle open. "I want to know why the bossiest man I know hasn't taken charge and stripped me naked already."

His eyes flare with heat, and he grips my waist with one of his hands while bringing his other one up my stomach, over my breasts, and to my face. "Something you need to know about me is that I have all the patience in the world when it's needed, and it was needed for you. If I'd taken charge when I wanted to, you would have been naked a long time ago." He shifts his body so he's sitting straighter and slides his hand down from my waist to my ass. "I've allowed you to come to me, Jenna, but from here on out, I won't be a patient man."

Holy shit.

That growly tone just made another appearance, and I'm almost at a level 30 of love for it now. Yes, love, not like. And I'm not even stopping to analyze that. Not when Beckett's sitting in front of me half-naked, ready to begin handing out orgasms.

"You know how you forced me to tell you I want you as much as you want me?"

His lips pull up, amused. "Yes."

"There's something else I want, and I won't make you force me to tell you."

He lets go of my face and glides his hand down to my chest. Pushing the straps of my dress to the sides, so the top of my dress falls away and reveals my breasts to him, he says, "What else do you want, Jenna?" The need I hear in his voice mixes with my own to the point where I'm starting to feel real desperation for his cock. Something I've never felt for a man before.

I place both my hands to his stomach and slide them up slowly to his chest, drawing the moment out before saying, "I want you to fuck me like I've never been fucked."

His eyes pin to mine. "How have you never been fucked?" His voice is raw. Rough.

Beckett's looking at me like I'm the only woman on the planet and the sexiest damn woman he's ever seen, and it's making me feel like a goddess. With this feeling racing through my veins, I run a finger over his lips and say, "Hard. Rough. With the kind of attention that makes me want to do filthy things with your dick."

"Fuck," he hisses as he stands, lifting me with him. With heat blazing from every inch of him, he demands, "Where's your bedroom?"

I direct him to my bedroom, and when we arrive, he places me down and strips my dress from me before I can catch my breath.

Spinning me, so my back is to his chest, he brings one hand to cup my breast and his other to my throat. Angling my neck to the side, he dips his mouth to kiss my collarbone, sending a shiver along my skin when his lips meet my skin. "How hard do you want this?"

Who knew six little words could make a woman's legs weak? Not me, but I do now. "As hard as you want to make it."

He tightens his hold on my neck and kisses a trail up it, bringing his mouth to my ear. "Careful what you ask for, Jenna.

You won't be able to walk tomorrow if I make it as hard as I want."

It's official: I've lost my mind. Completely. I'll take anything Beckett wants to give me, and I'll throw a freaking party if I can't walk tomorrow.

I wrap my hand around his forearm and practically beg him, "Fuck me as hard as you want, Beckett. I want to spend every second tomorrow thinking about why I can't walk."

He moves swiftly, stripping my panties before lifting me and throwing me on the bed. I've never been thrown on a bed before. I'm adding it to my list of "make him do that again," a list that's growing faster than any list I've ever put together.

I move onto my back and watch as he removes the rest of his clothes. He does this while keeping his eyes on mine, a hot-as-hell move of his I love. Beckett likes to watch me, and if he fucks me how I think he's going to—with the kind of attention I've never experienced during sex—I'm not sure how I'll ever let him leave here tonight.

He places a knee to the bed and slowly makes his way onto it, moving until he's over me, still with those blue eyes on mine. Bringing his mouth to mine, he pauses briefly before devouring me with a kiss that makes me want to tell him I'm kidnapping him. Not that I think Beckett's a man who could ever be kidnapped, but a woman can try. Especially when she's kissed in a way that makes her feel like she's everything he's ever wanted.

When he finally ends the kiss, I grip his biceps. "You should always kiss me like that."

I'm breathless with need, and my words come out a mess, but he understands them. I know this because his nostrils flare right before he rasps, "I plan to."

He then proceeds to show me the kind of attention I knew he would. The kind of attention that brings me close to orgasm over and over until I struggle to recall my own damn name.

He takes his sweet time with my body.

His mouth.

His lips.

His tongue.

His hands.

Every. Inch. Of. My. Body.

"Oh God," I moan, clutching handfuls of his hair as he works my pussy with his tongue. "I can't take much more."

A growl is his only response before he presses his face harder against me and continues with his tongue.

I'm going to die of pleasure.

Here in this bed.

And I'm okay with that.

But holy hell, I seriously don't think I have it in me to last another minute.

When Beckett pushes two fingers inside me, I'm done.

I fling my arms to the side and grip the sheet as my back arches up off the bed.

And I finally experience the kind of orgasm every girl should have in their life.

The kind that touches every nerve and causes enough pleasure that I could store some to keep me going for months.

Beckett moves over me as I come, peppering more kisses up my stomach and over my breasts.

When his face is inches from mine, I loop my hand around his neck and say, "You should also do that every day."

He kisses me. Hard and rough, and I take it as a sign of what's to come. When he comes up for air, he says, "I'm going to fuck you now, and then you're going to do those filthy things you mentioned."

I tighten my hold of his neck. "Yes I am."

"Wrap your legs around me and hold on tight," he orders, and for the first time ever, I obey him without argument.

Then, with his eyes on mine, he slams inside me exactly how I asked him to.

It's hard.

It's rough.

It's everything I want from him.

"Fuck," he roars, pulling out and thrusting in again.

I keep my arms and legs wrapped around him and take everything he has to give.

Beckett has the kind of stamina that makes me think he could keep going for hours.

He's fiercely masculine. Dominant and powerful in the way he moves. And by the time we orgasm together, I'm certain he could ask me to do anything, and I'd agree.

"Holy hell," I say as I lay thoroughly fucked once he's finished. "You were right."

"I'm always right, Jenna," he says, rolling onto his side to face me.

I turn my face to his, ready to tell him what I think of that statement but stop when I see the smile in his eyes. "You're baiting me, aren't you?"

His smile reaches his lips, and he kisses me before saying, "I told you that arguing with you is one of my favorite things to do." He pauses. "What was I right about?"

I roll onto my side and hook my leg over his. "I won't be able to walk tomorrow. Not after you do that a few times tonight."

"I like that we're on the same page."

"For once."

"I've got some ideas for how to get us on the same page more often."

"I bet you do."

He kisses me again and then moves off the bed. Jerking his chin at me, he bosses, "Up. I want you in the shower."

I don't move. "Do you?"

"Yes."

Every cell in my body wants to get off the bed and get in that shower with him, but I stay where I am. If Beckett likes arguing with me, I'm going to let him. "You know I'm not a fan of Bossy Beckett."

With a shake of his head, he walks around to my side of the bed and scoops me into his arms. Carrying me into my bathroom, he growls, "Soon you'll learn to do as you're told."

"You have no idea what's in store for you, do you?" I say as he puts me down and flicks the shower on.

"I'm counting on it," he says before brushing his lips over mine. "Now, get your ass in there and do some filthy things to me."

19

JENNA

"All I can say is thank God you finally came to your senses," Shona says late Friday afternoon, the day after my second date with Beckett, when she stops by my office. "How was the sex?"

I kick off my heels and pull my feet up under me on the sofa we're sitting on. "Beckett made good on his promise that I'd have trouble walking today."

Her lips curl up. "I knew he had it in him. Tell me you're not waiting until the party tomorrow to see him again."

"He has a work thing tonight, but seriously, I'm not sure I'd have it in me to go another round with him today. The man ruined my muscles last night."

"Looks like you can quit your gym membership and let Beckett take care of your body if you keep seeing him."

The thought of just how well Beckett took care of my body last night causes another ache of need to settle low in my belly. This has been happening all day because I can't stop thinking about him. He spent hours fucking me last night, finally allowing sleep just after 3:00 a.m. He then woke me at 6:00 a.m. for more before he had to leave half an hour later. The fact I succumbed to his demands at such an ungodly hour is proof my brain is all messed up over him.

Cora knocks on my door, interrupting my thoughts about Beckett's skills. I call out for her to come in and a moment later, I'm looking at the largest bunch of red roses I've ever seen.

Shona whistles and says, "He means business."

Cora's eyes are bright with excitement as she places the roses on my desk. "If you ever change your mind about him, please send him my way."

I take the card she passes me and read his message as she exits the office.

THE SOUND you make when I give you my tongue. I need that again.

HOLY. Fuck.

I look at Shona, holding the card up. "He's sexting me with flowers. The man is lethal."

"Good. God knows, after five months with no dick and two years with Declan, you're in desperate need of lethal."

Shona was never a fan of Declan. That should have been a red flag to me, but I was blinded by his smooth ways.

My phone sounds with a text and I snatch it up, telling myself I'm not doing that because I'm hoping it'll be a text from Beckett. The disappointment that slides through me when I see my sister's name on the screen tells me the truth.

Kristen: Jenna, I need you! Tell me you're free tonight for me to come over so you can fix my outfit for tomorrow.

Jenna: I'll be home all night. What's going on?

Kristen: I'll come over around 7. Will show you then.

Jenna: If you can give me a heads up now, it'd be better so I can be prepared.

Kristen: This is the dress my stylist chose for me. It's horrid and I need you to fix it.

She sends through a photo of a dress that is all kinds of

wrong for her body shape. I don't want to be the one to tell her this dress is unworkable. Especially not at this late hour before the party. Kristen is a highly anxious person. What she needs is for me to be calm and just work my magic.

Jenna: I'll fix this for you, babe. Don't stress over it, okay?

Kristen: I love you.

I look at Shona as I stand. "I have to make some calls. Kristen needs a dress for tomorrow."

Shona frowns. "Since when doesn't your highly organized sister have a dress lined up weeks in advance of her party of the season?"

"The one she has is awful, so I'm going to get her another one."

Shona stands. "Okay, I'll leave you to do that. I'll talk to you later."

We exchange hugs and kisses, and she exits my office at which point I get to work on securing my sister a dress she'll love. After I send Beckett a text, that is.

Jenna: Noted.

~

"Wow, how did you make this happen?" Kristen asks when she arrives at my condo just after 8:00p.m. She's never been known for her punctuality, so I didn't expect her until now even though she told me 7:00 p.m.

I eye the rack of dresses I managed to put together at short notice this afternoon. "I have great contacts and they were all keen for their dresses to be seen at your party. I think you're going to have trouble choosing. There are some gorgeous dresses in this selection."

She points at the glass of scotch I'm holding. "I'll take one of those please. Today has been the worst; I could do with a few drinks."

Everything that's happening with Kristen today is so out of

character that it makes me worry about her. "What's going on, Kris? It's not like you to not have your dress sorted or to drink the night before your party."

She stares at me, eyes wide, for a long moment before bursting into tears and collapsing onto my sofa. "Johnathon broke off our engagement on Monday. He told me he still loves me but needs time to figure out whether marriage is what he wants right now."

"Jesus, you do need a scotch." I head into the kitchen and pour her a glass. I bring the bottle back with me and sit next to her as I hand her the drink.

She guzzles half of it in one go before looking at it and saying, "This is good scotch."

I nod. "It'd want to be for the price." *Thank you, Beckett.*

She finishes the drink and holds her glass out for a refill, which I give her without hesitation. If she's feeling the way I felt when I broke up with Declan, she's going to need quite a few of these.

I drain my glass and pour myself another one too before saying, "Tell me everything."

Kristen gulps some scotch down and takes a deep breath. "I think he's cheating on me, Jenna."

Those are the words guaranteed to make me lose my shit. I'm super protective of my little sister, and the idea of someone hurting her in this way brings out my fight. "Okay, wait. Did you guys break up or did he just pause the engagement while he gets himself together?"

"He's moved out. We're on a break while he takes some time to figure out what he wants."

"What makes you think he's cheating?"

She bites her lip. "I know this is bad and I shouldn't have done it, but I went through his phone. I found texts from a woman called Julie. And photos." Her face crumples. "She sent him nudes."

"What did the texts say?"

"That's the thing; they were a little inconclusive. She was sending him suggestive stuff about hooking up and seeing him at work. But he never replied with anything sexual. He was just always polite back to her."

"That's weird. Maybe she wants something to happen, but he doesn't? Did you ask him about it?"

She pulls a face. "No. I was going to, but that felt too scary. Like, once I know for sure, I'll have to make a decision, and I'm not sure I'm ready to make a decision."

I reach for her hand and squeeze it. "I get it." I drink some more scotch. "What's the plan for tomorrow with him? Is he coming to the party?"

Kristen empties her glass. "Yes, he's coming, but.... God, it's such a mess. Everyone's going to notice there's something wrong with us. Mom's going to go on about it incessantly. Oliver will definitely notice, and I hate to think what he'll do if he discovers any of this. And God, if Grayson figures it out, he'll ruin the party."

She's not wrong about any of that, especially the bit about our brothers. Oliver has little time for Johnathon and will be swift to hurt him if he finds out what's going on, and Grayson loves Kristen fiercely and won't put up with anyone hurting her. He's a little unpredictable in how he'll respond, but fully predictable in that he will, and that it won't be pleasant.

Kristen swipes the bottle of scotch up and pours herself another one. Her movements are jerky, and I know from experience that when she gets like this, it's downhill pretty fast unless someone takes charge of her. That job falls to me tonight.

"Right, here's what we're going to do," I say, pushing up off the sofa. "That's your last drink because you will regret getting drunk tonight if you do. We're going to choose your dress and then you're going to bed. Here. Tomorrow morning, we'll leave early to set up. We'll make sure everything is perfect and that you have all you need to get through the party. One thing you're going to have to do is talk with Johnathon about what you require from him tomorrow. I mean, I would do this for you but we both know that would not be a good move."

A text comes through on my phone.

Mom: Jenna, do you know where your sister is? I've just arrived at her place and she's not here.

Jenna: She's spending the night with me. We're having a girls' night to celebrate her party success ahead of time.

Mom: You really expect me to believe that, darling? Kristen never takes the night off before her parties.

Jenna: I don't expect anything. I'm just answering your question. I managed to get her some amazing dresses today to try for tomorrow and we decided to make a night of it.

Kristen's phone sounds with a text and I snatch it off her so I can read it.

Mom: Darling, why are you with your sister instead of getting ready for tomorrow? And why is she lying to me about it?

I pass Kristen our phones. "Read what I told Mom on our messages and then reply with the same info."

She does as I say and after a few minutes of texting and then a phone call, she declares, "Our mother is hard work."

I laugh. "She really is."

"It's going to be up to you to keep her occupied tomorrow if we have any hope of her not sniffing out trouble between Johnathon and me."

How did I not see this coming?

She's absolutely right; someone needs to be on Mom duty and since I'm the only one who knows what's going on, it has to be me.

I pick up the scotch bottle and take a swig directly from it. A long fucking swig. I then stab my finger in the air at my sister and say, "You owe me so big for this." After one last swig, I say, "Right, let's choose a dress. And I take back what I said about it being hard to decide between them all. If Johnathon did to me what he's done to you, there's only one dress there I would choose." The stunning red dress that reveals so much skin and boobs that he will be unable to take his eyes off her. I know my sister won't choose that one, though, because she's all about maintaining her image, but I wouldn't hesitate to wear it if I were her.

BECKETT: You got my flowers.

I roll over in my bed and switch on my lamp. It's just after midnight and I've been struggling to get to sleep for an hour. I haven't heard from Beckett since lunchtime when we last spoke. The reason I'm having trouble sleeping is because I've spent the last hour after getting Kristen to bed thinking about him.

Jenna: Who knew you had it in you to send flowers and surprise a girl?

He calls and I answer immediately. "Something you need to know about me is that I require my beauty sleep, and midnight is reserved for that. Especially any night after a night where I don't get said beauty sleep."

"I'll keep that in mind," he says, his deep voice hitting all the spots that will ensure I continue struggling to sleep tonight.

"That sounds an awful lot like *noted*, and we both know you only truly note things that suit you to note."

I hear the smile in his voice when he says, "I missed you today, Jenna."

Dear. Lord.

I never imagined Beckett telling me he missed me could cause an instant flutter of butterflies in my tummy.

"How was your work thing?"

"Long. How was your night?"

"A little like yours. My sister came over and I spent the night trying to put her back together enough for tomorrow after her fiancé wrecked her. Well, actually, he's not technically her fiancé anymore, but that's a whole other story for another day." I exhale a long breath, trying to force the tension I feel over Johnathon from my chest. "Can I ask you something?"

"Anything."

"If a guy's engaged and is exchanging texts with another woman in which she's suggesting hooking up and sending nudes, and he's not doing anything to stop the texts, is he likely to be sleeping with her or planning on it?"

"You know the answer to this."

"I was really hoping you'd say no."

"This is your sister's fiancé?"

"Yes, but pretend you don't know, okay? If any of my family find out tomorrow, they'll ruin the party. Oh, and I'll have to meet you there rather than go with you sorry."

"Why?"

"Kristen stayed over, so we need to leave early tomorrow to get everything ready in time for the party."

"I can't leave any earlier, but you should take my helicopter to save time."

"Flowers and a helicopter. You really do like me, huh?"

"You've no idea," he says, all growly in the way I like. "What time do you need it ready for the morning?"

"Seven."

"I'll take care of it and send a car to pick you up."

"Thank you."

"You should go get that beauty sleep you think you need."

He also has no idea. I don't see sleep in my near future. "I loved the flowers. You should note that."

"Goodnight, Jenna."

"Night."

We end the call and I spend the next two hours tossing and turning while trying to stop thinking about Beckett. A futile endeavor; the man is stuck on replay in my brain.

20

JENNA

"What's going on with Kristen today?" Oliver asks as I stand at the bar waiting for the scotch I desperately need. We're only half an hour into the party, yet it feels like ten hours. Between my mother and my sister, I'm not convinced I'm going to make it through today without drinking all the drinks. Liquid cocaine is looking good right about now.

I eye my brother. "Huh?"

He gives me the look of his that tells me he doesn't buy what I said for even a moment. "Come on, Jenna, you can do better than that if you're trying to lie to me."

"I'm not trying to lie to you, Oliver. Kristen's anxiety over the party is at epic proportions as it usually is. I don't know why you're surprised by that."

He gazes in Kristen's direction, where she's standing with Johnathon and looking anything but relaxed. Gah, I need to get over there ASAP. "If you're trying to tell me that *that*"—he points at Kristen—"is Kristen simply being anxious over a party, you must think I'm a fucking idiot."

The bartender slides my drink across to me. "Thank you," I say with a smile before turning back to Oliver. "I don't know. I'll go check on her."

Before he can interrogate me any further, I start toward my sister, however my mother intercepts me on the way.

"Jenna, I need your help, darling."

"I'm busy. Oliver's free. Ask him to help."

Her lips press together. "No, he won't do." She takes hold of my arm. "This will only take a few minutes. Twenty at the most."

"Mom, there's a vast difference between a few minutes and twenty, and I'm in the middle of something that can't wait. Let me take care of this first and then I'm all yours."

"Fine, if you must. I'll be in the kitchen. Come find me there when you're finished whatever is so dreadfully important."

I fight an eye roll as I carry on toward Kristen who has started arguing with Johnathon. When I reach them, I cut in without hesitation. "Kristen, you either need to take this somewhere private or put it off until later." She made me promise her I would do this if needed. I know from experience, though, that she will likely argue with me in the heat of the moment, so I'm fully prepared for that.

She surprises me when she doesn't argue. It's Johnathon who does. He looks at me with annoyance and snarls, "You need to leave us the fuck alone, Jenna. This isn't the time for you to stick your nose into Kristen's business."

Wow, this is a side of Johnathon I've never seen before. He's usually all smiles and politeness, to the point that he bores me. "I'm not trying to stick my nose in, Johnathon. I'm just trying to look out for my sister because she asked me to."

He blows out a frustrated breath. "Of course, she fucking did. Your family can't do anything by themselves."

My brows arrow as I cross my arms. I'm feeling every ounce of defensiveness swarming through me. My family may frustrate me and annoy me, but don't come at me with this kind of shit about them because I will defend them like you've never seen anyone defend someone. "You'd be surprised what my family can do, Johnathon, and trust me when I tell you that you don't want to find out." I look at Kristen, my eyes and voice softening as I say, "Kris, go inside and finish this conversation. You'll regret it if you don't."

She glances around the party, observing the few pairs of eyes on us and nods while looking at Johnathon. "We need to finish this inside."

He shoots me one last glare before following Kristen into the house.

I watch them leave and take a few deep breaths. Johnathon has brought all my hurt over being cheated on to the surface. I don't know for sure if he has cheated, but I think Beckett's right; I believe he has. And that makes me angry on Kristen's behalf and also so disappointed for her.

With one last deep breath, I turn to go and see what Mom wants help with. I stop when my eyes lock onto Beckett who is coming toward me, his strides purposeful and his expression determined. He's wearing sunglasses, so I can't see his eyes, but I can imagine the intensity with which he's watching me. The intensity he brings to every interaction we have. The intensity that every part of my body now lives for.

When he reaches me, his arm goes around my waist, and he pulls me close. Brushing his lips over mine, he says, "You look beautiful."

My hands go to his chest while I try to catch my thoughts. The thoughts he's stolen simply by existing. "This suit needs to go on regular rotation."

He doesn't smile or give me one of his usual amused looks, but rather his nostrils flare and he kisses me. This time it's not a quick brush of his lips but a full kiss that makes me want to skip the party and spend the day begging him to ruin my muscles again.

When he finally lets my mouth go, he says, "I like that you're not fighting this anymore."

I keep my hands on his chest. "Me too." I really do. Fighting this was great foreplay, but what we're sharing now is the kind of next-level sexy I'm here for.

He lets me go and removes his sunglasses. "How's your sister?"

"Shit," I mutter, remembering my mother. "I have to go find my mom. Come with me."

While we walk, I fill him in on the fact Kristen wanted to cancel her party this morning, which is something she would never ever consider if she was thinking straight. My sister is like my mother and is all about social appearances. I also share with him how she went into a meltdown when Johnathon arrived, how she hid herself in the bathroom for half an hour afterwards, and that I feel on edge over the fact they're inside discussing stuff now.

It doesn't escape me that I'm merging my world with his in a way I never imagined. It also doesn't escape me how easy and natural this all feels. Three days ago, none of this would have felt possible; now the possibilities feel wide open, and I'm not running from any of them.

"Jenna," Mom says when we arrive in the kitchen. "Goodness, I wouldn't want to be waiting on you to save me in an apocalypse." She stops abruptly when she realizes Beckett's with me. The exasperation leaves her face and voice as she looks at him, batting her freaking lashes. "Oh my, it's a pleasure to meet you, Beckett."

Save me now.

The sweetness oozing from her is too much for me.

Beckett handles her with grace, though. He steps next to me and says, "You too, Maria," he says, enough gravel in his voice to cause my mother to practically swoon in front of me. I don't know if he did that on purpose, but he deserves my gratitude and I intend to deliver it when we're alone later.

"Jenna was very secretive about the fact you two are together. I have to say that I, for one, am very happy about this." She looks at me with what can only be described as triumph. "That auction was a success for you."

I roll my eyes and ignore the auction reference. I don't even want to think about how often she'll mention it in the future if this relationship with Beckett turns into something. "Mom, he's my date for the party. Don't get confused about what that means." Can someone please come and steal her away? I just know today is going to get worse before it gets better, and that knowledge makes me want to run back to the bar.

Mom waves her hand in the air like she's dismissing me. "Darling, I'm not confused. I can see exactly what's going on with you two."

Before I can correct her again, Oliver joins us, and if the look on his face is anything to go by, he's ready to rip someone's head off. Eyes to mine, he demands, "Is it true?"

"Is what true?"

"Don't fuck with me, Jenna. Is it true that Johnathon has fucked half of New York?"

My mother's sharp intake of breath is all I hear as I stare at my brother in shock. "Half of New York?"

Oliver rakes his fingers through his hair, growing more impatient with each passing second. "That's the rumor doing the rounds of this party. I'd like to confirm it before finding the motherfucker and letting him know what I think of him."

"Oliver," Mom says, holding her hand to her chest and looking as dramatic as if the world was about to end, "please don't use that language. You know I don't care for it."

"Honestly, I would have thought you'd care more about the fact your daughter has been betrayed by her fiancé," Oliver says.

"Okay, can we all calm down," I suggest as Mom's eyes widen at Oliver's tone. "I can't confirm this rumor, Oliver, so—"

"I can," Grayson says from behind me, his voice dark and murderous.

I spin to face him and suck in a breath at the hard stone of his face. "How?"

He looks at me. "I just dragged that confirmation out of him."

"Oh God. What did you do?" Visions of a beaten and bloody Johnathon fill my mind. It wouldn't be the first time Grayson has beaten the shit out of a guy Kristen or I dated.

"He's still breathing if that's what you're worried about," Grayson says.

"Where the fuck is he?" Oliver demands.

"He's gone," Grayson says. "I shoved him in his car and told him that if I ever lay eyes on him again, he won't be so fucking lucky to walk away again."

"Where's Kristen?" I ask, desperate to get to her. This is far worse than I imagined, and probably completely out of the realm of what she thought she'd ever have to deal with.

"I left her in her bedroom," Grayson says.

Looking at Beckett, I say, "I'll be back soon. I'm sorry about this."

"There's nothing to apologize for." His words are laced with concern, something I appreciate.

"Thank you." I eye my brothers. "Don't do anything to ruin this party for Kristen."

Oliver looks at me like I've lost my mind. "There's not much more to ruin. Johnathon already made sure of that."

My heart breaks for my sister. When I find her face down on her bed sobbing, it continues to crack some more.

"Kristen," I say, sitting next to her and smoothing her hair. "Come here."

She shakes her head, not lifting it, and mumbles, "Go away, Jenna. I just want to be alone."

"Being alone is the last thing you need. I'm not going anywhere."

Her sobs grow louder while she keeps her face shoved into her pillow. I don't try to force her to sit up; I just rub my hand up and down her back trying to soothe her even though I know nothing will soothe the ache of what that asshole has done.

We sit like this for a long time until finally she lifts her head and looks at me. "Grayson told you?"

I nod, taking in her puffy face and mascara-streaked cheeks. "Yeah," I say softly. Holding my arms out, I say, "Please come here for a hug."

She scrambles up into a sitting position and lets me hug her. "I hate him."

"I know."

A sob escapes her, and she wraps her arms around me. "I want to chainsaw his dick off and make him eat it, and then I want to stab his balls until they're a bloody pulp."

"I know, and I want to help you." God how I want to help her do that. I pull back to look at her. "I think, though, that you might have to get in line behind Grayson and Oliver."

"Grayson punched the crap out of him."

"Like, how bad are we talking? I need to visualize it."

She smiles. It's tiny, but definitely a smile. "Worse than he's ever punched any of the assholes we've dated."

"Broken bones?"

"Probably."

"Good."

Her smile grows a little. "I love you, Jenna."

"I love you too. Now, we need to talk about the party and what you want to do about it. I'll make whatever you want to happen, happen."

She thinks about that for less than a minute. "I want to get drunk."

"No, you don't."

"Yes, I do." She lets me go and moves off the bed faster than I can keep up. "And I want you to get drunk with me. When was the last time we drank together?"

"Ah, like pretty much never because you don't get drunk, remember?" It's true. Kristen is the good girl of our family who never does anything in public that will cause any kind of gossip.

"Yes, well today I do." She heads into the bathroom and cleans her face as best she can. Her face is a mess after all that crying, though, so I help her reapply her make-up. Then, after we also fix her hair, she announces, "Fuck Johnathon. I'm going to get drunk and fuck one of his friends."

With that, she exits the bedroom in a puff of what-the-fuck-is-happening-right-now. I follow her, but she's moving fast and I'm struggling to keep up. I need to get in front of her to stop her, but I don't see that happening.

"Kristen, stop! You will wake up tomorrow and wish you never did this if you go through with it."

She shakes her head madly. "No, I won't. I'll wonder why the I didn't do it sooner." She spins to face me while continuing to walk backwards. "I've suspected he was cheating for a while now. I never told you that. I should have listened to my gut, but Mom always taught us not to cause a scene and not to stir up trouble with our men, so I didn't. I was the good girl and look where it got me." She throws her arms out to the sides. "It got me nowhere! I am so done with being this girl. I want to be you now." She turns back around and stalks faster down the hall and stairs.

My sister is losing her ever-loving mind and while I definitely encourage all women to throw off the armor they wear to protect their hearts, I'm not convinced this is the right move for Kristen today.

I don't manage to stop her before she hits the bar. By the time I catch her, she's ordered us both drinks and is flirting with the bartender like she's being paid to.

I pull out my phone and text Grayson.

Jenna: Come to the bar. I need your help. Kristen is losing her shit.

He doesn't waste time doing as I asked. When he arrives, he says to our sister, "I don't know what you plan to do, but it doesn't look like anything good. And let me tell you, he isn't worth it."

The bartender places two scotches on the bar and Kristen ignores Grayson and downs almost all hers in one gulp.

"Grayson," I say, "we need to clear the party out."

Kristen's head snaps around to look at Grayson. "No! Everyone stays."

"You really want to go down that path?" Grayson asks her.

She finishes her drink. "Yes. I want to have a good time and forget everything that asshole did."

Grayson looks at me. "I can't argue with that."

"Seriously?" I widen my eyes at him. "You know this isn't the real Kristen talking. This is her pain talking. We need to look out for her."

"Maybe letting her hair down is exactly what she needs," he says.

"You two can stop talking about me like I'm not here," Kristen says. Then to me she says, "I'm tired, Jenna. Tired of trying to be perfect all the time. I promise you I'm fully aware of what I'm doing and if I do regret it later, that's on me, not you."

I inhale a deep breath and exhale it. Nothing's going to stop her from doing this, and hell, maybe it is what she needs.

"Okay," I say, moving next to her at the bar. "Let's do this."

21

BECKETT

I eye Jenna dancing with her sister on the dancefloor set up under the marquee. They've been dancing for the last ten minutes and don't look like stopping anytime soon. Jenna's sister has finally stopped drinking thanks to the dancing. I assumed she'd pass out hours ago with what she's consumed, but somehow she managed to keep going. Jenna did her best to slow Kristen's drinking, but her sister has been on a mission to get as drunk as possible. Not that I blame her. I understand her pain in a way I wish I didn't.

Jenna's gaze lands on me as I sit back watching her. Those lips of hers pull up in a sexy smile and she motions with her finger for me to join her. I finish my scotch and make my way over, my eyes firmly locked with hers.

"Do you like my dress?" she asks, bringing her hands to my chest.

My brows pull in. "Does it matter?" This isn't the kind of question I'd ever expect from Jenna. Her confidence is such that she's never given me reason to believe she cares what others think of her or any of her choices in life. Especially not her clothes since she's a stylist.

She smiles, biting her lip and giving me her vulnerability.

"No, but for some reason even I don't understand, I want you to like it."

"I like it," I growl, crushing her body to mine. "I like it a lot, especially that slit that shows me your leg. But I like you giving me what you just did more."

"Giving you what?" She hasn't drunk as much as her sister, but she's still consumed a fair amount of alcohol, causing her thoughts to slow down over the course of the afternoon.

"That honesty about you wanting me to like it."

Her hands move up to loop around my neck and her body relaxes into mine. "I've never been with a man who's said stuff like this to me. I mean, when I say 'with a man', I don't know what this is between us or whether I'm with you or whether this is just sex, and I'm okay if that's what it is, like, seriously okay if it's just sex for you, and God, now I'm just letting all my thoughts out and—"

"I'm not okay with that."

She frowns. "With me vomiting all my thoughts?"

"No, *that* I'm good with. What I'm not okay with is if this is just sex for you." Just how not okay I am with this is a feeling I'll need to work my way through later.

Her eyes widen for a moment before her face fills with a smile that lights every inch of it up in a way I want to see again and again. "Has any woman ever told you how growly you get sometimes?"

"No." My eyes search hers as my gut tightens while thinking about how fucking growly I feel with her. "You're the only woman who has brought it out in me."

Her lips part and her fingers grip my neck harder as she takes that in.

We're interrupted before she can respond. "Beckett!" Kristen says while cutting in on Jenna and me. "We need to talk."

Although it's the last thing I want to do, I let Jenna go so Kristen can have whatever conversation she wants to have with me. Jenna's eyes don't let mine go, though, and she sends a silent apology before looking at her sister and saying, "Kris, now's not the time."

"Now is most definitely the time," Kristen says. "I need to know Beckett's intentions with you."

"Jesus," Jenna mutters. "We've just started dating. No one needs to be talking intentions."

Kristen sways and then stumbles backwards into Grayson who has just made his way under the marquee. He steadies her and says, "I think it's time for you to exit the party."

She pulls a face and grumbles, "I'm not ready to leave, Gray Gray."

"If you're calling me that, you're more than ready to leave."

Kristen reaches for her sister as Grayson attempts to guide her off the dancefloor. "Jenna, you need to stay with me tonight."

"No, she doesn't," Grayson says. "She's drunk. I'll be staying with you."

"But we haven't talked about Beckett's intentions yet," Kristen slurs, still trying to fight her brother off.

Grayson's eyes meet mine and I don't miss *his* intention when he says, "Trust me, we'll find time for that conversation soon." With that, he moves Kristen off the dancefloor and takes her inside the house.

Jenna comes back to me after they leave. "I'm sorry today's been such a shitshow."

I pull her into my arms and rest my hands on her ass. "You don't need to apologize. Family has a way of taking over at times."

She runs her hands over my chest, her fingers dipping under my suit jacket. "Two things." Her dimple pops as she blesses me with her sexy smile. "First, I really like your hands on my ass. Make sure that preference is noted. And second, I'm not sure how I ever missed this patience of yours. Thank you for giving me the space to deal with my family today even though I pushed you into attending this party with me. I appreciate it all."

Fuck, she has no idea. But then, she doesn't know me well enough yet to know I'd live through this day with her over and over if that was what she needed. I don't know her well enough yet either, but what I do know is Jenna's the kind of woman who puts her family first, and that's the kind of woman I want by my side.

"Three things." I pause to take in the way her eyes light up at my words. "First"—I tighten my grip on her ass—"your preference is noted. Second, no one pushes me into doing anything. You should know that. And third, family always comes first."

She curves a hand around my neck and pulls my face down to hers so she can kiss me. It's quick and nowhere near what I need from her, but I don't push her for more because I won't be able to stop if I do. "I like everything you just said," she says when she lets my lips go. "And while family comes first, I'm sorry if this is all too much, too soon. When I invited you to this party, I imagined us dancing, eating, having a drink, and then leaving. I didn't imagine what's happened today." She pauses. "I didn't imagine three days into this, you'd have to deal with my family on this level."

I didn't imagine any of this either, however, it's not too much too soon. Not with Jenna. This is another thought I'm going to have to work my way through later. But for now, every fiber in my being is ready to see where this goes.

"This isn't too much too soon."

"Okay, but, still, you didn't sign up for this."

"We've known each other for years, Jenna. I know what I'm getting myself into."

"We haven't really known each other for years. I mean, I had no idea this Beckett I'm getting to know even existed."

I detect uncertainty in her voice, and I realize Jenna's family is the part of her life that leaves her feeling naked, exposed. I've only ever been witness to her confidence. Now, she's allowing me front row seats to the side of her that doubt resides in.

I tighten my hold of her. "Can you tell me you're not feeling this like I am?"

She doesn't have to think about that. A fact I like. "I'm feeling it, but it's all happening so fast."

"Fast is how I prefer to do things. Can you handle that?"

I know I'm pushing her, but it's in my blood to always push for what I want, and I want Jenna. After years of not being willing to contemplate a woman in my life again, she's woken a need deep inside me, and I'm helpless to stop myself from chasing what I know will satisfy that need.

She only hesitates for a second before giving me what I'm looking for. "I can handle that."

I knew she could. Jenna wouldn't be the woman for me if she couldn't. However, I also know I'll have to be far more patient than I want to be with her. And for the first time in my life, I'll compromise and make allowances. How any man ever let Jenna go is beyond me. I've never met a woman I want to hold onto more.

22

JENNA

Rolling over, I crack an eye open and survey the luxurious bed I'm in. Beckett's bed in his Hampton's home. He brought me here last night after we left Kristen's party. That was after giving me the option of going home or spending the night here. Having had a little too much to drink, flying home hadn't sounded like a great option, so I was grateful for this one. Unfortunately for Beckett, I practically passed out the minute he got me here. I blame his bed. Not the alcohol. It's the most comfortable bed I've ever slept on.

Pushing the sheet off, I leave the bed and go in search of him after I use his bathroom and then steal some of his tooth-paste to clean my teeth.

Beckett's home is spectacular.

An oceanfront estate with views of the Atlantic Ocean and Shinnecock Bay, it's a four-level house with floor-to-ceiling windows everywhere so that nearly every room has a water vista. Masculine grays fill the house and it's clear Beckett's style is minimalist. It's not a style I love, but I can appreciate it in this house because it keeps the focus on the location. I mean, is there anything better than seeing water and nature everywhere you look? I think not. I could live here simply for the tranquility.

It doesn't take me long to find him. His bedroom is on the main level just off the great room which leads out to the wood deck and infinity pool. Beckett is relaxing on one of the outdoor chaise lounges, his impressive muscles on full display. I can also see that tattoo of his I love curling over his shoulder. The eagle tattoo. His other tattoo turned out to be an intricate design featuring a compass, triangles, and circles on his back. I haven't had much time yet to fully check it out and ask him about the meaning, but I intend to. Beckett doesn't do anything without a reason, and I can't wait to discover what his tattoos mean to him.

Slowing my approach, I give myself some time to admire his body. The man has the best body I've ever had the pleasure of ogling. And touching. When I finally reach him, I slide onto his lap like it's something I've always done. His arm comes around me so his hand can rest on my ass like that's something he's always done. It's crazy how natural being with Beckett now feels, but it does, and after our conversation yesterday about how we're both feeling this, I'm fully embracing our relationship.

"Good morning," I murmur as I bring my hand to his jaw and kiss him. I only intend to be quick with his lips, but Beckett has other ideas and deepens the kiss to the point where I never want to let these lips go. When we finally come up for air, I say, "I want to spend all day doing that."

"That can be arranged." The gravel in his voice causes me to grind myself against him as he glides his hands around my waist to my stomach, reaching under the shirt of his I'm wearing. "How are you feeling?"

"Surprisingly okay." I felt okay when I woke, no hangover, but now that he's got his hands and eyes on me I feel like a goddess. I remove the sunglasses he's wearing so I can see those eyes of his. "That's better," I say once they're off, enjoying the desire I see in his gaze.

"How so?" he asks as his hands move lazily up my stomach to cup my breasts.

"Well, now I can see you."

He lifts the shirt I'm wearing over my head and lets it fall to the ground before dropping his gaze to my chest. Taking his sweet time, he brings his mouth to my nipple. Beckett may have told me yesterday that moving fast is his preference, but when it comes to how he prefers to explore my body, the opposite is true. His methods deliver both the most exquisite type of pleasure I've ever experienced and the most torturous.

When he's finished with both my nipples, he meets my gaze again and says, "You wanted my eyes?"

"Yes."

"Tell me where you want them."

"I just wanted to see them."

In one swift movement, he sits up straight and brings his arms around me so he's gripping my ass. Dipping his mouth to kiss one of my breasts, he demands, "Do you prefer them here?" Then in another swift move, he has me on my back laid out in front of him. "Or do you prefer them here?" he asks as he brings his mouth to my pussy, kissing me through my panties. Looking up at me, he adds, "I'm more than good with keeping them on your face, but I want to hear your preference."

Resting on my elbows, I smile at him. "My preference is for you to get rid of all our clothes and to get your eyes on every inch of my body. I can't choose my favorite place for them yet."

His fingers hook under my panties and he slides them down my legs. "We need to schedule some time for me to help you choose."

"I'm free every morning and night from here on out. Oh, and every weekend. All weekend." Can he just get his clothes off already and his mouth on me? The man is far too controlled sometimes.

"I see you're getting on board with my preference for fast."

I grip his biceps. "When I date a man, I don't need to put him on my schedule. And I prefer a man who doesn't need to pencil me in, just so you know. I'm wide open for you, Beckett. Can you handle that?"

His eyes flare with more heat. "Consider my calendar cleared."

"Good. Now can you please speed this up and get your eyes and your mouth on my pussy?"

"I thought you didn't have a preference yet."

"It turns out I do. And while I'm good with you going slow once you've got your mouth on me, I prefer you not take your time getting it there."

He watches me for one last moment before finally giving me what I want, and God if it isn't everything I never knew I needed.

~

"How can anyone not like chocolate milk?" I ask as Beckett and I clean up the kitchen after breakfast.

I cooked bacon and eggs for us after telling him not to be silly when he indicated his chef would cook for us. I told him to let his chef have the day off, that we were more than capable of feeding ourselves. I then searched his fridge, located the bacon and eggs, and took over.

We ate on the deck, looking out over the ocean, and spent a couple of hours talking. I'm not sure I can recall a more perfect Sunday morning. Amazing sex, breakfast in the sun, and great conversation, with a man I'm falling for more and more each moment I'm in his company.

And now this revelation about him not liking chocolate milk.

He chuckles and puts the last plate away before coming

back to me. Caging me in against the kitchen island, he presses a kiss to my neck. "How can anyone *like* it?"

"Do you like any flavored milk?" The sensations his attention to my neck is causing are very distracting, but I manage to continue a conversation. The way his body feels against mine, though, is a whole other story. *That* is distracting on a whole other level.

"Milk isn't meant to be flavored, Jenna."

"Everything is meant to be flavored if that's what we like. That's the magic of life, right? Flavor and fun. Try it all."

Something I've said has him looking at me like he's thinking hard about it. Whatever it is, he doesn't comment on it. Instead, he bends his face to mine and kisses me. Long and deep, which is fast becoming one of my absolute favorite things Beckett does. Like seriously, I need to have him and these kisses available on demand.

He ends the kiss just as I'm falling into it and says, "What were you thinking just then?"

I thread my fingers through his hair at the nape of his neck. "Huh?" He's caught me off guard. I was lost in that kiss and am struggling to catch up with the conversation.

"When you were kissing me then, you started smiling in the middle of it. I want to know what caused that."

"Oh that." I smile again and press myself harder against him. "I was thinking about how much I wish I could have you on demand."

I can tell by the way his eyes crease that he likes what I've said, but he doesn't get a chance to say anything because his phone interrupts us when it rings.

Glancing at it, he says, "It's Ruby. I need to take it."

"Of course. I'll give you some privacy."

As I move to step out of his embrace, he reaches for my hand and stops me. "Stay." He then answers the FaceTime call and his sister's voice fills the kitchen.

"Where are you?" she demands, and I'm struck by what

appears to be the Pearce way of doing things. Beckett isn't the only one in their family with those bossy genes. "Oh, I can see where you are. When are you coming back to the city?"

"I'll be home tonight. Why?"

"I've made a decision and I want to see you to tell you what it is."

"Just tell me now."

"No, I want to tell you in person. What time will you be home?"

"I don't know, Ruby." Beckett glances at me before adding, "It might be late."

"Who's there with you? You never take anyone to the Hamptons with you." She sounds as suspicious as my sister is with our brothers when they do something out of character.

I almost want to laugh at Beckett's response to her interrogation. It's like he's abandoned hope of controlling the conversation, which is something I've never seen him do. With a shake of his head, he pulls me next to him so she and I can see each other. "Ruby, meet Jenna. Jenna, meet my sister."

Ruby's eyes widen as she says, "Holy hell, you took a woman to your place? Wait, is this what I think it is? Oh my God, I never thought I'd see the day." A smile takes over her face. "Jenna, I love your name. Tell me, how long have you been with my brother? He never tells me anything."

I laugh, feeling completely at ease with her. "Beckett bought a date with me in a charity auction and we had that date on Wednesday, so not very long."

"Oh, this is gold," she says. "Keep talking. How much did he pay for the date?"

"My lips are sealed on that," I say.

Ruby opens her mouth to speak but Beckett cuts her off. "We're not going there, Ruby." And he's back to being in control with that firm voice of his.

"You know I'll keep hounding you until you tell me."

Beckett ignores her and asks me, "What time do you want to be home by?"

"Seven at the latest," I say.

He nods and then looks at Ruby again. "I'll drop Jenna off and then come over."

"I can come to your place," she says.

"No. I'll come to you." His tone is clear that he doesn't intend to change his mind.

"Fine, but you should expect a lot of questions. It's not every day a girl discovers her brother, who swore off relationships years ago, is in a new one."

"Goodbye, Ruby," Beckett says before ending the call.

I burst out laughing as he places his phone down. "I need more of your sister in my life."

The look Beckett gives me is the equivalent to an eye roll. "I can imagine. And thank you for telling her I bought our first date. She'll never let that go."

I move into him, slipping my arms around his waist, enjoying the closeness and the mood between us. I really liked how he felt comfortable enough to bring me in on the call. "You know that even though you somehow made me fall for you, I'm never going to go easy on you, right?"

"I'm aware of that, yes."

I grin. "I sense some fun ahead with your sister." When he shakes his head at me like he's resigned himself to this fact, I grin some more before changing the direction of the conversation. "Is she okay? I mean, I don't want to intrude on personal stuff, so tell me to leave it if this is too personal, but I remember she was texting you a lot the other night and now this."

"You can ask me anything, Jenna. I've told you, I'm an open book to you. Ruby sounds okay. She and our mother have been going head-to-head over her finding a husband. I tried to step in the other day and help Ruby, but Mom seems determined about what she wants. Ruby's just as determined about what she wants, so I expect fireworks for a while."

"She seems confident about her decision."

"Ruby's always confident about her decisions."

"It sounds like you don't think she'll go ahead with whatever it is." He actually sounds a little like my father when he's dismissive of my choices in life, but I'm withholding judgment on that because I'm probably reading him wrong. At least, I hope I am.

"Ruby makes new decisions all the time. She goes from one thing to the next, so I don't expect this to be anything that will last for any length of time."

"I hope she and your mom figure everything out soon. I know how difficult mothers can be."

"Trust me, they're both as difficult as each other."

"And what about Elon? Is he close to your parents?" Beckett hasn't talked much about his older brother which makes me wonder about him.

"He's close with Mom, but not Dad. They fell out when Elon chose not to go into the family business."

"Are you two close?"

"Yes, but not in the way you'd define it."

"What do you mean?"

"We don't see or speak to each other often, but there's no distance between us. I try to see him whenever he's home, however that's not often."

"He travels a lot?"

"Yes. He's in New York every four or five months." He pauses. "Has Kristen replied to your text from this morning?"

I reach for my phone and check the messages. "Not yet."

"Do you want to visit her before we fly home?" The concern in his eyes means the world to me. I'm not sure how I've missed the importance of family to Beckett in all the years I've known him.

"Yes, I would really like that. Thank you."

He nods and lets me go. Pulling his phone out, he says, "I'll organize the helicopter for five this afternoon. We can leave to go see Kristen whenever you want."

I run my hands up under his shirt, over his abs. I can't get enough of these abs. "We have plenty of time to hang out before we need to leave, and I know exactly what I want to do in that time."

He drags his gaze from his phone, a knowing look in his eyes. One I'm about to wipe away completely, but I'll let him keep thinking it for a moment. "Keep talking."

"We should watch a movie."

Beckett arches his brows. "We've got the afternoon free and you want to watch a movie?"

"Oh, you have no idea of my love for watching movies, Mr. Pearce. It's time I introduced you to one of my favorite ways to spend an afternoon."

"I could introduce you to one of *my* favorite ways of spending an afternoon and we could do yours another day," he says as he finishes tapping out a message on his phone. He then slides the phone into his pocket and lifts me into his arms.

I wrap my arms and legs around him, loving his playful mood. "No. I win today. We're watching *Crazy, Stupid, Love*. Take me to the television."

"You're serious about this, aren't you?" He might be trying to argue with me, but he's doing as directed and walking us out of the kitchen.

"Soon you will understand how hardcore I am about my movie reruns."

He takes me down to the next level of the house and into the theatre which is an opulent room decorated in dark gray and black, featuring three levels of plush sectionals, and a fully stocked bar. "Where do you want to sit? Front or back?"

I grin. "The back. Maybe I'll let you get lucky."

His lips pull up in amusement as he deposits me on the sofa. "If you think there's any chance in hell of me not getting lucky, you're dreaming. And just so you're aware, reruns aren't my thing. If I'm going to watch a movie, it's going to be one I haven't seen."

"Hmm, we'll see." He really has no idea what he's in for while dating me. New movies only, pfft.

I get comfortable on the sofa as Beckett moves to the bar.

"Do you want a drink?" he asks.

"Water please. I don't think my body can handle anything else today."

He pours himself a scotch and brings me a water before settling next to me.

I drink some water as he searches for the movie I've requested. "Have you seen this movie?" I ask.

"No." He stretches his legs out to rest his feet on the large square ottoman in front of him and brings his arm up over the top of the sofa behind me.

I shift so I can snuggle up against him, resting my head on his shoulder. "You're going to love it."

He locates the movie and I feel the familiar comfort I always experience when I rewatch movies I love. It's something I've always done. Kristen does it too. It's a tradition passed down from our mother. One I want to pass down to my daughter if I'm blessed to have one.

The movie starts and after a couple minutes, I say, "God I love Steve Carell."

Beckett shifts his arm from the sofa to rest over my shoulders. "Really?"

I glance up, finding him watching me. "Yes. You don't?"

"No."

"Why not?"

"Do you want to discuss him or watch the movie?"

"Both."

He watches me silently for a couple moments like he's connecting thoughts in his head before saying, "I don't like the movies of his I've seen."

Ryan Gosling appears on the screen, stealing all my attention. Clutching a handful of Beckett's shirt, I say, "Shh, Ryan's talking."

"When you said you wanted to watch a movie, I'm taking it that what you really meant was you want to check out the hot guy in between talking about everything that happens. Am I right?"

Grinning, I meet his gaze. "You're a fast learner, Mr. Pearce."

Before I know what's happening, Beckett pulls me onto his lap, settling me there with one arm around my waist and one hand gripping my hip. "I am. Are you?"

His growly tone isn't in full force, but it's teasing the edge of his voice. I like it. A lot. I also like the heat in his eyes and the way his fingers are digging into my skin.

I bring my hands to his stomach. "I can be if I have the right teacher."

"You have the right teacher." He's a little more growly this time. Ryan is completely forgotten. Beckett is the only man on my radar now.

I press myself against his erection and kiss him.

It's slow. Delicious. And oh so thorough.

When I come up for air, I say breathlessly, "I'm ready to learn."

Beckett drops his hands from my body and orders, "Take off the shirt."

After we showered this morning, he gave me another one of his shirts to wear since I didn't come prepared for a night away with clean clothes. I like wearing his stuff, but I really like taking it off because the way he watches me while I do that is everything I want in my life. The hunger in his eyes, the raw need, and the pleasure I see when he looks at me are things I've not experienced with a man before. Not to the extent I experience them with Beckett.

I do as he says. Not quickly, though, which is a good decision because by the time the shirt hits the sofa, Beckett's impatient and even more growly than before. He flicks my bra undone and slides it off, rasping, "Fuck, Jenna," as he sucks one of my nipples into his mouth.

My hands go to the nape of his neck and up into his hair while he dedicates time to my breasts. This seriously is the best day of my life this year so far. And I want many more days like this.

Beckett moves his mouth from my breasts up my body until he reaches my mouth, at which point I lift his shirt over his head and discard it. He kisses me as we both work fast to get rid of the rest of our clothes. What started out slow has become frantic.

I'm greedy for this man. I was crazy to think we'd make it through even some of a movie. I'm not sure we'll ever make it through one.

"Jesus," Beckett says, letting my lips go as he stands, taking me with him, and placing me on my back on the ottoman. "I was going to take my time with you, but I don't have it in me to do that." He takes hold of my legs and angles my body so he's holding me up off the ottoman with my legs up over his shoulders. Only my head and shoulders remain on the ottoman.

Our eyes lock and I let him know I'm with him completely, and without wasting another second, he thrusts inside me.

Fuck. Me.

This has to be one of the hottest positions a man has ever fucked me in. I'm on full display to him. I almost feel like he's spreading me apart while he grips my legs and drives his cock deep inside me. Every inch of my body and soul feels his attention, and when his gaze zeros in on my pussy, it's hot as hell.

He may have said he doesn't have it in him to take his time with me, but Beckett slows us down while he fucks me with the kind of rhythm that allows for maximum pleasure. He inches me close to orgasm but doesn't take me right to the edge, instead building us slowly to it, all the while giving me his eyes everywhere I want them.

When I think I can't take another second of this exquisite

bliss without coming, I reach for him and beg, "Make me come."

He likes that. I can tell by the way he grips me harder and thrusts inside me rougher. But rather than giving me what I want, he rasps, "Not yet. I need more time with you."

I can't decide if it's his voice or if it's the fact he can't drag his eyes from my pussy that makes me needier for him than I already am, but holy hell I can't get enough of him.

Beckett is pure fire and I'm caught in his flames, helpless to do anything but let them engulf me.

He fucks like he was built for sex.

He fucks *me* like he was built for me.

He's all hard muscle and strength and stamina, but there's a connection between us that takes it beyond the physical. It's that connection that's igniting this need inside me. The kind of need I've never known and am incapable of fighting.

I want him.

God how I want him.

"Touch yourself," he commands.

I comply instantly, rubbing my clit, loving the way this affects Beckett.

His rhythm switches up, his moves growing a little jerkier, a lot faster, like he's having trouble controlling himself. I am all for watching this man lose control when I'm the one causing that.

"Fuck," he roars as he thrusts so deeply and roughly I feel like he could break me in two.

"Oh God," I cry out, orgasming.

I shatter completely, lost in a moment of bliss my body won't ever forget.

I want so many more days like today.

"I think I might be into your way of watching movies," I murmur into Beckett's neck as he carries me into the bathroom down the hall from the theatre after we've both recovered from our orgasms.

He places me down and turns on the shower. "Thankfully."

I stand on my tiptoes and press a kiss to his lips. "Seriously, though, your legs have some strength in them. I need to come and watch you in the gym one day." The way he had to use his legs to fuck me like he just did is something else. Something I'm into.

Wrapping his hand around the back of my neck, he kisses me again. For much longer this time. "You do not need to come and watch me in the gym. You'd be too much of a distraction."

"Hmm, we'll see about that."

With a shake of his head, he bosses, "Get your ass in the shower. I'm ready for more of you."

I do as he orders but continue to give him a little hell. "Is this going to be a common thing with you?"

"What?"

"You telling me to get my ass in the shower."

He backs me up against the tiles and takes hold of my face with both hands. "Fuck yes." Then, with his signature intensity, Beckett kisses me and shows me exactly why I'll keep letting him boss me into getting in the shower with him.

23

@thetea_gasp

#BECKETTPEARCE AND @jennablaise were spotted together for the fourth time this weekend. Oh, the tea, my friends. So much glorious tea. We're predicting big things for this power couple. Sadly for her sister, things aren't looking as rosy. But the tea is spicy there. It looks like it's splitsville for @kristen-blaise and @johnathonswindle. The man lived up to his surname. Kristen, honey, maybe ask your sister for help. She knows how to trade up.

24

BECKETT

I can't recall the last time I took almost an entire weekend off. Possibly never. After this weekend with Jenna, I've made a note to have Louise look at my schedule with the intention of clearing more weekends. It's been good to take a break. The fact I did that with Jenna has made it even more enjoyable.

"You should take me to dinner tomorrow night," Jenna says from beside me. Davis collected us from the heliport five minutes ago and we're on our way to her condo.

"Do you have a restaurant in mind?"

"No. Surprise me with one of your favorite restaurants."

I already know where I'll take her. I also already know I'm going to struggle keeping my attention where it needs to be tomorrow. Jenna will likely spend most of the day front and center in my thoughts.

She shifts, angling her body toward mine and bringing her leg up to rest her knee on my thigh. My hand instantly curves over her leg. She's wearing a short white dress she picked up after lunch when I took her out for dessert. Jenna's preference for dresses that don't meet her knees is one I share.

I run my hand up her leg, my fingers dipping under the

hem of the dress while my gaze joins the journey. Stopping mid-thigh, I meet her eyes again. "Thank you for this weekend."

She smiles. It's one of delight. I get the impression she didn't expect that from me. Placing her hand on my forearm, she leans in close and brushes her lips over mine. "You are full of surprises, Mr. Pearce."

My hand goes to the nape of her neck, holding her in place. I need more of those lips before I let them leave me again.

I kiss her, my tongue sliding over hers as I deepen it, forcing her to give me far more than she gave me a second ago.

She moans and it elicits a growl from me. Jenna has mentioned my growly ways this weekend; they're ways that are all new to me. When she looks at me, touches me, surrenders to me, I'm powerless over my responses to her.

Neither of us are in a hurry to end this kiss. Jenna's hands move to my chest, a place she seems to like them. She slides onto me, straddling me, and I reach for the button to close the privacy screen.

I feel the smile in her kiss before she lets my lips go and gives me that smile. It's laced with the kind of sexy that shoots straight to my dick. "I've never been fucked in a car."

"Fuck," I growl, not enjoying the thought of her being with another man. "Let's not discuss all the ways you've been fucked before."

She presses herself to me, bringing her hand to my neck. "More surprises," she says softly before bending her face to kiss the side of my neck.

Keeping one hand on her ass, I find her breast with my other one while she dedicates time to my neck. The kind of time I never imagined I'd want to fill my days with. Sex has always been a purely physical release for me. Even with my ex-wife. With Jenna, it's more than that. It's fast becoming some-thing I crave.

"Tell me about these surprises," I say as her mouth draws closer to mine.

Lifting her face, she looks at me. "You'd rather talk than have sex?"

Tweaking her nipple, I say, "You're a woman with talents. I suspect you can do both at the same time."

More of that sexy smile. "I can, but the thing I like about sex with you is how you completely steal all my thoughts. All I can think about while you've got your hands on me is how much I want your cock inside me. You, Beckett, are a man I cannot multitask with. So, you're going to have to choose whether you want to talk first, or whether you can wait for that conversation."

"Jesus," I rasp as everything she says works its way through my veins. I fucking like that I do this to her. That I make her want me so much she can't think about anything else while I'm delivering her pleasure.

I'm about to make it clear this conversation can wait when my phone rings.

I want to ignore it, but I'm expecting a call from Ashton Scott regarding a development we're working on. A call I can't miss.

"I have to check this," I say apologetically as I reach for my phone.

Jenna goes back to my neck, murmuring, "You do whatever you need. I'm good here."

My sister is FaceTime calling me and I only hesitate for a split second before answering it. Ruby will continue calling until I do.

"I'll be at your place soon," I say, dropping my gaze to Jenna's body as I move my hand from her breast down to her ass.

"Change of plans. We're having dinner at my place. Come now."

"Who's we?"

"Mom, Dad, you, and me. I want to talk to you all together." The enthusiasm in her voice and all over her face is more than a hint that she intends for this dinner to go ahead. I may have had plans to spend time with Jenna at her place tonight, but I can kiss those plans goodbye now.

"I'm on my way to drop Jenna off at her place. I'll be there after that."

"Oh," she says with even more enthusiasm, "bring her with you. I want to meet her."

Jenna undoes the top two buttons of my shirt. Her fingers brush against my skin, causing me to lose focus on what Ruby's saying.

"Beckett," Ruby says, pulling me back. "Change direction and come straight here. Dinner will be ready soon." She pauses, squinting at me. "Wait, are you fucking her in the car right now?"

A laugh bubbles out of Jenna right before she says, "Not yet, Ruby, but it was high on my plans for tonight."

Ruby grins. "Finally. You finally found a woman without a stick up her ass. I'm so fucking proud of you, Beckett."

Dinner with my family tonight is not how I intend for Jenna to meet them. Especially not when Ruby is no doubt about to drop a bomb on our parents. Ignoring what she says about me finding a woman without a stick up her ass, I reiterate, "No, I'll come after I take Jenna home."

Ruby is nothing if not stubborn. "Put Jenna on."

Jenna's eyes meet mine. Their filled with amusement. She arches her brows questioningly. She's asking if I want to humor Ruby by bringing her in on the conversation.

"Knock yourself out," I say, turning my phone to face her.

She smiles at Ruby. "I feel like tonight may not be the best night for me to come to dinner. It sounds like you've got important family stuff to discuss."

"I do, but honestly, I could use your presence to my advantage. Mostly, though, I just want to meet you," Ruby says.

"You want me to distract your parents," Jenna says.

"I promise I'm not usually this calculating," Ruby says. "Beckett will vouch for that."

I nod. "That is true."

Jenna's eyes find mine again, filled with more questions. She doesn't know what to do here. Not wanting her to feel uncomfortable with this situation, I turn the phone back to me. "Ruby, I'm not changing—"

"Beckett," Ruby says, her voice losing all her previous enthusiasm. In its place is vulnerability that never fails to stir my desire to look out for her. "Please come now. Mom and Dad are here and I need you. Now."

Jenna gives me a nod to indicate she's good with this if I am.

Against all my better judgment, I give Ruby what she wants. "We'll be there soon."

"Thank you," Ruby says softly and disconnects the call.

I place my phone in my pocket. "I hope you know what you've signed up for."

Jenna presses her hands to my chest. "You survived my family this weekend. I can survive yours." She leans in close and shares her lips with me for too brief a moment before adding, "And just so you're aware, we're taking a raincheck on you fucking me in your car."

"IT's NOT TOO late to have Davis drive you home," I say against Jenna's ear after Ruby brings us drinks.

We arrived ten minutes ago and she's been spared my sister's interrogation so far, but I know it's coming. And while Jenna told me she can survive my family, I don't want her to have to. I may have a preference for fast when it comes to getting to know her and spending time with her, but I don't have that same preference when it comes to subjecting her to my family.

"I'm good, Beckett. You don't need to worry about me."

And that's it right there.

I've arrived at the place where I'm worrying about her.

That it took me less than a week to get here is a fact I'm surprisingly okay with. My assumption is that it took this short amount of time because we already knew each other. I already cared for her. Not that she knew that, but I did. Simply because she was dating my best friend. Anyone who was important to him was important to me by association.

"Jenna," my mother says, appraising her with a cool gaze, "It's surprising we've not already met. What, with the fact you dated my son's best friend for years."

I instinctively put my arm around Jenna, wanting to protect her from my mother. Margaret Pearce is a formidable woman who comes from a long line of formidable women. She hasn't liked anyone I've brought home to meet the family, that being my ex-wife and two serious girlfriends before Ellen. Hell, Ellen almost called off our wedding three nights prior thanks to my mother.

Jenna is stiff in my arms, but she doesn't show my mother any of what she's feeling when she says, "I don't find it surprising, Margaret. I think we're all aware by now of Declan's tendency to leave me at home while he pursued other women." She loosens up as she brings a hand to my stomach and smiles at me. Then, looking back at my mother, she adds, "You should be proud of your son. In the short time we've been seeing each other, he's already treated me better than his ex-friend ever did."

If there's one thing my mother doesn't like, it's being put in her place. Today is no exception. Her lips flatten as ice settles in her eyes. "I am proud of Beckett. That has never been called into question. Of course, he will treat you well. He was raised correctly."

"Mother," Ruby says, giving me the wide eyes she often does when our mother annoys her. "Let's not bring Declan into the conversation." Ruby never did like Declan.

Jenna raises her glass. "I second that."

Ruby smiles at her and opens her mouth to speak but Dad cuts in. "I'm ready to hear the reason you've brought all of us here tonight, Ruby." His tone leaves no doubt that he won't wait another minute to hear this information.

I don't miss the way Ruby swallows her nerves. It's a moment she moves past quickly, though. By the time she shares her news she's regained full confidence. "I'm buying an art gallery."

My mother pulls her face into an unreadable mask as she processes this information.

My father appears angered by her announcement.

This is the real reason Ruby wanted Jenna here. Sure, she wanted to meet Jenna, but she knew this bombshell would be enough to cause all sorts of problems between her and our parents. The kind of bombshell that not even Jenna's presence will shift attention from.

"Have you lost your goddamn mind?" my father demands, his anger unmistakable. He turns to me. "Did you know about this?"

I shake my head as Ruby says, "No, Beckett is as clueless as both of you about this. And no, Father, I have not lost my goddamn mind." She sips some of her wine. "If anything, I've found it. Finally."

"We're not paying for this, Ruby," our mother says. The flat, cold tone of her voice makes it crystal clear she doesn't ever intend on changing her mind.

Hurt flashes in Ruby's eyes right before pride does. "I don't expect you to." And there's the Pearce defiance we're all known for. Unfortunately for them, our parents raised three children who have an open disregard for rules and authority.

"Who *do* you expect to pay for it?" Dad asks, his meaning not lost on anyone.

"I love you, Dad, but that is one of the most offensive things you've ever said to me," Ruby says. "Yes, I like men. Yes, I've been with many of them. But contrary to popular belief around here, I've never once allowed any man to pay my way."

Dad's expression makes it obvious he doesn't buy that for a second. Not acknowledging anything she's just said, he continues, "Well, how are you paying for this art gallery?"

"With the money I've saved from the paintings I've sold."

My father stares at her. He appears to be working that idea over in his mind.

Mom, on the other hand, doesn't give it even a second thought. "Ruby, this is nonsense. I don't know why you're wasting our time with this."

I step in. Fuck knows, Ruby needs me to. "That's enough, Mom," I say with some force. I then look at my sister. "Tell us about this gallery, Rubes. Where is it?"

A look of pure appreciation flares in her eyes. "Thank you," she says softly before sharing some information about the gallery with us.

Dad listens intently. Something she's said tonight has caused him to look at her in a new way. Mom, on the other hand, still appears to be looking at her daughter with disbelief. I imagine the plans she has to marry Ruby off are still alive and well.

After Ruby has finished speaking, Mom says, "When is this supposedly going ahead?"

Ruby shakes her head at Mom and empties her glass of wine. "You know what? I don't think we're going to bother with dinner after all. I refuse to sit with you and pretend to like you right now, Mom, because I don't. I feel hurt by everything you've said to me tonight. Actually, change that to everything you've pretty much ever said to me. You can show yourselves out."

With that, she stalks out of the room, leaving me to deal with this mess of a situation.

"Jesus," I mutter, scrubbing a hand over my face. I look at my mother. "Are you happy now?"

"Happy?" Mom says, like I've just asked the dumbest question she's ever been asked. "Do you think I'm happy, Beckett? Your sister needs to grow up, and she needs to do that fast. She's almost thirty. I refuse to sit back and watch her continue ruining our family name."

"How is she ruining our family name?" It's a waste of my breath to ask this. I know how she perceives Ruby's lifestyle as a blight on our name, but I don't share her sentiments. This is a topic we've argued over many times. An argument I have no chance in hell of ever winning, but one I can't simply let pass me by. Not when it involves my sister and her happiness.

My mother regards me with disdain. "I would think you'd know the answer to that question. There are certain choices a Pearce makes that keep us all how we should be. Ruby's choices, to date, have not been in line with what our family requires. If she continues making those kinds of choices, we will have no other option but to cut her off. I would appreciate it if you ensure she understands this. God knows, she won't listen to a word I say."

This isn't the first time I've had to listen to this kind of bullshit from my parents. I was raised with this knowledge drummed into me. We didn't go a day without being reminded to watch everything we said and did when we were kids. "The Pearce family has a special kind of privilege, one that will bring you power" was often thrown at us, along with "but you must manage your behavior."

"I do know the answer to that question," I say, my distaste spilling all over my words. "However, I don't agree with it. And I think it's evident Ruby isn't going to change her mind."

"It doesn't matter whether you agree or not," Dad says, his tone clear that his decree is final. "This is the way things are. Speak to your sister."

Five minutes later, he and Mom exit Ruby's condo and I exhale a long breath as the elevator closes behind them.

"That was intense," Jenna says.

"I'm sorry you had to witness that." I glance in the direction Ruby left. "I need to go and talk with Ruby."

She nods. "Yes, absolutely."

I've only taken two steps when Ruby rejoins us, her face puffy and blotchy from crying. Surveying the room, she says, "They left?"

"Yes," I say.

The sting of that appears briefly on her face. She may have told them to see themselves out, but I imagine what she'd really hoped for was for them to change their mind and listen to what she had to say. My sister is used to hurt when it comes to our parents, though, and recovers quickly. "I'm buying this art gallery, Beckett," she says with determination.

Dedication to her cause, whatever it may be at the time, is a core trait of Ruby's. She's fiercely stubborn. However, I've never known her to be dedicated to her work. It seems my eyes need opening. She mentioned something to me recently about having made money from her art, but I didn't really take that in like I am now. If Ruby can afford an art gallery, she must be doing well with her paintings.

"Have you had someone look over the numbers?" I ask.

She rolls her eyes. "Of course, I have. I'm not an idiot."

"I never said you were, but I'd like to help you. Send them to me."

"I'm not sending them to you," she mutters as she moves to her bar. Then, looking at Jenna, she says, "Do you feel like a cocktail? To help me celebrate my new venture?"

Jenna takes a seat on the large white sectional sofa that

takes up a significant portion of Ruby's great room. "I'd love to celebrate with you. What cocktail are we talking?"

Ruby's face lights up. "How about an Eastside? Do you like gin?"

"I love gin. And I'd love to try an Eastside. I've never had one before," Jenna says.

"Also," Ruby says, motioning at Jenna, "I adore this dress. Where did you get it?"

Jenna glances down at the dress I had my hands under for far too short a time earlier. She rattles off the name of the boutique where she picked it up. She and Ruby then engage in a conversation about dresses and books while Ruby makes their drinks.

I decline a cocktail but accept a scotch as I sit next to Jenna.

Sliding closer to me, Jenna rests her hand on my thigh and sends me a smile when Ruby leaves us to go in search of a book she wants to recommend to Jenna. "You doing okay?" she asks softly.

I place my hand over hers as I digest the genuine care I hear in her voice. "I am, but I'm concerned about Ruby."

"You're the brother who takes care of her, aren't you?"

"Elon and I both do that, but yes, I'm the one she comes to more often."

Her eyes search mine for the longest time, and I ask, "What thoughts are running through that beautiful mind of yours?"

"A lot of thoughts. You have no idea. But mostly, I'm thinking that all those times I thought you were being over-bearing and arrogant and bossy, you were actually trying to help me."

"Now we're getting somewhere."

"Oh, we've been getting somewhere," she says sexily and I don't miss her meaning. But then, she turns serious. "You're a fixer, aren't you? Like, you can't help but want to look after those you care about."

"That is true. And Ruby would likely be in your camp of people who think I'm overbearing and arrogant."

She grins. "Well, you *can* be arrogant. Let's not get ahead of ourselves here."

"Fuck," I growl, leaning into her so I can kiss her.

It's not a quick kiss, and it's sure as hell not the kind of kiss that doesn't show her exactly what I'm feeling, which right now is a strong desire to be inside her. I need that to express all the other feelings she's brought out in me tonight.

I'm fucking grateful for her presence and her support, the likes of which I've never had in a relationship. And hell if that doesn't say something, because most would assume a man who was once married would have experienced this kind of support before. I can count with one finger the number of women who have ever asked me if I'm doing okay. That woman was my sister.

By the time I'm done with Jenna's lips, she's breathless. So breathless and alive I'm struggling not to lift her over my shoulder and take her home so I can do what I want to her. Gripping my shirt, she breathes, "What was that for? I need to know so I can make you do it again."

"You asked me if I was okay. You then called me out on my arrogance. And you were sexy as hell while you did it."

"Right, so be nice to you, then lay on some home truths, and make sure I flirt with you while I'm doing all that, and I'll get more of those kisses. Noted."

"I found it!" Ruby exclaims, joining us again. "This book changed my life." She hands the book to Jenna. "You must take it and devour it, and then we must powwow over it. I love me a good deep and meaningful with book talk and cocktails."

I eye the book. *Braving The Wilderness* by Brené Brown. I've not heard of it, and it doesn't look like a book I'd read, but Jenna appears interested. "I agree!" she says. "I love a good powwow too. I'll read it and let you know when I'm done."

Ruby brings their cocktails over, hands Jenna's to her, and

sits across from us. She pulls her feet up onto the sofa and holds her glass up in a toast. "To women who finally figure out how to follow their own path."

I drink some scotch and am about to ask her more about the gallery, but I lose my chance when she begins her interrogation of Jenna.

"So, Jenna, this date my brother bought. Are you really not going to tell me how much he paid for you?"

"No, he didn't buy *me*. He bought the date," Jenna corrects her.

Ruby nods. "Right, yes, of course. That's a good distinction to make. So, how much?"

"The amount isn't relevant," I say.

Ruby looks at me. "Oh, I'd say it's very relevant. If it wasn't, you two wouldn't be tripping over yourselves to keep it a secret. A hundred k? Two hundred? Come on, tell me. I won't tell anyone how much it was."

I spread my arm across the sofa behind Jenna and sip some more scotch as she answers Ruby. I'm not inclined to carry on this conversation and am more than happy for Jenna to take the lead.

"Let's just say that when your brother means business, he really means business."

"Ugh, you're no fun, Jenna," Ruby grumbles. "I can see we're going to need to spend some time together so I can teach you my ways."

"Going back to the gallery," I say. "Where are you in your negotiations?"

Ruby sighs. "You're going to force me into letting you take control of this, aren't you?"

"No, Ruby, I'm not. But I want to make sure you're not getting yourself into something that won't benefit you. The last thing you need is an asset that doesn't perform well and that causes you more headaches than you need." I'm concerned, too, that she's jumping into yet another fun project that won't hold her attention longer than a month.

"What if I don't so much want an asset as I want something that speaks to my soul?"

I frown. "If you want something that speaks to your soul, we can find you better options. A gallery is a business. An asset. It's going to mean hard work, and long days. Tell me you understand what you're buying here."

Displeasure creases her face. "Why can you never see things from my perspective? Honestly, are we even from the same parents?"

I wonder that at times too. I don't understand her perspective on many things, and as much as I try, I fail. "Business is business. It's not pleasure. I'm concerned you're trying to mix the two."

She stares at me while she takes a long sip of her drink. Finally, she says, "Let's not talk business tonight. In fact, let's not talk it ever again. I'll just go about mine my way while you go about yours your way."

Before I can reply, my phone rings. It's the call I've been waiting for from Ashton, so I excuse myself to take it.

I'm gone for ten minutes and when I return, Jenna and Ruby are deep in conversation about fashion. I join them, but not having any knowledge of what they're discussing, I mostly sit back and observe for the next half hour.

"We should eat," Ruby says, standing. "I have the most amazing Japanese you'll ever taste."

Jenna moves off the sofa. "I'm impressed. You're so relaxed. If I'd cooked for my family, I'd be super stressed by now."

Ruby laughs and waves her off. "Oh, girl, no. Us Pearces don't cook. I had my favorite chef make it."

I place my hand to the small of Jenna's back as we walk to the dining table. "Thank you," I say against her ear.

She looks up at me. "For what?"

"For being you."

The smile she gives me quiets some of the tension knotting itself in my gut. My family never fumbles its way through stressful situations. No, we get right on in there and fuck things up as much as we can. And often, I'm the one called upon to be the intermediary. It's something I don't enjoy, but it's a task that is mine nonetheless. Jenna's presence tonight has taken the strain I'm experiencing and halved it.

She reaches for my hand and threads her fingers through it. "Noted."

25

JENNA

"The next time your sister interrupts you fucking me in your car and invites me over for a spontaneous dinner, we're going to be late for said dinner. I'm not missing out on sex ever again."

Beckett backs me up against my kitchen island and drops his mouth to my neck, kissing me there. "You don't have to miss out."

The man has no idea how tempting he is. I really want to have sex with him right now, but I know it won't just be a quickie. It'll be hours of sex, and I don't have hours to spare.

I gently push him away. "Ugh, I ate too much. And I'm tired. And I have a million things I still have to do for work tomorrow before I can even think about going to bed. You need to leave. A girl can only say no to you for so long, and this girl can't afford to say yes tonight."

Dinner was a long affair.

We managed to leave the tension of Ruby's art gallery announcement behind and move onto safer topics. I discovered some interests that Ruby and I have in common, namely fashion, books, and knitting. Beckett appeared surprised to learn we both love knitting. I got the impression he never imagined in a million years that either of us would take that hobby up.

I enjoyed chatting with his sister. I enjoyed that a lot, but it cut in on my time alone with Beckett. And since this is all new with him, I want all the hours with him I can get.

I had to dedicate good time during dinner to dragging my thoughts away from how he was about to fuck me in his car when Ruby invited us to dinner. The way he watched me let me know he was struggling with the same thoughts. That only distracted me further.

He lets me go, but it's clear he doesn't want to. "The next time my sister calls while I've got my hands on you, I won't be answering."

I shoot him a sexy smile. "Now we're talking. But please let the record show that I did enjoy tonight with Ruby. Not so much with your mother, though. I get the distinct impression she already doesn't like me."

"My mother doesn't like anyone."

"Okay," I say slowly, processing this information. "Does she ever change her mind?" I freaking hope so because that woman was colder than any woman I've ever met.

"She's been known to, yes." The way he says this leads me to believe it doesn't happen often. Since I don't really want to get into a conversation about our families so soon in our relationship, I let it go.

"Good to know. Now, you need to leave because I do not have the willpower to keep saying no to you if you stay."

A smile teases his lips, not quite forming, but giving enough of a hint for me to know he likes what I just said. Bending his face to mine, he kisses me. "Goodnight, Jenna."

His deep voice stays with me long after he leaves, ensuring that it takes me far longer to do all the things I need to do before I can even think about sleep.

～

I'M tired at work on Monday. Cora is too, so between us we're messing things up all over the place.

It's just after 11:00 a.m., and I've already fixed three mistakes, repeatedly checked my texts for a message from Beckett (still none), bought two dresses online that I don't need, and consumed three coffees when Tilly texts me.

Tilly: So it looks like my job is safe.

Jenna: I didn't realize it wasn't. It's been two weeks since that fiasco. I thought your boss was okay now.

Tilly: One can never be sure, but he just told me he's found someone new to pursue to make up for the interview Beckett didn't do.

Jenna: This is good news.

Tilly: Yes, for you it is.

Jenna: Why for me?

Tilly: Because it'll be up to you to score that interview for me if I ever do need it. And I suspect Beckett won't be easy to persuade. Even if one is sucking his dick. And speaking of sucking Beckett's dick, did you see the posts about you two on Insta?

Jenna: No. What did they say?

Beckett constantly appears on social media. The gold diggers of New York ensure that. He doesn't have his own Instagram account, but he doesn't need one to have his own hashtag. People snap photos of him everywhere he goes and post them. However, we've been so low-key that I wouldn't have assumed to see anything about us yet.

She sends me a link to a post with photos of us at Kristen's party. I should have anticipated this. Kristen's party *is* one of the biggest of the season.

Tilly: Nice grope, my friend.

She's referencing the fact I have my hand on Beckett's ass in one of the photos.

Jenna: What can I say? He has the best ass I've ever seen.

Tilly: I'm saving that in case I ever need it for a quote.

Jenna: Please don't. His mother already hates me. I don't need to give her any more ammunition to use against me.

Tilly: We need drinks to discuss all this. Stat.

I'm distracted by an email I just scrolled past on my laptop. An email I need to shift my complete attention to in order to figure out if it's real or not.

Jenna: Gotta go, Till. We definitely need drinks xx

I place my phone on my desk and pull the email up. Reading it carefully, I conclude that it's very real. I also conclude that the universe is most definitely rigged in my favor today, even if Beckett has not called or texted me.

Jesus.

Who even am I right now?

I'm not the kind of woman who waits around for a man to call.

I snatch my phone up and tap out a text.

Jenna: Do you want to know what I'm imagining right now?

He only takes a minute to reply.

Beckett: I'm guessing it's NSFW, and since I'm in the middle of a board meeting, I encourage you not to share it with me just yet.

Jenna: When would be a good time to share it with you?

Beckett: I'll call you when it's time. This is something I'd prefer to hear from your lips.

Holy hell.

This man knows how to sext without even being inappropriate.

Jenna: Noted. Also, I hope you're having a good morning. Mine just improved and not only because I heard from you.

Beckett: Mine just improved too and that was completely because I heard from you. I look forward to hearing the other reason yours improved.

"You look like you're reading porn," Cora says, entering my office.

My head snaps up and I blink as I resume participating in life. Texting with Beckett is like entering our own little world. I didn't even hear Cora come in. "That's because I *was* reading porn."

Her brows pull together. "Seriously? I didn't know you were into that kind of thing."

"Beckett porn, not actual porn." I place my phone down. "I just received an email from Diana Black."

Cora's eyes widen. "Holy shit. Really?"

"Yes, really. She wants me to style her and some of her friends for a gala she's organizing to raise funds for a literacy foundation."

Diana Black is a famous actress. The kind of famous that you'd have to be a castaway on a deserted island to have never heard of. She's held this gala yearly for the past decade. To be invited to style for her and her friends is a huge win for my company, one I'm having trouble processing. It feels like something exciting I already need to prepare myself to lose in case it doesn't happen.

I take a deep breath as my heart races with both anticipation and nerves. I've styled celebrities before, but none as big as Diana. "Okay, I'm going to email her back and then we need to get to work."

Cora nods enthusiastically. "Right." She hands me a sheet of paper. "But first, after you email her, you need to take care of these things."

I run my eyes over the list of tasks I have to do for my current clients. God, I appreciate Cora's organizational skills. I look at her. "Perfect. Thank you." She's only worked with me for two months, but she's the best assistant I've had.

"I'm working through your expenses at the moment, but let me know if you need anything else done first."

"Will do."

She exits my office and I reply to Diana's email, high-fiving myself as I send it.

This is what hard work achieves.

My father can tell me all day long that my business won't go anywhere, but I'm proving him wrong. I'm *determined* to prove him wrong.

Diana comes straight back with a reply, setting a time for us to meet later this week to discuss her needs.

After adding that to my schedule, I work through Cora's list of jobs. I lose track of time, only noting it when my phone rings just before 2:00 p.m.

Beckett.

My core instantly makes itself known when his name appears on my screen.

I settle back against my chair as I answer the call. "How do you survive those long board meetings?"

"With great difficulty." Good God, that voice of his alone could make me do many things my mother would be ashamed of.

"Do you want to know what I'm having great difficulty doing?"

"I like that you're so willing to share all these thoughts with me."

I smile. "I'm having difficulty not thinking about how I want to use my tongue on you tonight."

"Jesus," he rasps. "You weren't kidding that day of the auction when you said there's some dirty underneath all that pretty, were you?"

"I don't kid when it comes to sex, Beckett."

"I've worked that out about you."

"I also don't kid about eating, and I'm sorry to tell you that the thing I texted you about earlier had nothing to do with sex and everything to do with food."

He chuckles. "Thank Christ you didn't break that to me then. Trying to figure out what filthy thing you were thinking about got me through that meeting."

"I'm glad I could be of service."

"What food were you imagining?"

"I was trying to work out where you're taking me for dinner

so I could plan my meal. I know I told you to surprise me, but I've decided I don't want it to be a surprise anymore."

"How about I tell you what cuisine you'll be eating but not the name of the restaurant?"

"How about you just tell me the name of the restaurant? In exchange, I'll promise to use my tongue tonight in all the ways I've been thinking about."

"You play a mean game of compromise, Jenna."

"And you play a long, drawn out one."

He chuckles again. It's ridiculous how much I like that sound. "I'm taking you to a new French restaurant a friend opened last week. I'll send you the link to their menu."

"Ooh, I love French food."

"I know."

Those two words nestle themselves deeply inside me. They just curl on up and make themselves at home. *They feel good.*

As I think about the fact Beckett knows this about me, that he's paid attention to me over the years when I thought all he was doing was arguing and being overbearing with me, I say, "I have to get back to work. I'll see you tonight."

We end the call and a minute later he texts me the menu. I proceed to drool over it for the rest of the afternoon. I also proceed to dedicate far too many minutes to thinking about how I'm going to use my tongue on Beckett tonight.

BECKETT ARRIVES EARLY.

He told me he'd pick me up at seven. He arrives just after six thirty.

"This suit is an eleven," I say when I open my door to him. This suit actually may cause me to manhandle him in the restaurant. Hell, who am I kidding? It may cause me to do that before we even leave for the restaurant.

Appreciation for what I've said flares in his eyes while his hand easily glides around my waist and pulls me close for a kiss. He takes his time with my lips, murmuring, "Good to know," as he finishes with them.

I put my hands to his chest. "I'm not ready."

"I didn't expect you to be."

"I like that you're catching on fast here." I also like his easy, relaxed mood. It matches mine.

"Who are you listening to?" he asks as he follows me inside, listening to the music playing from a playlist featuring some of my favorite songs.

"This is James TW." I walk into my kitchen to finish prepping my oats for breakfast.

Beckett joins me, watching with interest as I get back to work.

"How was your afternoon?" I ask.

"Good. I got through everything I had to. Yours?"

"Really good. I also kicked ass."

"What are you making?" he asks as I layer ingredients into the five jars in front of me.

I look up at him. "Peanut butter and strawberry overnight oats for breakfast. Have you never had them before?"

"I can't say I have."

When I see amusement flash across his face, I say, "Why does this amuse you?"

He moves closer to me, his gaze tracing every angle of my face while he pushes my hair off my cheek. "It interests me more than it amuses me. I've never known a woman to make her breakfast while also getting ready for a date."

"A girl has to make sure she has her meals organized. Especially when she knows she'll be busy the night before using all her energy in a way that will require nutrients in the morning to refuel her."

He slides his hand into my hair. "You fascinate me, Jenna. You always have."

Hello butterflies.

I reach for his waist as a new song fills the condo. "Cool Anymore" by Jordan Davis and Julia Michaels. One of my favorite songs at the moment. "Dance with me," I say softly, moving my hips against his.

His expression tells me this has caught him by surprise. The way his body doesn't relax against mine makes me wonder if he'll go with me on this. He danced with me at Kristen's party, but Beckett is a man who always has an agenda and a next move, and right now his agenda has one thing on it: getting us to the restaurant for dinner. I'm not sure he's the kind of man to make allowances for spontaneous deviations from the plan.

I put both my arms around him, resting my hands on his ass. "Can we please get this ass moving?" I say with a sexy smile.

His arms come around me as he finally gets on board with what I want. "I can't say dancing in the kitchen before a date is something I've ever done."

"You should prepare yourself to do more of it."

"Noted."

"I'm going to have a mug made for you. It shall say *Noted*."

Ignoring that, except for a lip twitch, he says, "So, what was the other thing that helped your day improve this morning?"

It has to be noted—yes, now I'm noting things—how much I like that he remembered this. Beckett's attention to detail is high on my list of things I appreciate about him. "I gained a new client today. Diana Black. She's hired me to style her and some friends for her literacy gala that she holds every year."

His smile reaches his eyes. "Congratulations."

"I've never worked with someone in her league. To be honest, I'm feeling a little nervous about it," I admit.

His arms tighten around me. "That's a good sign, Jenna."

"Why?"

"When the nerves aren't there, you're in your comfort zone. You don't grow in that zone."

He's right and I know this, but dealing with it is a whole other thing.

When I don't say anything, Beckett continues, "Push through the nerves. Diana wouldn't have hired you if she didn't believe in you."

I reach for his face so I can pull his lips down to mine.

I kiss him in my kitchen while we slow dance.

I make a little more room in my heart for him.

Beckett Pearce is one big surprise.

When the song finishes, I let his lips go and reluctantly stop dancing with him. I'm almost ready to tell him to cancel dinner so we can spend time in my kitchen doing this instead, but I *do* want that French food he promised, so I don't tell him that.

"Okay," I say, "I'll get these jars in the fridge and finish getting ready, and then you can introduce me to your friend's restaurant." I pause. "And thank you."

"What for?"

"For listening to me. And for giving me support and encouragement."

Beckett has no way of knowing, but I've never dated a man like him. One who actually listens to what I say rather than simply hearing it.

I've never looked forward to a date more.

Good food, good conversation, and time alone with the man who just keeps on showing me parts of himself I can't help but like.

26

BECKETT

"Did you hear from Ruby today?" Jenna asks as we eat.

She chose the ricotta and swiss chard ravioli with sage brown butter and parmesan, and watching her eat it is distracting as hell. Jenna has a way of eating food that is sexual. She dedicates her attention to the task in the same way she dedicates her attention to sex. I make a note to bring her back here soon. She's already told me four times how much she likes it here.

"I did," I say in answer to her question. "She called me after my meeting."

"How is she today?"

"She's still being as stubborn as usual, refusing to let me look at the art gallery numbers." We argued over this for a good ten minutes before she told me I could stick my need for control up my ass.

"She said she's had someone look at the numbers, though, right?"

"Yes, but Ruby's idea of that and mine are two very different things. She likely showed a guy she met in a bar rather than a professional."

Jenna gives me a look of disbelief. "You really think that?"

"I do."

"Beckett," she says, her tone full of skepticism, "Ruby strikes me as an intelligent woman. She was raised by the same parents as you and she's had you guiding her at times. Surely she's smarter than that."

"Ruby is smart. Absolutely. She's also fickle and bad at commitment. I don't see this art gallery holding her attention for very long. She tends to get grand ideas and pursue them against all common sense before quickly moving on to the next idea."

Jenna listens to what I say and thinks about that for a minute before saying, "I don't know her, but from what I saw last night, she's fighting against the same kind of thing I am with my father. Maybe she's still trying to find her feet in your family." Her voice softens and fills with emotion when she adds, "It can be hard to do that in a family of sons, especially with parents like ours."

I frown. "What does that mean?"

She puts her utensils down and takes a few moments to gather her thoughts. "I grew up with the awareness that my father fully believed in my brothers without them even needing to prove themselves or earn that belief. It was a given that they would grow up and make something of themselves, something my father would be proud of. Kristen and I, on the other hand, never had that unconditional belief or expectation that we would achieve great things. I mean, not unless we're talking a belief that we'd just find a man and marry him and be done with it. I watched a lot of my friends from school experience the same thing. Girls are for marrying off; boys are for carrying on the family greatness." She pauses. "I'm not saying you and my brothers never had to work hard to prove yourselves, but maybe Ruby feels the same way I do. Maybe she feels like she has to fight twice as hard to prove herself."

"Ruby has never tried to prove herself, Jenna."

She gives me a small smile. "That's how you perceive her

actions, but put yourself in her shoes. Perhaps she tried but never felt like she measured up. Perhaps she just gave up at some point."

I consider everything she's said. There's a lot to unpack there, and while I will think it all over, I'm not convinced she's right about my sister. She doesn't know Ruby like I do.

The waiter interrupts us to clear the table, and when he's finished, I ask her if she heard from her sister today.

"Yes. She's losing her mind, I think. Us Blaise girls don't do well with being cheated on."

"No one does well with being cheated on."

"True, but we take it to the extreme. Kristen burned Johnathon's belongings. She spent a huge chunk of his cash that they had in a shared account on clothes, shoes, and jewelry. She also booked a trip to Europe with his cash. And to top it all off, she made a post on Instagram about it all. My sister, who values above all things a clean and perfect image, shared all her dirty laundry on social media. I shudder to think what she'll do tomorrow."

"She did all that today?"

Jenna's eyes widen. "Yes!"

I reach for my scotch and take a sip. "How did you take being cheated on to the extreme?" I only recall Declan's response to the breakup. He didn't give a shit about it. He'd found a new woman to latch onto, one who he thought could help him move up in the world.

"My extremes involved a lot of food my hips did not need; alcohol they also did not need; many late night texts letting Declan know exactly what I thought of him; an embarrassing encounter with him and Katie at a party in which I'm fairly certain I managed to remove my name from many future party guest lists; and a sketchy Valentine's date with a guy I was trying to move on from Declan with, who taught me that I should never date men I meet in shady clubs I've frequented while heartbroken."

My desire to ruin Declan only increases with everything she says. How the hell he could hurt Jenna in this way is beyond me. "For the record, your hips have never looked better."

She smiles. "That's because I took up the gym in a way I never have before. Honestly, boxing does wonders for a cheated-on heart." She reaches for her glass of wine while crossing her legs and angling her body toward mine in the booth we're seated at. "Have you ever been cheated on?"

I asked to be seated in a booth in one of the darkened corners of the restaurant so we could have more privacy. My friend, who owns this place, has done an exceptional job with the ambience and layout of the space because although we're surrounded by a fully booked restaurant, I barely notice anyone else. Jenna and I are in a hushed world of our own. Having her this close and all to myself makes it difficult to keep my hands off her. Particularly when she slants her body to mine like she just has.

I nod. "Yes, my ex-wife cheated on me."

The honest look of regret and disappointment in her eyes is an expression I've only ever known from Ruby, Elon, and Josh. Not even my parents have shown me this kind of emotion. "Why do people have to be such assholes? Did you handle it in an extreme way like I did?"

"It was extreme for me."

Her eyes light up with interest and she moves even closer to me, something I didn't think possible. At the rate she's going, I'll have her in my lap soon and all bets will be off as to how I handle the desire for her I'm currently doing my best to ignore. "Oh, you can't just say that and not elaborate. Tell me everything."

"Has anyone ever told you how distracting you are?"

"If you're saying this to avoid spilling your secrets, you need to know I never let secrets go."

"I don't doubt that."

Her hand lands on my thigh. "Come on, Beckett. I told you mine. It's only fair that you tell me yours."

She has no idea how she's affecting me.

I've told her I'm an open book, and I am. To her. Generally, I don't feel the desire to share too much of myself with anyone, but Jenna's different. Her honesty and willingness to be vulnerable with me makes me want to give the same to her. I trust her and that's not something I can say about too many people.

I throw some more scotch down my throat. "Ellen and I met when she came to work for Dad's company. I was still working there at the time, and she and I worked together on a contract. I left the company a year after we married to start building my own. Ellen stayed at Pearce Industries. Dad wouldn't have allowed her to come with me even if she wanted to. She was his star and he paid her a fortune to stay. When I learned she'd cheated on me throughout most of our marriage, and not just with one man, I forced my father to fire her. He didn't want to, but I'd lost my goddamn mind and threatened to destroy his company if he didn't." I pause, gripping my glass harder as I recall that time in my life. "I would have too. And he knew it."

Jenna watches me silently, taking every word in like they're words she needs to study. Finally, she says, "I really like this side of you."

"Not what I was expecting," I murmur, placing my glass on the table.

"What were you expecting?"

"I just told you I threatened my own father while demanding he fire the woman I was married to. I would have expected that to perhaps not go down so well."

"You were hurt, Beckett. Really fucking hurt. And you showed it. You felt it deeply. If your family experience is as much like mine as I think it is, we don't ask our parents for a lot. We do our best to gain their love and attention, and don't often receive it in the way we want or need. You threatened your father because you knew that kind of action would speak to him and get you what you needed, which was simply for him to choose you. You needed him to show you he loved you." She pauses. "That's the Beckett I'm falling for. I've watched you be an island for years, and I'm really enjoying getting to know the Beckett who needs people by his side."

I take hold of her neck and kiss her, showing her how deeply I feel what she just said. I don't want to let her go, but I do. "We need to eat dessert fast so I can get you alone."

She bites her lip as she gives me one of her sexy smiles. "Well, since I'll be eating both my chocolate mousse and some of your pavlova, and since I never rush dessert, you may need to adjust your expectations."

I arch my brows. "I'm sharing my dessert?"

"Of course. You should note that's always a given when we eat together."

Fuck, she's beautiful and sexy and bewitching. I would give her my entire meal if that was what she wanted.

"Noted. And now you need to note something for me."

"I'll take it under consideration."

I move my mouth to her ear. "The faster you eat our dessert, the faster you'll have my mouth on your pussy."

She grips my thigh harder.

She inhales a breath.

She sways into me.

"You are the only man who has ever tempted me into considering skipping dessert. I'll eat fast."

27

JENNA

I ate dessert faster than I've ever eaten dessert.

A woman has no option but to do that when a man like Beckett Pearce is making promises all over the place about where he's going to put his mouth.

And holy hell if he's not making good on those promises right now.

I grasp his hair with one hand while madly flinging my other arm out to try to find something to latch onto. Anything. I need to brace myself for what he's doing with his tongue. "How do you know to do these things?" I demand, my thoughts a tumbling mess of letters scattering themselves throughout my brain. Useless, useless letters that don't even know how to go together anymore. "Why did I take so long to know you know how to do these things?" I arch my back on the seat of his car. "Oh God, Beckett, I am going to die. Just make me come already."

The man does not make me come already.

He doesn't even continue trying to make me come.

No, he lifts his head and looks at me. Granted, it's the kind of wild, impure look I like—*really like*—but still, he needs to put his mouth back where he just had it. And he needs to do that now. "Give me your hand."

Oh Jesus.

There's something way too hot about a man wearing a suit with the top few buttons of his shirt undone, looking at me the way Beckett is, with eyes like his, telling me to give him my hand in that deep, growly voice of his that gets me a whole lot more than bothered.

I mean, bothered isn't even really a word that should be in my vocabulary when it comes to Beckett. It doesn't convey well enough just how turned on I am.

I am in a state of disarray right now.

My thoughts are a jumble.

My body is alive in a way I'm not certain one orgasm will even begin to be enough.

My vagina, well, she's not certain she can ever live without this man.

And good God, if he doesn't touch my breasts soon, they may just unattach themselves from my chest and relocate to wherever his hands are. And yes, I'm aware unattach isn't even a word. See: state of disarray.

I give him my hand.

"I don't ever want you to wear a suit again," I throw out, my brain putting words together that I never imagined it ever joining in one sentence.

The way his mouth forms a sexy line that goes well with those seductive eyes of his only increases my state of disarray. "I'm not noting that," he says as he guides my fingers to my clit.

I arch my back again when he directs me to rub my clit, his fingers staying with mine, working with mine. This act coupled with his gaze remaining firmly on mine is hot as hell. The gentle vibrations of the car help too.

Beckett likes to direct me to touch myself.

I like that too.

A *lot*.

Mostly because it brings out the look in his eyes that I'm currently staring at.

The kind of desire no man has ever looked at me with.

"Please *do* note how much I want your mouth back on me," I say. Well, *say* is an understatement. It's more like a beg.

"Give me your other hand," he growls.

I almost orgasm at that order and the way it's delivered.

I give him what he wants.

This time, he directs one of my fingers inside me, and then he finally bends his face back to my pussy.

Our fingers work together on my clit and inside me while his mouth and tongue work their magic on me.

I spread my legs as wide as I can and continue living in disarray.

It's my new preferred way of living.

Beckett dedicates himself to what he's doing and it doesn't take long for me to orgasm.

I lose myself in the waves of pleasure.

My state of disarray levels up with all the pleasure he delivers, so much so that it takes him growling against my ear, "You are so fucking beautiful when you come" for me to unlose myself in the pleasure.

Actually, scratch that, I'm still losing myself. I'm just more aware of it now.

I grasp his neck when he brings his face to mine. "You should do that every day."

I feel his smile as he kisses me. "I should," he rasps before kissing me again, letting me taste myself. That's another thing that I'm learning turns him on, and it turns me on simply because of what it does to him.

I reach for the buttons on his shirt that are still done up. "How do you have so much control over yourself? I need to know your ways." I mean, his dick is hard as hell. I am here for a man who ensures his woman comes first, but I also have no clue how he didn't abandon me in favor of his own pleasure. I think this says more about me than him, though. Yes, I'm a selfish, selfish woman who lives for pleasure.

He kisses his way down to my breasts while answering me. "I don't have much control at all."

"I beg to differ."

He circles my nipple with his tongue before glancing up at me. "You think that I have control because of what I just did?"

"Yes."

He sucks my other nipple into his mouth while keeping his eyes on mine. "Jenna, I'm barely hanging on here. Making you come with my mouth is me losing control. I think about fucking you like that far more than is healthy." He licks me again, tweaking my nipple with his fingers. "Control was me not insisting you were my meal at the restaurant tonight."

Deadly.

That's what he is.

Deadly and lethal and ohmigod so damn good with that tongue of his.

I frantically finish making my way down his buttons and move onto the button of his pants.

Beckett continues giving my breasts the attention they deserve.

By the time I've freed his cock, I want to force him to stop everything he's doing and just get inside me.

Beckett has other ideas.

Of course, he does.

He moves his mouth from my breasts to my stomach.

He kisses every inch of my skin.

He takes far too long with every inch of my skin.

It feels good, but goddamn I just want his cock.

"Beckett." It's a beg. I can't even bring myself to care that it's a beg. I wrap my legs around him and try to force his dick to go where I want it. "Just fuck me already."

He allows me to almost get his dick inside, but it's just the tip. Heated eyes gaze down at me. Hungry, heated, eyes. "How do you want this?"

"I don't care. I just want it and you need to hurry up and give it."

His eyes flash with more of that heat. I swear I see some amusement in there too, but I'm not really paying enough attention to be sure. "Tell me your preference."

I tighten my arms around him. "Hard. I want to feel you all day tomorrow."

"Fuck," he growls and thrusts inside without another word.

Hallelujah, the man does know what he's doing.

And goodness if he doesn't do it the best he's done it so far.

He fucks me exactly how I asked, and by the time we both come I'm certain I'll feel him all week.

After, when we're clothed and I've sorted through some of my disarray, I say, "We're doing that again when you get me home, and if you had plans not to stay for a while tonight, you need to change those plans."

This time I don't miss the amusement in his eyes. "Consider my plans changed."

28

JENNA

I squeeze my eyes so they stay closed.

Without looking, I know it's still dark outside. I know it's still early. Way too early for Beckett to be waking me up.

But that's exactly what he's doing.

He's spooning me and has his hand on my breast. His mouth is at my ear. His erection is against my ass. "Jenna," he rasps, using one of his biggest weapons against me.

"No," I mumble, still refusing to open my eyes.

He keeps his hand on my breast while kissing my neck. He doesn't speak again, but he doesn't have to. His hands and mouth and dick are doing all his communicating.

"What time is it?"

He kisses my shoulder. "Four thirty."

Is he joking?

"Go away."

His mouth smiles against my skin. "I have to go home."

"Whatever for?"

"I want to hit the gym before I leave for work." He grinds himself against me. God that feels good, but at this time of day, sleep always trumps anything else on offer.

"Go. I'm good here."

More of that smiling against my skin before he presses kisses to my back. Then, ramping up his efforts, he reaches for my clit. The fact I'm wet only encourages him. My traitorous vagina will hear about this from me later.

Against all better judgment, I open my eyes and look at him. I mean, it's barely a squint, but my eyes are more open than they should ever be at this time of the day. "I feel the need to educate you. Four thirty is for sleeping, not sex."

He smiles down at me and says, "You surprise me," using that raspy, rumbly, sexy voice that should be banned between the hours of two and six in the morning.

"I surprise myself all the damn time, but right now I'm making more sense than I've ever made. You should run along to the gym and let me go back to my slumber."

He runs his gaze over my face for what feels like a long time before finally bending and kissing me. "No sex at four thirty in the morning. Noted." He gives me one last kiss. "Sleep well, beautiful."

With that, he leaves me to go back to my dream. I swear, if I don't go straight back to my dream about George Clooney, Beckett will pay for this later.

~

Shona: Four thirty? Is the man insane?

Jenna: Apparently.

Shona: Jesus, if Graham ever starts wanting sex at that time, we'll be getting separate bedrooms.

Jenna: He ruined my dream.

Shona: *gasps* Not a George dream?

Jenna: YES, A GEORGE DREAM. It was a good one too.

Shona: I mean, when is it too soon in a relationship to get separate bedrooms?

Jenna: I'm going to put serious thought into that question today.

Shona: Oh shit, I have to go. Judy is coming my way and by the look on her face I don't think it's going to be a happy Tuesday here.

Jenna: Go. Love you xx

Shona: Right back at you xx

Shona is a cake decorator and Judy is her boss. Judy hates Tuesdays almost as much as she hates cake decorating. Actually, she hates every day almost as much as she hates cake decorating. Shona and I aren't even sure why she still runs a cake business.

I place my phone on my desk as Cora knocks on my office door and comes in. "Do you want the good news or the bad news first?"

I lean back in my chair. It's just past eight. Far too early for bad news. "Can we just do the good news and then you go take care of whatever the bad news is? I've already had to give up a George dream this morning. I can't take any more bad."

She fakes shock and gasps. "Not a George dream."

I make wide eyes at her. "Yes, a George dream!"

She rolls her eyes. Cora is barely twenty-two, and while I'm only seven years older than her, it may as well be twenty-seven years. She has no concept of how hot George Clooney is. "We really need to work on your daddy issues. I could get behind Chris Hemsworth dreams, but this George dude is way old."

"What is it about Chris Hemsworth that everyone and their damn dog goes on about?"

It's her turn to make wide eyes. "Are you sure you're not blind, Jenna? Also, have you not noticed your boyfriend has Chris Hemsworth eyes and lips?"

My boyfriend.

That slows me down.

"He's not my boyfriend."

She gives me a pointed look. "I feel like he is."

"We haven't even been dating for a week, Cora."

She shrugs. "So? Besides, it feels like way longer than a week."

She's right about that. The day of the photo shoot a couple of weeks ago when this all kind of started feels like an eternity ago. I'm struggling to recall a time when I didn't like Beckett.

"Right, we'll agree to disagree on that. Tell me the bad news so we can get to the good."

She grimaces. "Kristen called before you arrived. She couldn't catch you on your phone, so she rang here. Something about wanting to organize dinner with you soon. She also mentioned she's getting her hair done today."

Oh God.

Cora's grimacing because we both know what getting her hair done means when Kristen's upset. She'll either cut it dramatically or color it just as wildly. I'll be the one left to pick up the pieces when she hates it tomorrow.

My sister is the good girl in our family. She does what our parents expect of her. She never causes a scene. And she doesn't behave badly, not even when awful things happen to her. The way she deals with disappointment, and anger, and pretty much any bad emotion is to get her hair done.

Cora's actually never seen her go through this, but I've shared enough stories of past experiences for her to know this is most definitely bad news.

I motion at her. "Give me the good news."

Now, her face breaks out in a huge smile. "Our Instagram blew up overnight. We had so many inquiries that I'm putting together a new plan for the week to get through everyone. It's almost ready for you to take a look at and okay before I send it to the girls."

I stare at her, a sense of calm washing over me.

Putting together plans and directing our team isn't Cora's job. It's mine. But I really like that she's taken the initiative to do this. It makes me think that my goal of expansion might be a little easier than I originally thought because having someone like her who can think on her feet takes a lot of pressure off.

When I don't respond straight away, she rushes out with, "I

know it's not my place to make a plan, but I thought it might help. I'm sorry if I shouldn't have done this."

I shake my head and smile at her. "No, it's perfect, Cora. Thank you. Go and finish it and send it to me. I'm going to call Lisa and make sure she's got everything she needs to keep this momentum going."

Lisa's our social media manager and has been kicking ass on Instagram and TikTok for the last few weeks since coming to me with a new strategy that we ended up putting in place.

She nods and it looks like her excitement could actually burst out of her. "I'm on it!"

After she exits my office, I get to work.

I spend all morning going over our social media needs with Lisa, finalizing the new plan for our stylists to get through all the new work coming in, putting in calls to the retailers and designers we work with to ensure they can meet our demand, and working on our projections going forward.

By eleven thirty, I feel like I've worked an entire week in one morning. I've just closed my laptop with the intention of heading out so I can move my body and source some caffeine when Cora calls to let me know Beckett has dropped by.

Butterflies instantly make themselves known in my stomach and I wonder if he'll always cause this response in my body.

I then wonder how long "always" will be.

I then think about what Cora said about our relationship.

This all leads me to think about Christmas and whether we'll still be dating then, which leads me to think about New Year's Eve, which gets me thinking about my clients and the dresses I'll be sourcing for them at the end of the year.

All this in the space of ten seconds flat.

My multitasking game is strong today.

"Jenna." Beckett's deep voice pulls me from my thoughts as I step out of my office.

Our eyes meet and my butterflies swoon all over the place.

Beckett has gone for the casual suit look today, and while a three piece is always my preference, he may just be causing me to doubt that.

He's wearing a blue suit, white dress shirt, no tie.

His suit jacket is buttoned.

The top two buttons of his shirt are undone.

I think it's those buttons causing me to melt over his look. They're giving me a hint of skin and flooding my mind with memories from last night. Memories involving undone buttons and the most talented mouth on this planet.

He reaches for me, and I move easily into him, my hands going to his chest.

It doesn't escape me how good this feels between us.

His lips brush mine and I like that he's good with public displays of affection because I am not the kind of woman to ever hold myself back from anything I'm feeling.

When he's done with my lips, he says, "Are you free for lunch?"

I smile up at him and nod. "I am."

His eyes crinkle with a smile. "Good."

I talk with Cora for a few minutes about what needs taking care of while I'm gone and then Beckett leads me out to his car.

We settle into the back seat, and Davis pulls out into the traffic as Beckett places his hand on my thigh and says, "You look beautiful today."

I glance down at the black pants and camisole I'm wearing today. It's not often I wear pants, but I fell in love with them when one of our retailers gave them to me yesterday. I also don't often wear all black, usually opting for more color. The understated elegance of the outfit is what sold me on it this morning.

I meet his gaze again. "I'm in mourning."

His brows furrow. "Someone died?"

"You killed my George dream this morning."

"Your George dream?"

"I was dreaming of George Clooney when you woke me up. I couldn't get it back after you left."

His lips twitch. "Are George dreams a common occurrence for you?"

"Oh, you have no idea."

His phone sounds with a text but he ignores it. "Right, so no sex in the early hours of the morning, and don't interrupt any dreams in case they're a George dream. Is there anything else I need to know about your sleeping habits?"

Another text comes through for him as I say, "They're the most important things. The rest will be fun for you to discover." When his phone goes off again, I say, "I'm good if you want to check that. I don't expect you to ignore your phone when you're with me."

His eyes spend a long moment with mine before he says, "*I* want to ignore it when I'm with you."

Oh, my.

I've dated a lot of guys in my time. None of them have given me the kind of attention Beckett does.

Another text comes through, and he curses softly before finally reaching into his pocket for his phone. We spend the rest of the drive to the restaurant on our phones, which works well for me because I've had some emails come through that are time sensitive.

When we arrive at Amorosis, Beckett puts his hand to the small of my back and guides me to our table. I find it fascinating that he enters through the back door, and watch with interest as he chats with the dishwasher and some of the other staff. The way they engage leads me to believe Beckett spends a lot of time here, and that he's spent some of that time getting to know these guys. Frankie, the manager, also appears to know him well. I learned that on our first date, and it's only reinforced to me today.

Frankie gives me a smile as he seats us. "It's lovely to see you again, Jenna."

I return his smile, not missing his reference to the fact he didn't expect to ever see me again. "I do believe you promised me a special meal the next time I was in. One that not even Beckett has had."

Frankie eyes Beckett for a moment before looking back at me. "I did. Is that what you'd like to order?"

"Yes, please."

He looks at Beckett who nods.

Frankie leaves us after taking our drink orders, at which point Beckett says, "What are your plans this weekend?"

"I was thinking I might try for another George dream." His amused smile at that settles deep inside me. "Other than that, I'm hoping for some sun and time with a man who's talented with his mouth."

"I've got a gala on Saturday night I'd like you to come to, and then I was thinking we could go in search of some sun on Sunday."

"And you'll use your mouth at some point, right?"

"My mouth is all yours this weekend."

I reach for my glass of water. It's suddenly hot in here. Why must it only be Tuesday? The number of days between now and the weekend is four too many. "That mouth may be your ticket to not having to sit through movie reruns."

"You mean movie commentaries," he says playfully.

"I do like Fun Beckett, so I don't want to discourage you from embracing him, but you need to know I take my movie watching very seriously."

He's trying not to grin. Trying and pretty much failing. "Watch would imply you're looking at the movie. Except for the amount of time you dedicated to checking out the actor, there was more talking going on than watching."

He's referring to the second time we watched *Crazy, Stupid, Love*. The first time we didn't get very far into it before Beckett convinced me to have sex instead. The second time was that afternoon after the sex. I *did* do a lot of talking. But that's what movie reruns are for. You don't talk the first time you watch a movie. Every other time after that is open for discussion, and I have a lot of things to say. It doesn't matter how many times I watch a movie, I always find something new to consider and discuss.

"How have you made it to this age without learning the intricacies of movie reruns?"

Our waitress brings our drinks and Beckett takes a sip of his scotch before saying, "It's a mystery to me too."

"This may be one of the reasons why I was brought into your life."

His gaze turns intense. "I can think of other, better reasons."

I can too.

And good God if they're not pooling deep in my stomach with the way he's looking at me.

My state of disarray from last night feels dangerously close to returning. How he's now managing to cause that without so much as laying a finger on me is beyond me.

That disarray is rudely interrupted when a blonde woman with the waist of a freaking six-year-old stops by our table. "Beckett," she purrs. Yes, fucking purrs. Like a cat. I mean, I've never heard a cat purr anyone's name, but I have zero doubt that if I did, it would sound like this woman's voice when she's talking to Beckett. "This is a lovely surprise," she carries on, and the way she says it makes me think this is far from a surprise. She then eyes me, her expression turning to dislike. She doesn't speak a word to me, but she doesn't need to; her face and body language say it all.

"Annabelle," Beckett greets her, and now I know she really is a cat. Beckett has said only one word to her, but observing her, you'd think he just dedicated a chunk of his time to her. I almost expect her to start grooming him like a cat does their owner with how delighted she is.

He looks at me and introduces us. "Jenna, this is Annabelle, an old friend of mine."

I smile at her even though I don't want to. Such an odd response from me. I'm usually open to meeting everyone, but I have an overwhelming sense that this is not a woman I should let my guard down around. "It's lovely to meet you."

She gives me another cool look. I think she must have taken the same etiquette class as Beckett's mother. "Yes," she says before moving closer to Beckett and placing her hand on his arm. "How fortunate I ran into you today. I'm going over some last-minute preparations for the gala. Do you have a minute to quickly discuss some things?"

I know many women like Annabelle. Sadly. This city is filled with them. And I don't have time for them. Not even one tiny second.

Beckett shakes his head. "No, we're having lunch and then I have to get back to the office."

Now, she gives me a smile. Perhaps the fakest smile I've ever been given, and that's saying something because I've received many in my lifetime. "You don't mind, do you, Jenna? I'll only take five minutes. This is important."

Before I can tell her I do in fact mind, Beckett says, "Annabelle, no. Email me whatever it is and I'll take a look at it."

Her hand on his arm settles in like it has no intention of ever leaving. "Honestly, darling, it will just be five minutes."

Darling.

He opens his mouth to respond, but a commotion at a nearby table catches his attention. Then, his phone rings. A look of regret flashes in his eyes when he looks at the phone. "I'm sorry," he says to me, "I have to take this. It's Josh."

I nod. "Of course."

Beckett excuses himself to take the call and I reach for my wine. If the way Annabelle is eyeing me is anything to go by, I'm going to need it.

She slides into Beckett's seat. "I'm surprised we've never met, Jenna. You dated Declan for a few years, didn't you?" She injects a little bit of warmth into her voice. It doesn't fool me. She's a snake; one I will do well to keep at arm's length. Also, what's with these women in Beckett's life telling me how surprised they are we've never met? And making sure to reference Declan?

I want to tell her to fuck off. Again, an odd response for me. I may not be the good girl my sister is, but my parents raised me with the same manners as Kristen. I'm usually more inclined to tend toward friendliness than a "fuck off".

Ignoring the Declan reference, I say, "How do you and Beckett know each other?"

A look of triumph fills her eyes, like she's just won something. "We've known each other since school. Our parents are good friends. We grew up together."

A sense of unease lodges itself in my stomach. Or maybe it's jealousy, but since I don't usually experience that emotion, I doubt that. "You're organizing the gala this weekend?"

"Yes. Beckett has graciously agreed to emcee it. His mother has been very helpful with the gala too. She's managed to convince most of her friends to attend. I think it's going to be my most successful event to date."

One might wonder how Annabelle and I have never crossed paths. This is the reason. I don't enjoy attending the hottest parties and galas on New York's social calendar. My sister likely knows Annabelle. I add it to my list of things to discuss with her. I feel the need to know everything about this woman.

She narrows her eyes at me. "Is Beckett helping you with something?"

I take a sip of wine. "Yes." I mean, he's helping me have the best orgasms of my life. I only just manage to keep that to myself. I don't elaborate on my yes. I know exactly what she's asking me, and I don't want to enlighten her.

Something shifts in her. I see it in her eyes. It looks a lot like relief. "He's always been such a giving man. He's helped me with so many things over the years."

I sip some more wine. "Yes, super giving. He always makes sure I get what I need."

That relief I saw in her eyes a moment ago disappears and she resumes looking at me carefully. "What's he helping you with?"

I want to tell her.

I really do.

I think she's a snake who wants my man.

Whoa.

My man.

Calm down, Jenna.

I'm still deciding what to tell her when Beckett comes back.

Annabelle stands and moves far too close to him.

She puts her hand to his chest.

My chest.

"I'm going to call Louise and schedule a time to come and see you this week," she says.

He frowns. "What for?"

Why has he not removed her hand from his body?

"I really want to go over these things for the gala in person. I have some problems that I just know you'll give me a new perspective on and help me solve."

"I'm not sure I have any time this week."

She waves him off. "I only need half an hour. Louise and I will find it." She says this like she's good friends with his assistant. She then eyes me and says, "Isn't Louise the best? She always looks after me when I need Beckett."

Beckett resumes frowning, glancing between Annabelle and me.

I can't respond to Annabelle's question about Louise. I don't know Beckett's assistant. And bam, just like that, my thoughts crash like falling dominoes.

I don't know Louise.

I don't know his friends.

I didn't know he went to school with Annabelle.

I'm not friends with his mother like she is.

Would *I* be able to call Louise and find half an hour to steal from Beckett's busy schedule?

Jesus.

Why must I be so good at multitasking with my thoughts while doing other things?

Also, I didn't miss that the five minutes Annabelle needed with Beckett today has morphed into half an hour.

He *finally* removes her hand from his chest. "Email me," he says, and I *really* like the tone he takes with her. Firm. Bossy. Not to be argued with.

Annabelle waves him off again.

Seriously, does this woman not understand social cues?

"I'll let you get back to your lunch." She glances at me briefly. "I know you're busy helping Jenna with something." She touches his chest again and I somehow refrain from demanding she stop it with the claiming of his chest. "I'll see you soon."

She breezes away and I stare at Beckett as he sits. He's watching me with a look I can't quite place. If I had to guess, I'd say he looks mildly entertained. "What?" I throw out, feeling a whole other, different state of disarray taking over my mind. One I don't like.

"I'm helping you with something?"

I sip some more wine. I may begin guzzling it soon. "Yes. Orgasms."

At that, his mouth spreads out in the kind of smile a girl could get used to. "Right."

"Tell me, do you spend a lot of time with Annabelle? Like, am I going to have to do that if we keep seeing each other?"

That look in his eyes disappears completely, replaced with the intense Pearce gaze that does so many wrong good things to me. "Are you planning on not continuing to see me, Jenna?"

"No. I didn't say that. Don't change the subject."

"As far as I'm concerned, I'm addressing the only subject you mentioned that requires addressing."

Jesus, there may come a time I need to mute him. I'm concerned I'll never win an argument with him thanks to that voice of his. Not to mention that intensity he likes to use on me. Another top weapon in his arsenal.

I take a deep breath to center myself. To clear my thoughts. To figure out what I actually want to say to him.

I may never have had a problem with jealousy before, but it seems I've found a man who I feel all kinds of possessive over. I truly don't think Annabelle is a woman Beckett's interested in, but holy hell if she hasn't made me want to stake my territory.

Territory that is not even a week old, but territory I'm feeling nonetheless.

"Annabelle wants you."

He watches me silently and takes a sip of his scotch. "The feeling is not mutual."

"Has it ever been?"

"No."

I sip some more wine, not feeling the need to begin guzzling anymore. "I may cut her hand off if she insists on resting it against your chest again."

I throw this out flippantly, but Beckett is all intensity when he comes back with, "Her hand will never touch my chest again."

It's a good thing our meals arrive directly after he says this.

I may have demanded he choose me as his meal otherwise.

29

BECKETT

Louise: Annabelle is hounding me to get her on your calendar. Yes or no?

Beckett: No. Tell her to email.

Louise: Perhaps you could handle her better the next time you see her. This is a waste of my time.

Beckett: I intend to.

Louise: Thank you.

"Traffic is a bitch today," Davis says from the front of the car as I slip into the back seat. "Are you in a hurry to get to the office this morning?"

"No, I want to stop at Jenna's on the way."

He nods and pulls out into the traffic.

Jenna and I had lunch together yesterday, but we were both unable to get away from work to have dinner together. I worked through until just after one this morning, and she managed to take over my thoughts far more than was productive. The fact I didn't end up at her place during the night astounds me. It was an idea that kept resurfacing.

I work my way through some emails while we sit in traffic. Davis wasn't wrong: it's horrendous this morning. I've handled three problems by the time I arrive at Jenna's just after seven thirty.

She answers her door half dressed.

My eyes are unable to look anywhere but at her body, in particular her breasts that are only covered by a strapless, black bra. "Tell me you don't answer the door to anyone else dressed like this." The level of possession I feel over her is something else. Something I've never experienced.

Her lips kick up into a sexy smile and she moves into me. One hand comes to my waist, the other to my neck, and her mouth is on mine in a way it should be every morning. Her kiss lets me know she missed me as much as I missed her last night. "There are only three people I would answer the door to like this, and the other two are both into men, so you have nothing to worry about." She shifts her mouth to my ear before letting my neck go. "I like that you were worried, though."

I take hold of her face with both hands and demand another kiss. Hell, I practically fuck her with my mouth. When I'm done, I growl, "I'm not sure I even want to share you with them."

Her fingers dig into my waist. "Jesus, Beckett, you know how to mess with a girl's thoughts," she says breathlessly.

"Something we have in common."

She lets me into her condo. "I didn't get a lot of sleep last night, so I'm all kinds of disorganized this morning. Did I know you were coming by?"

I track her ass to the kitchen. She's wearing a figure-hugging red skirt that only just reaches her knees. It's not the length fucking with my dick today; it's the zip on one side that runs the length of the skirt and is only zipped halfway down her leg. It's also the sexy, black, strappy stilettos she's teamed the skirt with. Today, my eyes don't stay on her ass as long as usual; they're too distracted by her legs.

"We didn't have plans, no," I say, taking in the oats she's halfway through eating.

"Have you eaten? I have spare oats."

I nod. "Yeah, I ate after my workout." I like that she's trying to feed me, though. "I dropped by to organize dinner with you tonight."

"I can't tonight. I'm having dinner with Tilly." She finishes her oats and rinses her bowl and spoon before placing them in the dishwasher.

I pull out my phone and bring up my calendar to check the rest of my day. "Are you free for lunch?" I can reschedule my lunch meeting.

"No. Work is hectic today. How about dinner tomorrow night?"

It hits me like a sledgehammer: I don't want to wait that long to see her again.

"Where's your phone?" I ask.

She frowns. "Why?"

"Because it's time to get me on your calendar." She told me she was wide open for me, but clearly our ideas of what that means differ.

This catches all of her attention, and she moves into me, wrapping her arms around my waist. "Have I mentioned how much I like Growly Beckett?"

One of my hands finds her ass. "I can't think straight where you're concerned, Jenna. And I sure as hell can't wait until tomorrow night to see you again. I'll pick you up for work in the morning. And I'll take you this morning."

She arches her brows. "Will you just? Have you considered that I may like to walk to work?"

"There's no fucking way you can walk to work in those heels."

"You noticed them."

"There's no way I couldn't notice them."

"So, is this going to be a thing now?"

"What?"

"Your bossy, presumptuous ways are going to make a return?"

I tighten my hold on her face, brushing my thumb over her lips. "This isn't me being bossy or presumptuous. This is me asking for what I need."

"I didn't hear any asking," she says, and I know I've affected her by the way her voice has softened.

"I'm not good at asking, Jenna."

"You're going to have to try because I'm not good at being told."

I continue stroking her lip with my thumb, taking my time with it; bewitched by it, by her, by everything she's got me feeling. "Noted."

She takes that in and then says, "It's probably another ten minutes until I'll be ready. I'm having trouble locating the top I want to wear."

I kiss her. "I'll wait for you in the car."

As she steps out of my hold to go and finish dressing, she says, "We can get you on my schedule on the way to work."

I DROP Jenna at work after syncing calendars and spending nowhere near enough time with her, and then head to my office. My day is filled with meetings to work on a government aircraft contract we're trying to win. Just after 3:00 p.m., Johnson stops by to go over some security issues.

After we've finished discussing those, I say, "My sister is buying an art gallery. I'll forward you the information on it. I want you to dig into the financials. I also want you to keep an eye on it and any potential threats or issues it faces."

He nods. "Will do. And before I go, some new info has surfaced about Declan."

That gains my interest. "What?"

"Apparently, he's involved in a property development that's shady as hell."

I lean back in my chair. "How so?"

"My source tells me they're selling it as extreme luxury but plan on pocketing most of the cash rather than delivering on the luxury."

This is exactly Declan's style. Always taking the shortcut to build wealth. And stealing from others to do it.

"Who's your source?"

Johnson relays what he knows so far and who's shared that information with him. He doesn't have anything concrete yet and wanted to run it by me first to see if he should continue investigating.

"Yes," I say. "Follow this through. I want to know everything there is to know about this."

The rest of my afternoon after Johnson leaves is spent going over budgets. I don't go home until 9:00 p.m. and after I eat dinner, I continue working on the budgets. The government contract we're bidding on is the first one we've ever chased. Pearce Manufacturing has focused on private contracts until now. Acquiring Pride Industrial was part of our plan to expand into government contracts. I'm putting the hours in on this to ensure we win.

Jenna texts at ten thirty.

Jenna: Are you awake?

I call her back.

"I saw my first public threesome tonight," she answers the call with. "Well, I mean, there wasn't any public sex, but it was three men going for it in a restaurant. No blatant dick action, but still, lots of tongue action and groping. Have you ever seen something like that in a restaurant?"

"I never know what I'm going to get from you," I say, feeling my smile in every part of my body.

"I hope that won't be a dealbreaker because I have to tell you, I'm never going to change."

"Don't ever change."

"So, don't keep me in suspense. Have you ever been blessed with that kind of sight?"

"I can't say I have."

"It was hot. Like, it's a good thing it was Tilly with me at dinner and not you. I may have started groping you."

Jesus, I've been thinking about her all day. The thoughts flashing through my mind now are thoughts that only she can help me with. "Are you on your way home?"

"Yes, I just left the restaurant."

"Come here instead."

"Are you horny after thinking about the threesome?"

"It's got nothing to do with the threesome."

She makes me wait far longer than I prefer before she finally says, "Okay, but if I'm sleeping over, you better not disturb my dreams at your ungodly gym hour."

I text her my address and she arrives fifteen minutes later, looking like she just stepped off a fashion shoot.

Her long hair falls in waves over her shoulders.

Her face is beautiful perfection.

Those lips I have trouble leaving alone wear her signature red.

One bronzed shoulder is bare while the large ruffles of the black and white top she's wearing cross her body diagonally from her other shoulder to this one. Her black, metallic, pleated skirt may be the first one I've ever seen her wear that doesn't reveal her knees.

I eye her strappy stilettos. The same ones from this morning. "How the hell do you survive in those?"

She moves into me, sliding her hands around my waist. "Years of practice." She kisses me. "Also, it helps when I find men who like to massage my feet."

I settle my hands on her ass. "You came here for a foot massage?"

"No, I came here for the orgasms, but I wouldn't say no to your hands on my feet."

I brush my lips over hers again before leading her to the sofa in my living room. "How was dinner?"

She sits next to me, and I pull her leg closest to mine up so I can remove her shoe. "Well, you already know about the hot groping that was a favorite part of my dinner. Besides that, the food was good. Not as good as that pasta Frankie prepared for us yesterday, but still good. And Tilly's job is safe, so we didn't have to spend the night going through new job options for her. Mind you, we did have to dedicate time to a phone call in which we talked Kristen off the ledge over her new haircut. Honestly, women should have to verify they haven't just gone through a breakup when they go to the hairdresser."

I glance at her as I lightly tap her other leg, indicating I want her other foot. "You thought Tilly's job wasn't safe?"

She hits me with a sexy smile as she gives me her other foot. "This is going to be the best foot massage I've ever received, isn't it?"

"I thought we'd agreed not to discuss all the ways other men have had their hands on you."

Her smile grows and she leans in to kiss me. "I just decided, I'm definitely sleeping over."

"There was nothing to decide."

"Sometimes I'm a fan of Bossy Beckett. This is one of those times." She leans back against the sofa. "And yes, I thought Tilly's job wasn't safe after the mess of that photo shoot with you and that god-awful photographer. Her boss was intent on her getting you back for a do-over, but he's found someone else he wants now."

That's a good thing because I have no intention of ever going back for a do-over.

I take her foot in my hand and massage it. Her hand instantly comes to my bicep and squeezes it while she says, "Oh my God, Beckett, I may have trouble choosing between foot massages and orgasms going forward."

"I've got you covered. I'm good with taking charge."

Her phone sounds with a text as she says, "That's the truth." She then reaches for her purse. "I'm sorry, but I need to check this message. I took on a new client today and promised I'd help her with an urgent last-minute thing."

I work on her feet while she goes back and forth for five minutes with her client.

When she slips her phone back in her purse, she says, "It's Adeline Spencer. Do you know her?"

I know of Adeline, but don't know her. She's a model who has built an impressive fashion brand. "I've not met her, no."

"Signing her as a client will give me the kind of exposure I need for expansion." She takes a breath. Her eyes are shining with excitement. "I've decided to find an investor to help me with that expansion."

I look at her, my hands slowing. "Do you want a list of possible investors?"

"I would love a list." She leans across and takes hold of the back of my neck while pressing a kiss to my lips. "Thank you."

I let her foot go. "I'll have it to you tomorrow. And now"—I stand—"it's time for me to get my mouth on you."

She stands, and before she has a chance to utter a word, I lift her over my shoulder and carry her upstairs to my bedroom. The need I feel to get her naked and under me is intense. And it's the kind of need that's going to take more than one orgasm to sate.

30

It's dark out when I wake.

This time, Beckett doesn't attempt to wake me.

I reach for him as he rolls away from me to leave the bed. Threading my fingers through his, I pull him back to me.

"What happened to no sex at four thirty?" he says as his body meets mine again.

I smile and open my eyes. "There's still no sex at four thirty, but I want your eyes for a minute before you go."

His eyes crinkle.

Goddamn, they're beautiful.

"My eyes are yours whenever you want them." His voice at this time of day is maybe even better than at any other time. All gravel and depth, it makes me wonder if one day he may convince me to have sex at a time I should be sleeping.

He presses a kiss to my lips after giving me what I asked for. "What time do you want breakfast?"

"Are you cooking for me?"

"No. Martha will be here at six."

"Is Martha your other lover?"

He smiles. "She's my housekeeper."

"Thank God. You need to conserve all your energy for my orgasms."

"At the rate this conversation is going, we could have been halfway toward one."

"No, we couldn't have. I'm still trying for a George dream."

"You didn't have one last night?"

"You wore me out. My brain passed out as much as my body did. There wasn't a dream in sight. I'll be ready for breakfast around seven. I'm going to use your shower first."

"It's all yours. Any preferences for breakfast?"

"Surprise me. There isn't anything I don't like for breakfast."

"Okay. Get back to your dream chasing."

I sigh a happy sigh as I listen to him dress and leave the bedroom.

Being with Beckett feels easier than being with any other man I've ever dated.

I sleep until six thirty. There's no George dream, but there is a Beckett dream, and holy hell if it isn't far better than any George dream I've ever had. I lament the fact Beckett isn't here in this bed to experience in person.

I didn't get a chance to check out his condo last night. All I saw was the living room, the elevator, and his bedroom. From those few things I can see his decorating style is super masculine with a range of grays, browns, and black. His bedroom is impressive and easily one of the most luxurious bedrooms I've ever slept in with floor-to-ceiling windows, a ceiling that has to be at least 20-feet high, and opulent dark furnishings. It's the space in here that I really love, though. He could easily fit five rooms in this space. Between that and the view over Manhattan, I'd spend hours in here if it was my bedroom. I've lived with wealth my entire life, but Beckett's is next level.

He left a towel in his bathroom for me, and after I shower, I take it upon myself to find one of his dress shirts to wear. Beckett told me he was an open book, so I take that to mean his clothes are available to me too. I mean, goodness, the man has more shirts hanging in his closet than I could even begin to count.

I team his shirt with my skirt from last night, knotting it at my waist and leaving the top few buttons undone. I then exit his bedroom and head downstairs to find his kitchen.

Beckett's penthouse is spread across four floors. The kitchen is on the second floor and the minute I lay eyes on it, I know I'm going to cook in here. Mostly gray, with hints of black throughout, this kitchen is spacious and sleek. The countertops and backsplashes are made from luxurious crystallo gray quartzite, and although he's told me he doesn't cook, Beckett has every appliance one could ever ask for.

"Good morning, Jenna," his housekeeper greets me.

I return her smile as I recall asking Beckett if Martha was his lover. This woman looks to be around seventy. "Good morning, Martha." With her gray hair that's pulled into a bun, her round glasses, her apron, and the pen and pad she's holding, Martha is giving me the kind of efficiency vibes that make me think of my grandmother. That woman ran a tight ship in her home, and I imagine Martha does the same for Beckett.

She motions toward the long dining table situated in front of the windows that overlook Central Park. "If you'd like to sit, I'll bring your coffee to you."

I eye the kitchen and the breakfast she's preparing. I make a mental note to mention to Beckett that when I say "surprise me", he doesn't need to surprise me with so much food. Martha has bacon, eggs, sausages, pancakes, croissants, and fruit for us.

Meeting her gaze again, I say, "Would you mind if I made my own coffee? I'm fussy. And also, I really like to cook, and this kitchen is unlike any I've ever seen."

She smiles. "Beckett has given me instructions on how you prefer your coffee, but absolutely, you can make your own."

I pull out my phone. "Also, are you okay if I put some music on?"

Her smile slowly grows as she watches me silently for a few moments. It feels like she's assessing me; it also feels like that assessment may be a good one. "You can connect it to the sound system if you'd like."

She's speaking my language, and a minute later I've connected my phone and the song "Slow Dance" by AJ Mitchell and Ava Max fills the kitchen.

Martha gives me a quick tour of the kitchen and shows me where everything is. She then tells me she'll be back to serve breakfast after taking care of something in another room.

Beckett joins us as she's relaying this information.

"You can leave us, Martha," he says. "I'll take care of breakfast from here."

I watch as they have a conversation about this and also about some errands he has for her today. The impression I get is that she's either worked for him for a long time or they've established a good relationship in a shorter time. Either way, the affection they have for each other is obvious.

Beckett's blue eyes find mine as Martha leaves.

My eyes then find his suit.

Actually, they already found that the minute he entered the kitchen. They're just rediscovering it now.

"I like you in my shirts," he says, coming closer.

"I'm not sure you own enough of them." I'm trying hard to stop staring at his suit. Today, he's chosen a dark gray three-piece suit, white dress shirt, and black tie. All very distracting.

His hand snakes around my waist and his mouth comes to my ear. "Keep this one. It looks better on you than on me."

My hands move to his chest. The chest I claimed as mine two days ago. I think even Beckett is aware I did that. As my hands find his chest, he kisses me. Not quickly, and most definitely not in a way that simply says "Good morning." No, this is an "I want to fuck you" kind of kiss, and I am here for it.

I find it a little hard to remember how to breathe after he's finished with my mouth. I also find it hard to remember where my thoughts are located. So instead of saying something intelligent, I throw out, "Those windows were made for sex."

His lips twitch at the same time heat fills his eyes. Then, his arm around me tightens. "You want me to fuck you at the window?"

I grip his suit jacket. "Yes."

"Noted."

"That is a very important thing to note. Most definitely not something to be forgotten."

"I don't intend on forgetting anything you tell me to note."

I may not make it through today.

I may end up spending it in a haze of Beckett lust.

The song that's been playing ends and a new one starts. "Fallin' All In You" by Shawn Mendes. It's one I've been dancing around my condo to lately and it inspires me to say, "Dance with me."

This is the second time I've asked him to dance with me and this time he doesn't hesitate.

"Your breakfast is getting cold," he murmurs as he moves with me.

"Your kitchen is fully loaded, and I know how to use all the appliances in here. We can reheat food. What we can't do is ever get this moment back."

His gaze turns thoughtful for a long few moments and then he brushes his lips over mine and says, "I like the way you think."

I smile up at him. "So, you have a gym here? Or did you leave and come back?"

"I have a fully-equipped gym and squash court."

"I've never played squash."

"We'll play a game."

"Ah, no, I don't think we will."

"Why not?"

"I've seen how sweaty that game is. There's no need for you to see me that sweaty."

His eyes flash with amusement. "You're good with me seeing you sweat while I fuck you, but sports are off the table?"

My eyes widen. "I do not sweat during sex."

He chuckles. "You do. And if you don't, I'm doing it all wrong."

"I'm choosing to ignore this part of the conversation. As far as I'm concerned, I don't sweat during sex. I look amazing while you're busy giving me orgasms."

Still dancing with me, he slides his arm further around my waist and draws me closer as he drops his mouth to my ear. "You look fucking beautiful while I'm busy doing that. You should note how much I'd like to see you play squash."

If Beckett thinks I'm going to play a game with him anytime soon, he's dreaming. What he's not dreaming about, or should I say, what *I'm* not dreaming about, is how many butterflies he's unleashed this morning.

Needing to contain all these butterflies, I press my hands to his chest and say, "I'm ready for breakfast now."

He doesn't let me go straight away, and when he does, he gives me a knowing look. But he doesn't acknowledge what he's aware of, namely the fact I'm dangerously close to a state of disarray. Instead, he goes along with my wishes, and we make coffee and serve ourselves breakfast.

We've just sat at the table when he receives a text from Ruby. I eat my pancakes as he texts back and forth with her for a couple of minutes.

When he places his phone down, I say, "How is she?"

"Dad just told her they're cutting her off financially."

"Oh, wow, they're going ahead with that. How is she taking it?" I'd assumed they only threatened that to encourage her to do what they want her to. Having observed Beckett's mother the other night, though, I should have realized they were serious. His mother was cold as ice.

I see the worry in his eyes as he says, "She appears to be okay with it."

"But you're concerned."

He eats some of his eggs before answering me. "Yes. Ruby has little concept of the cost of things. She spends money like there's an endless supply of it."

"Maybe this will be good for her."

"Our parents shouldn't have spoiled her for so long. This will either be good, or it will be a rude awakening."

I'm surprised to hear his parents spoiled Ruby. They didn't come across as the spoiling kind of people the other night. But, if anyone knows about parents who spoil their children, it's me. My parents fund Kristen's life. I stopped taking money from them years ago, but she still relies on them to enjoy her luxury lifestyle.

My phone sounds with a text and a quick glance alerts me to the fact it's news I'm not going to like. Not when Kristen's using our code for bad news.

Kristen: CODE RED

"Oh God," I mutter, swiping my phone. Then to Beckett, I say, "Prepare yourself. My sister is about to give me bad news."

Jenna: Can we pretend we live with unicorns and rainbows today?

Kristen: A heads up, Mom will be calling you today to organize a family dinner.

Jenna: Why is that a code red?

I mean, Mom is often organizing family dinners.

Kristen: All that sex you're having is getting in the way of your quick thinking.

She's not wrong there.

Jenna: Perhaps. Tell me.

Kristen: She wants Beckett there.

Jesus.

No.

He's already been subjected to my family once. We need more time together before I make him sit through them again.

Kristen: I told you it was a code red.

Jenna: On a scale of 1 to 10, how hard is she going to push for this?

I need to be prepared for the onslaught.

Kristen: *insert a million laughing emojis*

Kristen: I'm almost certain that if you resist, she'll just go straight to the man himself.

My head snaps up and I find Beckett watching me with interest as he drinks some of his coffee.

"What?" he asks, taking in the expression on my face that must be screaming "Kill me now."

"My mother." Seriously, she and I need to have strong words about her level of interference when it comes to my love life. She always does this. It's like she thinks I can't find a man and keep him by myself.

His brows pull together. "You're going to have to elaborate, Jenna."

"If my mother calls you or comes to see you, and asks you to attend a family dinner, say no. Apparently, her current mission is to drag you to one of our dinners."

His brows stop pulling together. "What if I want to say yes?"

"Why in the world would you want to do that?"

"Why wouldn't I?"

Jesus, he has no idea what he's saying or thinking. Maria Blaise is not a woman to underestimate when it comes to this matchmaking business.

I take a deep breath and proceed to educate him on my mother. "She does this when she knows I'm dating a guy. She swoops on in and tries to take over. First, she'll sweet talk you and make you like her. Then, she'll engineer ways for you to spend more and more time with me, and also with the family. That's her goal, you see. She wants to marry me off. And she thinks I need help with that. Before you know it, she'll have taken over all your time and will be inserting herself into your life while she meddles with your thoughts. She'll confuse the ever-loving heck out of you, and you won't even remember what your goals in life are because all you'll be thinking about is how to escape marrying me." I pause. "That is how Johnathon became engaged to my sister. Not that I would ever point that out to Kristen, but it's the truth of the matter."

Beckett processes all that and then simply says, "I'm good with that."

I blink.

And I stare at him.

"What?" I mean, did he even hear a word I just said?

"Jenna," he says, "Let your mother do her thing. I'm a grown man and can handle myself."

"I know you are, but I want time with you alone before I have to share you. And honestly, my mother needs to learn to back off and let me run my own relationships."

He finishes his breakfast. "I want time alone too, but I also want to get to know the people who are important to you. Consider agreeing to this dinner."

I don't get a chance to respond to that because Beckett receives a call he has to take. What I would have said to him was I have no intention of agreeing to this dinner. My mother will need to learn some patience.

I finish my breakfast while he's on the phone, and then clear the table. He finishes his call, and we gather our belongings and make our way to the elevator.

"I'll drop you at home on my way to the office and then Davis can circle back and pick you up to take you to work," Beckett says.

"Thank you, but I'm meeting with Adeline Spencer at her home this morning."

"Davis can drive you."

"You don't need to have your driver take me places, Beckett."

"I don't need the car this morning." His eyes flash with his signature intensity as he adds, "I want you to have it."

My natural instinct is to tell him no, but I sit with this for a moment, trying to feel into it. Trying to figure out if I really don't want what he's offering or if I'm just being stubborn. "I'm not used to men like you," I say softly.

"Men like me?"

"Yes, men who look after me like you're trying to. I'm finding it a little overwhelming I think."

His intense gaze demands I pay attention as he says, "You're going to have to get used to this because I don't intend on looking after you in any other way."

With that, he continues taking charge and ushers me into the elevator when it arrives.

I let him take charge.

And every step of the way, I realize how good I actually am with this.

@thetea_gasp

@ADELINESPENCER WOWED last night on the red carpet in a
dress styled by @jennablaise. The two were spotted deep in
conversation on Thursday at @littlecollinsnyc the home of
Aussie coffee in Manhattan. Adeline gushed about her new
stylist to @rodriguezgarcia who dropped a Jenna mention in
his regular Friday fashion shoutout yesterday. @dianablack
also gave her a shoutout this week. Jenna's follower count
bumped to just over 1M overnight. Gather in for the tea: this
girl is going places. Sidenote: who knew Aussie coffee tasted
so good? We skipped down to Little Collins to try it after
seeing Adeline there. It is #fire.

32

JENNA

Jenna: Saying yes to this gala was the worst decision I've ever made in my life.

Shona: Really? I do recall some bad decisions in your time.

Jenna: Beckett's family is sitting at our table and Beckett is busy emceeing.

Shona: OMG his mother.

Jenna: Right.

Shona: Is his father being nice to you?

Jenna: Well, he's not being rude but nice may be a stretch. All I can say is thank God for Ruby.

Shona: I think I'd like Beckett's sister from everything you've told me about her.

Jenna: You really would.

I eye Beckett coming my way.

Jenna: I've gotta go. I hope Graham is making good on his orgasm promises this weekend.

Shona: Oh girl, you have no idea. Talk to you later xx

I stand as Beckett draws closer, moving into him when he reaches me. "Has anyone ever told you your voice was made for these kinds of events?"

His lips brush mine. "It wasn't. It was made so I could convince you to do wicked things with me."

"Jesus. A girl needs prior warning when her man is about to say something inappropriate in public."

His eyes heat. "No, she needs to know her man prefers watching her caught off guard by the things he says."

We're interrupted by Annabelle when she joins us. "Beckett, if I could have a minute, please?" She's talking to Beckett, but she's looking at me. Actually, glaring is more like it.

From the minute we arrived, Annabelle has been shooting daggers at me. She was more than pleased when she was able to drag Beckett away to prepare for his emcee role. I had to refrain from announcing to her that rather than just being my helper on something, he's actually making it his mission in life to kill me with orgasms.

Beckett glances at her, keeping his hand on my waist. "What's up?"

She shifts her gaze to him. "I want to discuss what you need to cover when the auction is finished."

"We went over all this yesterday, Annabelle." I detect a note of frustration in his voice. I'm really here for that note. Jesus, this woman is turning me into a bitch. I must work on that.

"Oh, darling, no we didn't. Not properly," she says.

I want to tell her to stop calling my man darling.

However, I do not tell her that.

Really, I deserve a medal for my outstanding ability to keep my mouth shut.

I look up at Beckett in time to catch him working his jaw. "Give me a minute," he says.

She waits expectantly for a few seconds and then, when she realizes he really did mean a minute, she says, "I'll wait for you out back."

Full credit to her, she's done an amazing job with this gala. From the stunning white and gold decorations to the glittery lights throughout the ballroom, to the guest list, she's nailed it.

And with the bids coming in for the art, she'll raise millions for charity.

Beckett turns to me after she leaves. "Don't go too far. I've got thirty minutes before this break is over and I want to spend them with you."

I smile up at him. "I'll be here."

Ruby joins me when he leaves. "How are you doing with Annabelle?"

I look at her, taking in the knowing look in her eyes. "You say that like you expect me to be having trouble with her."

"She's been after Beckett since they were twelve. I do expect you to be having trouble with her."

"That's a long time." I want to ask her if anything has ever happened between them, but I don't want to pry like that. If I want to know something, I'd rather go directly to him for that information.

Well, mostly.

There is a small part of me that wants to beg Ruby for all the dirt, so I know what I'm dealing with here. But I don't. I decide to have a conversation with Beckett about this at some point in the future.

Her brows arch as she nods. "Yes, it is, but you have nothing to worry about there. And when I say nothing, I mean absolutely not one thing." She throws a glance around the room. "Let's get a drink."

"You go," I say as I spy my sister coming our way with the kind of look on her face that lets me know she's got something to tell me. "I told Beckett I'll wait here for him."

"You want me to get you a drink?" Ruby asks.

"No, I'm good."

Kristen reaches me a few moments after Ruby leaves. "You are never going to believe what I just heard," she says.

"Probably not." Also, I'm probably not going to care. Kristen's love of gossip isn't a love I share.

Her lips purse. "Humor me for once, Jenna. Please."

"I always humor you."

"You do not. Also, before I tell you this, swear to me my hair doesn't make me look like a pixie." The tone of uncertainty and anxiety in her voice can't be mistaken, something I feel sad about because my sister looks beautiful.

Before she entered the hairdresser the other day, Kristen had long, blonde hair. After, she had a pixie cut. Still blonde, thankfully, because I shudder to think what I would have had to deal with this week if she'd cut that much hair off *and* colored it. The cut is a long pixie cut, which I think looks stunning on her. Mom couldn't withhold her opinion, though, and threw out words like tomboy and gamine. I mean, I'd actually never heard the word gamine before that. I had to look it up. I told our mother that Kristen most definitely does not look like a neglected girl who was left to run the streets. That sent Kristen into another spiraling round of tears and regret.

"Kris, you look beautiful. Please believe me."

She smooths a hand over her hair, self-doubt clinging to her eyes. "Really? Like, seriously, can you ever see any man being attracted to me now? I should never have cut my hair."

I reach for her hand and remove it from her hair. "Stop this. You look stunning. And your hair will grow back. But for the record, I love this cut."

"It's all well and good for you to love this cut, but don't think I didn't notice your lack of answer to my question about whether any man will ever be attracted to me now."

"I didn't answer it for two reasons. Firstly, of course men will be attracted to you. Just look around the room. They're paying attention. But secondly, don't you want to take a little break and gather yourself back together after the breakup?"

She looks at me like we don't speak the same language. "Ah, did you or did you not get straight back out there after Declan cheated on you?"

"Yes, I rushed straight into a few dates, and all of them were a bad idea. That's why I think you should take a breath and work through what Johnathon did. You haven't had any Kristen time for years."

"I don't know what you mean when you say things like that. Is this part of your whole recharging your vibration thing you've been going on about for months?"

"No, it's basic self-care. Spending time by yourself can be a good thing."

She waves me off. We really are speaking different languages. "Pfft, I don't need to spend time by myself. I need to find love, and I'm not going to do that sitting at home on a Friday night drinking tea and petting my cat."

Kristen doesn't drink tea, nor does she have a cat, but I get the sentiment. I also decide to let this conversation go. We all find our way through life differently. My sister will figure herself out in her own time.

"Okay," I say, "tell me the thing I am never going to believe."

"Oh," she says, her eyes coming alive. "Apparently Annabelle has slept with half of New York. I did not know this before today. And, she's turned down marriage proposals from Tommy Dune, Marc Diamond, and Samuel Benson. You're welcome."

I asked Kristen what she knew about Annabelle after I met her earlier this week. Kristen gave me the few facts she knew: Annabelle comes from old money; she doesn't work, but rather dedicates her time to finding a husband; she's a gossipy snake just like I assumed; and she's got a reputation for going through friends fast.

The three men Kristen has mentioned are all men the women in Annabelle's circle would classify as worthy husband material.

When I don't respond, Kristen makes wide eyes and says, "Clearly she's holding out for someone else."

I don't miss the reference to Beckett. "He's not interested."

Kristen's lips pull together. "Still, I'd keep an eye on that if I were you."

"What are you keeping an eye on?" Mom asks as she joins us.

"Beckett's ass," I say, not wanting Kristen to bring Mom into our conversation about Annabelle. God knows our mother likes her gossip. We do not need to give her anything to run with.

"Where is that man?" she asks. "I need a minute with him."

"You do not," I say. She's asked me three times over the last twenty-four hours to invite him to dinner tomorrow night. I've said no each time. I have no doubt my sister was right when she said Mom would simply go straight to Beckett if I didn't say yes.

She gives me that look of hers that says she has no intention of listening to me. "Darling, we want to get to know the man you're dating."

"I want to get to know him too, Mom. Have you forgotten that we've only just started seeing each other? You need to give us time alone before you force our family on him."

She waves me off. This is a favorite move of hers and Kristen's where I'm concerned. "You've known the man for years, Jenna."

"Not in the way I'm getting to know him now," I say, exasperated with her and her meddling ways. "Please let me decide when it's time for him to be subjected to our family."

I spot Beckett walking our way. I also spot Annabelle right next to him. I then spot her grip his arm and stop him so she can say something to him.

"Subjected?" Mom says. "That's hardly the correct term to use, Jenna." She sounds offended, but I only vaguely process that. I'm too busy processing what I'm looking at.

Annabelle's hand goes to Beckett's chest.

He removes it instantly.

This only causes her to step closer to him while they talk.

He doesn't appear interested in the conversation, a fact I high five inwardly.

It has to be said, though, that there are many other feelings happening for me inwardly at the same time as that high five. There's just something about this woman I do not like.

"Jenna!" Mom says sharply, drawing my attention back to her. "Did you hear a word of what I just said?"

"Ah," Kristen says, "I think she's a little distracted right now."

Mom follows Kristen's gaze, and the moment she lays eyes on Beckett, her eyes light up.

"Oh dear God," I mutter. Then, looking at my sister, I say, "I need a drink to deal with this."

I told Beckett I'd wait here for him, but I can't be a witness to my mother inflicting herself on him, so I make my way to the bar. It takes me far longer to get there than I plan because I keep getting stopped by women who want to say hello. Most also drop something in about working with me in the future. My new connections with Diana Black and Adeline Spencer have done wonders for my business this week. Not to mention Rodriguez Garcia's Instagram post last night. If I ever meet Adeline's old modelling friend, the drinks will be on me.

I finally arrive at the bar and order an Eastside. It's become a new favorite cocktail of mine after Ruby introduced me to it. The bartender has just placed my drink in front of me when Beckett's hand slides around my waist.

"I thought you were waiting for me," he murmurs against my ear.

I smile as the sensations from his touch and voice move through me. "I was, but my mother changed my mind." I turn to face him. "Did she ask you to dinner?"

"She did."

"And?"

"I told her we haven't finalized our plans for tomorrow night yet." He pauses. "You should tell her yes."

I move my hand to his hip, resting it there. Touching Beckett is something I don't seem able to stop myself from doing. If we weren't in public right now, I'd have my hands all over him for what he said to my mother. I expected him to say yes to her. I like that he's leaving this up to me. "I'll think about it."

His eyes search mine. "You have no intention of saying yes, do you?"

I exhale a breath. "I don't know. My mother can be hard work and my father can mess with my confidence. I'm not sure I'm ready to deal with either of those things when I'm on a high after this week."

He starts to say something, but Misty Parker interrupts us. "Jenna! Ohmigod, that dress you chose for Adeline was to die for! I need you to help me with my dress for the Northrup Gala next month. Tell me you can fit me in."

What I want to tell her is that I'm in the middle of an important conversation and she needs to learn some manners, but I don't. I am a Blaise after all. My mother would be horrified to learn I was rude to a Parker. Misty's family is one of the most influential in New York and Mom is close to her mother.

I smile at Misty. "I'm your girl. Call my office and we'll set a time to meet."

Her eyes relay her excitement. "Thank you, darling." She looks at Beckett briefly before giving me her attention again. "I'll leave you two alone. I apologize for the interruption, but I didn't want to miss my opportunity." With an air-kiss, she glides away from us.

Beckett pulls me close. "It turns out I'm not a fan of sharing you."

I look up at him. "I'm not a fan of sharing you, either."

He takes a few moments with my eyes, looking down at me silently. Finally, he says, "Maybe you're right about this dinner tomorrow. I want an entire day with just you."

I curl my hand around his neck and pull his lips to mine. After I kiss him, I say, "I think that may be the first time you've ever told me I'm right about something."

A smile plays on his face, not quite forming, but there nonetheless. "You've been right about many things, Jenna." Then, threading his fingers through mine, he says, "I need to get back to work."

We head back to the table where Beckett's mother is deep in conversation with Annabelle. And surprise of all surprises, well, really, I guess it shouldn't be since they've known each other for a long time, they look super friendly. Gone is the ice queen I've been sitting with all night, and in her place is the queen of warmth.

Knots form in my stomach.

Which I hate.

I'm not jealous of Beckett and Annabelle, but I do think I'm a little jealous of the fact Annabelle has managed smiles out of the woman I want to encourage smiles from. I do not like feeling this emotion. Not when it causes a range of other emotions and thoughts to cascade through my mind and body, namely insecurity.

Annabelle glances our way when we arrive at the table. I don't miss the venom in her eyes as she says, "Oh, Jenna, there you are. I was just telling Margaret how amazing Beckett has been to you, helping you with that thing." She frowns a little. "What exactly has he been helping you with?"

Beckett has been drawn into a conversation with his father, so I'm in this one with Annabelle and his mother on my own. Oh, the joy. Margaret is watching me with the kind of interest that confuses my thought process. I want to excuse myself before I throw thoughts out that make little sense, but my manners dictate I stay. "Actually, he paid for a date with me in a charity auction and we've kind of gone from there." I mean, this news has circulated on social media, so I can't tell if she's pretending not to know or if she's actually unaware.

Annabelle blinks.

Okay, she was not pretending.

Margaret eyes Annabelle. "It was a tax deduction."

Annabelle regains her composure. "Oh, yes, that makes sense."

I mean, yes, it does, but no, the rest of our dates don't make sense if we're talking a tax deduction. Orgasms cannot be claimed. I refrain from sharing that thought.

Margaret gives me one more cool glance before turning her full attention back to Annabelle. "I'm hosting a morning tea next month and would like you to come. It's on the tenth. I think you'll find it beneficial to attend."

They go back and forth on this morning tea for several minutes while I stand here like an idiot waiting to be brought back into the conversation.

When it finally occurs to me that Margaret has no intention of involving me, I look around for someone else to talk to. The awkward and brushed-off feelings surging through me are ones I'm not used to, ones I don't know what to do with.

I don't want to cut in on Beckett's conversation with his father, so I don't do that. Instead, I find my sister who's standing a few tables away talking with a friend of hers, and I zero in on her.

Kristen frowns when I reach her. "Are you okay?"

Her friend leaves us as I say, "No, I'm not okay! I was just very rudely dismissed by Beckett's mother, and Jesus, if I have to endure any more conversations with Annabelle today, I may stab her in the eyes."

Kristen's gaze shifts to someone behind me and a moment later, our father joins us.

"Are you still considering bidding on that Mitchell painting?" Kristen asks him.

"No, I've changed my mind," he says before looking at me. "Did Grayson talk to you about what we need from you at the company dinner next month?"

Our family company, Blaise Corporation, holds an annual dinner every July. It's a big event for Dad and Grayson, and all the Blaise children are expected to contribute in some way.

Grayson asked me to make myself available at the dinner to mingle with the guests. And by mingle, he means turn up the charm by a million and ensure their investors and advertisers stick with them. Saying no was not an option.

Beckett comes to stand next to me as I answer my father. "Yes, everything's taken care of."

Dad's serious expression remains in place. "Good. We've got a lot riding on this dinner this year. There's no room for error."

There's never any room for error. Not for a Blaise. This isn't something he needs to tell me; he's drilled this into us since we were born.

Dad eyes Beckett and greets him, "Beckett."

"William," Beckett says. Dad and Beckett met at Kristen's party. They spent a little time chatting and my father told me later that he approved of my new choice far more than he ever approved of Declan. It seems I finally found a way to gain my father's approval. Unfortunately, it's not a way I care to gain his approval.

"Did you see that Jenna's now working with Adeline Spencer and Diana Black, Dad?" Kristen says excitedly.

I exchange a smile with her. My sister and I may be almost complete opposites, but we always have each other's back.

"Do you think that's a wise move?" Dad says.

My father pretty much never thinks the same way I do, but I, at least, imagined he'd support my business growth. It turns out he never fails to find ways to think differently than me.

"I do," I say, sounding more confident than he's making me feel. I chastise myself for allowing him this power over me, but that's what I always do.

His lips flatten. "Use your brain, Jenna. You don't want to surround yourself with tacky women who will downgrade your business profile. Think smarter. I taught you better than this."

His words are a slap in my face.

I literally feel them.

My face burns, my chest burns, my heart burns.

Before I can respond, not that I think I have any words to respond with, he excuses himself, leaving me staring after him, wondering how I never saw that coming.

"Shit," Kristen says, looking bewildered. "I would never have said that if I thought that would be his response. I'm so sorry, Jenna."

I swallow my hurt. "It's okay. I mean, no one would expect their father to say that to them. You couldn't have known."

She glances between me and Beckett, looking desperate for his help. I catch his nod out of the corner of my eyes. A second later, he's moved to stand in front of me and is taking charge of the situation.

"He's wrong. I hope you know that," he says.

I swallow more of my hurt. There's a lifetime of it lodged in my throat after what Dad just said to me, though. I'm unsure how I'll swallow it all back down. "Rationally, I know he's wrong, but when it comes to my dad and all the things he says to me and all the ways I process those things, there's nothing rational about any of it. He always finds a way to say things that cause me to doubt myself, and today is no different."

"Beckett," Annabelle calls out, "It's time."

He nods at her. "Give me a minute." He then comes back to me. "Put him out of your mind. Focus on the numbers. You've seen them grow this week. That's all the proof you need to know he's wrong."

I nod, but I don't say anything.

"Jenna," he says, his voice taking a firm tone. "You told me your numbers, and they're good. I would invest in a business with those figures. Your father doesn't know what he's saying."

That catches my attention.

Beckett never bullshits and never says something he doesn't mean.

"Thank you for saying that," I say softly, every word coming directly from my heart.

He looks at me questioningly. "Are you going to be okay, or do I need to delay Annabelle?"

The fact he would delay her is all I need.

"I'm good. Go, before she comes over here and gives me hell for keeping you."

He bends his mouth to mine and when he's finished with his kiss, he says, "We're leaving as soon as I'm finished up on that stage."

I smile. "That is the best thing you've said since we arrived."

This night has been intense. Between having to sit with Beckett's mother, who has barely exchanged a word with me, to having to converse with Annabelle, to having to listen to my father tell me to use my brain, I wish I'd stayed home, drunk hot chocolate, and watched old movies. When Beckett says we're leaving as soon as he's finished emceeing, I hope he knows I'm taking that to mean the absolute second he's finished.

33

JENNA

"There you are," Beckett says, walking my way. When he reaches me, he repositions me so he can sit behind me on the chaise lounge. Then, wrapping his arms around me, he says, "You couldn't sleep?"

It's just after 2:00 a.m. Monday morning, and no, I couldn't sleep. My mind is still working on my thoughts and feelings over my conversation with Dad at the gala on Saturday night.

Beckett made good on whisking us away from the gala the minute he was finished emceeing. He took me to his place and helped take my mind off Dad. He then flew us to his place in the Hamptons early Sunday morning where we spent the day swimming, talking, and having some great sex before flying home after dinner.

We declined Mom's dinner invitation. In fact, Beckett made it clear he didn't want us to attend. I don't think he was impressed by what my father said to me at the gala. He didn't say that, though. He simply told me he wanted me to himself all day. We came back to my place where we fell asleep just after 11:00 p.m. I woke about half an hour ago, and knowing I was too wired for sleep, I came up to my rooftop to think.

"I'm wide awake," I say, snuggling against him.

"You're still thinking about what your dad said, aren't you?"

"Yes."

He's silent for a moment before saying, "I received a text from Sarah tonight. She's going home to her husband."

I smile, loving that he's trying to help shift my thoughts. I also love hearing this update on his cousin. He's been keeping me updated on her since our first date when he went to see her. "How is she?"

"She sounds raw. She's unsure if they can make the marriage work, but they're both willing to try. Josh has told me she's making good progress. He's made sure she's found the professional help she'll need, and he's hopeful she can turn her life around."

Josh was supposed to attend the gala. I'd been looking forward to seeing him again, but at the last minute, he was unable to come.

I stare out into the dark night, thinking about marriage and relationships and the work they take. "Do you want kids one day?" The question falls out of my mouth before I can stop it, and unlike the past me who would stumble over herself to backtrack on it—because, hello, we haven't even been dating two weeks yet—I let it sit between us.

Beckett takes it in his stride. "I do. Two would be good. I don't want a large family. You?"

I smile. "I'd like five kids." I don't really; I just feel the urge to have some fun with him.

He kisses my neck and murmurs, "At the rate you beg for orgasms, five kids isn't a stretch to imagine."

"I do not beg."

He keeps pressing his lips to my neck as he says, "You do."

"I don't have to because you can't keep your mouth off me."

He takes hold of my neck so he can angle my face around and kiss me. When he's finished with my lips, his eyes meet mine, full of amusement and heat, and he says, "How many kids do you really want?"

"Three."

"A much better number than five."

I play with him some more. "I also want two dogs and a cat. Oh, and I think a pet bird for the kids would be fun too."

His lips twitch. "I imagine you also expect your husband to babysit all those kids and animals when you go away on girls' weekends."

"Ah, Mr. Pearce, I do recall you telling me it's not called babysitting when the husband looks after the kids."

He kisses me again. This time, he goes slow, stealing all my thoughts and breath. His eyes don't let mine go when he's finished. "Will you travel much with your family?"

A smile spreads slowly across my face. "I like playing this game with you."

When he doesn't reply to that but rather just waits for my answer, I say, "I love to travel, but I imagine it would be hard with three children."

"I imagine your husband would make it easier."

"He would, otherwise I'd kick his ass."

This gets me a smile. "I have no doubt about that."

I suddenly feel the need to be in his lap, facing him, with my arms around him. A few moments later, I am, and his arms circle me.

Dipping my face to his, I claim his lips in another slow, deep kiss. When I come up for air, I say, "I feel like a hot chocolate."

"I'm taking that as you want me to make it."

"You are a smart man."

He smacks my ass. "Let me up."

I don't let him up.

I kiss him again, and then I let him up.

I spend the time he's making my drink staring out over the city I love, thinking about what I've got going on today. As I run through all the work appointments I have, and the jobs I have to take care of, I realize Beckett did shift my thoughts away from my father. I also realize how supported I feel after this weekend with him.

I'm in the middle of those thoughts when he returns. He hands me my drink and sits behind me again.

After I take a sip of hot chocolate, I say, "This is good. I think we've found your thing in the kitchen."

"What, you didn't like the waffles I made you yesterday?"

I laugh. "Right, sorry, I forgot about your masterpiece yesterday. I mean, toasting waffles is super tricky and you excelled at it."

He gives me his teeth, lightly biting my neck before growling, "Careful, Jenna, I may never treat you to my cooking talents again if you keep wounding me like this."

"I can live without your cooking talents, but please never take your dancing talents from me." Beckett danced with me twice over the weekend in his kitchen. The man has moves, and each time we dance, I'm treated to a few more of them.

"Where did you pick this dancing thing up from? Your mom?"

"Uh, you've seen my dad, right? There's no way he'd dance with her in the kitchen. Also, she doesn't cook. Their kitchen is run by Nancy, the housekeeper they've had for over a decade."

"So where did you learn to cook and dance?"

"When I was twenty-five, I shared an apartment with a girl called Donna. She was this weed-smoking, art-loving, free spirit who embraced all the ways of living my parents had tried to ensure I never took up. We met at a party and became fast friends. Donna taught me to challenge everything, to live life full out, to never take a moment for granted, and to dance in the kitchen. She also taught me how to cook. 'The kitchen is for soul therapy' she used to tell me."

"So it's Donna I have to thank for you challenging me all these years? What happened to her?"

I laugh. "Well, to be fair to her, I was already good at challenging everything. She just taught me to own it. I'm not sure where she is at the moment. She's travelling the world. I receive postcards every now and then. The last one came about four months ago from Tasmania in Australia. Oh, and don't bring Donna up with my parents unless you want to hear them go on about the year I lost my mind."

"I take it they didn't like Donna."

"That's an understatement. It was their extreme disapproval that caused me to move in with her and to stay living with her for a year. Honestly, I loved her, and she was a huge influence in my life, but I will admit to you that I found living with her hard. She was always on the go, and inviting people over, and having parties. It was a little too much for me in the end." I pause. "How about you? Who have been your influencers?"

"Josh mostly. He'll tell you I changed his life, but he changed mine far more."

"How so?"

"I know you'll find this hard to believe, but I was an asshole when I was younger. My only goal in life was to impress my father. In business, in my marriage, in the way I spent my spare time. I didn't care who I used to achieve that goal. Declan was right there by my side, aiming for the same goal with his father, so between us, we were two assholes who never called the other on their bullshit. It was Josh who pulled me aside when I was twenty-six and told me he couldn't imagine being my friend anymore if I continued being the person I was."

"His friendship must have meant a lot to you for you to change."

"Yes, it did, even though I never showed him that."

"I really liked Josh when I met him."

"We'll have dinner with him one night. You two will get on well."

There's something in the way he says this that makes me question him. I turn to face him as I ask, "What do you mean by that?"

He smiles, and it's such an easy, carefree smile that I can't help but think if thoughts of Josh bring this out in Beckett, I really am going to get along well with him. "He likes fun in the same way you do. Any time I've been spontaneous in my life has been thanks to Josh. And now"—he slides some hair off my face—"I find myself behaving in similar ways with you."

"Did you get your tattoos when you were with Josh?"

"You're fascinated with my tattoos, aren't you?"

I grin. "Well, they are hot, but mostly they surprise me. In the very best way."

"I was with Josh when I got the eagle tattoo. It was the first weekend we spent together after I started working on myself and on our friendship. He suggested it because of the symbolism of courage and strength."

"And the other tattoo?"

"That one I got a few months ago. There's a lot to that one."

The way he stops talking, and the look in his eyes make me think he's maybe not ready to tell me any more about that, but then he continues, "I've been questioning a lot of things in my life since my divorce, and have been making small changes here and there, trying to be a better person and give back where I can. I've also been clearing people out of my life who don't fit anymore. Fuck knows where it's all come from, but I've been seeing life and people differently. I got the tattoo on a whim one weekend in Vegas. The compass and clock together signify the passing of time and fragility of life, along with guidance through life. The triangles mean many things, but for me it was about a higher perspective."

I curve my hand around his neck and pull him close so I can kiss him. This man is full of surprises, and I'm having trouble believing that until just recently I didn't like him very much. Now, I think very highly of him and can't wait to peel back more of his layers.

"We wasted so much time," I whisper when I end our kiss.

"No," he disagrees, "I wasn't ready for you until now, and you sure as hell wouldn't have stayed with the old me."

The spiritual side of me loves what he just said. "I think you're right."

"Those are four words you would never have given the old me."

I wiggle around to look out over the city again, leaning against his chest. Pulling his arms around me, I say, "Do you want to know one of my favorite things to do?"

"I want to know all your favorite things to do, Jenna."

"Watching the sunrise."

"I find that hard to believe."

"Because I like my sleep?"

"Yes. You don't even give up your sleep for one of your other favorite things."

"Beckett, I would have thought you'd understand by this age in your life that women are contradictory creatures and as such are allowed to change their mind on a whim, are allowed to choose options you never saw coming, and are allowed to make one choice today and a different choice tomorrow."

He chuckles and his lips graze my neck. "We're staying here for the rest of the night, aren't we?"

I smile at what I hear in his tone.

Beckett wants to give me what I want.

And as that thought makes itself known, another thought pops up too.

He's always tried to do that.

All the times I thought he was being overbearing and treating me like he thought I was incapable of doing things for myself, he was actually just trying to ensure I got what I wanted.

A whole lot of memories flash through my mind of the times I've spent in Beckett's company. Memories in which I was irritated with him because I misunderstood him.

I put my hands over his. "Yes, we're staying here for the rest of the night because one of my other favorite things to do is have long conversations in the early hours of the morning."

I love my sleep the most, but I adore the connections that are made in the AMs, and I always feel a sense of peace when I watch the sunrise. I will go without my sleep every now and then to experience those things.

"You do realize we've both got work in a few hours?"

I laugh. "Life is for living, Beckett. You can take a nap during the day."

He kisses the nape of my neck. "I've got no time for a nap."

"And still, you're going to stay up with me and tell me all your favorite things to do, aren't you?"

He presses more kisses to my neck, murmuring, "I'm unable not to."

"You should note that this is one of my favorite things you've done with me so far."

His mouth moves to my ear. "Noted."

BECKETT and I stayed up all night talking. I discovered his love for all forms of water sports; his extreme dislike of chess (it stems from his father forcing him to play it repeatedly as a child); that he enjoys road trips even though he can't recall the last one he took; his dislike of strip clubs; and that he quite likes stand-up comedy (this may have been my biggest surprise). He also learned my favorite things. Well, I mean, I have so many favorite things that we'd need a few nights to get through them, so he only learned some of my favorites. I think he realizes that and is preparing for some more sunrise sessions. We talked about the places we want to visit in the world and discussed taking a trip to Hawaii together soon. He's been there before, but I haven't, and I really want to go. Possibly, sharing that trip with him might not be the best move because we'll likely not see much more than our hotel room, but a girl can always plan a second and third trip to see all the sights.

We also talked about my business and the meeting I have on Thursday with a potential investor. Gordon Roth was one of the men on the list of possibilities Beckett gave me. I worked through his list on Friday and Gordon came back to me late Friday night with an email setting up a meeting. Beckett gave me some advice on how to approach the meeting.

The sun rose just before 5:30 a.m. It was beautiful like it always is, but this time it was more beautiful simply because I watched it rise with Beckett.

"I found a way to encourage you to have early morning sex," he'd said against my ear as the small ball of light cracked through the sky.

"You should make use of it," I'd said.

That was all he needed to hear. We sat on the rooftop for a little while longer, and then he carried me down to my bedroom and started my day off right with two orgasms.

We're now in my kitchen making breakfast. I'm feeling a post-sex, post-best-night high that's counteracting any and all tiredness. Nothing will bring me down any time soon.

"Are you still free this Wednesday night?" I ask as I slide his coffee across the kitchen island to where he's sitting on a stool.

He glances up from his phone. "Yes. For your work dinner?"

I nod. "I have to let them know final numbers today."

"What's it for again?"

"One of the designers we use is hosting it for her clients. It'll only be a small affair. Probably no more than twenty people. You'll likely be suitably bored, so no rooftop sesh for you the night before or you may fall asleep at dinner."

He's amused by that. "Trust me, I've sat through some boring dinners. I'm sure this one will be interesting."

"There will be a lot of fashion talk and a lot of gossip. You won't find any of it interesting."

My phone rings and I check who it is. When I see it's Tilly, I answer it and put her on speakerphone so I can drink some coffee and continue making breakfast while we chat.

"Hey, Till," I answer. "You're on speaker."

"Jenna." She sounds off. Like something bad has happened to her. "Are you okay?"

"Yes, but are you? You sound like someone's died."

"Okay, right, so you haven't seen the news yet."

"No. What's happened?"

"Shit." She pauses. "Fuck. Declan released that sex video you guys made. I'm so sorry, babe."

34

BECKETT

I listen to every word Tilly's saying while keeping my eyes firmly on Jenna.

Declan released the sex video.

"Send me the link," Jenna says to Tilly, her voice wavering.

"No," I cut in. "Don't do that." The last thing Jenna needs is to see that damn video online.

Jenna looks at me questioningly. "I want to see it."

"You don't need to see it," I say, a little more forcefully than I mean to, but I'm too angry to rein it in. "Trust Tilly that it's there."

I see the moment Jenna's hurt and fear and anger kicks in. I also feel it because she lets it loose on me. "Don't tell me what to do, Beckett," she snaps. Then, to Tilly she says, "Send me the link, Till. And thank you for calling to make sure I'm okay."

"I'm going to send the link," Tilly says. "But for the record, I think Beckett's right. You don't actually need to see this."

I am right, but I know Jenna's not going to pay attention. I understand this because I'd likely do the same as her, but I fucking wish I could convince her otherwise.

I pull up my messages while Jenna and Tilly finish their conversation.

Beckett: Reschedule all my morning meetings. I'll be in late.

Louise: You've got a Zoom call with Ted McMaster at 9:00 a.m. Surely you don't want to reschedule that.

She's right; I don't want to. Ted is the government representative I've been liaising with on the contract my company is bidding for. It won't look good for me to reschedule at this last minute.

Beckett: Reschedule it to tomorrow if he can fit me in then.

"I can't fucking believe he did this," Jenna rants.

I can.

And I should have anticipated it.

She stalks out of the kitchen into her bedroom, continuing her rant about what an asshole Declan is. I follow her into her bathroom where she applies lipstick.

Eyeing me in the mirror, she says, "I need to get to the office and begin major damage control. How is this going to affect my meeting with Gordon? Do you think it will influence him at all?"

"It may."

She stops what she's doing. "Give me more than that, Beckett. Would it affect your decision if you were considering investing in my business?"

"It would depend on how this pans out from here."

"So, how I handle this now is super important for that."

"Yes. I have a guy I use occasionally for this kind of thing. I'll call him for you."

She exhales a long breath. "Thank you."

Jenna finishes getting ready faster than she ever has, and five minutes later Davis pulls out from her curb to drive us to her office. She spends the entire trip on her phone, fingers madly flying over it as she starts her damage control. I call Nicholas, the guy I've used to handle problems like this. He's not your usual PR handler; Nick tends to color outside the lines when needed. If anyone can help Jenna, it's him.

After I finish my call, I say to her, "Nick will call you this morning."

She glances across at me. "Oh, thank God. This is worse than I thought it would be. I think if this had happened before I started working with Diana and Adeline, it wouldn't be this bad, but wow, people are nasty online."

"Don't read that stuff."

Her lips pull into a straight line. "It's a little hard when my brand relies so heavily on social media."

"You have a team, Jenna. Let them do their job while you do yours."

"This *is* my job, Beckett."

"No, your job is to look after the clients you style and to be the visionary who guides your team through the expansion you're working on. Checking social media is not part of that job."

Her lips are still in that flat line. "We may need to agree to disagree on this."

"If you want to take your company to the next level, you'll need to find a way to block the bullshit out so you can remain focused. Reading garbage on social media won't help you do that."

"Anything else you want to lecture me on this morning?"

"Fuck," I curse, regretting that we've gone from where we were this morning discussing our Wednesday night dinner plans to this. "I'm not trying to lecture you."

"Well, it feels like a lecture," she says before going back to her phone when a string of texts light it up.

We don't return to our conversation again, and when Davis pulls up outside her office, Jenna says, "Thank you for driving me to work," before reaching for her bag and opening her door to exit the car.

I'm out of the car and around to her side before she has her door closed. I don't usually walk her in, but I want to today. I also want to ensure we move on from the last conversation we had.

Frowning at me, she says, "What are you doing?"

"I'm walking you in."

"I don't need you to walk me in. I'm fine."

Jenna is one of the strongest women I know. I've seen her handle Declan's bullshit over the years and stand strong afterward. I watched her father cut her down on the weekend and saw how she dealt with that. And now, I'm watching her cope with this.

She may be fine, and she may be able to handle everything by herself, but I don't want her to have to do any of this on her own. Not anymore.

"There's a difference between fine and kicking ass, and I know you prefer to kick ass. So let me walk you in, kiss you goodbye, and see for myself that you've got everything you need to get back to kicking ass."

Her chest rises as she takes a deep breath. Letting it out, she moves into me. "I'm sorry I argued with you in the car," she says softly. "I know you're just trying to help."

"I am, but I can see I need to work on my delivery."

She brings her hands to my hips. "You've got a million things on with your work. You don't have time to be walking me in and looking after me."

"I have all the time for you, Jenna."

She stares up at me, taking another breath while her eyes fill with that same hurt I saw in them when Tilly told her about the video going public. "How could I have been so wrong about him?"

I slide my arm around her waist, feeling her question deeply. I worked through all these thoughts after my marriage ended. "Betrayal isn't something we move through quickly. It keeps rearing its head, sometimes at the most unexpected times. You'll question yourself repeatedly, and maybe for a long time, but never forget that you did nothing wrong. You loved well, he didn't, and loving well is what life's about."

She smiles through her hurt. I suspect that hurt might linger for a while. "I did love well. You're right."

I return her smile. "I'm always right."

That gets me an eye roll. Exactly what I was going for. "I do recall times you weren't right."

I put my hand to the small of her back as we walk into her building and listen to her recount the times I haven't been right about something.

I don't bother pointing out that she vividly remembers times from the last couple of years during which she told me I was far too arrogant and overbearing for her.

I also don't tell her that I too vividly recall these moments.

I simply allow her to talk because the more she's thinking about something other than her current problems, the better.

"WHERE TO?" Davis asks when I slide into the back seat of the car after dropping Jenna at work.

I clench my jaw. "Katie Stein's condo."

Katie and I go way back. Davis knows where her condo is because I've been there many times.

I don't pull up my emails on the drive.

I don't check my stocks.

I don't make any calls.

I stare out the window, thinking about Declan.

When I told him he'd regret it if he ever made his sex video with Jenna public, I meant it. However, that was before I started dating Jenna. The dirt I have on Declan that would hurt him could also hurt her. It wouldn't affect her reputation, but it may hurt her to learn these things about him.

I can't decide which way to go with this, which is an unusual predicament for me.

I'm still working through all these thoughts when we arrive at Katie's place. As I enter her building, I call Johnson.

"What's up?" he answers.

"Where are we with that information on Declan?"

"I'm still digging. They've done a good job of keeping this all hushed. Either no one knows the truth, or they've paid people well to keep it hidden."

"Fuck," I mutter. "I need you to work faster on this."

"I'm working as fast as I can, Beckett. This may require time for the development to progress more before the truth will start to show itself."

"Time we don't have." I'd rather use this information to achieve my goal.

We end the call as the elevator arrives. A couple of minutes later, I stride into Katie's foyer where she stands watching me with an expression that reveals her utter contempt for me.

"To what do I owe this non-pleasure?" she says. "Oh, wait, that's right, your dick has led you here."

My contempt matches hers. "Where is he?"

She crosses her thin arms. "He'll be out any minute. He's been waiting for this moment. We both have."

"I wasn't aware you had an issue with Jenna."

"For a smart man, you're being dumb."

"That's because he's fucking pussy-whipped," Declan says, entering the foyer with a smug look on his face.

I look at my old friend, wanting to rip that fucking smug expression from him.

"It's not Jenna we have an issue with," Katie says, "It's you."

I've known Katie since I was eleven. She was part of the set of friends I had that included Annabelle. We remained friends until just after my divorce, although I use the term loosely because she slowly became the kind of woman I want nothing to do with.

Katie became better friends with my wife than with me. She then showed what a good friend she was to Ellen when she made a move on me while we were still married. I turned her down. That was the beginning of the end for us.

It appears Katie has never let that go.

"You put that video out in the world because I refused to fuck you years ago?" My chest is growing tighter with anger every second I stand here staring at these two.

If there's one thing Katie Stein doesn't like, it's being rejected. I should know. She didn't handle it well when I said no to her. It seems she also doesn't like being reminded of rejection. Anger clouds her face as she snarls, "We put it out there because you're an arrogant prick who deserves to lose things he cares about."

Declan steps closer to me. "You've had everything fucking handed to you since you were born. You need to know what it feels like to have things taken away from you."

"You're making no sense," I say as I try to figure out their angle. "We've all had things handed to us since we were born."

"Yes, but you're the only one not fucking losing things," Declan spits.

Something's happened that I'm unaware of. "What have you lost, Declan? From where I'm standing, you've gained ten mil and a fiancé."

Katie answers before he can. "Thanks to you, he's lost his inheritance."

This is news to me. Declan comes from a wealthy family, and while they don't fund his life, he's always anticipated a good inheritance, particularly since he's an only child.

"Dad wiped his hands of me," Declan enlightens me, venom in every word. "That was after a little talk with your father. So, yeah, fuck you, Beckett."

I glance at Katie. "Surely your money will be enough for you both to live on, or did you lose your inheritance too?" I'm being sarcastic, but I see it in her eyes that I've hit on something there.

She squares her bony shoulders. "We don't need their money. We're making our own."

I eye Declan. "Yes, so I've heard."

He reads me perfectly, his eyes instantly filling with menace. "You'd do well to stay the fuck out of that."

"You should know me well enough, Declan," I say a lot more calmly than I'm feeling, "to know I don't let people fuck with me and get away with it."

A knowing look crosses his face. "I imagine you've finally found an exception to your rule." He knows I'll struggle with potentially hurting Jenna if I share the dirt I have on him.

That smug look he wore before returns with a vengeance and so does my intense desire to knock him the fuck out.

Closing the distance between us, I grip his shirt. "Don't fucking count on it. And don't expect me to stay out of your new scheme. I'll expose you for the fraud you are if it's the last fucking thing I do." With that, I shove him away from me.

He crashes into a wall, his anger growing as he hits it. Pushing off from it, he stalks back to me and attempts to punch me. I duck to avoid his fist and then get a punch of my own in. My fist connects with his cheek. Hard. The sound of it is the most satisfying thing I've heard today.

"Fuck you!" he roars, coming at me again.

I avoid his punch. This only riles him up further, and then we're on each other.

Fists are flying.

Buttons are flying.

Blood is being spilled.

This is years' worth of anger and resentment finally being unleashed.

I've never wanted to hurt someone as much as I want to hurt Declan.

For what he's done to me and for what he's done to Jenna.

My fury sits deep in my gut and clenches my chest.

It's so entrenched I'm unsure I'll ever rid my body of it.

We fight so hard we break a vase, smash a mirror, and scatter furniture.

In the end, it's Katie who stops us. If she wasn't here, I'm unsure we would stop until one of us was unable to continue.

Stepping into the fray, she narrowly avoids my fist as she screams, "Enough!"

"Fuck!" I roar, stabbing my fingers through my hair as I survey the damage we've caused.

The foyer is a mess, and Declan and I are too. We've both got cuts and bruises all over us, and our clothes are bloody and torn.

He glares at me. "Get the fuck out of here and don't ever fucking come back!"

I leave.

I have no intention of ever returning.

Davis whistles low as I get in the car. Looking back at me, he says, "You wanna hit up the hospital?"

I reach for the bottle of scotch I keep in the car and pour myself some. "Take me home."

He nods and pulls out into traffic.

I throw some scotch down my throat and call Josh.

He picks up on the second ring. "A Monday morning call. Something must be up. No one interrupts your Monday mornings."

"Declan released a sex video featuring him and Jenna."

"Jesus. How is she?"

"Not great."

"How's he? I imagine you've paid him a visit."

Josh knows me well. "He's not in enough pain as far as I'm concerned."

"So this is a conscience check-in?"

"He needs to be stopped. I can help with that, but it may be at the expense of Jenna's feelings."

"Ah, I see." He turns silent for a moment. "What's Declan up to these days?" Josh knows all about Declan's past deeds. He also knows Declan is a piece of shit who needs to be stopped. I'm not telling him anything he doesn't know here. The difference between us is that Josh has a better moral sense than me when it comes to some things.

I fill him in on what Johnson has learned regarding the shady property development Declan's involved with.

"You're right that he does need to be stopped," Josh says. "How sure are you that your way of doing that would hurt Jenna?"

"I'm not sure at all. It's just a feeling I have."

"Well, the only way you'll know is to talk with her about it. But you know that, Beckett. Why are you coming to me with this?"

I glance out at the city. "For your perspective. I needed to hear you agree that Declan has to be stopped."

"We agreed on that years ago, my friend. It's you that has slowed that process down. Your loyalty is to be commended, but it has been misplaced for a long time."

We end the call and I'm about to phone Jenna when she calls me.

"How's it going? Have you spoken with Nick?" I ask when I answer the call.

She's like a wild gush of energy when she comes back with, "Oh my God, Beckett, I just saw a post from Katie on Instagram. Are you okay? Tell me he didn't hurt you."

"Slow down. What post?"

"She posted a photo of Declan after your fight and said you went over to their place and beat the shit out of him."

This is why I detest social media and refuse to have any part in it. "Don't worry about me. I hurt him more than he hurt me. Talk to me about Nick. How's your damage control going?"

"I don't want to talk about Nick. I want to talk about you! I am so fucking angry with Declan that I could go over there and punch him myself. All the times I looked out for him and fixed his problems were for nothing. That man is the most selfish man I've ever met. I hate that Katie can just spin things to make him look like the victim. The world needs to know what an asshole he really is. I'm so sorry they've put this all on you and made you to be the villain."

"Jenna, there's something I need to—"

"Oh, shit, Beckett," she cuts me off, "I have to go. Sorry. Something has just come up that I have to take care of. I just wanted to make sure you're okay."

"I'm okay. Go. I'll call you later."

I disconnect and pour another scotch.

After I drink it, I call my lawyer and advise him of the situation and that I want that video removed from the internet. He advises that once a video is published, you'll never be able to remove it completely. I tell him to put my team to work on ensuring that fucking video is removed as fast as it continues to surface.

I then call Johnson and fill him in on the sex video situation.

"I need you to look into Declan and Katie. This won't be the last I hear from them; of that, I'm fucking sure. And release the information we have on him."

Josh is right; my loyalty has been misplaced for far too long.

Jenna wants the world to know what an asshole Declan is.

Now, they will.

@thetea_gasp

BIG YIKES, did you all see the tea that's been served on @declanjames? This is some serious tea, no cap. Gather round: he was involved in the #MonarchClub years ago #gasp. And dodged his taxes so he could pay for all that sex #doublegasp. We wonder what @katiestein will make of the fact her fiancé likes high-priced hookers. Oh, the scandal, my friends. We bet she's big mad about it. Only this morning she was posting about #beckettpearce beating her man up. Now, we imagine she's beating him up. It seems that while @jennablaise made some questionable choices in the sex department, she made a good one letting the #thief go. Also, sidenote: scandal is good for Jenna. Her followers just bumped past the 2M mark #straightfire

36

JENNA

Kristen: OMG did you see the news about Declan? The Monarch Club!

Jenna: Yes.

Kristen: That dirty, dirty asshole.

Jenna: Yes.

Kristen: Where do we find these men?

Jenna: This leads me to believe Johnathon has done something new?

Kristen: He's started dating Julie Marx. Can you believe that?

Jenna: Honestly, nothing much surprises me anymore.

Kristen: How's Beckett? I saw he got himself into a fight with the thief. I think we all need a Beckett in our life.

I eye the glass door of Beckett's building that I'm standing in front of.

Jenna: He told me he's okay. I'm about to see for myself. Also, yes, we all do need a Beckett.

And who would have thought I'd say that a month ago?

Oh, how times have changed. In so many ways.

It's just after 2:00 p.m. and I've spent the day sorting through the mess Declan created for me. I've also spent far too much time talking myself out of going to see him.

I want to give him a piece of my mind, but at the same time I don't want to bring his negative energy anywhere near me. I've worked hard on myself since we broke up, and I've reached a good place. Some of that is due to Beckett; most of it is due to me.

I'm feeling more positive and confident in myself than I ever have.

I refuse to allow Declan to mess with that, and being in his space will definitely do that.

The PR guy Beckett put me onto, Nick, has come up with some great ideas to help my brand after Declan tried to ruin it. And interestingly, the sex video seems to have raised my profile rather than trashed it.

I've tried to get hold of Beckett a few times after our call this morning that I had to cut short, but every time I've called, he's been busy. And every time he's returned my call, I've been busy. I had lunch at one thirty and decided I was too tired to keep working. Staying up all night with Beckett was fun, but I'm paying for it today. I've made a mental note to only do that with him on a Friday or Saturday night in future.

I left my office and came straight to his, hoping to catch him in between meetings or calls. I'm just about to step into the elevator when my father calls.

"Hi, Dad," I answer, stepping back from the elevator to let other people in.

"Jenna." His stern tone says everything he doesn't. "I heard about the video Declan shared. What are you doing about it?"

I wonder if I'll still feel like a little girl being chastised when I'm forty? Or when I'm fifty? Or even when I'm sixty? Like, does this ever end between fathers and daughters, or do fathers always have the ability to slay their daughter with one question?

"I've hired someone to help me. It's being taken care of. You don't need to worry."

"I am worried. The company can't afford something like this." When he says "the company", he means his, not mine.

"Honestly, this hasn't affected my business negatively. I doubt it will affect the company."

"Good. Make sure it stays that way."

He disconnects without a goodbye, but then, he often does that. Still, it never makes me feel good, and it really doesn't today.

The ugly feelings left over from the call cling to me as I ride the elevator up to Beckett's office and are still there when I reach the receptionist. She greets me with a smile and calls Louise to tell her I'm here. She then directs me to another elevator and tells me which floor to exit on.

I expect to find my way to Louise when I reach that floor. Instead, I'm greeted by Beckett.

My eyes don't go straight to his suit. They go directly to his face. And all my ugly feelings scatter because now all I can think about is Beckett.

"Oh my God." I step off the elevator and move into him. Bringing my hands to his face, I say, "You told me you were okay. You do not look okay."

Beckett's face is an angry mess of bruises, cuts, and swelling. Clearly his idea of okay and mine are two vastly different things.

He removes my hands from his face. "The swelling makes it look worse than it is."

That's because one of his eyes is swollen almost closed. Soon, he won't be able to see out of it.

"Have you been icing your face? Tell me you have." Maybe I'll go and see Declan after all. I think I want to punch him a few times too now.

"Jenna, stop." He uses his firm voice on me. The one he likes to pull out when he's trying to assume control of a situation, or of me. "I've iced it. I've taken painkillers. I've done everything but go to the damn hospital. Stop fussing over me."

"Right, so just to get things straight; you can fuss all you like over me, and you can give me lists of investors, and you can call your friends in when I have a scandal on my hands, but I need to hold back when it comes to you suffering physical trauma?"

Amusement flares across his face, right before he bends to brush his lips over mine. "Correct," he murmurs, giving me some of the gravel I can't get enough of.

I take hold of his suit jacket. "We'll see about that."

Now, he smiles. "I wouldn't have it any other way."

We watch each other silently, sharing a moment in which no words are required. Then, I say, "You should show me your office."

He directs me into the biggest office I've ever laid eyes on. Just like his home, it's super masculine and screams Beckett from every corner with its grays and black. It also has a spectacular view of Manhattan.

Walking to the window, I say, "More windows that were made for sex."

Beckett sits on the sofa in front of the window. "Is this a fetish I need to be aware of?"

I turn from the view and smile at him as I walk his way and curl up on his lap. His arm comes around me as I say, "Is your body also covered in bruises? Am I hurting you?"

His arm tightens around me. "Don't you dare move."

I gently thread my fingers through his hair. "Today has been the longest, shittiest day of my life. I need a nap."

"This is the worst day you've ever had?"

"Maybe not." I pause, searching his eyes as I add softly, "But I've been worried about you. Plus, I'm really tired. That never helps."

"I do recall it was you who wanted to stay up all night."

"Are you complaining?"

"No, that would be you."

I smile. Then, I kiss him. Very gently because this face of his looks like a masterpiece of pain. "I hate that I brought this to your door. I'm sorry."

"You've got nothing to be sorry for, Jenna. This fight was long overdue."

"Was it you who leaked that information about Declan?" I suspect it was. The timing is too coincidental for it not to have been.

He nods. "Yes. I wanted to prepare you for it before it was published, but we kept missing each other today." He's watching me carefully, like he's concerned about me.

I frown. "Why are you looking at me like that? And why would you need to prepare me for it?"

"I was unsure how you'd feel about it."

"About Declan sleeping with prostitutes?" At his nod, I say, "This all happened before he and I got together." I pause. "Wait, was he still sleeping with them while I was with him?"

"Not that I was aware of, but I think we're both learning that we never truly knew the real Declan."

Beckett is still watching me with care, Like, extreme care. The kind of care that touches me deep in my heart.

This man, who I thought way too many bad thoughts about for too long, has become one of my greatest supporters and protectors.

I kiss him again. "I want you to tell me what you know about all this. I also want you to know that this doesn't make me feel anything you might have been worried about me feeling."

I don't miss the relief in his eyes as he says, "You've heard of The Monarch Club?"

"Yes, my father had a friend who was involved in it."

The Monarch Club was an escort service that supplied high-class prostitutes to politicians and anyone else who was willing to pay their exorbitant prices. The federal government investigated the Club after becoming aware many politicians were involved. Underage prostitutes were being used, and five politicians were arrested, including the governor of New York. The investigation really only focused its efforts on the politicians. Speculation was rife as to who else was involved but never identified.

The club was also well known as the source of any illegal substance your heart desired. In amongst the photos released of Declan today, one showed him snorting coke off a prostitute's stomach. I never saw him indulge while we were together, but then, I never imagined him sleeping with prostitutes. I never imagined any of the things I've discovered about him.

"Declan used the service for a while and got himself caught up in a sting that one of the prostitutes ran after the government began their investigation. She blackmailed him, sending him photos of them together and demanding money to stay quiet. It would have ruined him at the time if it had come out, so I helped him by paying her off and ensuring she never uttered a word of it."

"Was she underage?"

"No."

"I doubt this will really touch him. I mean, years ago when this all went down it would have hurt him a lot, but not now. He seems to have a way of escaping things that would ruin most. Although, the tax evasion might affect him."

"The tax evasion will hurt him."

"I hope so. People need to know who he really is." I run my gaze over his face and down to his throat and chest, looking for more damage. "My father called me. He's not impressed by the sex video."

Beckett tips my chin up to bring my eyes back to his. "What did he say?"

"He told me to make sure this doesn't affect his company."

He works his jaw. "Are you okay?"

Tears unexpectedly well at the back of my eyes. I'm not the kind of woman who cries over things; I just get on with life and make the most of bad situations. But today feels overwhelming.

My father's response, coupled with what he said to me last weekend, feels too hard to deal with today. Damn it, though, I do not want to cry in front of Beckett.

I swallow my hurt as well as I can and nod. "I'm okay."

Beckett's eyes fill with concern, and he softly curses, "Fuck, Jenna, it's okay to not be okay. Your father has said some hurtful things to you."

"Jesus," I mutter as my tears threaten again. "I don't want to cry. I am not a crier. My dad can be mean, yes, but I need to just keep on going." I put my hands to his chest. "What have you got planned this afternoon?"

He doesn't answer me straight away. I think he's assessing the situation and deciding whether to push me to keep talking about my father or not. In the end, he lets it go and says, "I've got some budgets to go over."

"Are they the kind of budgets you could go over in bed?"

He narrows his eyes at me. "Where are you going with this?"

"I need a nap and I was thinking I'd really like to take it in your bed. With you. And since I know you won't blow work off, I was thinking I could nap while you do your work next to me."

Judging by the way Beckett's looking at me, he's never worked from his bed before. How sad for him. I feel it's up to me to rectify this situation for him.

"I promise I won't demand orgasms," I say. "Also, I still have work to do after my nap, so you won't be the only one working."

"Jesus," he says. "We both know where this is going to end up."

I think we're on the same page here.

I'm pretty sure he knows that when I say I won't demand orgasms, what I mean is I won't demand ten of them.

37

JENNA

Shona: How are you after yesterday?

Jenna: I napped all afternoon after convincing Beckett to leave work early with me. I'm good today.

Shona: Nap is now code for sex? Did I miss that somewhere? Also, I may need tips on how to convince your man to leave work early.

Jenna: I promised him no sex.

Shona: And then had all the sex?

Jenna: There were three orgasms in total throughout the afternoon and night. But the thing I'm most proud of is that Beckett Pearce took an actual nap in the actual afternoon.

Shona: Wait, I thought nap was code for sex? I'm so lost.

Jenna: No, I literally napped all afternoon (after one orgasm to begin with) and Beckett literally napped for an hour. Then, he gave me two more orgasms after dinner.

Shona: I feel like all these orgasms are messing with your ability to communicate clearly.

Jenna: Highly likely. Also, Declan James can rot in a hole.

Shona: Attagirl.

Jenna: Are you good?

Shona: Never better. Looking forward to seeing you tomorrow for coffee and a chat xx

STYLING IS A SCHLEP, and I mean a *schlep*.

Before I started my own business, I assisted other stylists. I logged tens of thousands of hours honing my skills. I lugged thousands of garment bags, returning items my clients didn't buy. I gave up nights selecting the right pieces for clients, looking for that one outfit that would suit their particular body shape, coloring, and body image issues. "It can't show my arms", "My boobs are too big for that", "I hate my legs". We all have our thing. We have so many *things*.

It's a schlep.

But it's one I love.

I've developed my own process for working with a client now. One that cuts many hours I used to waste trying to understand their needs. I also have my team these days, and they do most of the grunt work for me.

Except when it comes to my high-profile clients like Adeline and Diana Black. My girls help me by sending links to potential outfits they've seen, but I still put in the hours searching and shopping. I refuse to leave anything to chance. Finding the perfect outfits for these clients spreads amazing word-of-mouth that I need.

I've spent this morning doing a pull for Adeline. She's got a photoshoot and another red carpet this week, and thank God the showroom had some perfect options.

"You've saved me hours," I say to Naomi who has helped me find what I need.

"I hope Adeline loves these dresses as much as we do."

"I think she will."

"What's she like to work with? I've heard she can be difficult."

"That's not been my experience. She knows what she wants and doesn't waste time being delicate, though, so maybe that's why she's got the difficult tag."

"I saw that she came out in support of you yesterday after the video went public."

"Yes. I really appreciated it." Especially after people started slut-shaming me. Both Adeline and Diana Black lent me their support yesterday. The bitchy side of me wanted to forward those Instagram posts to Declan with a big "fuck you". The Blaise side of me refrained.

A text hits my phone and I check it instantly in case it's work. I'm due to meet with Adeline in an hour but she mentioned she may need to push the meeting.

Kristen: CODE RED

Jenna: NO. I can't handle any more bad news this week.

Kristen: I just heard that Katie Stein has been spreading doubts over a Manhattan development that Beckett's involved with.

Jenna: What kind of doubts?

Kristen: She's been pushing for a land use review and trying to get some community groups involved. From what I've heard, it's gathered steam.

Jenna: Oh God.

Kristen: Yes. Exactly.

Those reviews can take a year to unfold, and in some cases can stall a project for years, especially if there's fierce community pushback.

"Everything okay?" Naomi asks.

I glance up at her. "No, I don't think so." I take the garment bag when she hands it over. "Thanks for these. I'll let you know how things go."

I call Beckett on my way back to my office.

"Hi," he answers. I detect the note of stress in his voice. Not something I really ever hear from him.

"Hey," I say softly, feeling a little anxious. I'm worried that dating me is bringing a world of issues his way that wouldn't otherwise have found their way to him. "I just heard something about Katie that I thought you should know."

"What?"

I relay what Kristen told me.

"Yes," he says. "I'm aware. We're working on this today."

"Is it likely to develop into anything, do you think?"

"It looks like it could, but we don't know for sure yet."

"God, I hope not."

"Jenna, don't worry about this. We're handling it."

Beckett sounds distracted, and not wanting to add to his stress, I say, "Okay, I just wanted to make sure you knew about it. I'll let you get back to work."

"I'll see you tonight, but I may be later than I originally said."

Beckett's taking me to Amorosis for dinner and told me he'd pick me up at seven. "I'll see you then."

We end the call and I exhale a long breath.

I really hope the sex video scandal doesn't hurt Beckett's development.

"THIS ONE IS GOOD," Adeline says, running her hands over the royal blue dress I selected for her red carpet this week. "This one"—she eyes the black dress I thought could work well for her photo shoot—"I'm not sure of. I was hoping for color. Red, maybe. Or even white."

I nod. "White could be perfect. Especially with your tan. Oh, wait!" I grab my phone and pull up a dress I found last night while working in Beckett's bed. "What about this?"

She takes the phone and her face breaks out in a smile. Good God, Adeline is stunning, even more when she smiles. "Yes. This is the one."

"I'm on it. And I'll also have a wardrobe for you to go through on Friday for next month's events."

She leans back in her chair and appraises me. "You work fast, Jenna. I'm impressed. I'm also impressed with the clothes you're choosing for me. I've never worked with a stylist so in tune with me."

"I'm glad to hear that. I'm really enjoying working with you."

"How are you doing with the sex video bullshit?"

I smile. I like Adeline's approach to life and inability to suffer fools. I've heard her on the phone a couple of times since working with her when she's put a stop to problems before they blew up. "Mostly it hasn't affected me, but we'll see where that all ends up." I don't mention that I think it's going to hurt Beckett more than me.

"I've had thousands of followers share my shout-out to you in their stories. And I saw Diana Black and many others make positive posts about you. Women want to support women. We're tired of watching each other being dragged down by this kind of stuff. You made a private video for God's sake; Declan had no right to share that with the world."

"Thank you. I appreciate your support."

"Any idea why he shared it?"

"Because he's an asshole. He gave me a necklace when we were together, and he asked for it back. I didn't want to return it, and after I discovered that Beckett was actually the one who paid for it, I didn't return it. Beckett thought he'd managed the situation, but I guess Declan's pissed off he never got it back."

She narrows her eyes at me. "What did you mean when you said you'll see where it all ends up?"

"I'm currently searching for an investor to help me grow the company. I have a meeting scheduled for Thursday and am hoping this video doesn't cause the investor to change his mind on hearing my pitch." Beckett was successful in having the video removed from the site Declan uploaded it to, but copies are everywhere. This won't ever disappear.

She nods slowly, thinking, before reaching for her purse

and standing. "I wish you all the best. Hopefully the investor is switched on enough to know you're going places."

After Adeline leaves, I put a call in to secure the white dress she wants. I then spend time searching for dresses for Diana Black and her friends for her event. In amongst all this, I handle a few issues that Cora brings to me.

By five, I'm exhausted. I do a little more work, though, because there's so much to do, and leave the office at six. I've just walked into my condo when Beckett calls.

"Hey, you," I say, happy to hear from him.

"I'm not going to make it for dinner tonight, sorry."

My disappointment is high but hearing the stress in his voice wipes it away. "You sound stressed. Are you okay?"

"Yeah," he says, but like he was this morning, he's distracted. Distant.

"Do you want me to order you some dinner?"

He doesn't answer me for a few moments. "Sorry, I missed that. What did you say?"

"I was just thinking I could order you some dinner. What do you feel like?"

"No, I'm good. Louise will order something." He pauses. "But thank you."

"If you need anything, let me know."

"I'll talk to you tomorrow."

"Should I cancel you from LaChelle's dinner tomorrow night?"

"No, I think I should be able to make it."

"Okay. I hope you don't have to work too late tonight. I'll talk to you in the morning."

We end the call and I contemplate again how much my video has affected him. I try to put that thought out of my mind, though. It's useless to worry over something I can't control.

TILLY: How was your dinner last night? Did LaChelle reveal any new designs?

Jenna: No, but she gave a hint of what she's working on, and I think I'm in love.

Tilly: Ooh exciting! Was Beckett bored out of his mind?

Jenna: He couldn't make it. Work is kicking his ass this week.

Tilly: *sad face* I wanted to hear all about how he made it through his first fashion dinner.

Jenna: You are too much, Till. He'll be fine with these dinners.

Tilly: Says you. The rest of us know Beckett Pearce and fashion and gossip do not go together. But then, the man is besotted, so who knows.

Jenna: Besotted? I hardly think so.

Tilly: Umm, are we talking about the same man here? I bet you a thousand dollars that if I begged you to beg him to do that interview with me, he would.

Jenna: He wouldn't. I can assure you of that.

Tilly: Shit, gotta run xx

I PLACE my phone on my desk as I scroll my emails. It's just after seven and I've come into work early to do my final pitch preparations for my meeting with Gordon Roth today. Truth be told, I'm as prepared as I'm going to be, but I'm more nervous than I've ever been. I'd hoped to have time to discuss this with Beckett this week, but I haven't seen him since Tuesday morning and there's been no time to chat on the phone either.

"You're early," Cora says, coming into my office.

"You are too."

"Do you want a coffee? I'm gonna go grab one."

"I would love one. Thank you."

She narrows her eyes at me. "You're nervous, aren't you?"

"Yes. There's a lot riding on this." Every other investor I've reached out to from Beckett's list has said no. Two of them made it clear the publicity surrounding the sex video didn't impress them.

"I know, but, Jenna, if anyone can make shit happen, it's you. If this guy says no, you'll find someone else to believe in you. And seriously, have you seen your Insta follower count today?"

I shake my head. "No."

Her eyes widen. "Girl, you just hit five mil. The whole reason I came in early today is because I logged into our emails this morning and saw how many I have to go through. I'm pretty sure we're gonna need to hire more staff soon."

We do need to hire more staff. That, I already know. Expansion is tricky, though. Walking the fine line between managing the finances we have to meet current demand while investing in the resources to meet the growing demand. I really need to find an investor to help me with this.

"Thank you for being so on the ball. I appreciate all the hard work you're putting in, Cora."

She smiles. "I'm excited. Shit's happening. Okay, I'm going to get coffee. Be back soon."

After she leaves, I return to my emails. I've worked my way through three of them when Beckett calls.

"Good morning," I say, leaning back against my chair and smiling as I hear his voice.

"You're not at home."

My smile grows. "You're there?"

"Yes. Where are you?"

"I'm at work."

"I wanted to see you before your pitch today and make sure you have everything you need."

"I think I'm good." As much as I'd love to go over the pitch with him, I know he's busy with his own work.

"Jenna, talk to me. Give me the truth."

"The truth is you're busy. The fact I haven't seen you and

have barely heard from you in two days tells me just how busy. You don't have time for this."

"I've made some time this morning. I'm on my way." His tone conveys he won't be argued with, so I don't bother.

We end the call and I go back to my emails.

Cora returns with coffee, and we have a conversation about what I want her to get done today.

I continue on with my emails. There are a lot today. Between my inbox and Cora's it may take us all day to go through them all.

Cora calls through when Beckett arrives, and he's just entered my office when a new email lands in my inbox.

It's from Gordon Roth.

My heart sinks as I skim it.

He's cancelled our meeting today.

He has no interest in my company anymore.

"Jenna."

My head snaps up at the sound of Beckett's deep voice.

I meet his eyes. They're full of questions. Clearly my disappointment is written all over me.

I try to gulp that disappointment down as I say, "Gordon just cancelled our meeting." I fail bitterly to gulp any of my disappointment down. It paints every word I utter just as much as I'm sure it paints my face.

"Did he give a reason?"

"He said he doesn't think our core values are in alignment, hence we wouldn't be a good fit. I'll add him to the list of people who think I sleep with every man I meet."

Displeasure creases Beckett's features. "No one thinks you do that."

I stand. "They do. You'd know that if you were on social media."

More of that displeasure of his. "This is why I wish you *weren't* on it."

I move into him, needing his arms around me. Brushing my lips over his, I say, "I've missed you."

His arms circle me, and he kisses me again. "The feeling is mutual."

I rest my head against his chest, inhaling his scent, the rich wood one I love. He tightens his arms around me and allows me the space to take a minute here in silence with him.

"I've had enough of this week," I say.

"I have too."

I look up at him. "Are you making progress on your issues?"

"Slowly. We've got a lot of work ahead of us."

"And this was all caused by Katie?"

"Yes, she and Declan seem to have made it their personal mission to stop the project. They've bitten off more than they can chew, though, and will regret it."

"How so?"

"Ashton Scott and Jameson Fox are my partners in this development."

That's all he has to say. I don't know much about Ashton, but I do know that Jameson isn't a man to be fucked with. The same as Beckett. I can imagine the lengths these men will go to in order to ensure their project goes ahead.

His phone buzzes with a few texts and he reaches into his pocket for it to check them. I watch as he works his jaw while reading the texts. His eyes then find mine again, filled with regret. "I cleared time for you but something urgent has come up. I have to handle it."

I nod and step out of his hold. "Of course." I grip his suit jacket, not wanting to let him leave even though I know I have to. "Call me this afternoon if you get time," I say softly.

"I'll make the time." He pauses. "I'll think about who else might invest in your company."

"No. Don't even think about that while you've got so much on your mind. I'm going to figure this out."

His phone buzzes again and he kisses me once more before leaving.

I stare after him, hating Declan and Katie for doing this to him. I can deal with everything they do to me, but I hate knowing I brought all this on Beckett.

38

@thetea_gasp

THE STRESS IS SHOWING FOR #beckettpearce while he scrambles to keep his hotel development with #jamesonfox & #ashtonscott together. Trouble is also brewing for his old bestie @declanjames who has the eyes of the IRS on him now. We can report that Declan still also has the eyes of @katiestein on him. There's no tea to be spilled there #love-birds. As for @jennablaise, her sex video has done wonders for her. She styled @anastasiabrady for a red carpet this week and is also now working with @jettvaughn and @diesel #blaisinghot. She and Beckett seem loved up too. They were spotted last night at @rubypearce's art gallery opening. Jenna is clearly soothing some of his stress if the way he was looking at her is anything to go by. We're keeping our eyes on #jeckett. So many predictions there #staytuned

39

BECKETT

Ruby: Thank you for coming to the opening last night. I know the last two weeks have been crazy for you with work.

    Beckett: It was a great night, Ruby. Congratulations.

    Ruby: We didn't get a chance to catch up last night. Any end in sight for this land review bullshit?

    Beckett: No. I suspect it will drag on for a while.

    Ruby: I'm sorry.

    Ruby: Are you free for dinner tonight? Jenna too? Just casual at my place.

    Beckett: I'll get back to you.

I glance up as Mac enters the boardroom where I'm working. "You got a minute to go over some figures?"

I nod. "Yes."

He places his laptop on the table and spends the next fifteen minutes running through projections for a property development in Florida we're working on. "It's tracking well and will come in on budget if things progress as well as they are."

I exhale a long breath. "Finally, something's going our way."

The last two weeks since the day I confronted Declan have been hell. It's been one fucking problem after another. I've had to dedicate more time than I have to spare working with Jameson and Ashton on the hotel development that Declan is hell-bent on blocking. I've also had to keep up with my other projects. Finding time for Jenna has proven difficult and I've canceled more dinners and time with her than I preferred.

"Yes," Mac says, but his tone is hesitant.

"What?"

"I think we may have an issue with the government contract."

"What kind of issue?" It wasn't well received when I asked to reschedule my Zoom call with Ted McMaster, but I was not aware we had a problem.

Mac appears pained to volunteer the information I've requested. "To put it bluntly, your association with Jenna Blaise could impact your success with the contract."

"In what way?"

"I've heard McMaster doesn't approve of her."

"What the fuck does his approval of her have to do with an aircraft contract?"

"One would think nothing, but it does. He's known for awarding contracts based on factors that have nothing to do with the key criteria. Personal preference for who he works with is one of those factors, and McMaster is a conservative who, I've heard, wasn't a fan of her sex video."

I stand. "So, what, we won't win it?"

"I'm keeping an eye on the situation. I just wanted to bring you up to speed for now."

"You have a contact with an in?"

"Yes. He's advised me that McMaster hasn't ruled us out, but that he's watching Jenna's profile." He checks his watch. "I have another meeting."

"Thanks for this information."

"I'll let you know when I hear more, but think about what I've said."

After he exits the room, I contemplate what we discussed. I

come to the conclusion that the bid we submitted was competitive enough to win the contract, and McMaster would be a fool not to award it to us.

Johnson calls me as I'm thinking about this.

"What's up?" I say as I go back to the documents I've got spread across the boardroom table.

"A competitor of Ruby's is looking at renting space in a building near her. They're not a big gallery at the moment, but this building will give them the ability to expand, and from what I've learned they intend on being quite aggressive in their campaign to attract the best artists and collectors. I'm emailing you the info on the building."

"Any update on Declan's development?"

"I've got a new lead I'm following up. It's one of the architects involved. I'm hoping she'll either be able to give us documents to support what I've heard or help us find someone who can give us those documents or other evidence."

"Good. Thanks for the information on the art gallery."

Johnson disconnects as Annabelle's voice sounds from outside the boardroom. "I'll only be a minute, Louise," she says before entering the room.

Louise is right behind her, a look of frustration on her face. She looks at me apologetically. "I'm sorry for the intrusion, Beckett. I was just explaining to Annabelle that you don't have a spare minute today."

Annabelle waves her off with her signature dismissive gesture. "That's all I'll be. One minute."

I nod at Louise. "Give us a minute."

Louise is correct in that I don't have a spare minute today, but I do need to have a word with Annabelle and ensure she understands I have no feelings toward her, so now is a good time for that conversation.

After Louise leaves us, Annabelle says, "I wanted to stop by and make sure you're okay after all the nasty Declan business the last couple of weeks. I also heard, on the hush, that he was sleeping with your wife while you were married and also after the divorce. I'm so sorry you had to deal with that, Beckett."

My ex-wife was paid well in our divorce settlement to not utter a word about it, so I know she's not the one who has shared this information with the world. The only other person it could come from is Declan. Or Katie.

"There's no need to worry about me," I say.

"I feel sorry for your friend too. Poor Jenna. How must she feel knowing Declan cheated on her for their entire relationship?"

"I'd appreciate it if you didn't repeat any of this, Annabelle."

"Oh, of course. This goes no further."

"Thank you."

"I also wanted to invite you to my annual family weekend at the Hamptons next weekend. I know my father would love to see you there."

"I'm busy next weekend. But regardless—"

She moves close to me. "It's not something you can reschedule? I would love to have you with me for the weekend, darling." She places her hand to my chest as she says darling.

My hand is around her wrist before her fingers have had barely a second to rest against my body. "No, it isn't something I can reschedule." I remove her hand from my chest. "This isn't going to happen the way you want it to, Annabelle."

"Okay, well how about we plan another weekend together, then? We could—"

"No," I say more forcefully. "I'm dating Jenna."

She blinks. "I know you made a tax-deductible donation in a charity auction for a date with her."

"The money I paid for that date had nothing to do with a tax deduction and everything to do with me wanting dinner with her."

She's silent for a long moment. "You can't be serious. Jenna is.... Well, she's hardly marriage material."

"I'm deadly serious."

"Right," she says matter-of-factly, "I see."

"What do you see?"

"I see you're still working your way through Manhattan. I can be patient."

"Patient for what?"

"Oh, come on, Beckett, you and I have been dancing around each other our entire lives. I'm just waiting for you to finish doing what you need to do before you're ready to finally settle down. I have to say, though, I'm growing impatient."

"We've been friends for a long time, but that's all we've been and all we'll ever be. I'm unsure what gave you the impression I was interested in something more."

The boardroom phone rings, and since only Louise knows I'm in here and I'm waiting on important information, I say to Annabelle, "Sorry, I need to take this."

I answer the call. "Yes?"

"I know you're busy, but you gave me clear instructions to always be interrupted if Jenna calls."

"Put her through."

"No, she's here. Shall I send her in?"

"Yes."

I place the phone down and Annabelle comes close again, placing her hand to my chest, again. "I understand what you're saying."

I remove Annabelle's hand as Jenna enters the boardroom. My eyes are instantly drawn to her and unable to look away. She's wearing a multi-colored, metallic skirt that looks like an array of rainbows with a black T-shirt that has a rainbow strip of colors in the center of it. The words *Spank Me, It's The Only Way I'll Learn* are scrawled across the top of that strip.

She glances at Annabelle for a brief moment before giving me all her attention, and hell if I don't feel all that attention in my dick. It's only been four hours since I've seen her, but these days, four hours feels like an eternity where Jenna's concerned.

"Hey, baby," she greets me, using a term of endearment

she's never used with me. Moving into me, she places her hands to my chest and brushes her lips over mine. It's not a long kiss, but it's not short either. Then, staying right where she is, she looks at Annabelle and says, "Hi, Annabelle. How are you?"

My hand curves over her ass while Annabelle looks her up and down. "That outfit is interesting. Where did you find it?"

Jenna glances down at her clothes. "Isn't it fabulous? I have a range of boutiques I frequent, but I can't recall which one I got these pieces from. I'm more than happy to send you my list if you'd like. Actually, I'm thinking of dragging Beckett shopping with me on the weekend. I'll let you know if I see anything similar."

Annabelle looks anything but pleased with that offer. Ignoring it completely, she says, "Right, well I have to go. I'm having lunch with the girls. You know how it is; one can't be late."

Jenna presses herself harder against me, her fingers curling around my neck as she says, "Oh, I'm a little jealous. I've been so busy with Beckett and all the sex we've been having that I haven't had lunch with my girlfriends for weeks. Have a wonderful time."

Annabelle stares at her, not uttering a word. I'm fairly certain it's the only time I've ever seen her speechless. Then, recovering, she looks at me and says, "I'll call you."

With that, she exits the boardroom.

I bend my mouth to Jenna's ear. "Baby?"

"I thought I'd try it out. I'm not convinced it's for us." She kisses me. For nowhere near long enough. "Do you like my T-shirt?"

I untuck her T-shirt from her skirt so I can slip my hand under it. Finding skin, I make my way up to her breast while I murmur, "There are a lot of things I like right now."

"It's my shoes doing it for you, isn't it?"

I glance down at her pink heels before meeting her gaze

again. "For the record, I won't be going shopping with you on the weekend. Or ever."

A sexy smile takes over her face. "For the record, there is no way I would ever allow you to come shopping with me. Ever."

I drop my mouth to her neck and kiss her while I lift her shirt over her head.

Jenna begins working her way down the buttons on my shirt. "Do you want to know what's doing it for *me* right now?"

I unclasp her bra and let it fall to the floor. "What?" I ask before taking her breasts in my hands and a nipple between my lips.

Her fingers thread through my hair as she arches into me. "Two things. Firstly, that you're going to fuck me on this table where anyone can walk in. This might be the hottest thing I've ever done. And second, seeing you remove Annabelle's hand from your body. That might be the hottest thing *you've* ever done."

"Fuck," I growl, lifting her and placing her on the boardroom table, on top of all my documents. "Spread your legs for me."

She lies back on the table and does as I say, kicking her heels off, bending her legs at the knees, and spreading them wide.

I grip her hips and pull her closer.

I lift her skirt and bend my mouth to her pussy.

I kiss her through her panties before removing them.

"You are so fucking wet. Did you come here for this?"

She reaches for my hand and directs my fingers to her cunt. "No, but that doesn't mean you shouldn't hurry up and get inside me."

I slide a finger through her wetness before rubbing her clit and bending to give her my mouth.

"Oh, God, that feels good," she moans, arching up off the table.

She grips my hair as I circle her clit with my tongue. Her fingers grip me harder when I push two fingers inside her.

I suck and lick and finger her.

Her body curves up off the table over and over as I work her towards her orgasm, and she grips and releases my hair while the waves of pleasure consume her.

I edge her close and then pull back, lifting my face to kiss her inner thighs before going back to her pussy.

"You're trying to kill me, aren't you?" she says. "Give me my orgasm already."

I lick her pussy as I meet her gaze. "I'm teaching you some patience."

"I don't need to learn patience, Beckett."

I slide my tongue inside her, not taking my eyes off hers.

I fuck her with my tongue, watching as her orgasm teases its way through her.

When she arches her back, I stop and circle her clit with my tongue.

I repeat these things again, inching her closer and closer until she can't take any more.

Jenna loses herself on my boardroom table and I make a note to fuck her on it every chance I get.

"Beckett!" she cries out when she finally comes, flinging her arms across the desk, and pressing her cheek against my documents as I keep working her clit with my tongue.

When it becomes too much for her, she sits up and forces me to stop. Then, reaching for my belt, she says, "I need you inside me."

I kiss her while she undoes my belt, making my way down to her breasts so I can dedicate time to them.

"Beckett." She pulls my face back up to hers so she can kiss me again. She's rough. Demanding. "I need you to fuck me with your dick on this table."

"Jesus," I growl. "This mouth is getting filthier."

"That's because you're bringing it out in me." She madly

undoes the button on my pants. Then the zipper. And then she has my cock in her hand.

"Fuck," I hiss as she strokes me.

Her hand curls around my neck and she pulls me in for another kiss.

I'm fucking drunk on her kisses.

Drunk on her body.

Drunk on her.

Wrapping one of her legs around me, I grip her hips and growl against her ear, "Hold on tight," before thrusting inside her.

She cries out with pleasure and holds on tightly as I fuck her how she prefers to be fucked.

Hard and rough.

Her nails dig into my skin.

Her legs cling to me.

Her teeth graze me.

Sex with Jenna is the best goddamn sex of my life, and not just because we're a match physically.

There's more to it with her.

I feel her in it with me.

Her soul.

Her heart.

Her.

She's right there by my side.

Giving.

Taking.

Needing me as much as I need her.

Even here, on my boardroom table, fucking each other wildly, this is more than purely physical.

This is us chasing everything we've ever wanted.

With each other.

As she finds release, Jenna grips me harder.

Her pussy squeezes my dick.

And she cries out my name.

She kisses me after I come. Then, her eyes find mine. "Do you think anyone heard us?"

I claim another kiss. "Not a chance. You barely make a noise while I fuck you."

She swats me playfully. "You are the worst, Beckett Pearce."

"I'll soundproof the room if you're worried."

She smiles. It's sexy as hell. "While you're at it, soundproof your office. Those windows are calling my name."

"Jesus, I'm never going to get any work done in there again."

We use the bathroom to clean up, and once we're both dressed, I say, "Was there a reason you dropped by?"

She surveys the mess of documents on the boardroom table as we walk back into the room. "Next time, I'm giving you a blowjob before you fuck me on that table." Then, stopping and moving into me, she says, "You were a little distracted this morning. I wanted to check in on you."

My hand goes to her ass. "You could have called."

"I could have, but I wanted to see you. The last couple of weeks have been a blur. I feel like I haven't seen you enough. And"—her voice softens—"you didn't dance with me this morning. I feel like we haven't danced enough this week."

I've learned over the past month that for Jenna, dancing in the kitchen is akin to having sex. She craves the connection both provide, with dancing giving her a slightly different way to be close with me. She wants time together in which the world is shut out while it's just the two of us. Sometimes, there's no talking, but usually it's the time she uses to catch up on my day with me and to share the things from her day that were important to her.

What she's telling me now isn't so much that she's missing my body moving with hers in the kitchen, but that she's missing the chance to connect with me.

"Can you clear your weekend?" I ask.

She thinks about that for a few moments before nodding.

"I've got that meeting with Geraldine Matheson early tomorrow, but after that I'm free."

Jenna's meeting with Geraldine to discuss her potential investment in her company.

"We'll go to the Hamptons."

Her brows pull together. "Can you take the time off?"

I can't, but I will for her.

"I'll have to take some work with me, but I can do it while you shop and swim."

Still frowning, she argues, "Beckett, no, I don't want—"

"Let me worry about what I can and can't do. I want this time with you. Also, Ruby invited us to dinner tonight. Just casual, at her place."

A smile replaces her frown. "That sounds good."

"I'll tell her yes."

"Will you pick me up or should I meet you there?"

"I'll pick you up. Around seven." I bend my mouth to her ear. "Afterward, I'll take you home and fuck you in front of my windows."

The kiss I'm blessed with after that is the kind of kiss that will make it hard for me to concentrate for the rest of the day.

40

JENNA

After I leave Beckett's office, I spend the afternoon seeing clients, replying to emails, and finalizing my pull appointments for tomorrow to grab pieces for Diana Black. Her event is coming up and we plan to finalize her selection on Monday.

I receive a text from Tilly just after 4:00 p.m. that ruins my afternoon.

Tilly: Holy fuck, babe, have you seen what Declan's done now?

Jenna: Honestly, I've decided I have a strong aversion to the words "have you seen what Declan's done now?" Feel free to never text them to me again.

Tilly: I'm taking that as a no, you haven't seen.

Jenna: Right, so now that we've started this conversation, I'm going to need you to finish it with the aforementioned information.

Tilly: Are you trying to impress me with your big words today?

Jenna: Tilly! Spill.

Tilly: He posted shit about you sleeping with Beckett while dating him. He says he always suspected something between the two of you.

Jenna: WHAT???

Tilly: IKR. I'm actually wondering if he was drunk when he posted it. His sentences were a little disjointed.

Jenna: I WILL FUCKING KILL HIM.

Tilly: Oh thank, God, the real Jenna is back. Does this mean you've stopped working on recharging your vibration? Like, I have no clue how you haven't already killed him.

Jenna: Trust me, I've wanted to, but I've come to the point where I know it's not healthy for me to be around him. Me killing him today isn't for me. It's for Beckett. Declan has caused enough problems for him.

I pack up my laptop and gather my things to leave the office. I know I won't be returning to work after I see Declan. I'm fairly certain seeing him will mean I get no more work done today.

I say goodbye to Cora, and after answering her questions as to the tasks I want her to complete before she goes home tonight, I exit the office and head to Katie's condo where I'm hopeful Declan will be.

I read the post Tilly alerted me to, and I have to agree with her that Declan came across like he was drunk. God knows where his mind is these days. I imagine having the IRS looking at you wouldn't be a pleasant experience, so perhaps that's fueling his hate and lies.

The post he made this afternoon was filled with hate. Lies, too, but it was the hate that struck me the most. And I have no idea where it's coming from because he was the one who cheated on me and caused us to break up.

When I arrive at Katie's place, she's not home, but Declan is. He lets me in and meets me in the foyer when I step off the elevator.

I suck in a breath at his disheveled appearance. I've never seen him like this. His hair is sticking out everywhere, his face is unshaven, his clothes are wrinkled, and everything else about him screams neglect.

His eyes flash with the same hate I read in his Instagram post. Taking a swig of the scotch he's holding, he snarls, "You finally deemed me worthy of a visit, Queen Jenna."

Everything about what he just said, down to the tone he took, provokes deeper anger in me. "I don't deem you worthy of anything, Declan. And I can't believe I ever did."

"Let's be honest here, Jenna All that time you were with me, you were just trying to get closer to my best friend. Trading up was the name of the game, wasn't it, sweetheart?"

I stare at him, unable to believe the words coming out of his mouth. But then, Beckett was right when he told me we're both learning that we never really knew the real Declan. This hate spewing from him can't be new; he hid it well all those years we were together.

"Do you truly believe I was sleeping with Beckett while we were together, or is this just part of your plan to ruin me?"

"I have no doubt you were fucking him while we were together. Why the fuck else would he pay for your necklace twice?"

That slows me down, causing me to frown. "What are you talking about?"

Some kind of realization spreads across his face. "Well, fuck me," he says before throwing some more scotch down his throat. "He didn't tell you."

"Tell me what?" I snap, my patience with him waning.

"Why did you think I stopped asking for the necklace back?"

"Beckett told me he paid for it originally and that I should keep it."

"And you thought that would be enough for me to stop asking for it back? Your naivety of the world you live in knows no fucking bounds. Mommy and Daddy did a superb job of sheltering you from shit."

"Fuck you, Declan." This is something he said to me a few times during arguments we had. He knows it never fails to miss its mark because I've always disliked the men in my life sheltering me from things. My father does it to my mother, Kristen, and me. My brothers do it to Kristen and me. They say they're trying to protect us, and I understand that, but I don't like being blindsided when life slaps me in the face with the things I know nothing of.

A nefarious smile works its way onto his face. The bastard is enjoying this; me standing here like an idiot waiting for whatever he's about to tell me.

He drags the moment out, slowly drinking his scotch. Finally, he says, "Beckett paid me off. He knew I only wanted the cash I could get for it, so he gave me the fifty k instead. He bought that fucking necklace for you twice."

And there's the slap.

I meant absolutely nothing to Declan.

When I continue standing in front of him like an idiot, a silent idiot, he says, "How does it feel, Jenna, to be nothing but a paid whore? He bought you, and I imagine he's still paying to get between your legs."

I stride toward him and slap him. "Beckett is so unlike you it isn't funny. Don't ever say that to me again."

He arches his brows as he recovers from the sting of my hand against his cheek. "Or what, you'll send him back over to beat me up again?"

I narrow my eyes at him. "Do you know what I'm having trouble understanding in all this? Why you shared that video. Why do you hate me so much that you did that? Because although you're standing here accusing me of sleeping with Beckett while we were together, we both know you don't actually believe that." I stop talking suddenly as a thought flashes through my mind. "Wait, you *do* believe that? You did all this because you're jealous?"

His lips smash together and his face clouds with fury. Leaning toward me, he spews his jealousy. "I fucking loved you and wanted to marry you, and you just walked away without a backward glance. And then you started showing up on the arm of my best friend. I have to listen to everyone going on about Jenna and Beckett. It's everywhere I look. Instagram, TikTok, TMZ. And Katie never fucking shuts up about it." He stabs his fingers through his hair. "There's no way you weren't sucking his dick while we were together, Jenna. You always wanted more than I could ever give you, and it seems you figured out how to get it."

I slap him again.

And again.

These ones are for me this time.

"First, he wasn't your best friend when I started showing up on his arm. Your memory is shit. Second, you had a funny way of showing how much you loved me. I mean, if sleeping with another woman is how you show love, then sure, I feel really fucking loved. Third, I'm glad you're being subjected to me and Beckett everywhere. And yes, I'm aware that makes me sound like a bitch, but since you already think that's what I am, I'll just go ahead and own it. Fourth, I see now that you never knew me. I don't want more money. I want more love. More fun. More life. And I want those things with a man who knows how to love deeply and who respects me enough to never allow another woman to touch him. And fifth, I wish I'd been sucking Beckett's dick for all those years. I wasted them on you instead, but you taught me well, Declan. I thank you for that."

With one last look at the man I hope to never see again, I turn and exit the condo. Walking away from him this time, I don't give the asshole a backward glance. Contrary to what he thinks, I did give him one last time. Now, though, I've cleared him from my system completely.

~

BECKETT: *Something's come up at work. I'll have to meet you at Ruby's now.*

Jenna: No worries. I'll see you there.

Beckett: I'll send Davis to collect you at 7.

Jenna: Thank you.

I place my phone in my purse as I enter my condo. I've just arrived home after seeing Declan and I plan to celebrate that visit with a scotch. I still have some of the Balvenie that Beckett brought with him the first time I invited him here. I pour myself a glass and sit on my sofa to drink it.

Beckett paid for my necklace twice.

He's always looking out for me.

I would have preferred to know, though, so that's a conversation we need to have.

But it can't be denied how cared for his gesture makes me feel.

It also can't be denied how clean of Declan I feel after visiting him. I thought going to see him wouldn't make me feel good, but it's done the opposite.

My phone sounds with a text, so I get up to check it.

Adeline: Are you free right now?

Jenna: Yes, why?

Adeline: I have a date and could do with your help.

Jenna: You want me to come over? Or do you want to send me photos of the outfits you're choosing between?

Adeline: I want you to come over and advise me here.

Jenna: I'm on my way.

～

BY THE TIME I'm finished with Adeline and her date stress (who knew a woman like Adeline would still experience nerves over a date?!), I don't have time to go home and change for dinner. I don't stress over that because it's Ruby we're having dinner with. She's so easygoing and casual that I could turn up wearing sweatpants and a messy bun for dinner and she wouldn't care.

After texting Beckett to let him know I wasn't at home, he

sent Davis to collect me from Adeline's home. We pull up outside Ruby's place just before seven thirty and I thank him for driving me.

He smiles at me in the rearview mirror. "I've worked for Beckett for years, and have never seen him as happy. You keep putting that smile on his face, and I'll keep driving you anywhere you want to go."

"You two look out for each other, don't you?" I've observed how friendly Beckett and Davis are at times, and I really like it. My father has had the same driver for decades and barely engages in conversation with him.

"Yes ma'am. Beckett has provided well for my family from the first day I started working for him."

I return his smile. "He's lucky to have you, Davis."

I exit the car and walk into Ruby's building. I spend the ride up to her condo replying to an email from Diana Black and am deep in thought over that when I step into Ruby's foyer. We may have a problem with the dresses I've selected for one of her friend's for the event, but since that's not something I can fix tonight, I slip my phone back into my purse and decide to relax and enjoy dinner with Ruby and Beckett. God knows, he and I could do with a night off all the stress we've been dealing with for weeks.

"Jenna."

My head snaps up at the sound of Beckett's mother's voice.

What? I didn't know she'd be here tonight.

I blink as I take in the fact Margaret Pearce is very much here tonight.

"Oh my God, I love that shirt!" Ruby exclaims as she joins us.

I look down at my T-shirt.

The one that suggests I want to be spanked.

What I actually want right now is to die.

Right here.

In Ruby's foyer.

Why did I think it a good idea to wear this shirt today?

"Where did you get it?" Ruby asks.

I don't miss the way her mother's lips pull together disapprovingly.

"I can't recall," I say.

Is it hot in here?

Like, I think I'm burning alive.

My face is so hot it could melt right off me.

"If you ever remember, you must let me know," Ruby says before ushering us into her great room. "What would you like to drink?" she asks as I sit on her sofa.

Everything.

I want everything she has on offer.

"What are you drinking?" I ask.

"A martini."

"That sounds great."

Ruby makes drinks while Margaret and I sit in silence. The kind of silence that leaves me feeling awkward.

In my desperation to not feel so awkward, I open my mouth and throw out, "I saw Annabelle today." *Oh my God, where the hell did that come from?*

Margaret eyes me, coolly as ever. "How was she?"

"Good. I think. I mean, I didn't really speak with her for very long. She was with Beckett when I arrived at his office. They were discussing, well, I'm not sure what they were discussing, but she and I talked about clothes shopping. I offered to send her a list of my favorite places to shop."

Dear God, please let the earth swallow me up whole.

Right. Now.

Or at the very least, please send divine intervention and force my mouth to stay closed. I must not speak again tonight.

Margaret remains silent, watching me, imagining ways to pry her son away from me. Well, that last thing is just what I'm guessing. Who knows what runs through this woman's mind.

Ruby glances at me, an amused expression on her face.

I commence praying. Not something I'm known to ever do, but a girl needs all the help she can get when she rocks up to a dinner wearing a *Spank Me* tee only to discover the mother of the man she's currently demanding orgasms from is also attending said dinner.

"How is the gallery, Ruby?" I ask.

She brings my cocktail over and sits across from me, next to her mother. "Really good. The sense of community among the Tribeca gallerists is strong, which makes it a nice change from the Chelsea galleries. They make an effort to work together and to get to know each other. I love that community feel, you know?"

I do know.

Business is hard enough; dealing with cutthroat, and sometimes vicious competitors only makes it harder.

"Business isn't for the weak," Margaret says. "You'll need to toughen up to survive, Ruby."

I'm going to need another martini.

"I know that, Mom," Ruby says. "But it's nice to be among humans who care for each other."

"Well, your father and your brothers didn't get where they are today thanks to getting on with people. They got where they are thanks to getting on with the work required of them." She glances at me. "If anything, the people you form relationships with can harm you more than help you."

I stare at her.

She's referring to my relationship with Beckett.

And without even knowing it, she's hit on a fear of mine.

All the problems Beckett is currently facing in his business are thanks to his association with me, and my ex's jealousy.

"That's utter bullshit," Ruby says, instantly drawing her mother's attention away from me and back to her.

"Language, Ruby," Margaret chastises.

Fuck.

Must watch my language.

I gulp some of my martini.

It really is hot in here.

My phone buzzes with a string of texts.

Margaret shoots me an unimpressed look when I reach for my phone.

"Sorry," I apologize. "It could be work."

It's not work.

Kristen: Johnathon is also dating Charlene Armand. AND Sheryl Braithwaite. Can you believe that?

Kristen: Seriously, how lonely is his dick?

Kristen: And to be honest, he barely knows what he's doing with that dick.

Kristen: Also, it's small. I never told you that, but it is.

Kristen: It's tiny and it's useless and I never liked sucking it.

Dear God.

Jenna: Are you drunk?

Kristen: No. Why do you always think I'm drunk when I share intimate information with you?

Jenna: Because sharing intimate information with me is something new for you. I can't recall you ever saying dick to me before all this blew up with Johnathon.

Jenna: Also, I can't chat. I'm at dinner with Beckett's mother.

I put my phone away and go back to the conversation with Margaret and Ruby.

"So," Ruby says, "I saw Anastasia Brady raved about working with you on Insta. Did you love working with her too? She's one of my favorite actresses."

"She's lovely," I say as my phone sounds with more texts. I ignore them. "And so easy to work with. I've been fairly lucky with the celebrities I've worked with. None of them have been too difficult."

My phone buzzes again and Margaret arches her brows. "Do you often have to work over the weekend?" she asks.

"Sometimes." I check my phone again.

Kristen: Oh God.

Kristen: How is she?

Kristen: Can you imagine how life will be if you continue dating Beckett? I'm not sure I could go on if she was part of the deal.

Jenna: Stop texting me. She's judging me for all my texts.

I would switch my phone to silent, but I never do. Not when I have clients who may need to reach out.

"I'm sorry," I say. "Work is super busy right now."

"Which is fabulous!" Ruby says. "You must tell us more about your work. I'd love to know how you got into styling and what it actually involves. Like, is it as glamorous as people think?"

I sip my drink. "It's definitely not as glamorous as people think." I then proceed to give them the basics of how I got started when I was eighteen and how I spend my days. And when I say "the basics", I mean I ramble far more than I would prefer because Margaret's icy gaze is putting me on edge and making sure words just keep on finding their way out of my mouth.

Ruby receives a call as I'm finishing my monologue and excuses herself to take it, leaving me alone with Margaret.

I finish my drink and stand to make another. My manners are completely forgotten as I do this. I can't wait for Ruby to return. I do locate one tiny manner, though, and offer to make Margaret a drink.

"No, thank you," she declines. Then, as I'm pouring the gin, she says, "This relationship you're in with my son won't go anywhere, Jenna."

I stop pouring for a moment.

I then resume pouring, adding extra gin.

God knows I'm going to need it.

I don't know how to respond to Margaret, so I don't.

"He's still working his divorce out of his system," she

continues. "And quite honestly, you're not the kind of woman he usually dates. This is clearly just some fun for Beckett, and I think you should be aware of that. I wouldn't like to see you get hurt."

Ah, no.

No, she doesn't get to do this to me.

I put up with enough of this shit from my father; I refuse to put up with it from anyone else.

I finish making my drink and return to my seat.

After I take a sip of my martini, I place the glass on the table between us. Then, in the calmest voice I can find, I say, "Please don't talk down to me and pretend to care about me, Margaret. You're not saying any of this because you don't want to see me get hurt." I pause and narrow my eyes at her. "I'm guessing you were the quintessential mean girl when you were younger. You do it so well now that it has to be a skill you developed early on. The thing is, I'm well-versed in mean girls and I can hold my own. As far as my relationship with your son goes, that's between him and me. And quite honestly, I don't think Beckett's just having some fun. You seem to have forgotten I've known him for two years and have seen what having fun with women looks like for him. I can assure you, I am far more than some fun for him."

Hot damn, someone needs to turn a fan on in here.

And I need to guzzle this martini in front of me.

Margaret's icy gaze turns positively Arctic (and yet, I'm still dying of heat over here). "We shall see," she says.

I mean, *that's it?*

That's all she's got after everything I just said to her?

I feel like my mother let me down by not sending me to the etiquette school that teaches one how to be an ice-cold bitch. Not that I really want to be one, but there are times, like right now, where the skill would come in handy.

I pick up my martini and proceed to try not to guzzle it when Beckett strides into the room. His eyes come straight to me and he watches as I inhale my cocktail. A knowing look passes through his eyes, followed by one of apology.

There's nothing to be forgiven. One can't choose their parents.

Ruby walks in after Beckett, and after he's greeted his mother, she hugs him. "Do you want a drink?"

He nods. "A scotch. What's for dinner?"

"Are you starving, or can you wait? I'm ordering pizza."

"I'm hungry now."

"Okay, I'll get your drink and then I'll order dinner."

Margaret stands. "I'll leave you to catch up and have your dinner."

I frown, wondering if she's leaving early because of me.

Her departure is a noisy affair thanks to Ruby who bombards her with a thousand questions about a lunch they have planned on Sunday. Margaret does say goodbye to me, but it's clear she's drawing on her manners for that.

I say goodbye from the sofa and sip my martini.

Beckett says goodbye to his mother, and as she and Ruby exit the room, he comes to sit with me. Placing his hand on my thigh, he says, "How brutal was that?"

I angle my body toward his, bringing my leg up to rest on his thigh. "Let's just say I'll be looking for many orgasms tonight to make myself feel better."

"I'm sorry. I'll speak with her about this."

I shake my head. "Don't you dare. Your mother needs to know I can stand on my own two feet."

"I don't want you to have to deal with her like that."

"Beckett, I'm a big girl. I can handle your mother. Also, I saw Declan today."

He frowns. "Where?"

"I went to Katie's place after he posted stuff on Instagram saying I was sleeping with you while I was with him."

His face instantly darkens with displeasure. "I'll fucking sue him for defamation."

I place my hand on his arm. "I didn't tell you this for you to do that. I'm telling you this to thank you for trying to help me by paying him for that necklace a second time. I appreciate you looking out for me like that."

"I should have done more. That clearly wasn't enough."

I shake my head. "There's nothing you could have done to stop him sharing that video. But, Beckett, you can't keep things like this from me. It didn't feel good to stand there, clueless, while he took great delight in telling me this."

"I'd hoped he would never tell you that, Jenna. I didn't want you to be hurt, and I knew you would be if you discovered it meant nothing to Declan to give you that necklace like you thought it did."

"I know," I say softly, "but still, I don't like being blindsided like that. Please don't keep things from me."

His eyes search mine and then he gives me a nod before leaning over and kissing me. "I'm sorry you had to discover that."

I grip his neck. "It sucked, but I feel better after saying everything I wanted to say to Declan."

"Good."

I keep a hold of his neck. "You're still going to get your lawyers involved, aren't you?"

"They're already involved."

Beckett's not the kind of man to let this go, and I'm not the kind of woman to tell him how to handle his business, so I don't, even though I think we should both find a way to leave Declan behind.

I let him go and settle back against the sofa as Ruby comes back.

"Okay," she says, "I've ordered pizza. It shouldn't take too long. They're normally fast with their delivery."

"Why did your mom leave before dinner?" I ask as she gets Beckett a drink.

"Oh, she was never staying for dinner. She brought some books over that a friend gave her for me today."

"So, you two are good? Even after everything that's happened with your gallery and your parents not being happy about that? And I'm sorry if I'm prying. I may have drunk those cocktails a little fast."

Ruby grins. "Girlfriend, you can ask me anything," she says as texts come through on Beckett's phone.

"Christ," he mutters before standing and looking down at me. "I have to make some calls."

Ruby and I watch him exit the room before she says, "I don't think I've ever seen him this stressed and distracted with work. And that's saying something because I've definitely seen him stressed and distracted many times. Declan's really caused issues for him, hasn't he?"

I nod as worry builds in my chest. "Yes, he has."

Margaret's words from earlier return to haunt me.

The people you form relationships with can harm you more than help you.

The last thing I want to do is hurt Beckett.

"He'll be okay, Jenna," Ruby says, placing Beckett's drink on the table in front of me and taking a seat on the sofa. "Beckett has the resources to fight this. And as for me and my mother, we're okay. We always are. And to be honest, I'm glad this has happened. I want to show my parents, and Beckett too, that I can do this on my own."

"I understand that deeply." God, do I understand that.

We chat about her goals with the gallery and her art until the pizza arrives. Ruby gets plates while I go in search of Beckett.

I find him in Ruby's library, pacing the room and having a heated conversation about zoning laws. He hears me enter and turns to me.

"The pizza is here," I say quietly.

He nods and I leave him to finish his conversation.

I contemplate the tension written all over his body and etched into his face as I walk back to Ruby. Going by everything Beckett's shared with me about this land use review he's facing, I don't think this is going to end any time soon. I'm concerned he's facing a long period of stress. And I hate watching him go through this.

41

JENNA

"You look like you spent the weekend being fucked," Shona says early Monday morning when she drops by my office on her way to work.

I sit next to her on my sofa. "That's because I did spend the weekend doing that."

Her brows arch. "I thought Beckett was too busy for sex."

"He is, but he made time for me."

"Attaboy."

"How was your weekend?"

"I was not as lucky as you. Graham was busy on Saturday, so I had to find other ways to occupy myself, and none of those ways were as good as sex."

"We need to plan dinner together. Can you let me know which nights work for you guys?"

"Yes. I'll text you, but Graham's super busy the next couple of weeks, and I know you've got the Diana Black gala and your Dad's dinner coming up, so we may have trouble finding a night that works for everyone. Not to mention all the stuff Beckett's dealing with."

I sigh. "If we can't find a night for dinner with Graham and Beckett, let's plan something for us."

"We haven't had a spa day for a while."

"No, we haven't. We need one."

We're interrupted by Cora. "Jenna, Adeline is here. She said she just needs ten minutes if you can spare it."

I nod. "Yes, just give me a minute."

Shona stands and slings her bag over her shoulder as Cora leaves us. "I'll work out some dates and let you know."

"Sounds good."

She exits my office and I usher Adeline in.

"This dress works so well on you," I say as she sits. It's a green dress I found for her last week, and although I've already seen it on her, I'm reminded now of how well it fits her.

"I would never have found it without you."

I sit across from her. "We didn't have an appointment scheduled for this morning, did we?" My memory is usually perfect, but I can't remember setting an appointment with her.

"No. What I want to discuss with you is time sensitive, so I stopped by in the hope you could squeeze me in."

I relax. "Okay, good." Now is not the time in our relationship to start dropping the ball. "What's up?"

"I know you're looking for an investor, and after discussing it with my CFO over the weekend, I'd like us to explore the possibility of working together."

"You want to invest in my company?" It's a dumb question, but my brain is trying to keep up with what's happening right now.

After every possible investor Beckett suggested turned me down, thanks to the sex video, I've worked hard to stay positive and find new potential investors. I had a meeting with one on Saturday, and while she's interested, I'm not convinced we're a good fit. She has a lot of ideas for how my company could expand that don't gel with my ideas. I have two more investors to pitch, but based on what I've read about them, I'm not convinced they'll be able to get behind the vision I have.

"I'd like to spend some time discussing where you see your company going and how you plan on getting there."

Adeline could be a great fit. She knows the fashion industry inside out and is the founder of one of the most successful worldwide fashion and beauty brands.

"Do you have some time this week?" I ask.

We go through our calendars and settle on tomorrow morning. We then spend ten minutes chatting a little about my vision. Adeline asks me some questions and appears very interested in my ideas. It's a good start, but I'm learning not to get my hopes up. We've scheduled two hours tomorrow for me to pitch to her. I'll wait until after that to gauge her real interest. And mine too because it's important I find someone who wants to build the same company I do.

After Adeline leaves, I work through the morning, taking care of the problems that have come up with the dress selection for Diana Black's event. I finish solving those problems just before 1:00 p.m. at which point I text Beckett to see how he's looking for dinner tonight. He dropped me at work this morning and we made a plan to eat together tonight, but I know his plans can change depending on what he's dealing with at work.

Jenna: How's your day going?

Beckett: I'm on track for dinner.

Jenna: You read my mind. See you then x

The rest of the day flies by. Beckett doesn't cancel dinner, and by the time Frankie is seating us at Amorosis at 7:30 p.m., I'm exhausted.

"You look like you could sleep for a week," Beckett says before he takes a sip of his scotch. "Work was busy?"

I exhale a long breath. "So busy. We hired five new stylists today, so that will help, but we need more. I've asked Cora to help me with that. She's been amazing in a way I never realized she could be." I sip some of my scotch. "How was your day?"

"Long." With that one word, and with what I hear in his

voice, I know Beckett's feeling as exhausted as I am. Probably more so.

I reach for his hand. Threading my fingers through his, I say, "Do you really want to eat here, or do you just want to go home, and I'll cook something for you while you either cook with me or do some work?"

"I can have Martha cook us something."

I smile as I lean across to him. Brushing my lips over his, I say, "Let me take care of you."

He contemplates that for a few moments before nodding. He then drinks some of his scotch and calls Frankie over to let him know we're leaving.

Five minutes later, we're in his car.

"This suit is new," I say as I curl into him and run my gaze over the dark gray suit he's wearing.

His arm comes around me as he murmurs, "Nothing gets past you, does it?"

"Not when it comes to your suits." I glance up at him. "I approve of it."

"I'll be sure to let my guy know."

"I'd be happy to pass on some suggestions to your guy. I have many suits I'm currently ogling."

"I imagine you do."

We chat about Diana's event that's on Friday night for the rest of the trip home. When we arrive at his penthouse, Beckett goes to his office to take a call that just came through while I head into his kitchen to find something to make for dinner.

I connect my phone to his sound system and put some music on before I check his fridge for ingredients. I've located what I need to make chicken tacos when Beckett's arms slide around my waist from behind me.

He kisses my neck and murmurs, "Dance with me."

The song "Conversations in the Dark" by John Legend is playing as I turn in his arms.

Meeting his gaze, I start swaying with him. "I'm making you chicken tacos for dinner."

His arm tightens around me. "And for dessert?"

"I thought you could have your favorite."

Heat fills his eyes. I love being the one who causes that. "At the dining table?"

Beckett's top two buttons of his shirt are undone. I kiss his chest that's showing. "Yes. Of course, you could have a second helping in bed. Maybe later, though. You don't want to eat too much at once."

His mouth grazes my ear. "There's no such thing as too much dessert, Jenna."

Desire pools low in my stomach. These days, it lives there thanks to Beckett. "When everything settles down at work for you, we should take a vacation. I can lie in the sun, and you can eat lots of dessert." I'm overdue for some time off and am feeling exhausted enough tonight to be thinking about a vacation.

He slides his hand down over my ass and rests it there. "Tell me your favorite thing to do on vacation."

For a man who was hesitant the first time I asked him to dance in my kitchen with me, Beckett has come a long way. He's embraced it and sometimes initiates it like he has tonight.

"What do you think my favorite thing would be?" I ask.

"Besides sex, which I think you'd demand double of, and sleeping, which I think you'd likely extend your hours of, I imagine your other favorite thing might be searching for secret places the average tourist doesn't know about."

"Why do you think that?"

"Because you're the girl who wears ballet skirts and *Spank Me* T-shirts with chucks, and the girl who doesn't go out of her way to fit in, and the girl who says inappropriate things at inappropriate times and just carries on. You love anything unique and different. And you find delight in the simplest things like a sunrise and a great view. I imagine you'd enjoy the standard tourist sights, but I think you'd find real joy in discovering something unexpected."

I'm a little lost for words.

This might be one of the most meaningful things a guy has ever said to me.

I've had men tell me I'm complicated.

I've had them tell me I'm a little too enthusiastic at times.

I've had them tell me I talk too much, laugh too loudly, change my mind too often.

Men have often made me feel like it's too much work to love me.

Beckett makes it seem so easy.

"Thank you for saying all that," I whisper.

"It's all true."

I smile. "You forgot my George dreams. Vacations are a perfect time for them."

"That was covered when I mentioned sleeping."

I pull his face down to mine and kiss him.

I take my time with it because kissing Beckett while dancing with him is something I love to do.

When I finally let him go, I say, "I do like finding secret places, although I'm not sure I realized just how much until now. What's your favorite thing to do on vacation?"

"I've always worked while on vacation."

"So what you're saying is you need to go on one with me so I can help you discover your favorite thing."

He dips his face so he can kiss my neck. "I suspect it may end up being the fact I have time to eat dessert three times a day."

Angling my head to the side while he continues kissing my neck and throat, I say, "How hungry are you?"

"Starving," he growls in between kisses, sending all my butterflies into disarray.

"Good, because so am I."

He lifts me into his arms at the same time I practically climb into them.

He then carries me to his bedroom.

We skip dinner.

He skips his dessert at the dining table but eats it in bed.

And I start planning our first vacation together.

After he gives me orgasms, of course.

I ARRIVE at work early Tuesday morning, ready for my pitch to Adeline. I'm only a little nervous. I can't decide if that's a good thing or not.

She arrives ten minutes early and we get started.

She lets me get through the entire pitch without saying a word. Every other investor I've pitched to has cut in at some point with questions or statements regarding something I've mentioned. I'm unsure what it means that Adeline hasn't said anything. This is when my nerves kick in, but I get control of them and finish the pitch.

Once I finish, I take a breath and smile at her.

Still, I can't get a read on her.

Finally, she says, "You need to think bigger."

I thought I already did that.

My pitch involved expanding my business throughout America; building an online styling program; creating a monthly styling subscription program; and branching out further into celebrity styling packages.

But holy hell, I'm excited to hear her ideas for thinking bigger.

"What are you thinking?" I ask.

"Everything you mentioned plus your own fashion brand, beauty products, style advice books, games, and possibly even lifestyle products. Also, with your celebrity ties, I could see a reality show centered around your work. And that's just to start." She smiles. "I see an entire Jenna brand driven by social media, celebrity connections, and strategic marketing."

My heart is racing. My mind is racing. I've never been so excited for the business I could build. I'm not interested in a reality show at all, but everything else she mentioned could be amazing.

"Finally," I say, "Someone who has the same kind of vision. And someone who isn't scared of a sex video. Thank you. I don't want to have to compromise the company I can see so clearly for the money I need to expand, and unfortunately, that's what I've been looking at with every other investor I've spoken to."

The determination in her eyes is fierce as she says, "Never let anyone take your company from you. Fight for it. Always." No wonder that determination is so strong in her eyes. Adeline lost her first company in a hostile takeover. I can't recall who to, but I do recall watching her rise again to build a new, bigger company.

She smiles. "I'm in, Jenna. So long as the numbers work out, you've got yourself an investor."

We spend the next hour going over what Adeline needs from me and agree on a deadline for me to get the information to her.

As she's exiting my office, she says, "I'm hosting a party tomorrow night and would love you to come."

"I'd love to."

"Good. I'll send you the details."

I'm staring after her as she leaves, my mind still racing, when Tilly texts me.

Tilly: My boss changed his mind. He wants Beckett to come back and do that interview.

Jenna: I don't think there's any chance of that.

Tilly: I AM BEGGING YOU, JENNA. Please talk with him about it.

Jenna: I'll try, but I can't promise anything.

Jenna: Also, I just had a meeting with Adeline Spencer. She's interested in investing in my company.

Tilly: Holy shit, girl! WOW. Congrats!

Jenna: I don't know if it will go ahead, but just knowing that someone like her can see the potential is huge.

Tilly: Drinks are on you next time we go out!

"Jenna," Cora says, drawing my attention from Tilly, "Diana Black called." Her eyes widen in the way they do when she thinks someone is being demanding. "You need to call her back. Girl is high on stress over her event and needs talking down. I think we're maybe going to have to reschedule your Thursday afternoon so you can spend most of it with her."

I frown. "Why?"

"I feel like you're going to have to do a lot of hand holding with this one. Between her and her friends we're styling, there's a whole lot of anxiety going on over there."

After I agreed to style Diana, stylist friends told me she was high maintenance. It turns out they were right. Diana is lovely, and I've enjoyed working with her, but she has proven to be a lot of work.

"I'll call her back and assess the situation. If we need to rearrange my Thursday afternoon, we will. Diana's brought us a lot of attention. We need to ensure that attention doesn't sour."

"How did it go with Adeline?"

"Good." I smile. "Really good. But I'm not getting ahead of myself yet. She needs to see the numbers first."

"We both know those numbers are going to blow her away."

She's right; the numbers are better than good. Still, I don't want to let myself get excited before it's time. If I've learned anything, it's that life has a way of disrupting you when you least expect it.

I go back into my office to call Diana, but as I reach for my phone, I think about Beckett. I've been thinking about him from the minute Adeline told me I need to think bigger. He also told me to do that when he went over my pitch with me. We had a conversation about thinking big, and while I told him I'd alter my pitch with bigger ideas, I didn't. I let all the negativity I've experienced online thanks to the sex video get in my head and cause me to doubt myself.

I call Beckett before I call Diana.

He answers immediately. He usually does when I call. "I've been thinking about our first vacation," he says.

The smile I hear in his voice causes my own. "That's because you've really been thinking about eating dessert."

"I'm always thinking about that."

"Where do you think we'll go?"

"Hawaii. I thought that was a given."

"You need to add swimming with the turtles to our list of things to do there. I forgot to mention that when we talked about it."

"I'm not the one in charge of making lists in this relationship."

In this relationship.

That settles deep inside me, in so many good ways.

"And here I was, thinking you liked to be in charge of everything."

"That's a common misconception about me."

"Hmm, what else are you not in charge of in this relationship?"

"Early morning sex."

"You really love your early morning sex, don't you?"

"It's a great way to start a day."

"So is sleep."

"Sunrises in Hawaii are spectacular."

"So I've heard. It's such a shame for you that sleep is higher on my vacation to-do list than seeing a sunrise. Also, don't think I didn't notice your attempt to take charge of our early morning sex there, Mr. Pearce. What else have you got for me on this list of things you're not in charge of?"

"The kitchen."

"Is that the best you've got? Give me something better than that."

His voice drops low and gravelly when he comes back with, "You might be surprised at what I have no control over when it comes to you, Jenna."

Oh. My.

Disarray, here I come.

And thoughts, there you all go.

When I don't say anything, because he really has stolen all my thoughts, Beckett says, "How did your meeting with Adeline go?"

"You were right."

I swear I hear his smile. "About what?"

"That I needed to think bigger. She told me the same thing."

"I thought you were going to change your pitch."

"I was, but at the last minute I didn't. I let self-doubt creep in," I admit quietly. Sharing this with Beckett feels safe, but it also makes me feel completely naked with him. Exposed in a way I don't allow myself to be with many people.

"You have nothing to doubt, Jenna."

"Rationally, I know that. But when I'm not being rational, I can come up with all the reasons why someone would laugh at me for thinking I can achieve those big things. How did you push past these kinds of doubts? And if you tell me you didn't have them, I will do bad things to you the next time I see you." Jesus, surely even Beckett experiences doubt when it comes to his business.

"I have doubts. No one escapes that. I just keep taking action. I make quick assessments and act fast because it's during that time of not acting that hesitation can take over. Just keep taking action because even the wrong one will help you grow. And don't factor in what others will think. They sure as fuck won't be laughing at you when you achieve everything you set out to."

"I feel like there may be a sunrise in Hawaii for you after all."

"Add it to your list."

"I will. I'll even put it above my George dream." I sigh, not wanting this conversation to end, but knowing it must. "I have to go, but let the record show that I could keep talking with you for hours."

"We'll pick this back up after dessert tonight."

"Yes, and I'm adding your yacht to the list of things to discuss. I'm imagining sunrise out at sea on your yacht might be one amazing sunrise."

"Jesus."

I grin at the growl I hear in his voice and say, "I'll see you tonight, lover."

"We're trying lover now?"

"No, I don't think it works for us either."

"Goodbye, Jenna."

He disconnects, and I spend far too many minutes that I don't have to spare creating lists in my mind for Beckett and me. And hot damn if I don't realize just how many lists I want to make with him.

@thetea_gasp

@JENNABLAISE WAS SPOTTED super tight with @adelinespencer last night at the party of the month. #beckettpearce was notably missing from Jenna's arm. Could there be trouble in paradise? There's definitely trouble in Jenna's ex's paradise. @declanjames and @katiestein were seen arguing at a party on Tuesday night and left separately. Could Katie finally have found a reason not to marry the #thief? Oh, the tea. We're thirsty for more #staytuned

43

JENNA

"We're sending the documents over to Adeline's team now," my accountant says over the phone as I enter the restaurant I'm meeting Mom and Kristen at for lunch.

"Fantastic. Thank you for taking care of this so fast."

"Let me know if there's anything else you need," she says. "But I think you've got everything."

We end the call and I slip my phone into my purse. I don't want another thing to do with it today.

It's been the Thursday from hell.

I woke tired after staying late at Adeline's party last night.

My mother called just after 6:00 a.m. of all times to discuss our family's company dinner that's taking place on Saturday. I had to sit through twenty minutes of a conversation regarding seating at the dinner. Twenty minutes! I then agreed to have lunch with her and Kristen today, at which we will no doubt discuss the seating again.

When I arrived at work, Cora had a long list of problems that arose overnight with our team. I spent an hour I didn't have fixing those issues.

Beckett has been unreachable all day. I've called him three times and left messages for him to return my calls. He hasn't returned any of them. I know he's busy, but it's unlike him not to answer a call, even if it's to tell me he can't speak. He's never left me hanging like this.

I've had Diana Black on the phone three times this morning. I've rescheduled my entire afternoon so I can be available for her. At the rate she's going, I suspect I may need to allocate some time to her tonight as well. Thank God her event is tomorrow. Things can return to normal after that.

The only good part of today so far is the fact my accountant is on the ball and has sent everything Adeline needs to assess my company.

Adeline and I talked some more about our ideas for the company at her party last night. She detailed some great brand concepts for me, and I discovered how good the two of us are when we brainstorm together. To say I'm embracing thinking big now is an understatement. My conversations with Adeline and Beckett have helped me shed enough of my self-doubt to start allowing myself to imagine just where we could take my company.

"Jenna," Mom says when I reach the table she and Kristen are seated at. "You look beautiful, my darling. Where did you get that dress?"

I sit and glance down at the sleeveless pink dress I'm wearing. It's an Antonio Bereti dress with a V-neckline and pleated skirt that billows to my shins. I've paired it with shimmery silver heels and Vita Fede earrings. "It's from a new designer I'm working with. I'll introduce you to him. I think you'll love his dresses."

"Introduce me too," Kristen says. "I adore that dress."

"I know you don't have a lot of time today," Mom says, "so I ordered you a gin."

"Thank you." I reach for the drink in front of me and take a sip. A big sip. I need it after my morning.

"We worked out the seating problems for the dinner,"

Kristen says, giving me a knowing look. "So, you don't need to sit through that again."

I mouth "thank you" at her while Mom flattens her lips before saying, "They were legitimate problems, darling. I can't sit Barry Jensen next to Martin Brown. I just can't."

Kristen rolls her eyes and I laugh. I also think about the subtle changes in my sister since she broke up with Johnathon. Although she's heartbroken and hurt, she seems a little lighter to me. Which makes sense, because that's what pain does. It either kills you or it forces you to work through it, shedding layers as you go.

"Can we please, for the love of God, talk about something other than Dad's dinner?" Kristen begs. "I'm all talked out when it comes to that dinner."

I raise my glass. "I couldn't agree more."

"Girls, your father and brother have worked very hard on this dinner," Mom says. "Please, let's help them by doing what they need to make it a success. I know your father is counting on you both."

I sigh. "When have we not done what Dad needed us to do?"

Kristen widens her eyes a little and nods in agreement. "We always do what he asks, Mom."

"I know, darling, but he's quite stressed over work at the moment. I think this dinner is even more important this year to ensure the company continues growing."

"Ooh," Kristen says, her eyes flaring with excitement, "speaking of companies growing, I really love the name you and Adeline came up with for yours."

"Wait, don't get excited yet," I say. "She still has to go over my numbers. And that name I texted you was what we came up with after a few drinks last night. Who knows what it'll end up being if this all goes ahead?"

"Well, I loved it," Kristen says.

"What is it?" Mom asks.

"Adeline + Blaise," Kristen says as her attention is distracted by something behind me. "Oh, God, isn't that Beckett's mother?"

Jesus.

No.

I turn and look.

It is.

Margaret Pearce is seated at the head of a table in the corner of the restaurant, surrounded by ten other women who are the epitome of women I find it hard to connect with. Socialites who look down their nose at almost everyone.

And sitting right beside her is none other than Annabelle.

I turn back to my mother and Kristen, and throw out, "Whoever chose this restaurant is dead to me."

Kristen laughs.

Mom frowns. "Why?"

"Because Beckett's mother is over there, with the woman who likes to put her hands all over my man. Annabelle, I can deal with, but Margaret Pearce is another story. She told me my relationship with her son won't go anywhere. That I'm just some fun for him while he works his divorce out of his system. Oh, and that I'm not the kind of woman he dates."

Kristen all but gasps. "She did not!"

My eyelids hit my eyebrows as I nod and take a gulp of gin. "She did."

"Didn't Beckett divorce his wife two years ago? How long does she think it takes a man to work his divorce out of his system?" Kristen says.

"Right?" I agree.

Mom watches Beckett's mother silently while Kristen and I carry on a conversation about Margaret and the mean things she said to me. Finally, she looks at me and says, "Darling, you just keep being you and don't pay any attention to that woman. She's not worth your time or your heartache."

I blink as I stare at my mother.

I try to speak, but no words come.

Mom has never, not once, not ever, said anything like this to me.

She's never told me to just keep being me.

All she's ever told me is to "change your outfit, Jenna, that one won't work", and "oh, darling, must you wear your hair like that?" and, "please don't say anything that might affect the family."

I've struggled to feel seen by my mother. Truly seen, for me. For the individual I am. Mostly, I've felt like just a family part that needs to be managed and directed into doing what she needs me to do.

The words she has just said to me are words I have needed to hear for my entire life.

"Thank you, Mom," I say softly, fighting back the tears that are threatening. Jesus, I cannot start blubbering in this restaurant.

"Your grandmother walked all over me," she says. "I've never shared that with you girls, but I think you need to hear this now. She told me similar things about your father, and I allowed her to keep saying those awful things to me for years." She pauses, determination filling her features. "I won't stand for anyone making you feel the way she made me feel, and I won't watch either of you shrink. I'm proud of the strong women you've both become. Don't ever let anyone tell you you're less than who you are."

I may need a day to recover from this conversation.

I start to respond to that when my phone goes crazy in my purse.

"Oh, God," I mutter, reaching for it. "What now?"

DIANA BLACK: *Is there any chance you can come now? Gianna is having a meltdown over her dress, and I feel only you can help her with this.*

.   .   .

TILLY: Any update on the Beckett interview? My boss is riding me hard on this, babe. PLEASE *prays*

CORA: I know you're at lunch with your fam, but holy shit, Jenna, the shit just exploded here. We kinda need you to come back. Maddy and Jane just quit because Lola stole some of their clients. And I don't need to tell you how much work Maddy and Jane have scheduled that now needs rescheduling, or that we don't really have anyone to take on their clients. I think I'ma just try creating clones while I wait to hear back from you.

MY HEAD SNAPS up and I eye my mother and sister before abruptly standing. "I have to go."

Mom frowns. "You just arrived, darling."

I take a deep breath, trying to force my lungs to stop feeling like they're strangling me. "I know, but there's no time to eat today. I'll see you on Saturday."

"Text me,' Kristen says as she hugs me goodbye.

"I will," I promise. One thing I love about her breakup is how close we're becoming. Kristen texts me daily now, whereas before, I was lucky to hear from her once a week.

I make my way outside and am about to wave a taxi down when my phone rings.

Cora.

"I'm on my way back to the office," I say when I answer the call.

"Oh, thank God. Maddy just came back in, and I had to break up a freaking catfight between her and Lola. I can't go on without you, Jenna."

I laugh.

Although I'm tired and stressed, I laugh.

"I do love you, Cora," I say. I try hard to keep the boundary between us professional, but I fail today. Cora has stepped up the last few weeks in ways I've needed her to, and in times of stress, she comes through for me.

"Does that mean you'll pick me up a coffee on your way?"

"That's exactly what it means."

"Okay, I think I can manage for that extra time."

"I have only one stipulation. No more texts or calls. *I* won't be able to go on if you do."

"Right, gotcha. I'll go old school and scribble my notes to you on paper instead. Prepare for a few when you arrive."

I smile as I slip my phone back in my purse and lift my arm to hail a taxi as Annabelle's voice sounds from behind me. "Hello, Jenna."

She catches me by surprise because I'm still thinking about Cora. "Annabelle."

She quickly inspects me. That's actually what it feels like: an inspection. "What a darling dress," she says, her tone communicating she thinks my dress is anything but that.

"I'm sorry, but I'm in a hurry to get back to the office."

"Oh, yes, you work. I won't keep you long. I just wanted to say I was sorry to hear about what Declan did to you."

All my senses go into overdrive.

And not in a good way.

I suddenly feel like I'm walking over dangerous terrain and I need to pay very careful attention to where I step.

"Thank you," I say, hoping for this to be the end of this conversation, and not just because I have to return to the office.

She steps closer. "Yes, I know Beckett wants this kept quiet, and I've assured him I'll keep it between us. I just can't imagine how difficult it must be to know your wife slept with your best friend for all those years."

I stare at her.

I try hard not to respond.

I try so damn hard.

I fail.

God, how I fail.

"Declan slept with Ellen? For all those years?"

Triumph fills her eyes. "Oh, you didn't know? Oh, my gosh, I thought you did."

In my next life, I will return as a mean-girl slayer. I will find ways to put these women in their place. Oh, how I will find ways.

In this life, I just need to get through today.

And I *really* just need Annabelle to fuck off.

"Cut the bullshit, Annabelle. Just tell me what you want me to know, so I can get on with my day. I've got too many other precious queens to deal with. I don't need to add you to my list for any longer than absolutely necessary."

She doesn't like that. Not one little bit. "I don't know what Beckett sees in you, Jenna. You're cheap and uncouth, and God knows, you're not doing him any favors at the moment."

"So I've heard."

Fuck her.

"Declan was sleeping with Beckett's wife throughout Beckett's marriage and also after his divorce." She pauses, gloating as she twists the knife. "Declan cheated on you with her throughout your relationship. I'm surprised Beckett has left you in the dark. This is something I would want to know if I were you."

I was right.

I was walking on dangerous terrain.

I was paying very careful attention, but when you don't fully know the lay of the land because some of it has been kept hidden, it doesn't matter how well you're paying attention; you'll fall and get hurt.

Beckett should not have kept this from me.

I don't care if he thought he was protecting me; I don't feel protected right now.

"I wish I could say it was lovely seeing you again," I say to Annabelle. "But it wasn't."

Then, without waiting for her response, I hail a taxi.

And instead of heading in the direction of my office, I go to Beckett's.

44

JENNA

By the time I arrive at Beckett's office, I'm a mess of anger. I'm so furious I can barely think straight. And while I'm aware my anger isn't fueled solely by Beckett (hello, years of being "protected" by the men in my family), he's the one in my firing line.

Louise greets me when I step off the elevator on Beckett's floor. She looks at me carefully. "Beckett is just on a call. He won't be long. I'll show you where you can wait."

She's looking at me carefully because of the mess I'm in.

When I arrived, the receptionist advised me that Beckett was unavailable. I asked her to please double check that information, which she did. When she still advised me he was unavailable, I demanded to speak with Louise. The receptionist argued with me over this, until finally relenting and allowing me to speak with Louise. Beckett's assistant apologized for the miscommunication, telling me she hadn't been made aware of my arrival, and that, of course, I could see Beckett.

The only excuse I have for my behavior is that I'm running on little sleep, I've had what feels like a thousand headaches to deal with this morning, and I've just been subjected to Annabelle and her mean-girl ways. I would never normally show up at my boyfriend's office and make demands to see him.

Louise directs me to a very luxurious waiting room and offers me a drink. I decline the drink and place my purse on the sofa before pacing the room.

I am not a pacer, but here I am.

Pacing like my life depends on it.

I wait ten minutes for Beckett.

It feels like ten hours.

And with each passing minute, my anger builds.

Also, with each passing minute, I receive more texts from God knows who. I count seven messages as they come in, but I don't check any of them. They do, however, add to my stress, and by the time Beckett joins me, I'm barely able to contain my emotions.

"Jenna," he says, striding into the room with concern etched into his face. "Is everything okay?"

Not even his dark blue suit can save him today.

"I just had a conversation with Annabelle," I say, my voice dangerously low and calm. "One in which she informed me that Declan was sleeping with your wife throughout your marriage and during my relationship with him."

Beckett listens to what I say and gathers his thoughts before responding. "I'm sorry you had to hear that from her."

"Yes, so am I. Especially after I asked you not to keep things from me."

"I knew it would hurt you to discover their affair."

"I understand that, but it also hurt me to have to stand there today and listen to Annabelle gleefully share this information with me. That woman took great delight in telling me something she knew I didn't know. She also took great delight in making sure I knew that the two of you had a conversation about this."

"I'll talk to her and—"

"No. Me coming to you now isn't about her. It's about you

and me, and that you need to know I won't go through this again. Is there anything else you've kept from me?"

His phone rings. He ignores it as he says, "I didn't want you to have to experience the same hurt I did when I discovered my wife had cheated on me for a very long time. Can you understand that?"

"Beckett, it doesn't matter if someone cheats once or if they cheat every day of their life. It hurts just as much. I do understand why you did what you did, but I don't ever want you to do something like it again. You should have told me about this when you agreed not to keep things from me."

He scrubs a hand over his face. "Fuck, Jenna, I've been distracted. I didn't think of it. And to be honest, I don't think knowing this helps you in any way."

The ball of anger in my chest expands.

It's tight and crowded in there, and my lungs are pushing my breaths out fast to clear space for new air.

"That just means you're not listening to me," I say angrily. Why can't he see my point here?

"I am listening to you." His voice now has traces of anger too. "But I don't agree."

"Well, this isn't something you need to agree on, or that we need to see the same way. This is me telling you how it makes me feel to have things kept from me, and let me tell you, it doesn't feel good. It makes me feel small. It makes me feel like you think I'm not strong enough to cope with that knowledge."

"That is so far from what I think, it isn't funny. I think you're one of the strongest women I know, and I want to help you stay strong. That's why I didn't tell you about Declan."

"Right, but by saying stuff like 'I didn't tell you that because I want to help you stay strong' you're effectively saying you don't think I can handle the truth. You're saying I'm *not* strong enough to handle it."

He works his jaw. "We're not going to get anywhere if we just keep going around and around on this."

"Oh my God, Beckett! No! I didn't come here to get some-where with you. I came here to tell you what I need from you, and that is for you to stop trying to protect me in this way. I like you looking out for me and standing by my side supporting me, but I don't need you to decide for me what I should know and what I shouldn't. That's not how I ever want to be in a relation-ship with anyone. We're either equals or we're nothing."

His nostrils flare. "I've never treated you like we aren't equals."

"No, but this doesn't make me feel equal."

His phone rings again.

"Fuck," he mutters, pulling it out of his pocket and checking it. Then, glancing at me, he says, "I'm sorry, I have to take this."

I expect him to exit the room to take the call, but he doesn't. He stabs at the phone and answers it while keeping his eyes firmly on mine. "What?" he barks.

The air in this room feels heavy.

As angry as Beckett and I are.

It clings to me while I stand here watching him on the phone.

He listens to what the person says before saying, "He's offering a sit down? For what? Me to change my mind?"

He listens again, and then says, "As far as I'm concerned, personal relationships shouldn't come into this decision. Mine doesn't affect whether I can deliver on what I've agreed to."

More listening, and more of his intense gaze concentrated on me before he barks, "I'll sit down with him, and I'll make it clear that we can deliver what they want at the best price they'll find, but I won't discuss my personal life with him when that has nothing to do with my business."

He stabs at the phone to end the call. He then slides the phone in his pocket and exhales a long breath.

"Our relationship is hurting your business," I say. It's not a question, because I know it is. This is more just me processing out loud all the thoughts and feelings that have been plaguing me since the day Declan uploaded that video.

Beckett looks at me with such care that my anger halves from that look alone. "No, it isn't."

This man.

I may be angry with him, but when I strip all of that back, I feel so deeply for him and the way he cares for me. Even when he's still trying to protect me in ways I wish he wouldn't. "Beckett, it is. You've spent weeks working your ass off to fix the problems Declan caused you on your hotel development. You can't deny that, or the fact it's because of me that Declan did all that."

"No, Declan and Katie have a personal vendetta against me, Jenna. They uploaded that video because they wanted to hurt me, not you. That was only the start of their plan to cause me problems. The hotel development issues are just another part of their plan. None of this was because of you." He pauses. "You had to sit through that video being uploaded because of *me*."

"What was that call about, then? What decision is your personal relationship affecting."

He shakes his head. "It'll work itself out. You don't need to worry about that."

Seriously, he has no idea.

"Okay, do you see what you just did?"

He frowns. "What?"

"I asked you a question that, instead of answering, you deflected and told me not to worry about it. I know you did it because you don't want me to worry, but that's what being in a relationship is about. Caring for and, at times, worrying about the other person. You don't have to carry everything on your shoulders all the time."

"I'm not good at this, Jenna," he admits.

"I know, but you're going to have to learn. Equal knowledge. Equal burdens. Equal care. I want it all or nothing."

He takes that in and thinks about it for a long moment

before finally saying, "My company has bid on a government aircraft contract. It's the reason I acquired Pride Industrial, to get into the government sector. We put a competitive bid in, and it should be enough to win us the contract, but the agency representative doesn't like my relationship with you. He doesn't want to align with me if I'm aligned with you."

I see every ounce of misgiving Beckett has over sharing this information with me, and I feel it from him too.

"So he wants to sit down and discuss this with you? Your company is still in the running for the contract?"

"Yes, we are, but I'm not interested in discussing my personal life when that has nothing to do with an aircraft contract."

"How long have you been planning this expansion into government contracts?"

"Years."

And just like that, my heart is in my throat.

Beckett has worked so hard to get where he is, and now, it's all at stake because of me.

"You can't just give up years of work, Beckett," I say softly, my words struggling to make it past my heart.

"I'm not. I'll fight this asshole and win."

I give him a small smile. "How?"

"I've got my team working on that."

"Yes, but how? What's the plan?"

I don't think there is a solid plan. I think that this government asshole can choose to judge me and not give the contract to Beckett without Beckett being able to stop him. I think Beckett's found something he can't control.

Unless he walks away from me.

I think that's the only way he'll win this contract.

"Jenna, we're figuring it out. I'll make sure we win that contract."

I shake my head. "If you had a plan that you knew would

work, you'd tell me. We both know the only plan that will achieve your goal is for you to end our relationship."

His face clouds over with anger. "That's not fucking happening."

"Beckett, you're not thinking clearly. Your company is the most important thing in your life. You've sacrificed everything to make it a success. You can't just give all of that up now. Not for me. I won't let you."

Even as the words are coming out of my mouth, I want to force them back in. It physically hurts to say them, but, I realize, that's what love is about. Giving everything you have to give to the person you love.

And whereas a minute ago, I didn't know I loved Beckett, I do now.

I've fallen in love with this man who I never saw coming.

I love his thoughtfulness; I love his attention to detail; I love the way he cares for his people; I love his arms around me; I love talking with him; I love laughing with him; I love his kindness; I love dancing in the kitchen with him; I love how he makes me feel like I'm the only woman alive. Hell, I even love his bossiness and protective ways. We just need to work on how he practices that protectiveness.

But, no, we won't be working on anything because I can't let him walk away from something he's wanted for years.

I have to take charge here and ensure he wins that contract.

"Jenna," he says, looking concerned, "I'm not giving anything up. I will find a way to win this contract."

"You don't have to give anything up. I'll walk away so you can win."

"No," he says in his bossy voice. But this time, it won't work.

"Yes, this is the only way." I take a step away from him.

My heart is trying to climb out of my throat so she can throw herself at him.

She does not want me to be saying the words I'm saying.

I ignore her as much as I ignore the pain slicing through me.

Beckett reaches for me, the concern on his face intensifying. "I won't allow you to walk away."

I grab my purse off the sofa, pulling my arm out of his hold. My throat feels so full it could burst. How did I not know a heart was so big? "You can't boss me, Beckett. Not today."

"Is this because I didn't tell you about Declan? I won't do—"

I place my hand to his chest.

Shit.

Mental note: it's a very bad idea to touch the man you love when you're attempting to break up with him.

I pull my hand back. "No, this has nothing to do with that. This is because I want you to have everything you've ever wanted."

"I want you."

He says that so clearly and so firmly that I almost stop.

I almost take back all my words and let my heart breathe again.

But I don't.

I can't.

"No." I take a deep breath. "I'll make it so your government guy knows you're no longer aligned with me."

I move past him to leave the room, but his hand curls around my arm and he stops me. "Don't go. I don't want you to do this." More of that firm, strong voice that won't work on me today.

I avoid his intense gaze and pull free of his hold to carry on toward the door.

As I turn the door handle, he uses a voice I've never heard him use when he says, "Jenna. Stop." It's a command, but all I hear is the fear and vulnerability laced all through it.

I open the door.

I look back at him.

And then I take the step that will end everything.

45

BECKETT

"Jenna!"

Fuck.

I go after her, closing the distance between us in four strides, regretting the hell out of the fact I took that phone call from Mac in front of her.

"I won't let you do this," I say, catching her before she steps into the elevator.

Before she can answer me, Mac comes our way. "Beckett, I need a minute."

I look at him. "Not now, Mac."

"Yes, now," he says, his tone drawing my attention. "McMaster just emailed. You're going to want to take care of this. *Now.*"

With a firm shake of my head, I say, "No. I'm busy. I'll come find you when I'm free."

He clenches his jaw as he glances between Jenna and me. Without another word, he leaves us and I give all my attention back to Jenna.

I need to make her understand there's no way I'll allow her to walk away from me.

"Stop running and talk to me," I say.

"I'm not running."

"Yes, you are. Why?"

Her phone buzzes with a text and she grabs it out of her purse. "I won't come between you and your company, Beckett. Don't ask me to."

"I'm not. I'm asking you to stay and talk, and to understand I have the resources to win this contract without you walking away."

"I don't think you do. I think you're so used to always being successful that you're not seeing this clearly. I think you should take the time to step back and look at the big picture. You'll see what I'm seeing when you do that. You need me to walk away."

Another text comes through on her phone as I say, "You're not going to listen to me, are you?" Jenna's as stubborn as I am about most things. It's a trait of hers I admire, but right now, I could do with less of it.

The elevator doors open.

"I have work," she says, looking at me like she doesn't want to leave but is determined to, regardless. Then, stepping close to me, she places her hands to my chest, and adds softly, "Goodbye, Beckett."

"Fuck," I growl, my hand going to her neck, my mouth to hers. I kiss her like my fucking life depends on it. There's no slow to this. It's rough and demanding. It's me drowning in her.

I can't lose her.

Jenna's everything I never knew I wanted.

Everything I never knew I needed.

For the first time in my life, I've found something I want more than the company I've spent years building.

I will walk away from this government contract before I'll walk away from her.

Jenna's body presses to mine as she kisses me back with everything I'm kissing her with.

By the time we come up for air, she's breathless. Her arms

are wrapped tightly around my neck, and when she attempts to unwind them, I hold them in place.

"I can't lose you, Jenna."

She looks at me like she's drowning too. "I know. I can't lose you either. But this has to happen."

With that, she enters the elevator.

I want to follow her.

To the ends of the earth.

But I know she won't listen to anything I say right now, so I don't.

It fucking kills me, but I let her go.

And I start work on the most important thing I'll ever do in my life.

I start figuring out how I'll win her back.

I try to concentrate on what Mac's telling me about the contract, but my mind is distracted by Jenna. She left here an hour ago, yet it feels like a year. I took my time finding Mac after she left because I needed time to think about how I'm going to proceed from here. In the end, he came to my office to discuss the developments with the contract bid.

"McMaster has an hour this afternoon that he's set aside for you," he says. "It's our last chance to win him over."

"I'm not giving Jenna up."

He looks at me with frustration. "You're thinking with your dick, Beckett. Is she worth it?"

"Don't ever ask me that again, Mac. I'm thinking with far more than my dick on this one. Trust me on that."

He studies me for a long moment. "Fuck me, you've fallen in love, haven't you?"

"Yes. So instead of standing here arguing with you over this, I need to come up with other ways to win this asshole over. The first being for you to run some new numbers so I can decide whether it's worth it to me to present McMaster with a new bid."

We discuss what I need from him, and he leaves to get to work on it while I spend time going over other options.

Three hours later, I'm on my way to the meeting with McMaster when Ruby calls me.

"Hi," I say, taking a sip of the scotch I just poured myself.

Ruby blows in like a wild storm with, "I love you to death, Beckett, but goddamn I'm angry with you right now. Why can't you stop trying to fix everything for everyone?"

"Jesus, Ruby, calm down."

"Don't tell me to calm down! I'm allowed to express my feelings, and today they're all about you, and how you piss me off when you decide to take charge of my life."

"It might help if I know what you're referring to."

"That building near my art gallery that you bought! A gallerist friend of mine was about to sign a lease on some space in it, and then bam, the owner tells her he sold the business to you. I'm no idiot, Beckett. When things appear coincidental, they never are. And I know how your brain works, so I figure you've had Johnson watching over me like you sometimes do and decided to help me out by stopping her from signing that lease." She takes a breath. "You can't keep doing this. You need to let me do this my way, by myself, so I can prove to you all that I *can* do it."

"I believe you can do it, Ruby. That wasn't why I helped you out on this. I bought that building because it's what I'd do if I was you. I'd neutralize my threats."

"Did it ever occur to you to bring me that information and let me decide what I wanted to do?"

"Johnson brought the issue to me. We discussed it, and I acted straight away. I didn't want to waste time."

She sighs. "God, it's hard to stay angry with you. Not when you're always just doing what you think will help me." She pauses. "Do you remember that time when I was about fifteen, and I had that huge fight with my best friend? I came home from school, utterly devastated that she'd turned my other friends against me. You consoled me and stayed with me all night while I cried myself to sleep. You wanted to fix it all for me, but you couldn't, and you knew it. So you did the only thing you could; you sat by my side and gave me your time and love."

I do remember that. I remember feeling useless. There wasn't a damn thing I could do to help Ruby solve her problem.

"I remember," I say.

"It was one of the best things you ever did for me."

I frown. "What, sitting with you all night?"

"Yes. Beckett, I don't need your money, or your protection, or whatever else you think will make me love you, or whatever else you think will show your love for me; I just need you to sit with me. I know Mom and Dad taught you that money and things fix all situations, but don't you remember how we always just wanted their time and their love? We just wanted them to sit next to us, and wrap their arms around us, and tell us they'd always be there. That's all I need from you."

A memory tugs at me.

Something Jenna said to me on our first date.

Time and love.

Two things I've never been good at giving.

I drink some more scotch.

"What do you want me to do with the building?"

"It's your building. You do whatever you want with it. Except don't give it to me. I won't take it."

"Do you want me to lease that space to your friend?"

"Only if that's what fits with what you want to do with the building."

"I have no plans for the building."

"Good God, you are too much."

I think about how similar Ruby and Jenna are and find

myself doing something I've never done. "Jenna tried to break up with me today."

"Shit. What happened?"

I share with her about Jenna's visit to my office today, the argument we had, and then the outcome of Jenna discovering my contract is at risk.

"So," Ruby says, sounding confused, "She did break up with you? I thought you said she tried to?"

"She did, but it will only be temporary."

She laughs. "Oh, God, she has no idea, does she?"

"About what?"

"About just how stubborn you can be."

"I think she's aware," I murmur, thinking about Jenna and the intense discussions we've had over the years thanks to our stubborn tendencies.

"Beckett," she turns serious, "Don't fuck this up. I adore Jenna, but mostly, I think she's absolutely perfect for you."

"I don't intend on fucking this up."

"Good. Keep me updated. And for the love of God, if you feel the urge to buy her a building, or a plane, or a country, or anything to fix this, don't. Just sit with her and make sure she knows you'd love her even if everything was stripped away."

Davis pulls up outside the building where I'm meeting McMaster.

"I have to go," I say.

"I love you, Beckett."

"I love you too." I pause before adding, "Thank you for this conversation."

I disconnect and exit the car. Ten minutes later, I'm sitting in front of Ted McMaster.

"It's good to meet you in person, Beckett," he says, looking like the smug asshole he is.

I've dealt with a lot of assholes in my life, and most don't bother me. Not on a deep level. But McMaster has angered the fuck out of me.

"I can't say the same, Ted."

That surprises him. And annoys him. He sits back in his chair and assesses me. "Well, this isn't a great start, is it?"

It was when Ruby told me she just wanted me to sit with her that I decided how this meeting was going to go down. It was also in that moment that I knew I was a fucking idiot for how I've handled everything with Jenna.

Jenna's been facing bullshit slut-shaming on social media since her sex video went public. She's battled her way through it, kicking ass as far as I'm concerned, but still, she's had to read the hateful things people who don't even know her have had to say.

I haven't read any of it because I don't enjoy social media, but I've heard what she's told me. I also have staff who keep me updated on anything related to me on social media, so they've shared information about it with me.

I've tried to encourage her to stop reading everything on social media. I've told her she has staff for that. What I haven't done is *listen* to her. I haven't paid careful attention to what she's said. I also haven't given her credit for knowing what her business needs from her. Instead, I've taken the way I work in my business, and assumed she should replicate that.

It was Jenna who said to me a while ago that creative people work differently than I work. Jenna is one of the most creative people I know, so it makes sense for her to approach her work differently. And social media is a huge part of her business; of course, she needs to stay connected to it.

Having to deal with nasty slurs in the course of a workday isn't something anyone should have to do. The same as having to deal with them in life isn't something anyone should have to do. Jenna's dealt with this bullshit every day since that video went live. And while I've supported her privately, I haven't done so publicly.

"Tell me, Ted, what is it exactly about my bid that isn't

getting it over the line?" He hasn't plainly stated his disapproval of Jenna. I want to hear him say it.

"As you know, this meeting can't go on the record, nor can anything I share with you about your bid. This is strictly between us. I can't be seen to be favoring anyone, you understand?"

"I understand."

"Right, so now that's out of the way, your bid is good. You meet all our requirements and then some."

"So, you'll award the contract to me?"

"Now, now, let's not get ahead of ourselves. I do have some concerns to discuss with you."

"Go ahead."

He clears his throat and shifts in his chair. "Your association with Jenna Blaise is troubling."

"Why? She's not involved in this."

"I prefer not to align the government with anyone who could create an issue at any point. And let's just say that Jenna has quite the flashy, celebrity profile online. And then there's the matter of the sex video she produced. It doesn't look good, Beckett."

I work my jaw. "So if I'm understanding correctly, you've judged Jenna based on a private video her ex-partner made and took upon himself to make public without her consent? And you don't approve of her social media popularity?"

He eyes me with distaste. "She flaunts an immoral lifestyle. I won't be tied to her."

"She flaunts hard work, fashion, and fun. Those are hardly immoral things."

"We disagree on this."

"And because we disagree on this, I won't win the contract?"

He takes a moment, but then he nods. "Correct."

"Good to know before I waste any more of my time." I stand to leave.

"Surely you're not walking away from a billion-dollar contract for a woman you've only recently started dating?"

"That's exactly what I'm doing. I don't want to be tied to a man like you in the same way you don't want to be tied to Jenna."

His lips flatten. "Do you have any idea what you're actually walking away from here, Beckett? This would be the first of many contracts. You're essentially walking away from billions of dollars' worth of contracts."

"I'm aware, and trust me when I tell you the day will come when you are no longer the one handing these contracts out."

With that, I stride out of the meeting and downstairs to where Davis is waiting for me.

"Where to, boss?" he asks after I slide into the back seat.

I check my watch for the time. Jenna might be home from work by now. "Jenna's."

He nods and pulls out into the traffic.

We sit in traffic for quite some time, and when we arrive at Jenna's she's not home.

I pull out my phone and call her.

She doesn't answer, so I text her.

Beckett: You're not at home.

I make my way back out to the car. She replies to my text in that time.

Jenna: I'm working.

Jenna: Beckett, please don't call me. It'll just make this harder than it already is.

I want to call her. Fuck, do I want that. But, I don't.

Beckett: I won't call you while you're working, but I will call you, Jenna.

I listened to everything she said today.

And I never intend to make those mistakes again.

I intend to win Jenna back and spend the rest of my life loving her.

46

@thetea_gasp

Oh no, the tea has been spilled by an anonymous source. @jennablaise and #beckettpearce have called it quits #gasp No confirmation from either camp, but we can report that Jenna was spotted outside @dianablack's home with puffy cheeks and heartbreak written all over her. We think this might be the kind of tea we all need some soothing over. We, for one, were big fans of #jeckett.

47

JENNA

Kristen gives me a slightly horrified look when I arrive at the hotel for the Blaise Publishing dinner on Saturday night. "Have you showered today? Eaten? Taken a breath? Dear God, Jenna, you are a mess."

"May I remind you of how supportive I was when you broke up with Johnathon? I did not tell you that you were a mess."

"You may as well have. I was." She eyes the garment bag I'm carrying. "Why aren't you dressed already?"

"I've been working all day. I didn't have time to go home and change."

She frowns. "Why are you working on a Saturday? I thought your team worked Saturdays for you now."

"Two of my girls quit on Thursday. I had to take on their clients today. And I had to reschedule my Thursday afternoon and a lot of yesterday to take care of Diana Black and her friends. Trust me when I tell you the last forty-eight hours have been hectic, and I am due many hours of sleep."

She gives me a look of sympathy. "And you had a breakup in there too. How are you today?"

I hold up my hand to stop her. "No, we're not going there

today. If I think about him, I'll start crying, and I cannot cry tonight."

"Okay," she says, taking charge. "Go up to your room and get changed. And maybe take a minute to breathe and relax. You've got plenty of time."

I'm so glad I reserved a room at the hotel. I knew I'd want to collapse into bed the second the dinner finishes, so I called this morning to arrange a room. I go up there now and take a quick shower, dress, and fix my hair and makeup. It's a good thing I'm skilled at doing these things quickly. It gives me ten minutes to lie on the bed and take that breath Kristen suggested.

I close my eyes for a couple of minutes, deep breathe, and then reach for my phone. I have some messages from Beckett to check.

He called me this morning while I was with a client. I couldn't answer, and I haven't had the time to contemplate returning his call. I haven't even had the time to read his texts. Well, that's not quite true. I have had the time; I just haven't wanted to cry in between clients, and I knew I would if I read them. So, I didn't.

Taking a deep breath, I read them now.

Beckett: *Please don't ignore me, Jenna. Please call me back.*

He then sent this a few hours later.

Beckett: *Congratulations on the success of your gala last night. You looked beautiful.*

Ruby must have shown him a photo.

And his texts do make me cry, just like I knew they would.

The fact I'm exhausted doesn't help, but it wouldn't matter if I'd had all the sleep in the world, I'd still cry reading these messages.

I miss Beckett in a way I never knew I could. I've had to restrain myself many times from running back to him and begging him to forget everything I said.

I wipe my tears and will them to stop.

I blame Tilly for all of this.

If she hadn't forced me to style Beckett at that photo shoot, none of this would have happened. I'd still think Bossy Beckett was all there was to him. I wouldn't know all the other things about him that have made me fall so hard.

As I reread his texts, I know he's not going to make this breakup easy. He's as stubborn as I can be, and he made it clear the other day that he didn't want me to walk away. Knowing this, I know I should not reply to his texts. But knowing what's good for me, and doing it, hasn't always been my strength. Not when it comes to men.

Jenna: Thank you. I survived Diana, but only just.

He comes straight back to me.

Beckett: Are you free for a call?

My stomach does some kind of awkward somersault. It's a mixture of "God yes, please call now" and "this is a really, really bad idea."

I call him.

"Jenna," he answers immediately, his deep voice hitting my veins like it's their drug of choice.

"Hey," I say softly, my entire body alive with both anticipation and uncertainty. This was perhaps not my best idea, and yet I'm unable to do anything but this.

"How are you?" The concern in his voice is so clear and honest. God, how am I going to survive this man?

"I'm exhausted. It's been two days of non-stop work and problems to solve. I'm pretty sure I'm going to sleep twelve hours straight tonight." I pause. "How are you?"

What are we doing?

This is not how a breakup should go.

"I miss you."

And just like that, I'm crying again.

I feel those three words from him just as much as I hear them.

It's right there in his voice.

Beckett is hurting.

My heart, who hasn't forgiven me for shredding her, makes herself known all over again.

This is not how a breakup should go.

"This was a bad idea," I say, my voice strangled by my heart. "I shouldn't have called."

"Fuck," he curses. "Are you crying?"

"I have to go, Beckett," I say, ending the call and dropping my phone on the bed so I can let all my tears out before I have to go down to the dinner.

It takes me ten minutes to get myself under control, and my face cleaned up enough to face everyone. I've got hours ahead of me talking with everyone at the dinner like Dad wants. All *I* want to do is crawl under the covers of this bed in this hotel room and cry for the entire night.

I take a deep breath and make my way back down to the ballroom.

People have started arriving, and many of them greet me as I weave my way through the crowd to find Kristen. I need her like I've never needed her.

"Jenna, darling," Mom says when I reach the family table at the front of the room. She frowns as she runs her eyes over me. "You look dreadful. What happened?"

"Thanks, Mom," I say, wanting to cry all over again. "It's been a long day, that's all." I glance around the room. "Where's Kristen?"

Oliver joins us, narrowing his gaze at me. "Have you been crying?"

"That's the generally accepted form of handling a breakup," I say with more than a trace of sarcasm.

"Kristen told me you and Beckett broke up. What happened?"

"Can everyone please stop asking me that?"

I am not going to make it through this night.

Oliver and Mom assess me like I'm fragile and could break

at any moment, and then Mom takes charge. "Oliver, give us a minute, please."

He does as she asks, and when we're alone, she looks at me with concern. "Do you want me to stay with you tonight, darling?"

I stare at her.

Who is this woman and what did she do with my mother?

When I don't answer her, she says, "Yes, I think I should stay with you. For as many nights as you need. I can also call Shona and get her to come over. Kristen will too."

When she stops to take a breath, I say, "What are you doing right now?"

She looks at me like I've just asked a silly question. "You need us, Jenna."

Before I can quiz her any further, my father joins us. His steely expression matches the hard set of his shoulders. "We'll be starting in ten minutes," he says to Mom.

"Okay, darling. Do you need anything?"

He shakes his head before looking at me. "I've heard you're considering using our family name in your new business name."

My brain is a little slow to catch up tonight, so I take a moment figuring out what he means. When I realize he's referring to the business name Adeline and I came up with, I nod. "Yes. Adeline + Blaise. I mean, if she invests in my company, that is. She may not."

"You'll need to come up with a different name. I don't want Blaise attached to that woman."

"That woman?" I ask, a hard edge creeping into my voice.

"She's an unsuitable match to our name, Jenna," he says with the tone he likes to use with me to indicate that what he's said is final.

"Why, Dad? She owns one of the most successful world-wide fashion brands. What makes her unsuitable?"

"She peddles clothes and sex. I don't want our name to be tied to that."

"William," Mom says with a berating tone. "Jenna's right; Adeline Spencer's brand is very successful. And she doesn't peddle sex. I don't know where you got that idea from."

"Her clothes barely cover her skin," Dad says. "It's not appropriate for the Blaise name to appear next to that."

I stare at my father and wonder why I still strive for his approval.

I'm never going to get it.

And I'm not sure I even want it anymore.

I don't think I care what a closed-minded man thinks of me and how I choose to live my life.

"You gave me that name, Dad," I say, straightening my shoulders and standing tall, "and I'm going to use it however I want."

His lips flatten. I'm not sure I've ever seen him look so unimpressed. "You're making a mistake, Jenna. Going into business with her won't work out well for you."

The part of me that used to want his approval would listen to that and commence the self-doubt cycle. Tonight is proving that part of me doesn't exist anymore.

Beckett's advice comes back to me: Just keep taking action because even the wrong one will help you grow.

There's nothing to doubt.

I've done my due diligence on Adeline.

I've gone over the numbers with my accountant.

I've researched the hell out of everything.

Taking this action will help me grow either way.

"I don't agree with you," I say.

I have never uttered those words to my father, and damn they taste good.

He doesn't respond to that. He simply turns and walks away from me.

"Darling," Mom says, "Your father has a lot on his mind at

the moment. You shouldn't pay any attention to what he just said. I know he doesn't mean it."

"We both know he meant every word he said." I smile. "But I love you for trying to make me feel better. And as far as you and the girl gang staying with me tonight; there's no need. I'm staying here and I'm going to sleep all night long. And when I wake up tomorrow, I'll feel much better. I just need some sleep."

"Jenna, what you need is to work things out with Beckett. I've never seen you as happy as you have been since you started dating him. And I'm not just saying that because I want grand-children."

"You want grandchildren?" She's never mentioned babies before.

"Yes, and I'd like them before I'm on my deathbed and unable to enjoy them."

I refrain from rolling my eyes.

Honestly, she can be dramatic at times.

"You're hardly nearing your deathbed, Mother."

"I will be if you don't work things out with Beckett."

"I do believe you have three other children to help you out with this."

"Yes, and I'm working on them too."

Of course, she is.

Kristen joins us. "So, I just ran into Dad, and he was not happy. Any idea what caused that?"

"Yes, me," I say. "I just stood up to him for the first time in my life. He didn't take it well."

Her eyes go wide, and she forgets how to speak. Then, she says, "Are we actually in an apocalypse this year?"

I laugh.

I laugh so hard that tears stream down my face.

I don't think many of those tears are due to my sister, though.

"Oh, God," she says, "We need to fix you."

I stare at her through my tears. "How do you fix a heart that is actually broken?"

"You've done this many times. You can do it again."

I shake my head. "No, this is different. I thought I knew what a broken heart was. It turns out I had no idea." I start crying harder. "And I think I just got my period."

"I hate men," she declares.

It's completely out of the blue, and so random that it makes me begin a whole new round of crying laughter that turns into actual sobbing. Through that sobbing, I manage to ask, "Why do you hate men?"

"Because they get to have dicks that don't bleed blood while we have to have vaginas that do."

I'm wailing like a banshee, probably with blood gushing down my legs by now (yes, I can be as dramatic as my mother when I put my mind to it), looking like I just stepped off a horror movie set when a deep voice my soul knows better than anyone's voice says, "That's a solid reason to hate men."

48

@thetea_gasp

OH MY HEART, gather around for the tea, girlfriend. @beckettpearce has joined Insta #gasp He just posted some #suitporn, ahem, a photo of himself with the caption 'dinner with @jennablaise at the annual @blaisepublishing dinner tonight' #swoon We are so pleased to know the rumors of their split weren't true. Now we can get back to #jeckettwatch We can't get enough of these two. In related news, where are @katiestein and @declanjames? They haven't been spotted together for days. Ooh, we think there may be some tea there #staytuned

49

BECKETT

Jenna is fucking beautiful, even when she's a mess.

"Beckett." Her eyes come to mine and I suck in a breath at the pain I see in them. It matches mine. Jenna and I were not made to be apart. "What are you doing here?"

I eye my seat at the family table. "I was invited." Technically, it's true. Jenna never rescinded my invitation.

Kristen looks at me before looking at her sister. "I'm going to leave you two to chat." It doesn't come out as a question, but that's what it is.

I wait to see if Jenna tries to send me away.

She nods at Kristen who hugs her, whispers something in her ear, and then leaves us.

I run my gaze over Jenna.

She's wearing a sexy, shimmery, navy dress that takes figure-hugging to a new level. I'm unsure she'll be able to sit while wearing it. Her hair is down, falling in loose waves. Her makeup is done, but those tears tracking down her face have messed it up a little.

The thing I notice the most is that she looks like she hasn't slept since I last saw her. I know this feeling; I've barely slept since then either.

"You shouldn't have come," she says.

"Yes, I should have."

"Beckett, we broke up. This is not how a breakup should go."

"Have you ever known me to do things the way they should be done?"

She opens her mouth to say something, but snaps it closed almost as fast. When one of her brothers takes his seat at the table, she mutters, "Shit," before grabbing my hand and dragging me out of the room.

"You don't want to stay for dinner?" I ask as we exit the ballroom and walk toward the elevators.

She lets go of my hand. "Not really, but mostly I need to go up to my room." We reach the elevators, and she turns to me. "You should leave."

Her tears have stopped, and yet, I still want to wipe them from her face. "I'm not going anywhere."

At that, she bursts into tears again.

I curse and attempt to pull her into my arms, but she resists, refusing to allow me to do so.

"No," she says, wiping her tears. "You can't come here and say nice things to me and make me fall in love with you all over again. Stop it. We broke up!"

While she's doing her best to keep me away, I'm stuck on what she's said.

Fall in love with you all over again.

The elevator doors open, and Jenna practically runs into it.

I follow her.

She selects her floor and the doors close.

"Do you understand what a breakup is, Beckett?"

She's wedged herself into the corner of the elevator like she's trying desperately to escape me. If I wasn't a wreck at the moment, I'd find this amusing. However, the very thought of Jenna trying to escape me only makes me feel worse.

"I wish I didn't, sweetheart."

Her eyes widen, tears still falling. "We are not trying that word out. Take it back."

"It works for us. I'm not taking it back."

Her eyes stay wide. "So, what, now you just get to decide things? We're going back to Bossy Beckett?"

"The last time I let you decide something, we ended up here. We're going back to Bossy Beckett until I fix this."

"This can't be fixed."

"Well, it looks like you've got Bossy Beckett for life, then."

The elevator arrives at Jenna's floor. She finally leaves her corner and pushes past me to exit the elevator.

"Stop looking at my ass," she says as I follow her to her room.

I smile.

It's my first in days.

I don't remove my eyes from her ass.

We reach her room and I follow her in. I then watch her rummage in her bags for something. She's still crying, and I wish she'd just let me pull her into my arms and hold her close.

"What are you looking for?" I ask.

Still rummaging, growing increasingly frustrated, she says, "A fucking tampon because"—she looks up at me—"of course, I got my period. I mean, what else goes as well with a breakup as a period?"

I place my hand on hers, stilling her. "You've already searched three times in all your bags. There's no tampons. I'll go and buy you some."

She finally stops rummaging.

"This is not how a breakup should go," she says for the second time before more tears stream down her face. She madly wipes them while looking at me like I've done something very wrong. "Oh my God, no, I cannot get through a breakup, and a period, and you all in one night. I can't."

I've tried hard to give her space until we talk and work

through this. I figured that's what she'd want. But, for the life of me, I can't do that for a second longer.

Moving into her, I gather her in my arms, and pull her close.

I wrap my arms around her tightly.

And finally, I feel like I can breathe again.

Jenna's arms go around me.

She doesn't fight me

She clings to me.

And she cries harder.

I don't say anything; I give her the space to cry, or talk, or do whatever she needs to do.

We stay like this for a long time.

When she finally lifts her face to mine, she says, "You suck at breakups."

I smile down at her. "Add it to your list of things to never forget. I don't intend to ever go through one again."

"You need to go and buy me tampons before I bleed to death all over the place."

"You need to give me those lips of yours before I'm even considering stepping foot outside this room."

"So bossy," she grumbles, but she hooks her hand around my neck and pulls my face to hers so she can give me what I want.

Two days without Jenna is two days too long.

This kiss is only the beginning of me showing her that I mean it when I say we're never going through this again.

I kiss her so thoroughly she'll have trouble thinking of anything but my lips, my tongue, my love when I'm finished.

She kisses me back just as thoroughly.

She arches her body into mine and wraps her arms around my neck exactly how I like them.

And she gives me one of her sexy moans that I can't get enough of.

When she ends the kiss, I say, "If you ever try to break up with me again, it won't go down the same."

Keeping her arms around my neck, she says, "We're still broken up, so technically I don't have to try."

"The whole reason you left me isn't relevant anymore."

She stills. "Why not?"

"I walked away from the contract."

"Why would you do that? You've been working toward this for years."

I don't miss the fact she still has her arms around my neck.

"There will be plenty of other contracts, but there will never be another you."

Those arms tighten around my neck.

"This hasn't fixed your problem, Beckett. There will be other people who won't want to work with you because of me."

"I don't want a thing to do with anyone who doesn't want a thing to do with you." I pause. "I listened to everything you said to me the other day. I want the same things you do. All of it. And I understand now that you don't need me to clear the way for you in life; you need me to stand next to you while you clear your own way."

"Yes," she says, her eyes softening. "That's exactly what I need."

"Noted."

Her arms are so tight around my neck now that I don't think we can get closer. Jenna proves me wrong. She presses herself harder to me and kisses me. Her fingers thread through my hair at the nape of my neck as she gives me everything she's got.

When she's finished, I say, "I love you, Jenna, and I will show up every day and walk by your side, equals. I'll share everything with you. Information, days, nights, vacations, dessert, me. It's all yours. *I'm* all yours. And if no one wants to work with me ever again, I'm good with that. So long as I've got you, everything else in my life is a bonus."

I've barely finished speaking when Jenna's mouth is on mine again in a kiss that steals every last breath I have. I thought she'd already given me everything she had; now, I know she has because she's as breathless as I am when she finally lets me go. "I love you too," she breathes. "I never, in a million years, imagined falling in love with you, but being apart from you has taught me that I never even knew what love was until you."

"Fuck," I growl, my gut tightening. "We're never spending a night apart again."

"Agreed."

"And we're never going through another breakup, or a hint of one, Jenna. Don't ever put me through that again."

Regret flashes in her eyes. "I'm sorry. I was trying to help you."

As the words leave her mouth, I realize what we've experienced. She did what I tend to do and took charge without giving me a say, while I was the one who had no control.

"Never again," she whispers before brushing her lips over mine again. With one last arm tightening around me, she says, "Okay, I really need tampons now."

I leave her, in search of a pharmacy. I locate one down the street, and less than fifteen minutes later, I arrive back at her room.

I let myself in and find her struggling to lower the zipper on her dress.

Moving behind her, I help her while pressing a kiss to her bare shoulder.

"Thank you," she says, turning to face me. She takes the bag of tampons off me and frowns as she looks in the bag. "So when I said I could bleed to death, I didn't mean there was literally that much blood."

I watch as she looks through all the boxes of tampons I bought her. "It occurred to me while I was standing in front of all the tampons at the pharmacy that I don't know which brand you use. I didn't want to chance your wrath by choosing the wrong box."

"Smart man," she says. She then locates her pajamas. "I'm going to have a shower."

I frown. "You're not going back down to the dinner?"

"No. I texted Mom to let her know I'm cramping and not feeling well. She told me to get you to put me to bed."

"Do you need anything else?"

She smiles. "No, I have everything that I need now."

I remove my shoes and suit jacket while Jenna's in the shower.

I reply to a text from Johnson when he lets me know he finally has the information on Declan that we've been trying to source.

I wait for Jenna to return.

And I think about how much I never want to be separated from her ever again.

When she exits the bathroom, dressed in her silk pajama shorts and camisole, I pull her into my arms. "Dance with me."

Her face fills with happiness as she slides her arms around me. "Dancing with no music. I like it."

"I have music." I press Play on the song I found on Spotify, and "Beautiful In My Eyes" by Joshua Kadison plays on my phone.

"You surprise me all the time, Beckett," she says as she dances with me.

"I hope I always do."

"I think you might."

I take hold of her hand. "What's a movie you haven't seen that you want to watch?"

She looks up at me, and I know I've managed to surprise her again. "I still haven't seen 'Crazy Rich Asians'."

"We'll watch it tonight."

She narrows her eyes at me. "Did you choose one I haven't seen so I don't talk all the way through it?"

"No. I chose it because I want one of your firsts." I search her eyes. "I want as many of your firsts as I can have, Jenna."

She curves her hand around my neck. "This is the first Blaise dinner I've ever missed. That's one of your firsts. And if you crawl into bed with me, snuggle with me, watch that movie with me, and hold me in your arms all night, that'll be another first for us. Our first night together in a hotel bed. Everything I do with you is a first, Beckett."

50

JENNA - 2 WEEKS LATER

"He's late," Tilly says, eyeing the time on her phone. "Are you sure he's coming?"

"He's coming," I say as Adeline scans the dresses I've chosen for the photo shoot.

"Which one do you like the most?" she asks.

"The red one." The plunging neckline is going to drive Beckett wild.

"This is my favorite," she says, pulling out a black dress I don't recall selecting.

I frown. "That wasn't one of my choi—" I stop talking as I realize what I'm looking at. "Tilly, did you get this dress sent over?"

She glances at the dress, distracted, and says, "No, that's the one Beckett asked for."

"Huh?" Beckett isn't the kind of man to order dresses.

Her phone lights up with texts, and she waves me off with no answer while replying to the messages.

This black dress is the dress I wore at the original photo shoot I styled him for.

"So," Adeline says, slinging her bag over her shoulder, "I'm going to go. Let me know if your plans change and you can make it on Saturday." We spent the morning working on our brand plans after she decided to invest in my company a week ago. She wants to introduce me to some business associates at a party she's hosting on Saturday.

"I will, but I don't think our plans will change. Beckett seemed insistent that I keep this weekend free for him."

Adeline nods, but she's distracted by something behind me.

I turn to see Beckett and Jameson Fox striding in. I'd forgotten that Beckett told me this morning that he was spending the day with Jameson. I didn't expect Jameson to come to the shoot, though. He and Beckett have been working through the last few issues they've got with their hotel development, so I assumed Jameson would stay at the office working.

"What the fuck is that asshole doing here?" Adeline asks, catching my attention with her tone. I've never heard her sound so hateful.

I look at her. "Do you know Jameson?"

She doesn't remove her eyes from him. "He's the asshole who stole my company years ago."

I take in Jameson as he comes my way. Tall and dangerously sexy is how I'd describe him with his dark eyes, dark hair that's often pulled into a man bun, and tattoos. Beckett and I had dinner with him last night, and I discovered he's driven and focused, and relentless in how he pursues what he wants.

My gaze shifts to Beckett as he draws close. The state of disarray I often exist in when he's around makes itself known. I hope to spend every day until I die in that state with this man.

"Your guy is slacking," I say, pressing myself to him and running my hands over his chest.

His lips twitch. "Why?"

I eye his black suit. "I've seen this suit on you far too often lately. He needs to sell you some new ones for me to ogle."

"I'll mention it to him."

Jameson's deep voice sounds beside me as he greets Adeline. "Adeline."

I glance at her in time to see her lips press together. "Why are you even speaking to me?"

Jameson's dark eyes settle on her. "I have manners."

She glares at him. "If you had manners, you wouldn't have stolen my company."

"I see you still hold a grudge."

Her eyes flash with disbelief. "When someone steals something from me, I don't forgive or forget."

"It's business, and the fact you think feelings deserve a place in business proves you shouldn't have been at the helm."

"I take it you've seen the business I've built since you stole my last one? Seen how much it's worth?"

"I have."

"And you still have the audacity to say something like that to me?" She cocks her head. "Tell me, Jameson, do you treat all women you deal with in business like shit, or is it just me?"

"I don't pay much attention to who I'm dealing with, Adeline. You know that."

"You're a Grade A asshole, and this conversation is a waste of my time." She glances at me. "Call me about Saturday."

She stalks out of the studio at the same time Tilly comes back to us and says to Beckett, "Thank God you're here. Jenna would have taken it out on your body if you didn't show."

Beckett eyes me, and while I read his thoughts and know he's thinking about how much he likes it when I threaten him with harm, he doesn't respond to tell her that.

Tilly looks at Jameson. "You can either sit in the corner over there, or you can sit in our reception room."

Jameson chooses the reception room, and while Tilly shows him to it, Beckett receives a text. He reads it and then says, "It looks like Declan could be charged with falsifying business records."

"I'm glad he's finally being shut down, but my thoughts are all currently centered around getting you styled for this shoot."

He slips his phone in his pocket and looks at me with heat.

"And when you say 'styled', what you mean is 'naked'. Tell me, sweetheart, were you imagining me naked the last time we were here?"

"I still haven't decided if that works for us yet." Beckett seems intent on using sweetheart as his preferred term of endearment; I'm honestly not convinced.

"It works. Now, answer my question."

"I was imagining stabbing you the last time we were here."

He chuckles and pulls me close. Dipping his mouth to my neck, he kisses me there before saying, "I got them to find the black dress you wore last time."

I angle my head to the side while he continues causing my disarray. "I saw that."

"I also got them to find the blue suit you chose for me."

"Are we reenacting that day? Because I have to tell you, it wasn't my best day."

He kisses his way up to my lips, his eyes meeting mine as he says, "It wasn't mine either, but it became one of the best days of my life." He takes hold of my face and kisses me, dedicating time to this kiss in a way that causes me to grip his suit jacket because my knees are going weak. "It was the beginning of us that day, Jenna. My favorite first with you."

I grip his jacket tightly as butterflies flap themselves into their own state of disarray in my stomach. There's something in Beckett's eyes today. Something that's making those butterflies pay more attention than normal.

"I want a million more firsts with you," he says. "And while I was going to wait until you were in the dress, and I was in the suit to ask you this, I can't wait because I'm an impatient bastard." He gets down on one knee and pulls a small box out of his pocket. Opening it to reveal the most beautiful diamond ring I've ever seen in my life, he says, "The first time I met you, we got into a conversation about gender equality. You were so damn passionate and knowledgeable that I found myself arguing against you just to keep you talking. I found myself looking forward to our next conversation every time I saw you. You're the most beautiful woman I've ever met, but it's not your beauty that made me fall in love with you, it's your soul. I love the way you challenge me to be a better man; the way you teach me to think differently and expand my views; the way you help me experience life and the people in it in new ways; and the way you give your heart to me without any conditions. I can't see a life without you in it now, Jenna. Will you marry me and dance with me every day in our kitchen?"

I look down at him through tears. "You remember our first conversation?"

He smiles up at me, those beautiful blue eyes of his shimmering with love. "Baby, I remember every minute of it. Every flick of your hair. Every eye roll. Every look of shock at what I said."

My damn heart has taken over my ears. I can barely hear my own thoughts thanks to her and her excitement.

When I don't give Beckett an answer to his question, because my disarray is at epic proportions now and I've forgotten how to breathe, speak, live, he says, "Do I need to boss you into this?"

That's all I need to return me to a state of not-as-much-disarray.

I practically slide onto his knee, and meet his gaze while saying, "Yes! Yes, I will marry you!" I'm an over-excited bundle of joy, and happiness, and love. So much so that I don't even know how it all happens, but one minute, I'm saying yes, and the next, I've got the ring on my finger, I'm standing, and Beckett's arms are around me tightly while he kisses me.

When we come up for air, Tilly is back, and is staring at us. "Did I just miss something? Like, were you just on one knee, Beckett? And did you just say yes? And did I just receive a bridesmaid request? The answer is yes, of course."

I grin at her and flash my ring. "Yes! You missed it all, but you are going to be a beautiful bridesmaid when Beckett and I get married on his yacht."

Tilly oohs and aahs over my ring.

I ooh and ahh over my ring.

Beckett arches his brows and says, "On the yacht?"

"Why else do you have a yacht if not to use it? Also, I take back my early assessment of 'baby' not being for us. It is most definitely for us, and you should feel free to call me that any time you want your dick sucked."

He looks at me with a mixture of amusement and heat. "Noted."

I slide my arms around his waist. "I love how you love me, Beckett. You've given me the world simply because you gave me you. And every day you keep on giving me the best of yourself. I can't wait for all our firsts together."

I kiss him again as Tilly drawls, "Right, and he's given you this photo shoot, babycakes, so how about a little less chatting now and a whole lot more smiling at the camera?"

Beckett puts on the blue Brioni suit.

I put on the black dress that is far shorter and low-cut than I remember.

And we relive the day that is one of our favorite firsts.

EPILOGUE

@thetea_gasp

Do we have the tea for you today, girlfriend! @jennablaise showed off her engagement ring #gasp from bae @beckett-pearce at a party hosted by her new business partner @adelinespencer last night. The massive diamond sparkler is rumored to have set Beckett back $3M #engagementring-goals The couple are tight-lipped on when the wedding will take place but #jeckettwatch is predicting the loved-up couple won't wait long. Our prediction is a summer wedding in the Greek Islands on zaddy Beckett's yacht #staytuned

EPILOGUE

@thetea_gasp

ORANGE IS the new black for @declanjames who will spend years paying for his sins #byefelicia We heard @katiestein ghosted him when she discovered he was looking at an extended #vacation We also heard his old bestie @beckett-pearce helped take the trash out. Oh, Declan, honey, keep your enemies close next time #facts

EPILOGUE

@thetea_gasp

Oh, the romance and glamour of a September wedding on a luxury yacht on the French Riviera #swoon @beckettpearce knows how to get married. He didn't waste any time doing it and he did it in style over the weekend when he said "I do" to @jennablaise on the Mediterranean coast of France. #jeckett were spotted at the Monte Carlo casino last week before making their way along the coast to Nice, Cannes, and Saint-Tropez. It was a small affair with only their families and close friends in attendance #couplegoals We're watching closely for signs of #babybeckett

EPILOGUE
12 MONTHS LATER

@thetea_gasp

WHAT DO you get when you mix a fashion icon and a style icon? Answer: #fashionheaven @adelinespencer and @jennapearce launched Adeline + Pearce today #OMG #ineedthisinmylife #dead Do yourself a favor, girlfriend, and check out their Insta @adelineandpearce for everything fashion and beauty you will ever need #snatched #youcanthankmelater

EPILOGUE

JENNA - FIVE YEARS AFTER MARRIED

"Dance with me."

I place my hands over my husband's after his arms circle me from behind. "I didn't hear you come in." I've been engrossed in my work at the kitchen island for the last hour and wasn't expecting Beckett home from the office for at least another two hours.

His lips graze the side of my neck as he murmurs, "That's because Alexander has all of your attention at the moment.'

I smile, swaying with him even though he hasn't put any music on yet. "I do love these possessive tendencies you have these days. The great news for you is that your mother came over today and asked if Alexander could have a sleepover with them tonight."

"I have you to myself tonight?"

And there goes the rest of the work I'd planned to finish before he arrived home. Not that I'm complaining. The last six months since our son's birth have been a blur for me, and I've struggled to find alone time with Beckett while juggling a new baby and work commitments. Adeline and I recently launched a line of Adeline + Pearce beauty products that have sold better than all our projections. On top of that, our fashion lines are in such demand that we can't keep up. Business is great, but I've had to admit to Beckett that I underestimated how difficult it would be to manage family and work now that we have Alexander. Beckett has been an amazing, hands-on father from day one, but he stepped right up after I shared this with him.

I turn in his arms, loving the familiar slide of his hands over my ass when I face him. "You do, and I've been thinking of all the things we could do."

Heat blazes in his eyes. It's the same heat that's been there for five years. Not a day goes by that he fails to experience it. Even on the days since Alexander's birth that I haven't showered until late afternoon, or that I've simply thrown sweatpants on, or that I've told him to go away because I'm too exhausted, Beckett has looked at me with desire.

"What's on your list?" he asks.

"Well, first, I'm hoping for some music to dance to with you."

He reaches for his phone. "Beautiful In My Eyes" by Joshua Kadison fills the kitchen a moment later.

It's our song.

It's the first song Beckett ever chose for one of our dances.

It's the song we danced to at our wedding.

It's the song Beckett paid millions to have Jett Vaughn sing when he hired a stadium for a private rock show with Jett, Diesel, and other singers as my thirtieth birthday gift.

It's the song he still often chooses when he asks me to dance.

My husband has an unexpected sentimental side that I cherish.

We sway silently for a few minutes, holding each other and kissing. I love sex with Beckett, but these days, with all the hectic juggling we do, it's these moments I look forward to the most.

I want to be held.

I want to be kissed.

I want to be adored.

And no one does those things better than Beckett.

"What else is on your list?" he asks after ending our kiss.

"Can you take tomorrow morning off work?"

He contemplates that for a moment. "Yes."

I smile. "Let's go to the Hamptons."

"For the night?"

I nod. "Yes. I want to go ice skating, and then toast marshmallows and curl up by the fireplace with you." I loop my hands around his neck. "If you're lucky, you can have dessert by the fireplace too."

"Ice skating and marshmallows." I know what he's thinking: a first for us.

"Sounds like fun, right?"

He bends his face to brush his lips over mine. "It does."

"I'm not sure why we've never toasted marshmallows."

"Possibly because you're too busy demanding dessert."

I grin. "Possibly."

"Okay, I'll get the helicopter ready. Mom's good to have Alexander until we get back?"

"I haven't asked her, but I think we both know she won't say no. And if she does, I can ask Mom to take him for the morning."

Beckett's mother changed her mind about me after learning I tried to end our relationship so he could win that government contract. I mean, she didn't thaw completely right away. It's taken us five years to get to where we are, which is her actually finding ways to spend time together, and me enjoying that time with her.

And who knew Margaret Pearce would take to being a grandmother like she has? Both Alexander's grandmothers dote on him and want as much time with him as they can get. I'm a little concerned there may be a fight over him one day.

I mentioned this to Beckett last week. All he could offer in way of a solution was for us to have another child ASAP so our mothers could have one each. I just shook my head at him. The man can be so practical at times it's ridiculous. He just gave me one of his sexy smiles and made it clear he intends on continuing his mission to get me pregnant again.

When the song finishes, Beckett lets me go and reaches for his phone. I know he's calling to get the helicopter ready, but I'm not ready for that yet.

I curl my fingers around his phone and take it from him. At his questioning look, I select a playlist and choose another song before moving back into him, and saying, "We're not finished dancing."

He puts his arms around me. "We're not?"

"No," I say softly. "I need at least one more dance today."

He cups my face while searching my eyes. "Tell me about your day."

I look up at my husband, who's watching me with so much love and care, and think about how well he loves me.

Beckett reads me better than anyone ever has.

He's spent five years learning all the intricacies of me.

My strengths, weaknesses, hopes, dreams, goals, hurts, joys, passions.

He knows all the ways to lift me when I'm down, and all the ways I like to have fun.

He knows how to navigate my moods.

He knows how to handle my tears.

He's stripped me naked, physically and emotionally.

Beckett has seen all my scars and fears and wounds.

He's seen me at my worst.

And he loves me anyway.

He loves me *because* of these things.

"Ruby came over this morning," I say. I then proceed to tell him every little thing I did today. I mean, not *everything*, but most things.

He listens like he always does.

Beckett never rushes me, never dismisses me. Not even

when I'm giving him so many details I wouldn't blame him for yawning.

I get to the end of my day, and say, "I'm ready for it to be Christmas already."

He frowns. "How did we go from the events of your day to Christmas?"

"Ah, how could we not? I spent time with Ruby and Alexander; I had lunch with Shona who told me about a painting she and Graham just bought; I got that text from Tilly about that guy she's started seeing; I messaged with Cora about my appointments tomorrow; I avoided Kristen's meltdown; Josh sent me that recipe I asked him for; Grayson and Oliver tried to escape our family chat; Elon checked in to let me know he'll be in town next week; I spent time with our moms. I mean, those are all our Christmas people, so naturally I'm thinking about Christmas. Honestly, how did your brain *not* think about Christmas after I mentioned them all?"

He chuckles. "I love you, sweetheart, but I don't think I'll ever understand your brain fully."

It's the sweetheart that does it.

That causes my disarray.

I used to tell Beckett that "sweetheart" didn't work for us. He always told me it did. I was more about "baby" back then.

Now, I have to stop myself from begging him to call me that because when those two syllables fall from his lips, I'm reminded that I'm his world. The woman he will do absolutely anything and everything for.

"You're having dessert early tonight," I throw out as my butterflies flap and flail all over the place.

"Am I?"

"Yes, and if you don't hurry up with it, I may hurt you."

"Jenna," he says, the heat now blazing in his eyes, "You should know by now that I like your threats."

I grip his shirt and smile sexily at him. "Baby, I do know

that. It's why I continue to issue them. Now, can we please move this to the table so you can do filthy things to me?"

"Fuck," he growls, finally lifting me over his shoulder. "But just so you're aware, I'm already feeling the need for seconds later. I haven't had enough dessert lately."

There's the man I love, and I wouldn't change a thing about him.

EPILOGUE

5 YEARS LATER

@thetea_gasp

WE'RE happy sighing over here. @beckettpearce and @jennapearce welcomed their third child into the world today. Isabella Pearce is sister to Alexander (5) and Saxon (3). The couple shared last month that they don't plan any more children, although in a rare playful moment, Beckett said he thought five children, two dogs, a cat, and a bird would make the perfect family. This appeared to be a private joke for the couple with Jenna rolling her eyes at him. Whatever they're having, we want some #couplegoals #jeckett

JAMESON FOX SNEAK PEEK
ADELINE

"Here's to Mr and Mrs Fox." Hudson raises his glass and smiles at me. "I wish Adeline all the best surviving my brother. I hope you know what you've gotten yourself into, gorgeous."

My husband's arm tightens around my waist right before his lips brush my cheek. "She knows."

I do.

I know very well what the future holds for me.

Turning to Jameson, I cup his face. "Maybe he's the one who needs the best wishes. Maybe *he'll* have to survive me."

Those dark eyes of Jameson's flash with a warning only I can see as laughter erupts among our guests.

"Oh, he'll survive you," Kurt, one of Jameson's closest friends, calls out. "How could he not? A man would be a fool if he didn't."

I look at Kurt in time to catch his grin and the wink he shoots me. Both help ease the nerves still racing through me. Thank God for him. This isn't the first time he's helped me and I'm sure it won't be the last.

"Eyes on me, Adeline," Jameson commands in a hushed tone for my ears only. His rough huskiness scatters desire over my skin. Desire I don't want anything to do with.

I meet his gaze again. What I see there sucks the breath from my lungs. Desire that matches my own. Jameson hasn't made any secret of the fact he wants to fuck me, but this, what I'm seeing now, is on a whole new level.

He tightens his hold on me, pulling my body hard against his. Far too close for my liking. Bending his face to mine, he kisses me. It's not our first kiss; that was after we exchanged vows, but this is the first time he's forced me to give him more of myself than I want to give.

I wasn't ready for this.

Certainly not in front of our 200 guests.

But fuck, the man can kiss. And I like it. I like it more than I should. I like it a whole lot more than I want to.

Keeping one hand on my waist, he brings his other hand up to my face and threads his fingers through my hair while deepening the kiss. His tongue slides over mine, as dominant as he is, and I have to use every ounce of control in me not to moan.

I've kissed a lot of men in my life, but none as skilled as Jameson. He kisses like he lives: intensely, demanding, and taking what he wants.

It sweeps me away.

Shuts my brain down.

Turns me into the kind of woman I swore I'd never be again.

The kind that gives a man too much control.

I press my hands to his chest and push, attempting to disentangle my lips from his. I don't push hard, only enough for him to feel it, not for anyone to see it.

He feels it, all right, and he ignores me, holding me in place, keeping our lips locked.

I push again.

A little harder this time.

Again, he ignores me, his lips demanding my submission. But I'm done. He might think he has all the power here, but he doesn't. Not by a long shot.

Taking charge, I pull my mouth from his. Our eyes meet and it gives me great satisfaction to see his displeasure. That's something I've started to strive for over the last three months, and every time I achieve my goal, it helps ease some of the pain he inflicted on me five years ago.

Our guests, who can't see our power struggle, cheer us on. They only see the love we take great care to project to the world. They want more of our whirlwind romance.

Ignoring them, Jameson leans in close and growls, "Don't ever do that again."

"Since when did the definition of husband change to dictator?"

He works his jaw, his eyes flashing with more displeasure. "You'll do well to remember what you're getting out of this marriage."

"And *you'll* do well to remember that I am not, and never will be, the kind of woman you can control. I went over every line of our marriage contract, every single word, and not once did it mention that I have to allow you to force yourself on me."

He keeps his hands on me, unwilling to yield. In the end, it's his phone that causes him to let go. A call comes in and he pulls the phone from his pocket.

Glancing back up at me after checking the caller ID, he says, "This conversation isn't finished, Adeline." Then, stabbing at the phone, he barks, "This better be important, Ashton. I'm at my wedding."

Ashton says something to him that causes him to walk away and exit the room. I watch him leave, my hate for him roaring to life.

How dare he think he can tell me what I can and can't do?

We survived our engagement, just, and I thought I'd made it clear I won't be ruled over. It seems I haven't been clear enough. Going forward, I will be. I'll make it crystal fucking clear that I have no intention of bowing down to his demands. We might be husband and wife now, and we might have to get through a year together, but that doesn't mean I have to ask "how fucking high" whenever he says "jump."

Jameson Fox might reign over everything in his kingdom, but he'll never reign over me.

∽

JAMESON FOX WILL RELEASE JANUARY 24, 2022

This is a standalone enemies-to-lovers, fake marriage, billionaire romance.

ninalevinebooks.com/ashton-scott-world#jameson-fox

ALSO BY NINA LEVINE

Christmas Hearts (#3)

Battle Hearts (#4)

Stone Ops Series

COMING 2022

Easton

Zane

Liam

Bronze

Axe

Billionaire Romance

Ashton Scott

Jack Kingsley

Beckett Pearce

Jameson Fox (coming Jan 2022)

Owen North (coming 2022)

The Hardy Family Series

Steal My Breath (single dad romance)

Crave Series

Be The One (rockstar romance)

www.ninalevinebooks.com

ABOUT THE AUTHOR

Nina Levine

Dreamer.

Coffee Lover.

Pilates Goddess

USA Today & Wall Street Journal Bestselling Author Nina
Levine is an Australian author who loves to write protective
heroes, sassy heroines, and lots of banter & heat.

When she isn't creating with words, she's busy being a pilates
goddess. Often though, she can be found curled up with a good
book and some chocolate.

www.ninalevinebooks.com

ACKNOWLEDGMENTS

2021 has been a huge year for me with my writing. It's been a hard year for me personally, but I think I must be channelling that into my writing because the five books I've written this year are some of my favourites to date.

I started writing Beckett's book early last year. I was actually writing it for a publisher and they had some guidelines for what I had to write. The original story I wrote was nothing like this book. It was actually a little sugary sweet. I have a memory of Jodie (my alpha reader) coming back to me and telling me that Beckett was no Nina Levine alpha lol. He was too nice.

Goodness, I struggled with this book back then. Like, really struggled. I couldn't get a feel for Beckett. I was trying too hard to write to a set formula (for the first time ever, I followed a writing craft book on how to plot a book and plan it to hit all the things you're supposed to hit in a book blah, blah, blah - like, seriously, kill me now, I cannot write to a formula to save myself).

I was talking with an author friend of mine, TL Swan, and she said to me "just pretend he's one of your bikers and put him in a suit", so I did. The Beckett we ended up with is a toned down version of that "biker Beckett". So, huge thanks to Tee for that advice. It got me started on the path to discovering Beckett. Also, I ditched that formula I was trying to write to and went back to my way of writing a book. It worked much better for me. If you're a writer, the best advice I can give you is to figure out how YOU write a book and do it that way.

The biggest thanks for this book must go to Jodie O'Brien, my alpha reader. She championed this couple like no other couple I've written. Don't get me wrong, JRO is here for all my couples, but she LOVED Beckett & Jenna in a whole new way and to a whole new level. I can't tell you the number of phone calls we've had or the number of hours we've discussed this couple. Jodie helped me so much to continue on when I got tired and my body got sore from all the hours I spent writing. The excitement I heard in her voice in those phone calls made me want to keep digging, to do better, to write the best damn book I've ever written. Thank you so much, JRO. Your support means everything to me. And maybe next time I'll let you go and buy me food for deadline time. Maybe.

I need to send a massive thank you to my cover designer, Letitia Hasser from Romantic Book Affairs. OMG you are a design goddess!! You took a stock image and made me my Hemsworth cousin and I can't tell you how much I adore him. I can't wait to see what you come up with for Jameson's cover!!

To Rose, my proofreader. Thank you so much for all your work on this book, especially with the Australian to US translations! I've learned so much about our different way of saying things!

To my readers. Gah. You have no idea, absolutely no idea how much I appreciate you for reading my books, and in particular for sticking with me over the last few years while I got my shit together after losing it in 2018 just after I published Ashton's book. You waited three years for Jack's book, and I love you for that. I hope you've loved Beckett's book. Thank you for being the best readers in the world.

To my bloggers & reviewers, thank you so much for always being so patient with my ARCS. I've never been great at getting them out early but you girls have always stuck by me. Thank you <3 Thank you for reading my books, for taking the time to write reviews and post them, for telling other readers about them, for posting on social media about them, and for every other type of support you give me. I wouldn't be here publishing if it weren't for you guys because you got me started and then you kept on sharing and getting the word out there for me. Thank you, thank you, thank you.

I've got to give special mention to my gym girls. Lisa, Catrinia, and Sally, you girls always give me inspo for my writing. I'm always certain I can go to pilates with not a clue as to what I'll write later that day for a chapter or for a Storm chat, and I'll leave class with exactly what I'm going to write. From the pink vulva pants, to the love garage, to Nude Tuesdays, to so many things, I thank you for making me laugh and helping me write!

Lastly, I want to give a shoutout to my Aussie writer friends who've been writing with me at 5AM the last couple of months. I've written two books, guys! TWO! Who knew that getting up so early could make me so productive! Thank you for the support and encouragement <3

PLAYLIST

"Cool Anymore" by Jordan Davis, Julia Michaels
"What Am I" by Why Don't We
"You & Me" by James TW
"Fallin' All In You" by Shawn Mendes
"Seeing Blind" by Niall Horan, Maren Morris
"Jealous" by Nick Jonas
"One Night Girl" by Blake Shelton
"I Will Always Be Yours" by Ben Rector
"Listen To Your Heart" by Roxette
"Conversations in the Dark" by John Legend
"Just The Way" by Parmalee
"Never Stop" by Safety Suit
"Next To You" by Little Big Town
"Incredible" by James TW
"Naked" by Jake Scott
"Beautiful in my Eyes" by Joshua Kadison
"Lover" by Niall Horan, FLETCHER

Made in the USA
Las Vegas, NV
30 September 2022